ALL
ABOUT
YOU

Dianne Venetta

ALL ABOUT YOU
Book #3

Silver Creek Series:
Romantic Mystery/Adventure
NOT WITHOUT YOU ~ #1
BECAUSE OF YOU ~ #2
ALL ABOUT YOU ~ #3
ONLY WITH YOU ~ #4

Other novels by Dianne Venetta

Ladd Springs Series:
Cozy Mystery/Romance
LADD SPRINGS ~ #1
LADD FORTUNE ~ #2
HOTEL LADD ~ #3
LADD HAVEN ~ #4
LOSING LADD ~ #5
LADD CHRISTMAS ~ #6

The Gables Trilogy:
Romantic Women's Fiction
JENNIFER'S GARDEN
LUST ON THE ROCKS
WHISPER PRIVILEGES

Women's Fiction
CONDEMN ME NOT

ISBN 9780996439121

All About You
Copyright 2015 by Dianne Venetta
ISBN: 978-0-9964391-2-1
Publisher: BloominThyme Press
Editor: Best Foot Forward
Cover Design: Seductive Designs

Dedication

This novel is for those who donate their time and energy to children in need. The world is a better place because of you.
Thank you.

Chapter One

Katharine Wainwright's stomach pitched as the aircraft, jolted about by the turbulence of hot dry air, made its initial descent into Silver Creek, Colorado. Seated in a posh leather chair at a table across from her father, she glanced out a round window of the Gulfstream G550, the newest addition to her family's air fleet, and felt a flurry of nerves skitter through her as a narrow runway nestled within the rugged Rocky Mountains came into view. The plane dropped suddenly and Katharine grabbed a glass of water before it spilled over the papers in front of her.

"We're here," William Wainwright announced quietly.

Her father's gaze simmered with a sadness that broke her heart, the severe navy color of his suit adding an uncustomary edge to his features. Silver-gray hair was combed back, revealing a soft spattering of age spots on his receding hairline. His skin was smoothly shaven and slightly folded over the neckline of his starched white shirt. Despite his years, her father's mind remained sharp, his determination strong. He was a vision of wealth and privilege, a vision of hard-fought success. But to anyone who knew him, William Wainwright was simply a man living a life he loved.

Pressure pushed into her chest. "Yes, we're here," Katharine repeated. Realizing her pen was clenched between her teeth, she yanked it free and set it on the polished wood table alongside her papers. "Stupid habit," she snapped at herself, one she'd repeatedly tried to break. But without fail, whenever her mind was fully engrossed in her work, the pen went into her mouth.

Her father smiled. "Your mother always fussed at you about that."

Katharine, it's not ladylike to put writing utensils in your mouth. You don't know where that pen has been. She could almost hear her mother's voice. But hell, at this point, what did it matter? There was no one on this plane to see but her father, and he adored everything about her, including her flaws.

A plump yellow-haired dog walked unsteadily down the center aisle, his large brown eyes pained as he stared at her. When he neared, Katharine cooed, "I know, baby. Turbulence is no fun on the belly." Cody was a purebred Labrador and her constant companion, but the flights out West took a toll on his system, mainly during takeoff and landing. Katharine scratched him behind an ear and the animal craned his furry head into her hand. Soon grunts of pleasure became a constant rumble. She laughed softly as she continued to scratch through soft fur. "Works every time."

"I'm sorry I can't stay and join you." Katharine's father's voice pulled her back to the moment, the business at hand, though she kept a hand on Cody's head. "I need to be in New York, now that the investigation is in full swing."

At the helm of his investment empire, she mused. Wainwright, Emerson was under investigation for high-speed trading operations. They were nothing but trumped-up charges aimed at taking the biggest investment firm in New York down a peg, but that didn't negate the need to address them. The Securities and Exchange Commission had filed charges and they had to be answered, though Katharine couldn't imagine anything criminal would come of them. How could the feds punish a company for using technology to its benefit? Progress was progress. It wasn't as if her father's firm conspired to cheat or engaged in fraud, but still, he insisted on being present for each and every deposition.

"Another time," Katharine replied. "Besides, this isn't a pleasure trip."

A deep sorrow swamped his gaze. "I wish you didn't have to go through this, Katie."

"There's no other way. I'm the only one suitable and we both know it." For a second, she swore her father was about to cry, but as usual, he held his emotion in check, stuffing it into a back compartment for release at some later date and time. It wasn't that her father was cold and insensitive. Quite the opposite. His emotion pulsed beneath the surface as a palpable indicator of where he stood on any given issue, plain for anyone to see if they knew how to read him. And she did. Unfortunately, when it came to her mother, his emotion was pure grief.

Overcome by a stab of melancholy, Katharine shot a glance out the window, her gaze filled with mountaintops that stood eye level as the aircraft made its approach. The jagged ridge of red stone was embedded in a cobalt sky, underscoring the intensity of blue. She'd never seen bluer skies than here. Add the green countryside, the plethora of wildflowers that covered the landscape, the abundance of trees and wildlife, and Colorado was one of the most magnificent places on earth. And she should know. She spent more days on the road than at home, and there was no place as bold and beautiful as the American West. This was her mother's home, the countryside that reflected her indomitable spirit and reminded Katharine of everything she'd lost when she'd lost her mother.

Swallowing back a rush of longing, she turned back to her father. "Once I arrive at the ranch," she said, "I'll call for an emergency board meeting to lay the groundwork for going forward." The plane dropped suddenly and Katharine bit back a gasp. Water sloshed over the edge of the glass and she grabbed her papers, pulling them out of the way. Losing their connection, Cody's head quickly found its place again as he pushed his entire body against her chair. "It's okay, baby," she said to the dog. "Don't worry. It will be over soon."

The rough and tumble ride was nothing unusual when flying into the small regional airport, but her sweet dog didn't understand. The ground was moving beneath him and it probably felt like his world was about to flip upside down. With a quick stroke of his head, she added, "We're almost down."

Katharine continued to pet Cody's wide flat head, warmed by the furry body pressed into her leg and said, "After the meeting, an audit of the records should reveal everything I need to know before the fundraiser."

"Frank should be instrumental in helping you get to the bottom of it. He's assured me you will have complete access to all records and accounts."

"Good." Frank Dillard was currently running the ranch. He'd worked side-by-side with her mother over the last half dozen years and if anyone should understand the financial landscape, it would be him. "Does he have any idea who could be responsible?"

"Frank suspects the new board member. He assumed the title only months before your mother's death."

Katharine steeled herself against the words, *your mother's death*. It had been almost a year, yet the pain felt fresh, hot. As the words wound through her system, she took a deep breath and asked, "What do you think? Do you agree with his assessment?"

Her father shrugged. "I don't know the players, Katie. This was your mother's baby, not mine."

Katharine almost heard him add, *Though I wish I'd spent more time with her and her kids.*

Eleanor Wainwright had established a children's charity ranch, a Western retreat geared toward allowing terminally ill kids to live their lives to the fullest while challenging their personal limits. Wainwright Ranch was a place where kids could learn new skills and test their wits against nature, allowing them to feel healthy and vibrant instead of the children everyone tiptoed around, afraid to upset their feelings. It was a place where children could feel normal. If only for a while, they were no different than anyone around them at Wainwright Ranch.

At the start of each session, Katharine's mother used to meet each and every child with open arms and a welcome hug, then put them right to work. Memories of her mother standing like a warden at the gate, decked out in her cowboy boots and jeans and speaking to the children, pulled at Katharine's heart. *This is no candy ranch, kids. This is real life, the way we live it out West, and we need your help to carry on operations.*

After informing her "guests" of the rules, her mother would break into a smile and entertain the children with a sense of humor that didn't quit. Hands-on, she'd demonstrate how to shoot a bow and arrow, build a fire, construct a shelter, tell direction without a compass, and navigate narrow trails through the mountains all while identifying animal poop along the way. Katharine had joined her mother for many such excursions and found each and every one memorable.

"Whoever's behind this has been at it for some time," her father said. "We need to stop them before the ranch goes bankrupt."

"We will." Katharine refused to allow her mother's good name to be dragged through the mud because of some greedy S.O.B. Whoever was stealing from the charity ranch had made a serious error in judgment, and it was Katharine's job to uncover the truth and do so before the annual fundraiser. Summer camp was winding down and rumors had already begun to circulate that this was the last season for Wainwright Ranch, and donors were nervous. No one wanted to spend good money after bad, a concept Katharine thoroughly understood. People would spend top dollar for a good cause, but no one would line the pockets of a corrupt organization.

During the final minutes of the flight, Katharine busied herself with Cody until the plane touched down, then collected her paperwork and slid it back into a Chanel briefcase. She pressed the shiny gold snap-buckle into place and swallowed hard, clearing the pressure between her ears. Smoothing her hands over the sleek black leather, she looked to her father.

"Are you sure you don't want me to call for a car?" he asked. He didn't bother to rise from his seat. The plane wouldn't be shutting down.

"I'm sure. Adele is coming to pick me up."

"Adele Simms?" Salt and pepper brows lifted in surprise. When Katharine nodded, he replied, "Why, I haven't seen her in ages. Does she make it back to New York often?"

"No. To be quite honest, I think she's happier here."

Her father nodded, his gaze drawn to airport personnel meeting the aircraft outside. Katharine felt another wave of regret emanate from him, but he said nothing. He didn't have to. This had been his wife's adopted home, as well. The place she had come to get away from the city, from the stress of her fast-living lifestyle. The turning point in their marriage had been her mother's permanent move out west. At the time, Katharine hadn't thought much of it. The two seemed happy. They seemed content with the frequent visits, explaining that not all marriages needed constant time together to remain strong. But over the years, Katharine saw the wear and tear on her father. It pained him to live without his wife, yet he couldn't abandon his investment firm. Wouldn't. As much as the ranch had been her mother's life, the investment firm was his.

It was a decision Katharine understood. She felt the same commitment to her career.

Turning away from the window, her father said, "Tell Adele I said hello, will you?"

"I will." Katharine slid from her seat and stood, then leaned down and pecked her father's cheek. "I'll keep you posted on my progress."

"Please do. And Katie?"

She stopped. "Yes?"

"I love you."

An automatic smile tugged at her mouth. "Love you too, Dad." With a quick whistle, she beckoned Cody to follow and headed for the door. "C'mon, boy. Time for some fresh air."

Outside, Adele greeted Katharine with a bear hug. "God, you look great!"

Katharine squeezed back, marveling at the strength of her friend's embrace. It was a pretty powerful grip for a woman of her petite build. Standing a hair above five-foot-four, Adele hadn't changed a bit. "As do you," Katharine replied then held her college roomie in outstretched arms. As she admired Adele's pixie hairstyle, Katharine thought her friend looked savvy and sophisticated with the shorter cut. It accentuated her prominent cheekbones and narrow nose. Add her heart-shaped mouth, huge brown eyes and creamy white skin, and Katharine thought Adele had an elegant, almost imperial look. It was a look right at home in the city, if not slightly at odds with the high country of Colorado. "I love that hairstyle on you."

Adele laughed. "Sure makes it easier in the kitchen."

"I'll bet." Katharine smiled but didn't elaborate. The first time Adele's hair had been cut this short had been right after her chemo treatment. At twenty-seven years old, she'd been diagnosed with breast cancer. It had been a shock—a freight train that punched to the core of her existence—and completely changed the course of her life. In short order, Adele divorced her husband, packed her bags, and moved to Colorado for a healthier lifestyle, leaving the decadent French cuisine of one of New York's finest restaurants for totally vegan gourmet fare in Silver Creek, Colorado, and she never looked back. Her current namesake restaurant had been in business for five years now and, from what Katharine could gather, was enormously successful.

Adele bent down and gave Cody a double-fisted shake behind his ears. "Hey, Cody-body. How's my favorite Lab?"

Katharine frowned. "Getting old, putting on weight."

Adele laughed and stood. "Not enough green space in the city."

"Tell me about it," Katharine groaned. "Even I'm getting tired of spending so much time indoors. I can't imagine what it's doing to him."

Adele picked up the smaller of Katharine's suitcases and glanced over her from head-to-toe. "Well, you certainly don't show it, though we are going to have to get you out of those city clothes and into some decent Western attire."

Katharine glanced down and made an instant reassessment of her clothing. A classic white shirt paired with a pencil-thin black skirt, met by knee-high black leather boots—what was not to like? It wasn't like she was jumping on the back of a horse anytime soon. She was headed for the office, not the corral, though she made a mental note to grab a jacket. Despite a cloudless sky, the temperature was brisker than she'd expected. "Hopefully I won't be subjected to any wagon rides this afternoon," she returned. "But you'll rest easy knowing that I packed a full range of clothing choices this trip." She'd even packed jeans and shorts, though didn't expect she'd be wearing them. This was a working trip with little time for recreation.

"One good thing about Silver Creek," Adele said, heading for her car, a shiny white Mercedes SUV parked in the front row on the opposite side of a chain link fence, "you won't lack for shopping options, should you need some."

"True." Katharine sighed, and breathed in the mountainous terrain that surrounded them. The airport was tucked within walls of rock cut by the striations of time, the landscape sharp and vivid, injecting the senses like a shot of espresso. Overhead, the sky was drenched in a brilliant cobalt blue, the sun tolerable, the temperature cool but pleasant. Try to find that combination on a July day in New York City, she thought dully.

Distracted by the piercing sound of jet engines, Katharine turned in time to see her father's jet race past. The pointed nose gently lifted from the runway as the aircraft took off, soaring up and over the distant range. Her gaze trailed its flight until it banked to the left and disappeared from view. Thoughts of her father's last words floated in her heart. *I love you.*

This little expedition of hers was more painful for him than for her.

Adele popped open the back hatch and they loaded Katharine's luggage, then walked around and opened the rear passenger door. "Hop in, Cody."

Katharine stopped suddenly. "Are you sure you don't want him in the far back?"

Adele closed the door behind him and slid into the driver's seat. "In Colorado, I've learned that dogs rule the roost. They aren't to be treated like luggage—they get a seat, like you and me."

"And you're okay with that?"

"It's fine." Adele handed her a white paper bag then started the engine.

"What's this?"

"A spinach wrap. I thought you might be hungry after the flight and I knew you wouldn't stop for food."

Katharine smiled. Adele knew her well. She was anxious to get to the ranch and get started on the business that had brought her to Colorado. The two had agreed to share an early dinner later, but business came first. "Thanks. And you're sure about Cody?"

"Another thing I've learned from living out west is to relax," Adele said, backing out of the space. "It's a car—pretty indestructible stuff. Cody won't hurt anything." She glanced over her shoulder and grinned. "Looks like he's settling into mountain life already."

Katharine glanced back at him and smiled. Cody was stretched out the length of the backseat, his chin resting on the supple tan leather cushion as he peered up at her, looking as if this was the most natural thing in the world for him. "You're spoiled rotten," she told him.

"Life's too short for anything else," Adele put in. "No stress, no worries."

Bands tightened around Katharine's heart as she gazed at her friend. If only she could feel so carefree. Unfortunately, her stay in Silver Creek felt more like an impending disaster than a relaxing reprieve from the city.

Chapter Two

Canyon Laredo strolled into the main office of Wain-wright Ranch and stopped short of the receptionist's desk. Fairly spacious, the room included a sitting area where a leather couch and chair were separated by a square wooden table, topped by a brass lamp. Walls were paneled and adorned with paintings of the Colorado countryside, giving an elegant feel to the space without being too fancy. Seated behind the desk, an attractive brunette ceased working the minute he walked in. She smiled at him, her heated gaze clearly more personal than professional.

Canyon removed his dark brown cowboy hat by the dent of its crown and held it before him. "Good afternoon, Amanda."

Amanda Bell perched her elbows on top of the desktop. "Good afternoon yourself, Canyon." Folding her arms, she leaned forward to reveal her ample cleavage. Pushed together in the V-shaped neckline of a pale blue frilly blouse, her skin was a creamy tan. "How can I help you today?"

He smiled, more because it was the polite thing to do than out of any desire to please her. Amanda's flirtations didn't mean anything. They were simply her form of communication. "Jacob informed me that we have an emergency board meeting in the morning. I came to let the powers-that-be know that I won't be able to make it."

Amanda pouted, as though personally upset to learn of his absence. "No?"

"No. I have a rodeo scheduled out at Bear Lake and it's too late to cancel."

"Okay, I'll let them know," she replied, slowly running a blood-red painted fingernail in a circle over the coffee-colored desk blotter, her gaze hanging on his as though her life depended upon his next word.

Canyon marveled at the blatant tease. Amanda made no secret of her attraction to him, but it was an attraction that would go unreciprocated. She was cute enough, with long waves of brown hair cascading about the shoulders of her shapely figure, her backside well-defined in the tight hip-hugging jeans she wore, but Amanda wasn't his type. Canyon didn't want a woman who was so casual with her affections that she flirted with every cowboy who walked past her. He wanted a woman who dated with both boots in, same way he did. Recalling his last girlfriend, Canyon thought, make that boots, clothing, hat and damn near his horse! He'd been so in love with the gal that he'd considered popping the question—until she'd revealed she wasn't interested in having children.

They'd been the wrong words in his book. No children meant no deal.

Jacob Hill strode into the office and came to a halt next to Canyon. He removed his black hat and waved gaily. "Hey, Amanda!"

Canyon turned. "Don't you have somewhere to be?"

"Yes, sir," Jacob replied without a glance in Canyon's direction. He was glued to Amanda and smiling so hard his expression looked cemented in place, his skin tinged red clear across his crew-cut shaven skull. He was a farm boy through and through, having more experience with heifers than pretty young ladies, though it didn't stop him from trying.

"I had a question for Amanda."

She giggled. "You always have questions for me, don't you, Jacob?"

"And you always have answers," he replied.

Canyon cleared his throat and gave Jacob a quick prod. "And your question was?"

Jacob clicked to attention and turned to Canyon. "One of the boys is refusing to carry the hay bales. Says he's allergic to hay and his parents will be mad if they find out we forced him."

Canyon eyed him suspiciously. "None of the kids on this track have hay allergies. Did you check his medical card?"

"Nope. That's what I came in here to do."

Amanda perked up as duty called. "Who is it?"

"Kyle Stevens."

"Kyle?" Canyon spit out a laugh. He happened to be well-acquainted with this particular child's medical history. He was recovering from leukemia with NKA—no known allergies. "Kyle isn't allergic to hay any more than you are to pretty women. That boy's playing you, Jacob."

Jacob's cheeks changed three shades of pink. Stealing several glances in Amanda's direction, he didn't say a word, his lips tighter than a roll of twine.

"Why so shy?" Canyon chuckled. "Everybody standing within ten miles of here can tell what's going on between you two." He flicked a glance toward Amanda and added, "Playing dumb isn't gonna hide it, son."

Jacob almost mouthed the word "dumb" but seemed to realize it would make him look all the dumber if he did. Instead, he shoved his hands into the front pockets of his jeans and kicked at an invisible speck of dirt on the floor. "Aw, shoot. I only came in here trying to do my job."

Canyon clapped a hand to Jacob's shoulder and ignored the hangdog expression on his face. Jacob was a good kid. He was a hard worker and a damn skilled ranch hand and Canyon shouldn't make fun at his expense. Though he had to admit, Jacob was easy prey. Shy as a two-day-old kitten and green as a grass blade, he didn't understand how blatantly he displayed his youth. "I'm sorry, Jacob. That wasn't fair." Turning back to Amanda, Canyon tossed out, "If you'll deliver the message, I'd appreciate it."

"What message?" Frank Dillard walked into the reception area, his aging eyes honed in on Canyon like the tip of a blade.

"Canyon can't come to the meeting in the morning," Amanda spoke up.

A snide smile pulled at the corner of Frank's mouth. "Let me guess...a rodeo?"

"Yes."

Frank scowled. "Since when is riding bulls more important than your business obligations?"

Canyon tapped his hat to the desk and replied, "Since the ranch meeting was scheduled without notice."

Frank took a few steps toward him, his contempt barely disguised. "That's why you'll never make anything of yourself, Canyon. You have your priorities screwed up."

Canyon allowed the insult to pass. Frank Dillard was as salty as he was frosty and totally out of line, but this wasn't the time or place to hash out old arguments. General Manager of Wainwright Charity Ranch, Frank was no fan of Canyon's and he made no attempt to hide it. After Mrs. Wainwright's death, Frank had tried to wrangle Canyon under his control but it was a losing proposition. Nobody controlled Canyon Laredo. Not Frank and not Mrs. Wainwright. Lucky for him, his former boss understood a man's need for independence and let him be. It was one of the reasons they had worked so well together. Unfortunately, Frank was a different animal. "The point stands. I can't make it. What's the meeting about, anyway?"

Frank shrugged and crossed his arms over his chest. "Guess you won't know, will you?"

Daggers of animosity flew between the men. If Frank thought he was going to get a rise out of Canyon, he had another thought coming. It wasn't worth the effort. Not on Canyon's part, anyway. "Thanks, Amanda," he said politely, and replaced his hat on his head.

"Sure thing, Canyon." As expected, she shot him a "this one's for you" wink, and threw in a smile for his trouble.

Canyon pushed his ranch hand toward the door. "C'mon, Jacob. We've got work to do." He reached for the door but it swung into him, forcing him and Jacob aside to avoid collision with a blonde woman barreling into the office—a beautiful blonde woman with honeycomb hair and tawny brown eyes.

She flung a hand up to cover her mouth. "Oh!"

"Ma'am, excuse us," Canyon said, removing his hat at once, startled by a push against his legs. He dropped his gaze to a huge yellow Labrador. The dog whimpered and Canyon shot a hand down to the animal. "I'm sorry, guy." He crouched down and stroked the fur to reassure the dog that he didn't mean any harm. "I didn't see you there."

"Cody!" The woman fussed and bent over, her face inches from Canyon's. Peering at him over the dog, she quickly registered the awkward proximity and bolted upright. "I'm sorry," she said, her gaze flushed with discomfort. "He belongs to me, but sometimes, I swear, he doesn't know his own size!" Her gaze darted between him, Jacob and the dog, allowing Canyon a few more seconds to enjoy the view. Soft, naturally plump lips were slightly parted, pulling him to her like a calf on a rope. He grunted inwardly with more than a bump of desire. What he wouldn't give for a taste of those...

Jacob whistled under his breath, yanking Canyon from his thoughts. He fired a silent glance to his side. *That's not how we treat women.* Not around here, it wasn't. The reprimand hadn't gone unnoticed, though the woman said nothing. On the contrary, Canyon noted a small smile had slipped into her gaze. He also noted her ringless fingers. No way this one's single, he mused. There must be an explanation for the absence of jewelry. Canyon straightened, a warm pleasure coiling around him as he replied, "No worries. He's a good-looking animal." The dog wagged his tail as though he understood. "I have a Golden myself, about the same size."

"You do?"

He nodded. "They're a great breed."

"I agree." She smiled up at him and the gesture felt so genuine, so guileless, it reached clear into his chest.

Pleasure surged and Canyon tipped his hat. "Good day, ma'am, and my apologies for the lack of manners displayed by my associate." Smoothing his tone, he added, "I assure you, it won't happen again." With that, Canyon replaced his hat and directed Jacob outside with a firm hand to his arm. As he passed the woman, he picked up a faint scent of expensive perfume.

Once outside, the door closed behind him, Canyon said, "Jacob."

"Yes, sir?"

"That's not how we treat women around here." He whipped a glance toward the office entrance then directed his fiery gaze back to Jacob. "You might talk to Amanda that way, but never a stranger. Not on these grounds."

Jacob shrank from him. He ran a hand along the side of his forehead and said, "Shoot, Canyon. All I did was whistle."

"We whistle for dogs, not women." Ignoring the disbelief pouring from Jacob's gaze, he added, "Don't let me catch you doing that again."

"Yes, sir," came the mumbled reply.

Canyon shook his head then took the lead as the two headed for the barn. While generally he saw nothing wrong with complimenting a beautiful woman, Canyon was on the Board of Directors now and felt obliged to tow a tighter line. Technically, Jacob worked for him, which meant it was his responsibility to keep the kid in line. Wainwright Ranch was a topnotch organization and he wasn't about to let the cowboys run wild. Mrs. Wainwright would have capped Jacob's behavior quick. Now that she was gone, Canyon would do the honors for her.

Besides, that woman appeared as refined as silk and probably crumpled just as easily. If she was a parent on the premises visiting one of the children, she would not be impressed by a staff that hit on every pair of legs that walked through the door. If she was a donor—and she looked every bit as wealthy—she'd be justified in calling him on it. Business was business. Pleasure was personal.

Across the grounds, Kyle's white-blond head poked out from the barn then immediately ducked back. Canyon felt a swell of frustration. Whether he was rebellious at heart or plain old-fashioned bored, Kyle was proving to be a handful, spending more time fighting his chores than doing them. He'd only been here over two weeks and had proven to be a quick study, but the boy fought tooth and nail when it came to his duties. All he wanted to do was hike the trails. He didn't want to ride horses or rope calves. He only wanted to hike. Said he wanted to be a survivalist, like some guy on a television show that he had watched.

Canyon rolled his eyes. Problem number one: kids watched too much television. Back in his day, kids couldn't wait to get outside. From sunup to sundown, Canyon and his buddies had either been on horseback or on foot, roaming the mountains. During the winter, they skied through the trees, jumping any hill or bump they could find. His father had to practically drag him inside under the threat of no rodeos for a year before Canyon would return indoors. He couldn't understand how kids today could watch television or play video games for hours at a time. He'd never been able to sit still that long, let alone sit still while staring at something on a screen.

Thinking back, Canyon chuckled. He had to admit, he'd been rebellious and ornery when it came to his chores, same as Kyle. Difference was, his old man had his number for sure and pinned it to his hide every chance he had. There'd been no cutting of slack in the Laredo household. None. Ever.

"Kyle!" Canyon called out and came to a stop outside the barn. Jacob continued walking past and disappeared around back to where the salt licks were stored. Canyon zeroed in on the spot where he'd seen Kyle and hollered again. "Kyle!"

No response. With determined strides, Canyon marched over and rounded the entrance to the barn. Three stories high with an interior ceiling pitched by angled tin sheets of roofing supported by huge beams, this barn was one of the biggest around. Industrial-sized globes served to light up the place, in addition to huge slants of sunlight spilling in from an open entrance. Walls were lined with tack and farming tools and the ground was a mix of dirt and hay. A tractor was parked in the rear of the barn near several bales of stacked sweet feed stacked, alongside which was an empty wheelbarrow, a pair of work gloves stuck on the ends of its handles. Several children, ranging in age from ten to thirteen, stood at attention about a dozen feet away. A boy on the end dashed a glance toward Kyle and snickered as his blond head darted behind the piles of sweet feed.

Canyon's stomach tightened. The scent of hay collected thickly in his nostrils. He didn't like to see the kids taking sides, rooting for one another to get in trouble, but Kyle seemed to bring it out in the others with his constant, outright refusal to share in the work load. This was a working ranch and chores were part of the deal, something these kids understood when they signed on for an extended summer stay. There could be no slack cut for Kyle.

"Kyle," Canyon stated flatly. "On your feet."

The twelve-year-old rose and reluctantly sidled out from behind the bales.

"Any reason you chose to lie to my ranch hand?"

Kyle dumped his gaze to the ground. "No, sir."

"Any reason I shouldn't make you haul all the bales in light of it?"

Kyle flinched. His dark brown-eyed gaze met Canyon's and revealed a mild panic. "All of them?"

Canyon skimmed the pile next to him and replied, "Yes. All twenty."

"But Mr. Laredo, that's not fair!"

"And it's fair that you tell stories to get out of work, leaving your partners to carry your load?" The children stood like a line of soldiers, and Canyon could see agreement streaming through their expressions, linking one like-minded child to the next. Nobody wanted to carry feed from the barn to the paddocks or refill the water bins. Nobody wanted to scoop poop or brush sweaty horses. They wanted to ride, round up the cattle, hike the mountains and camp overnight.

But mundane work instilled a sense of responsibility, a pride in knowing they contributed to ranch operations as a whole. At Wainwright Ranch that was the name of the game. These kids were part of a team where everyone was expected to do their part.

Kyle was a natural on the ranch but he couldn't be allowed special treatment. He needed to understand that Mr. Laredo meant what he said. Canyon slid a gaze over the line of children and the quivering gazes staring back at him. All of the children needed to understand it. Time to pull the trigger. Canyon cleared his throat. "Well," he began, taking a measured step toward the boy. "Around here it's one for all and all for one, and if we don't get these horses fed and watered, there'll be no trail ride this afternoon."

A collective gasp erupted from the group of them. But not Kyle. He stood defiant. "Mr. Laredo, that's not fair, either. You can't punish us by taking away our trail ride just because we didn't get a chore done. That's not the way the ranch is supposed to work."

Canyon held Kyle in his gaze. "Who said anything about punishment? I'm talking actions and consequences. I can't saddle horses for a two-hour ride if they haven't been properly cared for. I can't expect the animals to perform when we, their ranch hands, haven't done our duties to ensure their care and safety." The utter disbelief staring back at Canyon from Kyle's young face amused him, but he kept his tone direct and objective. "Your choice, son. You work, we ride. You don't, we don't." Canyon turned and walked away.

Kyle cursed under his breath, "Aw, hell."

Canyon turned on his heel and stormed over to him. Towering over him, he drove the point home. "And we don't use that kind of language around here. I'll put you on a plane home first thing in the morning, if you feel these rules are too much for you to handle."

Kyle peered up at him but said nothing, his mouth zipped closed.

Canyon felt a stab of remorse, but it didn't hurt for these kids to learn a little something about respect while they were here. He'd seen too many of them coddled, their parents focused so heavily on battling illness that respect for boundaries had been allowed to slip. Canyon understood there was nothing fun about what these kids were going through—or their parents, for that matter—but he believed that maintaining a strong sense of dignity would help everyone involved. Lashing out with anger and fear didn't solve anything. Self-respect did. It helped funnel the emotional energy through productive channels and gave these kids a fighting chance.

It had been true for Rebecca. She'd lived next door to him growing up and the two had been inseparable, sharing everything from their horses to their dreams. Canyon always believed they'd be friends for life—until she received a diagnosis of lymphoma. It had been devastating. In the beginning, they both had pretended it wasn't real. Then, when the treatments began, there'd been no denying it. Rebecca was sick. She looked sick and felt sick. The doctors said she was going to die. Canyon remembered the day she told him and recalled the flash of anger he'd felt. How could anyone say that to her? How could anyone be sure?

People were cured all the time. They could fight, they could heal. But as he watched Rebecca go back and forth to the hospital, a sense of defeat had begun to pervade their relationship. She was sick. They said she was dying. What Canyon remembered was a girl giving up, accepting what the doctors said without question. The adults around her seemed to agree, and everyone started treating her as though she were a fragile egg about to break open and spill its contents.

Canyon couldn't. Rebecca was his friend. She was tough and brave and still the person she used to be, and that's how he was going to treat her. And to prove this illness of hers was a setback and not a death sentence, he decided to focus on the stuff they used to do, the things she could still do. He got Rebecca back on a horse, back into the creek that ran behind their houses, and refused to feel sorry for her. Instead, he treated her like normal.

The tactic worked and she began to feel better, earning a span of remission. Her parents had been beside themselves with joy, same as he'd been, until the doctors came back a few years later with the news. The cancer was back. It had been the saddest day of his life. Rebecca swore to him that she'd never been happier than she had the last several years, but this time, she was finished. It was too hard. Her parents had suffered too much, and she couldn't bear to see them go through it again. She was done with the business of being sick.

Rebecca died three months later.

Brushing painful memories from his mind, Canyon planted his hands on his hips. Well, he wasn't done with the business of sick children, and at over six feet in height, he knew how to use his size to his advantage. "Do we understand each other?"

"Yes, sir."

"All right. Once the bales are moved, we need to fill the water bins and clean the stalls. Afterward, we'll take a break. At that point, anyone interested in learning to rope a calf can meet me in the paddocks for another go at it."

"I'm going to get a clean catch, today!" a black-haired boy called out. "Just you watch."

Canyon grinned and tossed back, "I believe you, Garrett. You nearly had that calf in knots yesterday."

Garrett Randall was a spitfire. At the age of ten, the boy was already showing signs of muscular definition, and he'd give any calf a run for its money, given the chance. At the hard lump in his throat, Canyon swallowed. That was the goal. *Give him the chance.* Garrett was a survivor of leukemia and Canyon intended for him to stay that way. "You missed that second leg by a hair yesterday, but don't worry. Today will be different."

The boy beamed and Canyon smiled back at him. Garrett reminded Canyon of himself twenty years ago. Content to spend hours at the rodeos watching cowboys run the calves, he'd pay special attention to their technique so he could practice on his own. Once home, he'd throw a rope at anything he could—posts, stumps, bushes. Whatever he could set his sights on, he'd try and wrap a rope around it. But it was the bulls that had held his true fascination. Two thousand pounds of solid muscle that couldn't care less whether you lived or died, yet those cowboys jumped on for the ride of their lives. As a man, it had become Canyon's passion. Fighting to hold on for eight seconds was a rush like no other, a thrill that coursed through his veins. Rodeo riding was in his blood. He lived it and breathed it, from bronco busting to calf roping and everything in between, Canyon loved the sport and he loved sharing it with these kids.

Tomorrow's rodeo at Bear Lake held a hefty purse for anyone who dared, and Canyon had decided he was up for it, especially in light of the current troubles at the ranch. Donations were down, investments weren't performing, and the ranch couldn't sustain the downturn for much longer. Frank Dillard claimed it was due to the poor economy, the rising cost of supplies and expenses and while all that was true, Canyon had his reservations. The economy had been bad for years. Costs were on the rise, but they were steady, not a series of unexpected spikes. And once Mrs. Wainwright had given him control of the cattle accounting, he'd managed to cut a lot of waste from the program. Like monogrammed paper napkins and cups. There was no need to spend money on something the kids were going to use to wipe the crud from their faces then toss in the garbage. Absolutely no sense in it. Same went for printed vendor agreements and invoices. They lived in the digital age. Why waste money printing something when you could email it and then file it away on a computer?

No, Canyon thought. Something else was going on, only he couldn't pin it down. The decline began right after Mrs. Wainwright's death. It was sudden and stark and Canyon didn't believe in coincidences. The two were tied together somehow and he needed to figure out how, and soon. If he wanted to stay on at the ranch, that is. Otherwise his primary life's passion would come to an end.

Chapter Three

Katharine looked at the closed door and felt a warm rush of pleasure. Well over six-feet tall and built like a skyscraper, the blond-haired cowboy with a red bandana wrapped around his neck looked as if he'd been peeled off the pages of *Gentlemen's Quarterly*—the western version—plucked from a horse in motion and put on the ground before her! Dressed in denim and boots and a long-sleeved blue chambray shirt rolled up to his elbows, the man was not only polite but gorgeous. Add a pair of dark brown eyes that practically caressed her out of her clothing and Katharine couldn't help but feel flustered. Expelling a sigh, she absently rubbed Cody's head.

"Hello." The young receptionist smiled broadly. "May I help you?"

Katharine brushed fallen strands of hair from her face and looked past her.

"Amanda," Frank cut in, "I'll take care of her." He walked over and took Katharine into his arms. He hugged her firmly, the musky scent of his cologne welcome. "It's good to see you, Katharine."

Sinking into the warm, comfortable embrace, she replied, "Wonderful." She was back on familiar terrain. Her mother loved this land like no other, and being here made Katharine feel almost a part of her.

Pulling away, Frank raked a hasty glance over her and smiled. "You look as beautiful as ever."

Katharine laughed in reply. "And you're as charming as ever!"

Frank was the same age as her father, the two having met while working at an investment bank in New York, but appeared decades older. It had been a shock to see him when she'd first walked in. His hair was no longer salt and pepper but a dull gray, and his eyes were reddened and glassy. What a terrible burden the last year must have been for him. Not only was he close with her father, but Frank and Eleanor had been longtime friends and associates, working side-by-side here on the ranch. His aging gaze relaxed, the stressed edge from moments before, softened. "It's true," he said. "You look more and more like your mother every time I see you."

The compliment stung. Staving off a wave of tears, Katharine replied quickly, "It's still hard to believe she's gone. Walking in past the front gate, I almost expected to see her standing like a sentry the way she used to do."

He frowned. "I know. We've struggled around here in her absence."

"Struggled" was putting it mildly, Katharine thought. The ship was sinking and the Captain was putting on his happy face. It had been Frank's job to see that the ranch continued on course and without interruption. The pain he must be feeling at watching it shrivel up before his very eyes...Katharine couldn't imagine. She shook the pessimism from her mind: she, too, had a job to do. "I hate to get right to business, but do you think we can go over some details before the meeting tomorrow morning?"

"Of course. I expected you'd want to jump right in, so I've set a few files out for us to go over." Frank paused, and sharp regret punctured his gaze. "I'm sorry you have to deal with this mess. We tried to avoid it, but the odds have been stacked against us. Between the failing economy and your mother's death, it's been a struggle to keep everyone upbeat and operations afloat."

"I understand. No one is blaming you, Frank. We have a problem, we need to solve it." Katharine glanced over her shoulder, uncomfortable sharing any further detail in front of the receptionist who was currently dishing out love for Cody which he was shamelessly lapping up. This was family business and should be kept private. "Can we go into your office?"

"Right this way." Frank stepped aside and extended a hand forward.

Katharine led the way down the hall and Cody automatically followed. Walking, she was struck by the fact that everything remained exactly as she remembered it, from the rich scent of pine wood paneling to the Oriental runner on the floor. Frank's door would be the last one on the right, but she stopped, noting the door to the office on the left was slightly ajar. Nearing it, she slowed and gently pushed it open. The sight hit her like a brick. As though frozen in time, everything looked exactly as it had the last time she was here. From the beautiful paintings of rugged landscape communicated through scope and color and a practiced eye, to the bronzed statue of cowboy and horse, the room evoked a sense of independence and free-spirit. It was bold, distinctive, and totally her mother.

Even the same burgundy leather wingback chairs were angled toward the massive mahogany desk, as though visiting parents would sit in them at any moment. Behind the desk, an entire wall was swallowed up by a bookcase lined with spines of all widths and colors. Katharine instantly envisioned her mother sitting there, gazing up at her daughter with a smile on her face and enough love in her heart to shower a ranch full of children.

"We didn't have the heart to touch any of it," Frank said quietly. Standing behind her, he added, "It's yours to use while you're here."

Katharine's heart squeezed. She had booked a hotel room in town, because she didn't want to stay at the family estate. Could she bear to work in her mother's office, surrounded by the memories infused into this space? Katharine shook her head and managed a small smile. "Thank you, Frank."

He waited while she lingered a moment longer then turned and walked into his office. Much like her mother's, it too had remained the same. Masculine with its chocolate-brown furniture and black leather chairs, brass appointments and similar western-themed bronze statues, Frank's office differed only in his choice of artwork. Lackluster by comparison, his landscape pictures lacked the intensity of emotion and vivid personality of her mother's, feeling more like mass-printed brochures of Colorado. But this was a job for him. For her mother, the ranch had been her life.

Frank circled around his desk as Katharine took a seat in one of the leather chairs. Cody dropped to the floor by her feet, settling his head on top of his front paws. He made no fuss or fidget. The dog was well-trained and well-loved and he knew his turn for attention was coming. Probably smelled the organic dog treats Adele had made for him and was biding his time until his momma dished them out. Adele said they were a new venture for her; organic gourmet dog snacks. For now, she doled them out as a form of advertisement for her restaurant, but who knew? Maybe one day she'd start selling them and Cody could be her poster boy. After all, the dog never met a treat he didn't like!

Frank opened one of the manila folders on his desk and slid it across to Katharine, his demeanor shifting from one of personal friend to business associate. She took the file into her lap and began to peruse the contents.

"The issues boil down to expenses versus revenue," he began. "Over the last year, our expenses have steadily increased, in part due to increased enrollment, but also due to a general hike in feed prices, livestock, energy—the list goes on. We could have handled the increases if we could have sustained the revenue, but we can't."

Katharine looked up at him. "Why not?"

Frank frowned. "Without your mother, people have lost their will to give, I guess."

He guessed? Sucking back a swell of disappointment, she objected, "But the tenets for their giving haven't changed. Terminally ill children continue to come to the ranch for the experience of their lives and walk away enriched because of it. Why stop funding it? Are you saying they were only donating to the ranch as some kind of personal favor to my mother?"

Frank paused, an odd glint in his gaze. "It's more complicated than that, Katharine. Your mother embodied this ranch and everything it stands for. When she passed, it wasn't a surprise that the transition would inevitably include fallout from investors."

"Our investments," Katharine said, picking up on his mention and using it as segue into the meat of the matter, "why are they performing so poorly? I've heard the routine line about the poor economy, but our investments at Wainwright, Emerson have recouped their losses and grown substantially since the downturn. I don't understand what could have changed so dramatically in one year that the ranch wouldn't have realized the same returns?"

Frank shrugged. "Perhaps we should have put ours with Wainwright, Emerson instead of Richmond Capital."

Except for the fact that Katharine's mother wouldn't hear of it. She wanted everything done at arm's length so no one could accuse her of questionable business practices when it came to the finances of Wainwright Ranch. An independent firm held the funds. An independent board comprised of non-family members made the decisions. Eleanor Wainwright believed the ranch should be able to succeed of its own accord and endure the test of time. If it didn't, then it shouldn't be in business. Ironically, the lengths to which her mother had gone in separating the ranch from her personal fortune had proven to be wasted. She would have been better off allowing her husband and daughter to manage the funds than Richmond Capital. Katharine dropped her gaze to the paperwork in her hands. The accounts were in shambles. The ranch was in jeopardy of going under and it might be too late to salvage the loss.

Mentally graphing the information, Katharine was dismayed to see the lines were all headed in the wrong direction. Expenses were up thirty percent, investments were down forty, and donors were dropping like mosquitoes in a buzz-kill light. Flipping through pages, Katharine skimmed the columns of numbers—the itemized list of expenses, the suppliers, the investment funds and returns—the gaps were outstanding. She didn't want to point fingers, but seriously, how had Frank allowed it to go on for so long? At some point, you must recognize you have a problem and work to stop the bleeding before the patient died a slow and painful death.

She lifted her gaze and settled it on him. Had he lost his touch? Was he getting too old for the job? William Wainwright was almost seventy years old yet he still managed to run an investment firm and mind the everyday details of the business, including the crises, spotting problems early and solving them before they careened out of control. Why couldn't Frank? He'd once been her father's right-hand man. If anyone had the skillset, it would be him.

Frank's expression hardened. "I know it looks bad, but I believe there's more going on here than meets the eye."

"How so?"

"The expenses have jumped in the last year, and I think our new board member might be skimming profits."

Katharine stiffened. Yes, he'd mentioned that prior to her arrival. "Do you have any proof?"

"I've got a man looking into it, but it's difficult. The guy is well-connected around Silver Creek and any single one of these companies could be a false front for him to siphon money from the ranch."

"That's criminal, Frank, and quite easy to dissect."

He nodded. "But it can get pretty sticky to prove when you have people willing to lie for you."

Anger swirled in her heart. "I will not tolerate a thief among our ranks." She didn't care who he was or how well-connected, she would prosecute in a heartbeat and to the fullest extent of the law. "Who is this man?"

"Canyon Laredo."

Katharine reached for a pen from Frank's desk and jotted down the name. "I'll take him aside after the meeting tomorrow morning and discuss the situation."

"Sorry, but he won't be attending."

"What?" Razors shredded her patience. "But I thought I made myself very clear. Attendance was *mandatory*, no exceptions."

Frank shrugged, a flicker of smile entering his gaze. "You might want to share that with him."

"I will."

"You can find him out in the stables right now."

Katharine stood. Cody lifted his head, suddenly alert to her motion.

"He's the one that almost knocked you over on the way in."

The blond cowboy?

"Canyon has a rodeo he plans to attend instead of your board meeting."

The kick to her gut was swift and hard. "A rodeo? *That's* his excuse?"

Frank nodded.

Katharine slapped the file down onto Frank's desk and Cody took it as his cue to rise. "Well, we'll just see about that, won't we?"

She strode out of Frank's office with Cody on her heel, a mix of disbelief and irritation churning in her chest. Part of her was admittedly disappointed to learn that the well-mannered good-looking man was potentially the problem. She wouldn't have minded a little eye-candy distraction while she was here, but in light of Frank's revelation, any notion of fun had been effectively crushed. She would not tolerate theft, no matter how handsome the thief.

Sailing past the receptionist, Katharine walked out the door and into a flood of sunshine. Instantly warmed, she looked toward the stables and barn and paused. Children walked from the barn to the stables where a few horse rears poked out from a line of exterior stalls. Several other horses stood idle in a nearby paddock, their tails swishing lazily across their backside as a male staff member approached with a bucket of water. He was the same young man she'd seen in the office. Beyond the activity, mountains were dotted by clumps of evergreen, punctuated by a few yellow aspen in an early show of fall color. The sign of impending fall and winter clashed with the plethora of colorful wildflowers that lined buildings and walkways, dotted the grassland that stretched between ranch and mountain range. In Colorado, summer meant flowers and her mother made sure the ranch was covered with them. They were everywhere—borders, window boxes, rock beds—you couldn't walk ten feet without seeing a beautiful array of lush flowers and healthy greenery, giving a shot of "happy" to the senses. Soon, the carefree happy would give way to hardcore snow and skiers.

Mr. Laredo emerged from the barn, his imposing figure hard to miss and snaring her attention immediately. Who did he think he was attending a rodeo instead of her mandatory board meeting? Did he not value his employment with Wainwright Ranch? Did he not care about the children he was serving?

Now was as good a time as any to find out she decided, and hurried toward him, thankful she had chosen to wear boots instead of heels on her flight from New York. There was no way her four-inch designer shoes would have survived the dusty gravelly trails around the ranch. As it was, her skirt and blouse were collecting more orange dust than she cared to think about.

Canyon Laredo. Homing in on the cowboy as she approached, the name sounded like some fictitious creation for his role as ranch employee rather than a real name, although it did fit him to a T. Her gaze meandered along the lines of his body, a long-legged stride that was almost graceful in its fluidity. A few children jogged to keep up as they followed him around the barn. He was tall and broad shouldered, his lazy swagger that of a cowboy who'd run the range more than a few times, confident he could overcome any challenge put before him. As she neared, Katharine saw the tufts of sandy-blond curls beneath the back rim of his cowboy hat, a tannish number that fit him like an extension of his body, similar to the bandana around his neck. It was an accessory that intrigued her, making him look almost as if he were wearing a costume to fit the part.

Katharine slowed at a black-brown four-board fence, careful not to touch the oiled wood. Cody idled around her feet, sniffing fence posts and bordering clumps of grass. Canyon and the kids had disappeared behind the barn but returned momentarily with an open wheelbarrow. The contraption looked more like a plywood carriage than a functional wheelbarrow, its wheels tall and narrow, its handle constructed of simple black metal. When Mr. Laredo saw her, he slowed his pace, but rather than stop, he continued leading his procession back into the barn.

Unwilling to confront the man in front of the children, Katharine decided to wait. He knew she was here. If he didn't come out and check to see what business she had, she'd seek him out and take him aside. The rules were clear. Strangers were not permitted access to roam the ranch unsupervised. And to him, she was a stranger. He had no idea that she owned the place.

Several minutes passed, and the crew reemerged with a load of hay bales headed for the paddocks. Several horses met them at the fence, their heads bobbing in anticipation. Seemed the animals knew sweet feed when they smelled it. Cody stopped abruptly as he detected the activity across the way. The dog stared, and she could feel his curiosity humming like an energy field between him and the horses. Cody bolted for them and Katharine commanded, "Stay."

Cody's rear hit the ground. She walked over to him and placed a hand to his head. "That's nothing for you to be involved in." Her dog seemed to disagree, his attention focused on the kids and horses like a laser beam.

Katharine laughed softly as she recalled the last time Cody visited the ranch. She'd gone for a trail ride with her mother and a few of the children when Cody slipped out from the office and followed them. Getting underfoot of the horses, the poor boy had nearly been trampled!

"You'd better watch yourself," she told him. "You forget these mountain horses can run over you without blinking."

Cody glanced upward at her then began to whimper. More beg than whine, her boy wanted to go investigate and get a closer look. Katharine did, too. "Okay. We'll go." Then murmured in afterthought, "There is a fence—how much trouble could you get into?"

Katharine stepped forward and Cody took off running. "Heel!" she yelled.

Chapter Four

Canyon saw the woman and her dog heading toward him, the animal's body jumpy and impatient as though fighting a tight leash. But there wasn't a leash. Canyon pursed his lips. Impressive. With so many dogs cavorting unrestrained through Silver Creek, he appreciated a dog that was well-trained. "Jacob! Take over."

Jacob looked up from the fence and saw the woman from earlier. He swiftly angled away and directed, "Okay, kids—let's get to it. The horses are hungry and waitin' on you!"

Pleasure kicked into Canyon as he watched her. She was definitely a looker with her long blonde hair falling in sweeping waves around the shoulders of her slim figure. She walked with confidence, the gold rims of her aviator glasses flashing in the sunshine as her chin tilted slightly upward. Dressed more like she was headed to a business luncheon than a barn, he wondered who she was and why she was here. She looked oddly familiar to him, but he couldn't place her. And if she was a prospective parent or donor, why wasn't Frank accompanying her?

Dismissing the questions as irrelevant, Canyon figured now was as good a time as any to find out and strode toward her. "Hello again," he greeted pleasantly.

"Hello." She stopped half a dozen feet from him and her dog did likewise.

Flashing a quick smile, Canyon said, "Your boy there looks like he's ready for a go-round with the horses."

She slid the sunglasses onto her head and briefly dropped the gorgeous topaz gaze he remembered so clearly from the office, to the animal as she replied, "Only because he doesn't know any better."

Canyon laughed. "My dog Buck isn't much different. Most of the time, he doesn't realize he's in over his head until it's too late."

"They're funny that way."

Canyon liked her smile. It was the kind born from a genuine love of animals. "Your dog is very well-trained," he remarked. "That's good."

She reached out a hand and introduced herself, "My name is Katharine Wainwright."

Canyon gaped at her. "Eleanor's daughter?"

"One and the same."

Shock gave way to astonishment as he quickly filled in the blanks. *That was it.* He knew he'd seen her before and now that she'd mentioned it, the resemblance was unmistakable. Eleanor had been in her mid-seventies when she passed, but had maintained an elegance about her clear up to the end. She'd worked every day, dressed as casually as a cowhand, but her hair had always been styled, usually swept into a twist at the back of her head, and she wore enough makeup to keep her looking refreshed and attractive. Canyon had admired Eleanor Wainwright on so many levels. It was an honor to formally meet her daughter.

"It's nice to meet you," he said. She shook his hand, but he could feel a hesitation in her grip. "What brings you out to the ranch?" he asked. From what he recalled, this woman lived in New York City. Was she here to take over? Part of him hoped so. They needed an injection of Wainwright blood into the leadership role, because frankly, Dillard wasn't cutting it.

"I'm here to address the financial difficulties the ranch has been experiencing and I understand you're one of the board members."

Pride lit into him and he thumbed the ridge of his belt. "I am."

"I understand you don't plan on attending the meeting tomorrow morning."

"Can't. I have a previously scheduled rodeo out in Bear Lake."

"One you deem more important than a mandatory emergency board meeting?"

"Yes."

"What does that say about your dedication to the children?" She flicked a glance toward the paddocks. "Don't you care about the ranch's success?"

Ribbons of resentment curled around his heart. "Of course I do."

"I'd beg to differ."

"Then you'd be begging wrong," he replied, wondering where this full-on assault was coming from. It was one board meeting—a hastily scheduled one at that. Why all the fuss?

Delicate lines around her mouth tensed. "Mr. Laredo, I'm going to have to insist that you cancel your appearance at the rodeo and attend the meeting. One of the larger issues at hand is the management of the costs associated with the cattle and horses, both of which are handled under your direction. I'll need you on hand as we discuss the way forward."

"Yes, ma'am." Canyon pulled his frame a bit taller and rested both hands on his hips, widening his stance a hair as he secured her in his sights. "Only one small problem. You don't tell me what to do. That's my job."

"Excuse me?" Her eyes glittered in the sun as she stared up at him, a distinct defiance churning in her gaze. "Do you value your job around here, Mr. Laredo?"

Canyon slowly pushed the lustful thoughts from his mind and replied, "More than anything in this world, yes, ma'am."

"Well then, I suggest you rearrange your priorities and start acting like a man who cares."

"I try my best to do so every minute of the day."

"Yet you're leaving for a rodeo in the morning."

"There's a mighty big purse at stake and I intend to claim it."

"Money?" Her light-brown gaze turned to stone. "This is about *money*?"

"Isn't it?" He suppressed a rise of amusement. "You mentioned the financial difficulties. That means money, right?"

"Don't get flippant with me."

"I'm sorry," Canyon replied and held up his hands. He wasn't here to fight. Ironically, he'd come over for wholly opposite reasons. With a glance toward the kids currently tossing feed for the horses under Jacob's supervision, he responded, "I'm sorry about missing the meeting, but you gave me no notice. And your lack of planning cannot become my crisis. These kids mean as much to me as they did to your mother, and there's nothing I wouldn't do for them. And that includes attending this rodeo." He tipped the brim of his hat. "Now if you'll excuse me, I have work to do."

Canyon turned, and ignoring her protest, returned to his duties. Truthfully, he was sorry to be missing the meeting. There were serious issues with the ranch that needed attention and he was glad to see Eleanor's daughter here in person to see and deal with them, but that didn't change anything for him. Bear Lake was a three-day run with some hefty payouts. If he won, he could take home over thirty grand, enough to finance one child at the ranch for a two-week stay. Not bad for a few seconds work. Make that eight seconds—on the back of a ball-busting bull looking to wreak sheer havoc on a man's body—and Canyon intended to outlast every cowboy to make it. It wasn't going to be an easy ride but it was a ride worth taking. Ms. Wainwright was right. This trip to Bear Lake was definitely about money and bailing out at the last minute would put a dent in his reputation, a definite no-can-do.

As he pulled up next to the kids, Canyon shook the confrontation from his mind, pleased to see Kyle with his hands full of sweet feed, half of it clinging to his navy T-shirt.

"What was that all about?" Jacob asked.

"That was Ms. Wainwright."

Jacob gave a double-take. "Huh?"

Canyon didn't follow his gaze but replied under his breath so the kids wouldn't hear, "Mrs. Wainwright's daughter. She's here to save the ranch."

Jacob's gaze wandered back to her, his mouth agape. "Do you think she can do it?"

"I hope so." Life would be a sadder place without it.

Not that there weren't other dude ranches and camps for terminally ill kids, there were, but none reached the level of Wainwright. Eleanor's vision had been bred from experience. She had lost her first child to leukemia, but confessed to him that worse than the pain of losing the girl had been the pain of watching her suffer the curious stares, the questions. *Why was she so thin? What's wrong with her? Why can't she come out and play?* The subsequent demoralization to her daughter's spirits sent Eleanor over the top.

It was a story Canyon recalled hearing on more than one occasion, usually when someone dared challenge Eleanor's premise for the ranch, accusing her of being too hard on the kids. She'd give it right back to them in no uncertain terms, telling naysayers that she understood these kids better than most. She understood what they longed for, what they needed, and she intended to deliver. Period.

Unable to resist, Canyon stole a glance toward her daughter. Standing where he'd left her as though uncertain what to do next, Ms. Wainwright looked out of place. She was city sleek, gorgeous and sophisticated and he hoped, half the woman her mother had been. Canyon swallowed back a lump. Wainwright Ranch had changed lives. He hated to think of a world without it.

Chapter Five

Seated at the head of a solid wood conference table, a handcrafted piece of furniture her mother had made from timber collected around the ranch, Katharine stood when Frank entered the room. He closed the door behind him and quietly took a seat at the opposite end of the table. Spacious, private, the windowless room gave way to minimal distraction. Unlike the rest of the luxuriously-appointed Wainwright offices, this room boasted no paintings, no bookcases, only a table and chairs. This space was strictly business. And it was time to get to the business at hand.

Taking a deep breath, she glanced around the room. Seven out of ten board members were in attendance. Of those missing, one was out of the country, one had taken ill, and one was attending a rodeo. Irritation curdled in her stomach. Because attending a rodeo was more important than answering the Chairman's call for questions regarding the state of affairs within the organization of Wainwright Ranch.

Katharine ran a hand down her midsection, flattened the front of her fitted blazer then set a finger to the closed file before her. While most in attendance opted for business casual, she preferred the formality of a suit. In her mind, it maintained the distinction between business and personal. As a woman, she found it an important line to maintain. Taking a deep breath, she began, "I'd like to thank you all for coming. I know this meeting was called on short notice, but under the circumstances, I believe it was warranted." Solemn faces stared back at her, experienced, aged, each intense and seemingly engrossed with concerns of his or her own. "Wainwright Ranch sits on the verge of insolvency. Our investment assets have declined considerably over the last year and expenses have risen, donations are lagging..." She paused and looked around the table, careful to make eye contact with each and every member. "I'm sure this is not news to you. The ranch is in a crisis situation and I need your help finding solutions."

"Are you looking to raise more capital, Katharine?" Gary Levine asked. Chief Executive Officer for a hedge fund out of California, his middle name was capital and everything about his appearance oozed the same. From his expensive silk dress shirt to his impeccably trimmed black hair, he was a man who turned fortunes like a chef flipped pancakes, making millions in the blink of an eye.

She turned to him and said, "Increasing donations must be a part of the equation, yes. However, it cannot be the only avenue we pursue." Taking her seat, she opened the folder and skimmed a finger down the top page as though checking her notes, a move totally unnecessary. She'd memorized the list down to the last penny in assets. "Our investments have suffered and our costs have risen. Currently, we spend thirty-eight thousand dollars per child, per two week visit. Sixty, for those who stay with us for four weeks. Averaging one hundred to one hundred and twenty campers each summer, that equates to about half a million dollars. Over the last year, we've added a second barn, a new henhouse, increased the herd by ten percent, excluding the calves born this past spring, and our liability insurance has spiked. Travel expenses for the children have nearly doubled. Add in the legal fees, medical fees, staff salaries..." She paused, allowing the information to sink in. "For the first time since the ranch's inception, contributions have fallen short of projected expenses."

The organization sat on three million dollars in cash, but that value was markedly less than what it was only three years ago, none of which should be a surprise. The board members received the financial reports. They were intelligent businessmen and women. They understood the repercussions. "Going forward, we need to reduce ranch expenses and take steps to ensure our financial investments are growing. Wainwright Ranch is a working ranch, but perhaps it's time to consider thinning the herds." It was a starting point, anyway.

"This is a conversation you should be having with Canyon Laredo," Frank said. He glanced at Gary who nodded, along with two women seated across from him, one an investment banker out of Denver, the other a wealthy philanthropist from Texas. "He's running that wing of operations."

"Thinning the herd that brings in revenue isn't the way I'd go," Zeke Roberts put in. He was an older gentleman sporting the classic western-style shirt with front and back yokes and pearlized snap-closed pockets. Black cowboy hat firmly rooted on his head, the man was a living, breathing cowboy and Katharine expected as much from him. Cattle was Zeke's business and according to Frank, Zeke was Canyon's partner in getting the animals to market, which in her opinion, gave him a less than an objective perspective on the matter.

Squelching her personal rebuttal, she replied coolly, "If we can't afford to feed them, it doesn't make sense to keep them, Mr. Roberts."

"Except for the fact that cattle prices are on the rise." Zeke glanced at his fellow members seated around the table, adding, "Doesn't make sense to cut a profitable revenue stream when you need it most, now does it?"

It was true that the cost of meat was increasing, but caring for the animals until they were ready for slaughter wasn't making current financial sense for the ranch. A vegan herself, Katharine would prefer they had nothing to do with the meat industry. In fact, if she were running the place, she'd be content to sell off the entire herd and deal solely in horse breeding.

But her mother had chosen cattle, so cattle it was. Katharine cleared her throat and stated simply, "I think everything should be on the table when it comes to cost-cutting. However, one of my biggest concerns is the lack of donations. Wainwright Ranch might be a working ranch, but we're also a charitable organization. What's going on there? Does anyone have any insight they're willing to share?"

"After your mother's death, several of our major contributors backed out," Celia Glenn, a banker based in Denver, spoke up. A well-put-together brunette in her mid-fifties, she reeked of success though she was somewhat sedate in nature. Looking at Katharine with a very serious expression, she said, "I spoke with one in particular, who shall remain nameless, who said, and I quote, 'No Eleanor, no money.'"

Katharine bristled. "Even though the money is supporting the same good cause as when she was alive?"

Celia shrugged, her narrow shoulders moving like pointed hangars beneath her nearly sheer silk blouse. "It's his money," she replied in a tone too cavalier for Katharine's liking. "He can choose his charities as he pleases, and he's not pleased to give to Wainwright Ranch."

"I've heard similar remarks," Gary echoed.

"I was told the new fundraising liaison is the problem."

Surprised by the statement, Katharine looked to the philanthropist, Susan Billingsworth. The older woman with a big blonde hairstyle, a palette of makeup, and a slew of gold and diamond accessories that any jeweler would covet, questioned, "Are you talking about Javier Suarez?"

"No. Paul Sutherland," Frank responded. "But he's been on the job for less than a year so I don't think we can lay all the blame at his feet."

"Twelve months and a dozen less corporate donors," Susan spit back. On the larger side, she was built like a Texas longhorn with a personality to match. "I'd say that's pretty significant."

Katharine stared at her. "How much money are we talking?"

"Over three hundred thousand between them," Susan replied. "Davis Construction, Huey Medical Systems and Strong Equipment have all dropped out."

"They're minor donors," Frank said.

Nothing was minor when every dollar counted! Katharine bit back her response and asked with measured control, "Anyone have any suggestions on how to correct the situation?"

Gary smiled. "Hire a new fundraiser?"

That's it? Katharine moved her gaze from face to face. These were the people responsible for the success of Wainwright Ranch and no one had anything better to offer? Zeke shot a disapproving glare toward the room at large then settled his gaze on the conference table. The women's gazes were teeming with opinion, though neither offered the first remark. The last gentleman remained silent. A grocer out of Boulder, he seemed as blasé as Gary Levine.

Across the table, Frank's flat expression reflected Katharine's disappointment. It was as if she were staring at a blank wall. The room lacked passion. There was no creative brainstorming, no critical eye offering a helpful suggestion. Back in New York, Katharine usually had to run for cover as ideas flew through the boardroom. Not here. These people were about as enthused as a string of wooden posts.

Exhaling a tight sigh, she stood. "The fundraiser is less than two weeks away. If we don't fix our numbers, prove that we remain viable, the ranch will fail."

A few nodded, but no one sitting at the table appeared to care.

Katharine had seen it before. This was a job to them. They had no emotional stake in the outcome, no financial interest. "Board member of Wainwright Ranch" was nothing more than a title to list in their professional profile. It wasn't a passion that burned in their heart. They were warm bodies filling chairs. "I'm sorry I wasted your time," Katharine said. Closing her folder, she picked it up and walked out of the room.

Bridling on the verge of temper, Katharine went into her mother's office and closed the door with a firm thud. Lying in a corner, Cody's head popped up. Ignoring the animal,

Katharine walked to the desk but didn't sit. Her emotions were running too high, too hot. Walking out on a board meeting was never in good form, but Frank could deal with the fallout. It beat risking what might come out of her mouth if she had stayed.

She couldn't force people to care. She couldn't make them want to salvage something they didn't care about. She slammed a hand on the desk. "What's the matter with people?"

Katharine balled her stinging palm into a fist and whipped her glance around the office. Didn't they care about the children? Didn't the good the ranch was doing matter to any of them? They were changing lives. They were making a real and positive difference. Cody was on his feet now, poking his nose against her leg. Katharine gave a brisk rub to reassure him she was okay, though every fiber in her being felt completely the opposite. There was nothing good about facing a room filled with complacency.

Katharine's gaze landed on a photograph of her parents. Perched on a corner of the desk, the framed image captured her parents in their western element. Dressed in jeans and boots, they stood smiling, two gorgeous horses behind them, a brilliant blue sky filled the horizon. They loved it here. Completely different from their home in New York, Colorado provided release, serenity, pure living in a pure environment. Katharine's heart ached as she lingered on the image. Her father had sent her here to fix the problem. He had sent her here to save her mother's ranch. How could she tell him no one cared? How could she tell him that his wife's dream was fading in the wake of her death?

Katharine looked away and tamped back an urgency she couldn't squelch. Through a window, she saw cattle grazing in the distance, a backdrop of mountains dotted with fall color. Fat cattle, black cattle, brown cattle. *Hungry cattle.* She didn't care what Zeke said. Thinning the herd was a viable option—as was cutting expenses across the board. Visions of Canyon Laredo entered her mind. Frank indicated that he was the man in charge when it came to the animals. He was the man in control of the barn and stables.

And he was the man potentially skimming profits.

Anger fired through her veins. He was also the man involved with the kids on a day-to-day basis. What kind of example was he setting? Was he good for them? Too hard? Uncaring? At this point, she had no idea, but when he returned from his rodeo escapade, she'd question him. She'd question staff, run through costs to the last penny, and every single one had better be accounted for. If not, Canyon Laredo would rue the day he crossed a Wainwright.

Katharine forced her gaze back to the photograph. Drawn to the indelible smile on her mother's face, the vibrancy of her gaze, Katharine understood what this ranch had meant to her. Eleanor Wainwright had lived the nightmare of watching a sick child die. It happened before Katharine was born. Her sister Sarah had contracted a rare leukemia and within two years, was gone. After only six short years on earth. Katharine closed her eyes and tried to imagine how horrible it must have been to watch your child die. The suffering, the heartbreak, the inevitable *why me, why her*?

When Katharine was a teenager, her mother had shared the story and said three words that changed Katharine's perspective on the subject forever. "Why *not* me? Why *not* Sarah?"

But that was her mother. It was the epitome of how she viewed everything. Katharine thought back to a letter her sister had written. Penned months before she took her last breath, the youngster seemed to understand what their mother had been saying. *If not me, then who? My best friend Gracie? My cousin Joey? If God needs an angel, why not me?*

Katharine's heart fluttered against a rush of tears. A deep wrench wound through her chest as she swam through memories. Wainwright Ranch was her mother's legacy to her sister's life. It was a project that had consumed her mother's existence for the last two decades, the last ten in the form of the ranch. It was a cause she lived and breathed. Touching a shaky hand to the file on the desk, Katharine was struck by sharp need. She couldn't stay here. She had to go. Grabbing the folder, she slid it into her briefcase, collected her purse and sunglasses and hurried out of the office. The phone rang. She froze, debating whether or not to answer it but automatically ran back in and yanked the receiver from its cradle. "Hello?"

"Ms. Wainwright," Amanda said. "I have the bank on line one. They asked to speak with Frank but he's still in the board meeting. I thought maybe you could handle it?"

"Yes, of course. Thank you, Amanda." Jabbing a button for line one, she answered with as much grit as she could muster, "Ms. Wainwright, may I help you?"

"Hello. My name is Dan Baxter and I'm calling from First Federal. We have some questions on your account regarding a recent international transfer."

"What kind of questions?"

"Are you an authorized member of the account?"

She hesitated. Not technically, no, but as owner of the company she had authorized access to all accounts. "I'm the owner of Wainwright Ranch. I should be listed as Katharine Wainwright."

After a brief pause, the man replied, "I'm sorry, but I don't see your name anywhere on the account. I'll need to speak with Mr. Dillard directly."

Katharine shot her gaze to the ceiling. Rules and regulations, rights, privacy... They were the name of the game when it came to financial institutions. "Of course. If you'll give me the account number, I will relay the message to him."

"I'm sorry, but I'm not permitted to do so."

"We have several accounts with your institution," Katharine said more directly into the mouthpiece. "I need to tell him which one you're referring to."

"Please tell him it's regarding the foundation account."

"Fine." Katharine jotted the information down on a small notepad. "I'll let him know."

Ending the call, she tore the paper from the pad and headed out of the office. She couldn't sit for another minute while her mission went down in flames around her. The board might not care what happened to the ranch, but she did.

It would have to be enough.

Katharine pushed out the side door of the Wainwright administrative building, her mind seething with questions as an early cold front pinched her cheeks. *International transfer? Why would the foundation be involved in anything of the kind? Was it a new donor?* A burst of sunlight poured down from overhead, adding warmth to the strange mix of cold and questions already pummeling her brain.

"Mrs. Wainwright!"

She stopped short and Cody's warm furry body bumped into her.

Turning, she saw a dark-haired man approach. Dressed in suit and tie, he appeared about her age but wholly unfamiliar to her. Had they met? Did he work here?

Katharine waited in place, uncertain whether or not she wanted to speak with anyone at the moment. Not that he appeared hostile. In fact, he was exceptionally good-looking. His jet-black hair was combed back revealing piercing blue eyes, a polished smile and an expression that was totally nonconfrontational. Actually, the man had a dashing flair about him, reminding her of the men she knew on Wall Street.

"Thanks for waiting," he said easily, as though he expected nothing less than her full attention. "When they told me you'd left, I was hoping I'd catch you."

"And you are?" she questioned.

"Paul Sutherland." He flashed a thousand-watt smile. "I'm your point man when it comes to securing donations. I was hoping we could sit down and discuss some of what's been going on over the last several months."

Shifting her possessions to a single arm, she shook hands hesitantly, finding his grip warm and soft. *Did he not under-*

stand that he was falling short of expectations? Did they not warn him that she was unhappy with his performance?

"Frank called me in."

"Frank."

He nodded. "We've been having some issues and I wanted to discuss a strategy for increasing our donor pool."

"Actually, I was on my way into town but I think I can spare a minute or two." He seemed sincere in his effort to help, and increasing donations was priority one.

"Great." Paul eyed the side door and asked, "Can we sit down somewhere?"

"Certainly," she replied, torn between his looks and her desire to confront him. The man was excruciatingly beautiful.

Paul opened the door and she stepped inside, the roast of heat instantly sucking her in. She pulled the sunglasses from her face and walked down the hall she'd traveled only moments before. Unwilling to go back into her mother's office, she detoured right and headed for the conference room, until she realized it was still occupied by disgruntled board members. At a sudden loss for direction, she stopped.

Paul stood beside her and Katharine felt awkward in the pause.

"Would you like to go into my office?" he asked.

"You have one?"

He smiled, unaffected. "Sure do. Right this way."

Katharine followed him down a hall that branched off before her mother's office. It led to a line of offices occupied by Frank's secretary, a ranch accountant, a schedule coordinator and an empty office once used by her mother's secretary. The medical staff was housed in a separate building, as were the maintenance people. Apparently, her mother's secretary's office now belonged to Paul, who wasted no time in taking a seat in front of a small desk while offering her an adjacent chair.

"Sorry my desk is a mess," he said with a sheepish grin. Unbuttoning his jacket, he continued, "But you know what they say, 'busy mind, busy desk.'"

Katharine wasn't sure she agreed with the logic, but it mattered little. She cared about what he had to say with regard to donors, not what his work space looked like. Sitting, she set her briefcase and purse on the floor. Cody automatically curled up on the floor next to them.

"Nice dog."

"Thanks." Paul didn't seem to mind his presence, but then again, in Colorado dogs indoors were almost as common as people.

"I'm sure Frank has informed you on the issues we've been having with our corporate donors," he said.

"Yes," she replied, her emotions cramped by the confines of the small space and the close proximity to this man. "We just concluded a board meeting where the sentiment was reiterated."

"I think it's an excuse. I think we need to sell harder, not close up our tent and walk away."

Katharine angled her head and thought, wasn't he criticizing *himself*? He was the liaison, after all. It was his job to bring in the money. But prepared to listen, she asked, "What do you propose we do to change course?"

Paul's smile reemerged with vigor, as if she'd asked the exact question he was waiting for. "Video. Radio. We need to get the word out about what we're doing around here. People need to see for themselves what great work the ranch is doing, and there's no better way than streaming live, accompanied by full-length interviews. Imagine it," he said, stretching his hands out between them as he sat back in his chair. "The screen is filled with images of joyful children riding horses, working the cattle, and viewers hear your voice explaining what's happening, what the kids are doing, and how it benefits their self-esteem and in turn, their health."

Katharine looked at Paul through his imaginary screen and thought, *that's his best idea?*

"Kids with huge smiles will steal the hearts and the PR will spread like wildfire," he continued. "We can even capture scenes of Canyon and the kids playing rodeo games."

The mention yanked her attention like a hand to the chin. "Canyon plays rodeo games with the kids? What kind of games?"

"The usual, they rope calves, ride horses around barrels. Some even act as rodeo clowns."

Alarm bells sounded in her skull. "*He does this with the children?*"

Paul stilled. "Is there a problem?"

"Only if you consider injuries to terminally ill children a problem! Their well-being is paramount to our success—we can't risk that by allowing them to be involved in risky behavior."

"I haven't seen any injuries," Paul murmured, his enthusiasm quickly dimming.

Katharine's stomach tightened. "Mr. Sutherland, while your idea sounds like a fine one, my mother made a strict practice of not involving the kids with public exposure. The ranch is a sanctuary from the world at large, not a fish bowl where we exploit their experience here." Or expose them to needless danger, she mused, though voicing the same would have no impact on this man. It wasn't he who was involved in risky behavior. That distinction belonged to Canyon Laredo.

"Who said anything about exploit?" Paul leaned forward, appearing genuinely shocked. "We simply share their experience on the ranch. Think of it in terms of inspiration, not exploitation."

She couldn't. Because it wasn't. Overwhelmed by a rush of cologne, she replied, "I appreciate your enthusiasm, Mr. Sutherland, I do. Unfortunately, opening the ranch experience up for public entertainment was never part of my mother's vision."

"Your mother isn't here anymore."

Katharine stiffened. Suddenly, it was easy to imagine why their donor contact was turning people away. This man took signs like a blindfolded cab driver. "No, she isn't, but her commitment to the children's privacy didn't die with her. It remains firmly ingrained in the operations of Wainwright

Ranch." Katharine stood quickly, and Cody lifted from the floor. "If you'll excuse me, I really must be going."

Slowly, Paul Sutherland rose. Penetrating blue eyes searched hers. "I think it's something you should consider."

"Thank you," she replied. But she would do no such thing.

"The donors of the past were here because of your mother," he said pointedly. "The donors of the future won't be."

Katharine felt the bite. Where the man might not have meant the statement to be insulting, it felt every bit as hurtful as a slap in the face. Without another word to him, she walked out of his office, his words ringing in her ears. *Did everyone on this ranch think the charity was doomed without her mother?*

Chapter Six

Katharine spent the next two days holed away in her hotel room, her time broken by infrequent visits to the ranch and meals with Adele. It was a tedious existence in a place known for fresh air and clean living at its finest, but an unavoidable one. After two hours navigating the maze of cabinets and computer files in the ranch office, she'd finally turned up the files she'd been searching for—the bank records from years prior to compare to the current ones. She loved Frank to death, but couldn't give him an "A" for organization. His system—if he had one—was terribly confusing. Instead of filing the information away by year or category, it had been scattered across computer program files and folders, with some of the information stored in print form, some in both digital and print. It was crazy. Even the donor information which should have been stored alphabetically and in one location had been filed away in three different locations. Katharine couldn't imagine what the poor accountant must have to endure in preparing their tax return.

Yet the exhaustive search had only raised more questions than answers. If she thought things were bad before poring over the numbers, she was now thoroughly convinced the ranch would be closed by the end of the year. Not only were they bleeding money in expenses, the investments were being soaked by fund managers. How could Frank let this happen? Had he been sleeping at his desk? It didn't make sense. Costs were definitely up, but according to the records, the ranch shouldn't be in as deep a hole as it was. The list of donors was incomplete. Comparing the list for the last three years, many of the names were the same, even through the current year, yet the board claimed donors had been lost. Where? Who was missing?

Katharine intended to make personal contact with each and every organization as part of her visit and touch base with everyone prior to seeing them at the fundraiser. But if she was going to initiate a phone call, she needed the list to be correct. Which led her to wonder, if the list of names wasn't correct, were the amounts? Based upon the taxes Wainwright had paid out on the most recent tax return, the ranch should be showing a much bigger profit.

Pushing back from the desk in her hotel room, she decided to call Frank and dialed his number, pulling the pencil from her mouth. *Darn it*, she silently cursed. Would she ever break the silly habit?

At the sound of Frank's voicemail, Katharine ended the call. There was no reason to leave a message. Not on a Sunday afternoon. She'd see him in the morning and go over her questions then. Scanning the papers in hand, she double-checked the list and jotted more checkmarks by the names she'd seen consistently over the years. The Boylston Group, Acme Lumber, Transnational, Grace Insurance, Allied American. But after her third run-through, she gave up. She'd ask Frank tomorrow. He'd know.

Trading one file for another, Katharine perused the list of funds in which the ranch had invested. Richmond Capital was an excellent firm with a sterling reputation. She knew several brokers who worked with the group and all were at the top of their game. Wainwright's capital positions should be healthy, if not stellar, and performing as expected. The market could take a hit, but a smart investor knew how to recover and quickly. Richmond Capital had good people who played the game as well as she did.

What bothered her more than lousy returns was the fact that some of the accounts looked as if they'd been churned. A definite no-no. It was investing 101; long-term growth was achieved by selecting successful growth funds and allowing time to work its magic. Assets traded any more frequently than six months was a recipe for disaster. For the fund *owner*, that is. It spelled big money in the form of commissions for the fund manager. But Frank knew better. He knew how the investment process worked and the only way this could have happened was if he hadn't been paying attention. It almost felt like he had allowed the fund managers to run rampant with Wainwright's investments, and now the ranch was paying the price.

Katharine closed the file. Unfortunately someone had been paying attention, only not the right person. Sliding the papers into her briefcase, she stood and walked over to a window. Outside the sun was shining over a spattering of tourists meandering cobblestone streets. This was shoulder season in Silver Creek. Not the height of summer, not the peak of fall, it was a time when the number of visitors was reduced, lending a quiet feel to the village. Year after year she had traveled here, and enjoyed the unhurried pace of resort living. She could walk these streets with her eyes closed and not miss a turn. She knew every storefront, every tree and bridge, every curve in the namesake creek as it flowed through town.

During the winter months her family skied. During the summer they golfed or rode on horseback over the acreage behind their home. Some of Katharine's best memories of her parents had been created in Silver Creek, and visiting the village without either one felt wrong.

Incomplete. Gripped by a sense of longing, Katharine reminded herself that she wasn't here for vacation. She was here to solve problems. Big problems. Softening her focus on the people below, flower beds layered with color, Katharine paused, and her thoughts went to Frank. It pained her to point the finger at him but it had to be done. She had to address his role within the organization and discern whether or not he was slipping in his duties. If he was, she had to let him know—a conversation that would be uncomfortable for both of them.

Katharine had always looked up to Frank. He was a peer of her parents, an equal in business and intellect. Her father had relied heavily on him in New York and then, when Frank moved out to Colorado, her mother's reliance on him had solidified that confidence. But now, it was clear he was failing. It was possibly due to his health. He didn't look good. She had noticed it the minute she saw him. He could be declining in mental acumen. He could be losing his faculties and not even be aware of it. But informing the man that his judgment was failing was *not* a conversation she wanted to have. It could permanently damage relations between Frank and her father. Another conversation she dreaded. The only bright spot she'd found in her trip thus far was in observing the children. Watching them work with the animals this weekend reminded her of why Wainwright Ranch existed. They worked and played and when one of the girls spotted her, the youngster jogged over with a handful of freshly-picked flowers. The image of her smiling face filled Katharine's heart with a fond warmth. Turning from the window, she called out, "C'mon, Cody. Let's go to the ranch."

She could use a shot of "happy" right about now.

A half-hour later, standing near the paddock fence line, Katharine watched as a circle of almost a dozen children gathered around a small calf, each taking a turn holding a bottle for the greedy animal while the calf's mother hovered nearby. With an eagle eye on the children, Katharine noted with amusement. Not that momma had anything to worry about. This was the younger set of campers with ages ranging from six to eight whose only goal was to help wean the young animal from its mother. Well, that and pet the calf relentlessly. In the distance, a group of teens on horseback looked to be returning from an afternoon ride. Definitely a beautiful day for it, the scene peeled right off the pages of a Colorado tourism magazine. Wide open grassland was home to lazy cattle and grazing horses, a mountainous range puncturing the brilliant blue sky. Only a scattering of dead evergreen marred the scenery, the rusted brown branches evidence of the pine beetle's presence.

Focusing on the patches of dead trees, Katharine thought it was terrible how much devastation could be caused by such a tiny animal. And dangerous. South of Silver Creek, wildfires had decimated thousands of acres of forest, because the dead trees provided ready fuel. Fortunately, this area had experienced a reduction in damage due to vigorous management efforts, paid for by Palmer International. As owners of the Silver Creek ski resort, they had a huge financial stake in maintaining the desirability of this area. Palmer put their money to work assisting the Forest Service as they thinned the forests and created fire breaks, swaths of empty space between tree lines and private land. It was an aggressive campaign and it was succeeding.

Drawing her thoughts back to the children, Katharine knew activities were divided according to age. Teenagers with an ability to ride worked the cattle on horseback by moving them from one pasture to another, while grade school children were tasked with the more sedate duties like feeding calves and collecting eggs from the henhouse.

Henhouse. Katharine shook her head and turned toward the structure in question. Positioned catty-corner to the barn, it was a small wooden building embellished with a stenciled painting of a hen just to the right of an open-arched entryway. It was cute, and fit in with the other architecturally stunning structures, but Wainwright Ranch needed a henhouse like they needed a bowling alley. What had Canyon been thinking when he built it? More work equals more pay? It wasn't like they were selling the eggs. They were consuming them. Katharine groaned aloud. Hens needed to be fed, cared for, housed—and at what price? Buying in bulk from a local farm had to be more cost-efficient.

"Is there a problem?"

Katharine whirled at the sound of the male voice. Biting back a gasp, she blurted, "Mr. Sutherland."

"Call me Paul, please," he said, sliding black sunglasses onto his head. "Mr. Sutherland makes me sound old."

Inhaling a deep breath, she replied as calmly as her pounding heart would allow, "Paul."

No longer dressed formally in suit and tie, he had donned the same jeans, boots and cowboy attire as the staff and children. Only this man looked like a cowboy model as opposed to a working rancher, the pristine white of his shirt proof-positive he hadn't been around the dusty ranch property for long. The fancy embroidered pattern taking up space on his upper chest and shoulders suggested the man was more urban-cowboy-wannabe than the real deal.

Cody was up and Paul rubbed his head. "Hey, buddy." The dog's whole body wagged with delight. Paul grinned as he found the sweet spot behind Cody's ear, the dog pushing his head into the man's hand. "Frank says you're from New York. I bet this big guy prefers Colorado."

"I'm sure he does," Katharine replied offhandedly, wondering why Paul Sutherland was standing here making light conversation with her after their last conversation had not gone very well. Was there a reason behind his presence at the ranch on a Sunday afternoon? She didn't imagine this was his normal schedule.

"Those kids are pretty cute handling that calf, aren't they?"

"They are," she agreed, instantly on the defense, her gaze darting between the children and the man, thankful she had left her sunglasses in place. No sense in giving away her position. If Mr. Sutherland—Paul—thought he was going to change her mind about filming them in action he was wrong.

"Listen, I wanted to apologize if I offended you the other day." He pushed his hat back on his head and set his hands to his hips. Katharine inwardly cringed as his elbows brushed perilously close to the top of the oiled fence. The marks he would walk away with on his gorgeous white shirt would be permanent should the two connect. "If I offended you with my comments about your mother, I'm sorry."

"No offense taken," she lied. Cody resumed position by her feet, his body lightly touching hers as he practically sat on her feet. It was his way of keeping tabs on his owner.

"But my job is to raise money," he continued, "and I feel like my hands are tied."

"How so?"

"Mr. Dillard thinks like you do. He wants nothing to do with advertising the features and benefits the ranch has to offer sick children, and it makes no sense. It's almost as though he hired me under false pretenses."

"False pretenses?"

"Nothing against Mr. Dillard," Paul said, a quick glance over his shoulder toward the administrative building, "but it feels like he wants me to fail."

"I'm sure you're misreading him. Frank loves this ranch as much as I do," she said, suddenly curious as to the three dropped donors Susan Billingsworth mentioned during the board meeting. "Why do you feel we're losing donors?"

Paul hitched a boot up onto the bottom fence rail. He set palm to thigh and looked her straight in the eye. "I have no idea."

"But you must know something."

He shook his head. "Nada."

"No one gave any excuses why they weren't making a contribution this year?"

"Nope."

Katharine narrowed her gaze. This line of conversation was going nowhere. "I see..." she mumbled, mentally distancing herself from this man. While he looked sharp and capable, his words led her to believe anything but.

"I hope you do see, because I have some really great ideas that can get this place rocking, but I need the freedom to pursue them." The piercing blue of his gaze seemed to drill his point into her.

Erecting a steel wall between them, she deflected his intensity. "If you're referring to the video, I think you should let that go. It's my decision not to go forward with it, not Frank's."

"Sure, no problem," he replied with a smile, though his gaze had lost its luster. "It's your ranch."

And her problem, she mused.

"But it's not the only thing I've been working on. I've been steadily adding names to the invite list for the fundraiser and a few look promising."

Katharine perked at the mention. "So you're having success attracting new money?"

"So far I've added ten new possibles, plus another five I think will come through for us with a little coaxing."

"Really? Who are they?"

"Glazier Foods, Sunshine Films, Canyon Falls Foundation, Children United and Fogarty International, to name a few."

She hummed quietly. "That's an impressive list."

"Deep pockets."

Katharine wouldn't have phrased it in those terms, but Paul was right. Those companies were sizable corporations with plenty of cash under their control. The fact they were willing to attend the fundraiser meant they were willing to consider Wainwright Ranch among their beneficiaries. Encouraged for the first time since she'd arrived, she replied, "I look forward to it. Oh, and by the way, do we have many international donors?"

"One, I think. Remington Northrop. They're actually based out of California but I think they have a pretty strong international presence. Why do you ask?"

"No reason, really. Just some financial housekeeping."

He nodded. "Can I interest you in a bite to eat?"

"Excuse me?"

Paul's award-winning smile was back in full force as he secured her in his gaze. "There's a great Mexican place over in Caribou Springs." He glanced toward the kids and said, "If you're not busy, we could head over for a late lunch. Maybe grab a couple of beers." He grinned. "Or margaritas, if you prefer."

Katharine almost laughed. Was he asking her on a date?

As though surprised she was taking so long to accept, Paul prodded gently, "You do eat, don't you?"

Katharine smiled. She couldn't deny the pull she felt toward this man. Not only were his polished looks definitely appealing, but Paul was a straight-shooter. Genuine to a fault, he seemed unaware when he misstepped, making it hard to hold anything against him. And the fluid desire swimming in his gaze? The man wasn't interested in a business lunch.

But dating was not on her agenda for this trip, especially not a man who posed a potential problem with Wainwright Ranch. "Yes, I do eat," she said, and brushed the hair from her eyes as she enjoyed a sweep of femininity with his nearness. "Unfortunately, I have too much work on my plate to get away. Maybe some other time?"

"Sounds good," he said then pushed off from the fence. "I'm going to hold you to it." Paul pulled his glasses forward with a wink and smiled. "See you around." With that, he walked off, headed for the parking lot behind the main office building.

Katharine chuckled, amused by the exchange. *Did that just happen*? Dropping her gaze to his muscular rear, she allowed herself the small indulgence. Paul Sutherland was definitely a hot commodity, and while his demeanor tended toward the brash, he actually reminded her of many New Yorkers she knew. His curt comments about her mother weren't appreciated, but generally speaking, Katharine was fine with blunt and matter-of-fact. It made for simple communication, and simple communication eliminated excess noise and misunderstanding.

Returning her focus to the group of children now following their instructor back into the barn, Katharine blew out her breath. Maybe she should head back into town. There wasn't much for her to do here and now that Paul had mentioned food, she felt a slight grumble of hunger pain. Maybe she could get a quick bite to eat with Adele at the restaurant before retiring to her hotel room for a final go-round with the records.

Tomorrow she planned to have meetings with Frank and Canyon. A squiggle of nerves flitted through her pulse. She was anxious to speak with both of them, but for wholly different reasons. Frank's conversation loomed troublesome, tangling years of loyalty with the present slate of poor conditions. Not only was he allowing investments to be churned, she hadn't been able to locate the foundation account the banker from First Federal had called about. Were there other account documents she didn't have?

Maybe it had been her mother who'd managed the ranch money and not Frank, as she had always believed. If that were the case, it made sense the accounts were in shambles. Either way, she'd have to remove him from his position. It was an untenable situation, but unavoidable. Canyon Laredo would be easier to cut loose, if only she could be sure that's what needed to be done. If she could prove he wasn't one of the good guys, she would see to it that he was removed from his board position and fired from his job on the ranch. Why the thought of seeing him go should bother her was something that made no sense at all. Probably because he seemed so good with the children. Not that he was alone in that skill. There were others equally qualified. Katharine heaved a sigh. How long that would take was anyone's guess.

Chapter Seven

Canyon's truck slowly rolled over the red dirt road as he pulled off the main highway and onto ranch property. After four days of rodeo, his body was stiff and sore, sensitive to every ditch and rut he hit. Bear Lake had always been a challenge, unleashing the biggest, meanest bulls around, but this year seemed to be stacked against the men. A lot of amateur cowboys on the circuit had steered clear of Bear Lake's bronco-busting event, leaving it to the seasoned professionals, but not him. There was too much money at stake. Besides, he'd never met a bull he didn't want to break. Canyon chuckled. Though this year, the bulls had nearly busted *him*. By the third round, his backside had been bruised, his leg muscles no stronger than jello and his neck pinched—but he'd won. He'd had the highest combined score for all of his bulls and it'd earned him a pretty payout. Thirty-two thousand dollars and some change. Warmed by the memory of his fellow bull riders' displeasure, Canyon smiled inwardly. It was his spurring technique that cinched it. While it wasn't required to spur the bull, he knew the judges liked to see it and would award extra "style points" for doing so.

As he pulled in next to Jacob's vehicle, the cab of his truck bumped over a pothole, clanging his keys together as he stopped. A cloud of dust billowed around him. Canyon tossed the gear into park, jerked the keys from the ignition and dropped them on to the floor then pushed out of his truck. It was time to check in and see what he'd missed in that board meeting. Instantly, thoughts of Katharine Wainwright came to mind—same as they had all weekend—and Canyon snorted. She was a beautiful woman but her management skills left a lot to be desired. She'd been coiled tighter than a rattler on the attack when she'd marched her way out to see him before he left, acting as if the ranch's troubles rested squarely on his shoulders. He understood the place was in trouble, but throwing accusations around wasn't going to solve anything. He also understood the woman's need to fill her mother's shoes, but that was a losing proposition. No one could replace Eleanor Wainwright. Not even her daughter.

Canyon adjusted his hat and strode across the patch of grass and dirt then fell into step along a sidewalk rimmed by flowers. It curved around the admin building and led straight to the front door. Eleanor had been a mountain of a woman and her socialite daughter from the city didn't stand a chance to fill her position with the same command and control. She was too delicate, too urban. She didn't understand how business worked in these parts. A man carried his own load, but he did so on his terms and no one else's. Canyon had set a goal and met his goal. Simple and straightforward, that's how he worked. If she needed it spelled out, he'd be happy to do the honors. He enjoyed spending his time staring into the eyes of a pretty lady.

Canyon broke stride, his attention caught by the sight of Paul Sutherland standing in the parking lot. He was speaking to a man beside a black BMW. The two were dressed in dark suits, and their identical black hair styles made them appear almost as twins, except the stranger had at least a decade on Paul. They appeared to be having some sort of discussion. Hopefully it wasn't another donor falling off the rolls. Ever since Sutherland set foot on the property, donations had taken a nosedive.

Whatever. Canyon ejected the gray cloud from his thoughts. Paul was Frank's boy which meant Canyon didn't have a say. He could claim the building was on fire and Frank wouldn't listen, not if the warning came from him. All because Canyon wouldn't do Frank's bidding. He wouldn't run his errands or take his hints. He wouldn't provide block when Frank ran into trouble. Canyon wouldn't lift a hand for Frank Dillard. He answered to Mrs. Wainwright and Mrs. Wainwright alone. Life had been good back then.

Until she called Canyon into her office and blew his world to pieces. Told him she was dying. Much like the children she served, she was dying from a terminal illness. And then she dropped the big one. She wanted Canyon to become a board member and keep watch over the ranch after she passed. She trusted him. She trusted his love for the children, his love for the animals, and feared what would happen in her absence without a man like him keeping tabs. She made him promise to keep the ranch true to her vision and not let anyone change a thing.

Canyon promised he would and during the remaining months of her life, she'd groomed him for the job. In addition to joining the board, she asked him to take over management of the expenses. Frank had been making some questionable choices when it came to vendors and Mrs. Wainwright wanted Canyon to look into it. He knew it wounded her pride to have to ask him, but in her condition she wasn't able to handle the rigors of day-to-day management.

But Canyon could.

In the beginning, he hadn't been sure he was capable but figured if she was willing to give it a go, so was he. With her guidance, running the numbers became a matter of common sense and not scary columns of dollars and cents. In truth, Canyon had learned it was no different than his own checkbook, a simple matter of what came in versus what went out. Mrs. Wainwright had assigned him the job of cattle and horses, gave him a budget and then set him free. He knew what he needed, what the animals needed, and the rest fell into place.

The trouble didn't start until after she died, when Frank stepped in and tried to take over. He claimed Canyon was in over his head and tried to sell the same to the board. Canyon stood his ground and after three hours of wrangling, walked out of the meeting with his position intact. Mostly thanks to Zeke Roberts. He'd backed Canyon and convinced a few other board members he was their guy. But where it was settled business as far as the board went, the vote in his favor had only made Frank angrier. To this day it irked the old man, but

Canyon couldn't care less. He'd made a promise to Eleanor and he intended to keep it.

Canyon swung open the door to the office and Amanda greeted him before he could get his hat off. "Did you win?" Anxious brown eyes clung to him. "Did you win the money?"

Canyon grinned. "Thirty-two grand, three-hundred and forty-six dollars."

Heavily-lined eyes widened and she smacked a hand to the desktop, her firecracker red nail polish almost identical to the color of her fitted T-shirt. "Get out."

"What? But I just walked in."

"Canyon Laredo, you seriously won that much? You're not teasing me?"

"Now, darling, why would I do a thing like that?"

"Because."

"Because nothing." He strolled over to the desk. "You can take it to the bank—I won it." He tapped his shirt pocket as if the check were folded inside. In fact, the real check had already been deposited. "Next, I'm headed to Texas for the big one."

"The big one?" Her mouth hung open.

"They have a tournament outside of Houston with big money up for grabs. After my body recovers from this week-end, I'll be looking toward Texas."

Slipping into flirtation mode, Amanda smiled coyly. "Well, we need to celebrate then. How about we hit Dakota's tonight?"

"No can do. I promised the kids I'd meet up with them tonight for a marshmallow roast."

Amanda frowned. "That's too bad." She hitched a shoulder up near her jaw and angled her head to peer up at him. "You know I could have showed you a good time."

Canyon stilled. Katharine Wainwright stood in the hall-way leading back to the offices. She was staring at him—at them—with a heavy dose of displeasure in her eyes. Decked out in black leggings and boots up to her knees, a fitted gray sweater that outlined her slim but curvy waist, she looked nice. Unhappy, but nice. "Good morning," he said, hoping to restart their relations on better footing.

"Good morning."

Amanda made fearful eyes at him, as if she'd just been caught by the Wicked Witch of the West. Silently, she pretended to get back to work by scribbling something on a piece of paper. Canyon smiled, signaling to Amanda that she was fine.

"Come to find out what you missed during the meeting?" Katharine asked.

"As a matter of fact, I did," he replied, marveling at the cool beauty staring back at him. Long blonde curls framed her face and seemed completely at odds with her stern expression.

"Do you have time to go over it with me now?"

"Yes, ma'am."

"This way," she said, and turned without waiting for his response.

It was Canyon's turn to make eyes at Amanda, as though he were the one in trouble now.

Amanda winked and waved him back then suppressed a giggle.

Canyon followed Katharine to her mother's old office. When he reached the open door, he watched her wordlessly take a seat. Beside her chair, her Lab lay sleeping. Canyon smiled. Lucky boy. He could have used a few extra hours of rest this morning, but it wasn't on the agenda. Lowering himself into a wingchair in front of the desk, he was immediately inundated by memories of Eleanor. The desk was the same, the chair, the artwork and wooden built-in lined with books. Nothing had been changed and he felt her watchful eye as he sat in front of her daughter. It was like she was here, a third presence sharing the space with them. Shaking off the uncanny sense, he asked, "Well? How'd the meeting go?"

"It went fine, Mr. Laredo. However, what's not fine is my audit of your expenses."

"How so?"

She opened a file on the desk in front of her and like a stiff-backed school teacher proceeded to rattle off the major expenses incurred in running a ranch. Buildings, utilities, feed, vet bills, fencing, vehicle maintenance and then finished, "And on top of all these rising costs, you increased the herd by ten percent." She looked up from her papers and took a breath before spewing, "Fifteen percent. Between that and the henhouse, I think you went over budget by fifteen percent."

"I recently culled the herd," he said. "You should have seen that revenue when you went through the records."

"Culled the herd?"

Canyon smiled. "Sold off some of the heifers."

Glancing down, Katharine pointed to something on her paper. "What are these new costs labeled vitamins?"

"Just like it sounds. Vitamins."

"For the cows?"

He nodded and pulled a booted foot over top of the opposite leg, setting his hat on his knee. "By improving the health of our current livestock, we're increasing revenue further down the line. We'll be doing less culling while reaping more productive market trips."

"You're seriously giving the cows vitamins?"

Canyon grinned. "Yes, ma'am."

"Why have the vet bills gone up, then?" Running a slender finger three-quarters down the page, she said, "Vet bills went from eighty-three thousand to one hundred and ninety-eight."

"We hired a new vet. By the way, the vitamins are also included in that total."

"Mr. Laredo," Katharine began, her voice tightly controlled. "I'm not sure you understand the severity of the situation. The finances of Wainwright Ranch are in need of a complete and thorough overhaul. For the first time, operating expenses have exceeded income, including all streams of revenue and donations. We need to cut and cut hard."

Canyon looked around the office. "Is that why I'm here? Because you want me to find some money to cut?"

"Yes."

"Have you looked at my projections for the next twelve months?"

"Projections?"

Exactly what he thought. If she had, she would have seen where his department is scheduled to overcome its deficit and skyrocket from there. "The cost of beef is up. The cost of feed is up. I acquired those new cattle from a rancher desperate to sell. When they're ready in another few months, we'll make three times our money back when we take them to market. Egg prices are up too, by the way, which is why I added the henhouse. The cost listed is the market value, not the cost paid. We didn't pay a dime for that building. A local charity outfit volunteered to build it when I suggested the kids would get a kick out of taking part."

Katharine stared at him, her lips slightly parted. As happened the first day he met her, Canyon couldn't help but settle on her lips. Today, she wore a pale shade of pink which made them appear almost nude but with a subtle gloss. As though picking up on his line of sight, she snapped her mouth closed and replied, "That's good to hear."

He chuckled. "I'll take that as a compliment."

"Do you think this is funny, Mr. Laredo?"

"Not a bit. But if I don't keep my sense of humor about me, I might get angry at being treated like an incompetent staff member instead of one of the key players on your team. Your mother entrusted me with this job and I don't intend to let her down."

"My mother?"

The mouth fell open again but Canyon forced himself to look into Katharine's eyes and not her mouth, a tough proposition to be sure. "Yes, your mother. She asked me to join the board and look after things when she passed. She personally guided me through the cattle expenses and explained how she wanted things run. I've done it. If you're losing money on this ranch, it's not from my section of the ranch."

Katharine didn't reply immediately. Instead, she appeared to be digesting the information, as if stunned to learn it. Canyon didn't know the Wainwright family dynamics and whether or not they'd discussed business over supper. He only knew Mrs. Wainwright and what she expected from him. "Like I said," he continued, "if there's a problem, you might want to check where the problem started—donations."

Giving a slight shake to her head, she glanced down at the paperwork in her hands. "Yes, I understand they're down in recent months."

"Try ever since Paul Sutherland came on scene."

She flipped her gaze back up to meet his. "I met him. He seems to be on the up and up. In fact, he suggested an idea for a PR campaign to raise money."

Canyon shook his head in disgust. "Then you understand what I'm talking about. He's a hustler. He's pushy, single-minded, and doesn't listen to a word of advice."

"He had an idea that didn't work," Katharine replied succinctly. "But at least he's trying. That's more than some of the board members and management personnel around here."

"You might want to check a little deeper. Paul isn't doing Wainwright Ranch any favors. In fact, I saw him outside just now in some kind of heated discussion with a man in the parking lot. Can't be good for business when your face to the community can't control his temper."

"The parking lot?"

"Exactly. The only reason a man holds a meeting outdoors is because he wants to avoid contact with the people indoors."

"What are you saying?"

"I'm saying he sounds like a man with something to hide."

At the sharp knock on the door, Canyon turned.

"Yes?" Katharine said.

Amanda poked her head inside with a stricken look on her face. No longer bronzy peach, her skin appeared practically ashen. "It's a child. One's gone missing from the ranch."

Katharine shot up from her chair. "What?"

Canyon's stomach hit the floor. Leaping from his chair, he confronted Amanda, "Who? When?"

She peered up at him like a frightened kitten. "Kyle Stevens."

Chapter Eight

Katharine circled her desk, catching her leg hard on the corner. She grimaced but ignored the pain and demanded, "Do we have any information to go on?"

Amanda remained in the doorway. "Jacob said they were packing up to head down the mountain this morning and that's when they noticed Kyle was missing. The other kids said he was with them when they woke up, but when they were taking a head count..." Amanda's voice faded.

"Kyle," Canyon practically grumbled the name.

"Do you know this child?" Katharine asked.

"I know him well." He gave a brisk shake to his head and said, "He's the kind of kid who might think it's funny to get people out searching for him."

"Funny?" His comment gave rise to a nervous lump in her throat. "Why on earth would he think that?"

"He thinks he's a survivalist."

Amanda looked up at Canyon, who towered over her. "What do you want me to do?"

"Call Hal Richardson. He'll get a search team organized and headed our way within the hour. I'll go fire up the ATVs. I know the area Jacob takes the kids for overnight trips. If we can get there fast enough, we should be able to hunt him down pretty quickly."

Hunt him down? Canyon sounded like he was going after some kind of dangerous prey, not a scared little boy! "I'm going with you," she announced, hurrying to keep up with him and Amanda as they headed for the reception area. Cody was on his feet and following but stopped when she did before the two of them collided into Canyon.

"You don't need to do that," Canyon told her, purposely blocking their way. "I'll handle this with some of the ranch staff."

"Fine, but you're taking me with you."

Frank Dillard walked in the front door. Confusion seized his expression as he zeroed in on the two of them. A hint of suspicion stole into his gaze. "Taking you with him where?"

Canyon stepped aside and Katharine looked to Frank. Her eyes misted. "A child's gone missing, Frank. Canyon is going to round up some of the staff to form a search team. I'm going with them."

"A child's missing?" Frank's gaze went to Canyon. "Are you sure?"

"Kyle Stevens."

A steely calm swept the confusion from Frank's expression and he moved farther into the office. "We can't let this get out before we find him."

Katharine blurted, "What?"

"Katharine." Frank lowered his voice and walked over to her. "If word gets out, our fundraising efforts will explode in our faces. We're having trouble with the donors as it is. If they get wind of something like this, we might as well close up shop and stick a 'for sale' sign out front." Frank flashed a glance to Canyon. "Let him go find the boy. I'm sure the kid can't be that far off." Addressing Canyon, he asked, "Where did they lose him?"

"Upper Payne's Creek," he responded, "where we take our usual overnight camping trips."

Frank nodded, as though it were settled. "Good." He took Katharine by the shoulders and looked her directly in the eyes. He spoke calmly, "They'll find him. The staff knows that area well. There's no need for you to join them. You and I can man the phones here. They'll call us as soon as they know something."

Where she hoped to be reassured, Katharine felt unsettled. Frank's gaze had an odd glint, an edginess that wasn't warranted and wasn't welcome. "If we can't find him, I'm not hiding the fact that we lost a child," Katharine replied firmly.

"He's not lost," Frank corrected. "He's wandered off. It's happened before and we found the boy within two hours."

Katharine gaped at him. They had? Her mother had never mentioned any such thing!

"It happens," he said, "but it's not the end of the world. Don't make the mistake of allowing it to be the end of Wainwright Ranch. Not this close to the fundraiser."

Katharine continued to sort through Frank's revelation as she held tightly to Canyon's waist, her cheeks stinging with cold. He had radioed ahead that they were en route to the campsite, a journey Canyon had wasted no time in taking. Amanda had agreed to watch over Cody while they were gone. It had been a tough decision, but one Katharine had no other choice in making. There was no place for her dog on this trip. Canyon was driving the all-terrain vehicle at top speed and it was all she could do not to fly off the rear. Save for the rubber antenna poking into her arm, it was all she could do not to notice the muscular torso within her arms. A fact she hadn't missed sitting across from him in her mother's office.

Despite her resolve to remain direct and unyielding, she couldn't escape his easy smile and the way it made her feel. He'd been unaffected by her negative appraisal of the ranch finances and then, when he'd mentioned her mother had hand-picked him for the board, Katharine almost took it as a sign he was one of the good guys. His response to the missing child sealed it in stone. Canyon hadn't hesitated. He called in a search and rescue team, rounded up some of the staff, getting the search underway in less than fifteen minutes. He'd also tried to call his friends in the police department, but deferred to Frank's decision to hold off.

If the child was playing a prank, and wandered off intentionally, there was no sense in blowing up the ranch's future over a situation that might be resolved in a matter of hours.

It's happened before. Katharine still had trouble wrapping her head around the revelation, but forced herself to accept it. These things happened. It happened once to a friend of hers during a scouting trip when she was a child in summer camp. It made sense it might happen when kids hiked the mountains during their stay at Wainwright Ranch.

It was her job to see that it didn't happen again. Despite her reservations to the contrary, she too, would defer to Frank's judgment and hold off on calling the authorities—for a little while. But if it became apparent the child was lost or in any danger, Katharine would make the call to the police herself.

As she and Canyon closed in on the mountains, the range stood like a fortress around the Wainwright property, walls of jagged stone dotted by the occasional clumps of yellow and red trees amidst a sea of evergreen and aspen, The Rocky Mountains. Thousands of feet high, miles and miles long and wide, this was the continental divide between the Eastern and Western United States. It was the scene where a child had gone missing. Drawn to the sheets of rock, Katharine's reluctant gaze scaled to the top and fear trickled into her heart. A child was wandering around up there alone. Lost and afraid, a young boy struggled to find his way home. Where did a child turn in a landscape of rock and trees and dangerous precipices? Did he huddle down in fear or set out for the bottom? And if he did, what would become of him?

Katharine shook a sudden chill from her body. Luckily it was morning and the day would only get warmer from here on out. The boy would be dressed. He would've been fed. Frank was right. He'd be fine and they'd find him in no time.

Minutes later, Canyon slowed the vehicle and Katharine closed her mind to everything but the mission before them. A group of men and women were gathered near the base where forest met grassland. Canyon pulled in a dozen feet away and parked. The two dismounted, she with his hand to assist her. Katharine combed fingers through tangled hair, her body continuing to vibrate as though still sitting upon the powerful engines of the ATV. She rubbed the cold bite from her nose, and looked through the trees, surprised to see similar vehicles already criss-crossing the terrain. How had they beat them here?

"Jacob is waiting for us at the campsite," Canyon informed her, already in motion and headed toward the mountain. Canyon no longer wore his cowboy hat, revealing a head full of wavy hair, ends curling over the red bandana at his neck. "I assumed you'd want to speak with him."

"Yes, yes, of course," she replied, following Canyon's lead. She was the senior staff member on scene. Peering at the swarm of activity, Katharine was struck by the daunting task ahead. How did one search for a missing child in the rugged Colorado Mountains? Did they follow a standard protocol? Did they look for a trail of evidence left behind by the child? Did anyone have any indication as to which way he might have gone? She looked to Canyon. "Do we have a plan?"

Canyon surveyed her from head to toe. "Are you sure you want to do this? You're not exactly dressed for the occasion."

Katharine nodded. Expensive leather boots with flat heels were not made for hiking, but they were all she had and she'd be darned if she were going to be left out of the mix. She could keep up. She'd make sure of it. Moving wayward strands of hair from her eyes, she replied, "I'll be fine. Which way?"

"Straight up and to the west."

"Good. Let's get started."

For the most part, Canyon hiked in silence. While others traversed the lower terrain, he opted to head straight for the campsite where Kyle went missing. Ground zero was usually the best place to begin searching in situations like these, then fanning out from there in measured patterns based on time of disappearance. A confined and measured search area within strategic points worked best, isolating the subject based on knowing the terrain, understanding how fast the target could travel and in which direction. Narrowing down the search was crucial to avoid wasting time. Most searches ended within the span of twenty-four to forty-eight hours. The longer the search went on, the lower the chances of finding your missing person alive and well.

They were techniques Canyon had learned from working with Dr. Hal Richardson, an orthopedic surgeon in town and one of the more experienced members of the mountain search and rescue team. And his buddy McIntyre Walsh. His experience came from the military but the tactics used were similar. When defining a search, the team liked to work up a subject profile sheet. In this case, Canyon had a pretty good grasp on the missing camper. Kyle was smart. He was clever, but he could only hike so fast and so far. At this point, he'd have to be close to the campsite.

Moving steadily uphill, Canyon darted an occasional glance over his shoulder to check on Katharine's progress. She was keeping up—he could hear her labored breathing—though noticing it didn't mean he'd slow down. It was her choice to join this search and rescue operation, not his and if she felt the need to rest or turn back, so be it.

From somewhere in the forest to the east, someone called out his name.

Canyon turned, and scoured the space between crowded aspen trees. About twenty yards in, he spotted two men. Mostly obscured by underbrush, they made eye contact as one shouted, "Any sight of him?"

"No, and you?" Both shook their heads. "We keep searching," he told them, the sound of his voice penetrating the quiet, "until we find him."

The men nodded and continued on their way.

"But we've been on the mountain for over an hour," Katharine complained from behind him. "Shouldn't we have found him by now?"

"Depends on where he is," Canyon shot back.

"Aren't you the least bit worried?"

"Wouldn't be here if I wasn't."

Canyon stepped up his pace, forcing Katharine to match his movements or turn back. Dodging a rock in the trail, she grabbed a branch, pulled herself forward and took three extra-long strides up to keep up with him. *Wouldn't be here if I wasn't.* Did he have to be so crass?

Annoyed by the remark, she watched his backside move farther up the trail ahead of her, his legs brushing through low-lying plants with ease. Canyon might not care for her presence along this hike but she wasn't turning back. Not until she found the missing boy. The mere thought of a child lost in this unforgiving environment squeezed her heart like a tourniquet. This was a challenging climb even for her, let alone a child recovering from leukemia. And where she might not have expertise when it came to search and rescue, it didn't take an expert to understand that the longer it went on, the less likely they were to find him alive and well. But giving up wasn't an option. They had to find him.

Taking a deep breath, Katharine forged ahead, a dry woodsy scent of pine filling her senses. Crisp cool air cut through her lungs and pinched her cheeks as she climbed. She considered herself to be in pretty good shape, but hiking a mountain was a far cry from working an hour of hot yoga in a comfortable studio. Maybe not aerobically speaking, but certainly it involved an entirely different skillset for her muscles. Add nature's obstacle course—layered with roots, littered with rocks, lined by knotty aspen trunks, and an abundance of creeks that wound through the underbrush, popping up in various places along the trail—and she had her work cut out for her. And if that weren't enough, the soles of her boots repeatedly slipped on the steep hard-packed ground. Luckily, the legging-style pants she wore allowed her free range of movement, a feature she needed at the moment. Hopping over a narrow band of running water, she landed hard.

"Need a break?" Canyon tossed back.

"No, thanks. I'm fine. How much farther?"

"About fifteen minutes, but we can stop if you need to."

"No," she replied, smoothing her breathing pattern into calm, easy streams.

Katharine hadn't questioned her ability to handle the hike. Not only the countless hours of daily yoga practice, but plenty of walking the lengthy blocks of New York City kept a gal in shape. The canopy of trees that covered most of the trail didn't hurt, either. Gorgeous scenery, challenging workout, and she felt good. Fine. She actually felt invigorated and more determined than ever to find the missing child.

Thirty feet ahead of her, Canyon detoured sharply to the right. He stopped between two aspen trees and pointed from his perch above her. "Beyond those boulders is where the kids make camp."

Katharine slowed behind him, her ribs hammered by a sudden pound of heartbeats. She didn't see any signs of tents or people, only a wall of enormous rock. Shrouded by foliage, it jutted straight up from the ground. She searched either side for a way around the massive impediment. "I don't see any-one. Do you think they've gone?"

Staring down at her, Canyon shook his head. "They know the procedure. They stay put until we rally forces."

"Oh." She hated to feel ignorant with regard to the most basic rules and expectations. It made her feel like an outsider rather than Wainwright Ranch owner and Commander-in-Chief.

"You can't see the camp from here," he told her.

She glanced uphill. "You can't?"

He shook his head.

"Then how do we get there from here?"

Irritation caught in Canyon's brown-eyed gaze. "That's where things get tricky." He dropped his gaze to her boots then back to her face. "We climb those rocks."

Climb them? As in straight up?

Canyon waited through her pause, as though he could read the thoughts steamrolling through her brain. "But you can't be serious," she replied, cursing the resistance in her voice. "The kids can't climb rock like that, can they?"

"They don't. They take a different trail up. It cuts down the opposite side of this ridge. But we haven't got time to waste. You can head back, if you want. The trail will take you straight to the base."

"No, I'm fine. Let's go," she said, but hesitated.

Canyon eyed her feet. "You won't make it in those boots."

"Of course I will." It wasn't as if she'd never climbed rocks before. Granted, dress boots might be less than desirable for the task, but they wouldn't prevent her from succeeding. Not if she was determined to do so. "C'mon," she told him, "let's get to it." As if to prove her point, she took off ahead of him.

"Suit yourself," he mumbled as she passed.

The ground was no longer a distinct trail, but a knee-high thicket of woody undergrowth. She had no idea what was beneath the mess of green, dotted by the occasional flower, but was grateful the ground seemed fairly level and easy to manage. Up to the rocks, anyway.

Disregarding the thin sheen of dust that coated her black leather boots, the drifts of cottonwood that clung to her pants, Katharine pressed forward, mentally sketching out her best mode of attack for the boulders ahead. Coming to a stop at the base, Katharine gazed upward. Shafts of light dropped through the trees overhead, illuminating sharp edges and jagged ledges embedded in the stone. They were a welcome sight. She could use them as grab-points to pull herself up and over. Assessing the task, she judged it to be approximately twenty feet in height. Intimidating, but not insurmountable. She could absolutely scale this rock and then some. *Take that, cowboy.*

Canyon moved past her.

"Oh!" Katharine flung a hand to her chest. How had he snuck up on her?

"Excuse me," he said. Reaching for the nearest ledge, he hoisted himself up and began climbing. His moves were quick and steady as he moved from ledge to ledge like a

mountain cat, no more strained than if he'd been climbing a
child's jungle gym. Canyon stood like a beacon at the top,
staring down at her with an expectant gaze.

Katharine's pulse fluttered as she grabbed the first pointed ledge. Wedging a boot into a recess farther down the rock,
she jumped up. Gritty stone dug into her fingers but she held
tight, fighting against the weight of her body as she fell
backward, landing on the ground with a thud. Long hair fell
over her face and she shoved it aside. Above her, Canyon said
nothing. He was impassive, waiting, watching.

Clenching her jaw, Katharine shook it off. She drew in a
deep breath and steeled herself against the sharp surface she
was about to grab. She latched onto a stone, adjusted her grip
then eased up slowly this time, leaning into the rock. She held
steady. When she felt ready, she reached up for the next
ledge. Securing her hold, she located a small opening below
her and stuck the toe of her boot inside. Up and hold. *Take
your time. Slow and steady wins this race.*

Exhaling a tight breath, she focused on the next niche
and ignored the small smile forming on Canyon's mouth. He
was probably enjoying watching her sweat—literally—and
counting the seconds until she lost it again. But she wouldn't.
She'd taken on billion-dollar hedge funds and won. She'd
taken on global corporate henchmen and won. She could certainly take on this inanimate rock and win.

Reaching up, she once again found her nook and hand
in, secured her grip. Leg up, foot in, she hit pause. Her heart
pounded, belying the outward calm she displayed. She was
getting higher now and the thought of falling loomed. The
adage "never let them see you sweat" popped into her mind.
Truer words were never spoken. *On so many levels.* Right
now, the concept resonated from the inside out. Despite herself, she ventured a peek upward. Through long clumps of
blonde hair, she estimated the top was less than ten feet away.
She could do this.

Hand up, in, leg up, foot in, she lifted her body another
foot higher. Tilting her head back slightly, she tried to shake

the hair from her eyes, but several strands caught in her lashes and served to irritate her. Tune it out, she told herself. Mind over matter.

As she paused in place, her arms began to shake, but her leg muscles remained firm. Challenged, but they were holding strong. Her arms, however, were about to give.

Think of the boy. This is about the boy.

Canyon shifted his weight overhead, a move which sent small stones flying through the air inches from her head. Katharine closed her eyes. She took a deep breath, held steady then continued up. Above her, the stone curved forward. A fact that worked in her favor. Pausing, she surveyed the landscape and decided the best route would be closest to Canyon. As though reading her thoughts, he stepped aside.

Katharine groaned inwardly. Perfect. The man held a first row seat to her grand finale. If she fell now, she could not only hurt herself but the sight would be humiliating. But she wasn't going to fall. Hot breaths reflected from the stone wall back into her face. She was going to finish scaling this wall. Why she found the situation humbling, she had no idea. She should be celebrating her achievement, not grumbling over the fact she had an audience. But she was.

Suppressing a swell of annoyance, Katharine set her thoughts to the rock and reached for the next ledge, this one more of an indentation in the stone than a protruding ledge. But it was all she needed. Cupping her hand inside, she pulled up, stepped on a narrow ledge and hoisted herself up and over, nearly landing in a face plant. In a burst of energy she scrambled toward Canyon. Her boot slipped, her knee dropped and Katharine cried out in pain. She grabbed for a nearby bush but leaves and branches slipped through her fingers.

Canyon gave a swift tug to her upper arm and hauled her onto her feet. Katharine's heart hammered. "Thank you," she voiced automatically and her knees buckled.

"You're welcome," he replied, his smile warm and genuine as he held her upright.

Realizing she had fallen into him, she stepped back. "I'm sorry." Eyeing the edge, she swallowed back a slew of nerves, moved farther away from it then spit gravelly dust and debris from her mouth.

"Nothing to be sorry for," he replied. "That was pretty impressive."

"What?"

"You scaling that rock." Dark eyes swam with pleasure. "I didn't think you had it in you."

Of course he didn't, she mused, victory ballooning in her chest. Katharine brushed the hair from her face and dust from the front of her clothing then pulled her shirttails down and forward. "A little worse for the wear, but I managed."

"Looks like you'll need a new pair of boots."

"Huh?" Katharine dumped her gaze to her feet and sighed. The toes of her black boots were scarred deeply, dust ingrained in the scratches of leather. "They're ruined," she said without thinking then lifted her gaze. Staring back at her was an I-told-you-so look. "It's not important," she said flatly. "Now which way from here?"

Chapter Nine

Canyon led the way to the campsite, his thoughts filled with Katharine. How she had managed that climb escaped him. He would have bet money she didn't have it in her and had been fully prepared to offer her the alternative route used by the campers. It would have taken longer, but was a simple trail hike up. But she didn't need it. She'd accepted his challenge and climbed to the top. Why he'd felt the need to test her in the first place, he didn't know. Maybe it was because she had inserted herself into his territory, accusing him of doing less than his best with regard to operating expenses. Maybe it was because Frank had. The man rubbed him the wrong way and always had. Together, they could override his choices and take him out of the picture, a decision that would cut clean through him. He had turned the cattle end of Wainwright Ranch around with room to grow. As a woman who made her living in the financial business, how did she not see that?

Whatever. Canyon shook the supposition from his mind. He had felt the need to test her and she had passed. Katharine Wainwright was definitely Eleanor's daughter, he mused. She might make her home in the city, but she could certainly handle the rugged outdoors. But that didn't mean he would let her push him around. He wouldn't. And the sooner Ms. Wainwright figured that out, the better.

Rounding a cluster of trees, Canyon spotted Jacob crouched near a child seated on a fallen pine trunk. It was a young girl named Caroline Sterling. Dressed in jeans and plaid shirt, one that hung from her slender frame like a bag of bones, Canyon thought she looked frail and afraid, her delicate features framed by long tendrils of strawberry blonde hair. The opposite was true. Inside the girl's feeble exterior lay a heart of grit and gold. Caroline was battling HIV, a battle Canyon believed she'd ultimately win due to sheer determination and positive attitude. The girl was a fighter. But at the moment, her face was intent upon Jacob's, wrenched by concern. With one hand clutched to a branch next to her, she rubbed her cheek with the other. Several other children stood nearby, their expressions glum. Becky Sawyer, a fellow staff member, stood behind them.

With a quick scan of the area, Canyon noted the tents had been packed, the fire ring had been cleaned and covered. The group was ready to go. But they hadn't.

Because Kyle was missing.

"Oh no, is she crying?" Katharine asked, seizing Canyon's arm.

At the panic scratching in her voice, he placed a hand over the one she'd placed on his arm. "Let's go find out." He kicked into action and called out, "Jacob!"

The campers turned toward him. Jacob stood at once and headed for Canyon. "Yes, sir?"

"How are the kids?" he asked, sliding a glance over Jacob's shoulder. "Are they holding up?"

"Mostly fine. Only Caroline seems to be upset. The others figure Kyle is just messing around and will be back any minute."

"He might be," Canyon agreed. "I certainly wouldn't put it past him."

"You think the boy is purposely hiding so that we think he's missing?" Katharine asked.

The disbelief in her voice warned Canyon not to reveal his true feelings but yes, that's exactly what he thought. "Sometimes practical jokes can get out of hand. I don't think Kyle wants to roam around this mountain alone, no, and I intend to make sure that he doesn't." Relief flooded into her gaze, loosening knots in his chest he didn't know existed. For some reason, when she was upset, he was upset. Probably because she was the closest thing he had to a boss on the premises. Turning back to Jacob, Canyon reverted to commander mode. "Retrace your steps this morning and don't leave out a single detail."

Jacob licked his lips and rolled his shoulders. "Well," he said, shooting a glance back toward the kids. "We woke up like normal, right, with everyone accounted for. The kids took care of their private business, going off in teams of two in the designated area, like always, then came back for breakfast. We ate, cleaned up, and packed our tents and backpacks. It was during this time Kyle went missing."

Stealing a peek at Katharine, Canyon noted she hung on Jacob's every word as if mentally recording every syllable he uttered. If she had pen and paper, he'd swear she'd take notes. Continuing his quest for information, Canyon asked, "Was Kyle acting unusual?"

"No different than normal, I'd say."

"Who was with him last, right before he left?"

Jacob hitched up his thumb toward the group and replied, "Derrick."

Canyon's gaze went to the boy. Surrounded by the others like a chief and his tribe, the brunette puffed out his chest like everything depended upon him at the moment. Would Derrick cover for Kyle?

The question was instantaneously answered in Canyon's mind with a resounding, *yes*. If he thought it would be good for a laugh, then yes. Absolutely. Resisting the urge to march over there and question the boy, Canyon remained in place, asking Jacob, "Do you recall exactly what time this happened?"

Jacob checked his watch. "About nine-twenty."

It was after eleven-thirty now. Running on two hours, Kyle could be down the mountain and back to the ranch by now. Evading Katharine's worried gaze, Canyon pulled the two-way radio from his belt clip and pressed a button. "Chase, you copy?"

After several seconds, static erupted on the line as the reply came back, "Copy, Canyon."

"Any sign of Kyle down there?" he asked, scanning the tree line for sight of the boy.

"Negative."

It seemed more likely the kid was up here playing survivalist. "Let me know if he shows up, will you?"

"Roger that."

Glancing between Katharine and Jacob, Canyon spoke into his mic again. "Weston, you copy?"

"Copy, Canyon."

"Any sign of the boy?"

"None."

"Where have your teams covered?"

"We've traversed the lower elevation, from Matter's Creek east, clear over to Bear Cub's Pass and as high as Devil's Lookout."

Canyon mapped the area in his head. Weston was acting as lead for the base search crew and his group had made impressive progress. If Kyle had headed down, they would have found him by now. Which meant he was still in the vicinity. "Thanks, Weston. Keep me posted."

"Roger."

Canyon re-clipped the radio to his waistband. "He's still up here."

"He is?" Katharine asked. "But how can you be sure?"

Canyon hated the worry etched in her features. It was needless. Kyle was messing around and putting people through needless worry. It was enough that this woman had the weight of Wainwright Ranch on her shoulders. She didn't need the frantic stress of a missing child on her plate. "I know the area." Canyon left it at that. The explanation would take too long, sucking up time they didn't have. "Jacob, you and Becky take the kids down from here, but not until I have a quick word with them."

"You got it, boss."

Boss. Canyon flicked a glance at Katharine and thought, *she might beg to disagree with you, son*, but didn't say a word as he walked over to the group of children. They were solemn-faced and mute. Acknowledging Becky with a quick nod, he asked gently, "How you kids holding up?"

Still seated on the tree, a tearful Caroline looked up at him. "Is Kyle going to be okay?"

Canyon squatted and smiled. He thumbed a tear from her cheek and said, "You bet he is. You know Kyle. He's probably building a fire right this minute so he can send up smoke signals." A couple of boys chuckled. "Isn't that right, fellas? Kyle prides himself on being an outdoorsman, doesn't he?"

"He thinks he's Bear Grylls!"

Canyon rose. "You know him well, don't you, Derrick?" Catching a quick exchange of glances between Garrett and Derrick, Canyon wondered if there wasn't some kind of conspiracy underfoot. Settling on the third boy, Avery Jones, Canyon prodded, "Anyone know where Kyle might be?"

Heads shook to the contrary, a fact that seemed to further upset Caroline. The only other girl on the camping trip piped up, "I think he left on purpose."

It was Melody Barnes. Threadbare wisps of brown hair fell around her face, evidence of her past chemotherapy treatment. A tomboy to her core, her body was strong, as was her spirit. When her dark eyes flashed with annoyance, Canyon recalled how she'd challenged Kyle on several occasions. If anyone would give him up, it was this one. In a heartbeat.

Canyon nodded. "You might be right, Melody. And if he were to set out on his own, any idea where he might be headed?"

Derrick zipped his lips. Kyle's trusted cohort wouldn't give him up except under the threat of severe duress.

Next to him, Garrett grinned. "I don't know exactly, but I bet he went down toward the river."

Derrick jabbed an elbow into Garrett's side.

Katharine gasped. "The river?"

Canyon could almost hear the worst-case scenario spinning through her imagination like a horror movie. River, water, boy drowning—it was predictable female anxiety—but nowhere near the truth. Kyle knew better than to get near the river. More likely he'd use it as a marker for his journey down—or sideways—as the case might be. The kids passed the river on the way up and knew the trail branching downward from the water's edge would lead them straight to the bottom. No detours, no worries.

"I bet Garrett's right," Melody chimed in. "Kyle probably went to the river."

Katharine clutched Canyon's arm. "We've got to get to him—before something awful happens."

Caroline latched onto Katharine, her feather-light hazel eyes widening. "You think Kyle is going to fall in and drown?"

"No, Caroline." Canyon reached a hand to the girl's shoulder. "We don't think anything of the kind." Behind him, he could almost feel Katharine chomping at the bit, but there was no way he was going to leave this child with anything but a sense of calm and security. "Kyle has set out for an adventure. He knows how to hike and I'm not worried about him at all, and neither should you."

Caroline's gaze darted between his and Katharine's. "Are you sure?"

"I'm sure," Canyon said. "And so is Ms. Wainwright."

"Yes, yes," Katharine stammered, following his script. "I'm sure, too. Canyon's right. Kyle is a strong young man and will handle himself accordingly while out in the wilderness."

Canyon turned to her and thought with mild amusement, *nice to know the woman didn't lie very well.* Straightening, he said to the group of them, "Okay, kids. You heard it for yourself. Kyle's going to be just fine and it's time you get headed down."

Jacob picked up on Canyon's lead and added, "That's right, kids. And if we don't hurry, we might miss out on our trail ride later this afternoon."

"Aw, man." Derrick kicked at the ground. "I wanted to take part in the search."

"Thanks for the offer," Canyon told him, cuing in on his lack of concern, "but I think we'll take it from here."

Once the children were packed and loaded with back-packs, Canyon watched them walk single-file down an established trail. True to form, Jacob was in the lead, Becky at the rear while a line of heads bobbed up and down as the kids hiked down, disappearing into a mountain of trees. Seemed Jacob's reminder about the trail ride was the spark they needed to light their bodies into action.

"Which way to the river?" Katharine asked.

"Same way the kids are headed, but I want to have a look around up here first."

"But you heard the children. They think Kyle went to the river."

Canyon searched her gaze, drawn in by the fluidity of emotion. It was an odd mix of strength and vulnerability, a combination of Joan of Arc and Cinderella which he found compelling. Alluring. It drew him in and not against his will. Canyon considered the woman standing before him. He could definitely lose himself in a woman like Katharine Wain-wright, if he were so inclined.

"The kids think he went to the river but they're guessing. Fact is, they don't know where Kyle is any more than you or I do. I have a hunch he's hanging out up here. As much as he likes to practice his survival techniques, he likes to play practical jokes even more."

Katharine gaped at him. "You still think this is a practical joke?"

"I'm not ruling anything out at this point." Canyon slid a gaze around the area, careful not to land anywhere in particular in the event Kyle was watching them. Lowering his voice, he said, "Now that he knows the kids are heading down, I bet he follows."

She moved her gaze around the area. "If you say so..."

"I do." Canyon handed her a bottle of water he'd borrowed from Jacob and said, "Drink up. Elevation and dehydration sneak up on you."

"Yes, thank you. I remember," she said, and drank without hesitation.

Canyon admired the fine bones of her face, her fingers as they held the bottle. He wondered if her hair ever looked this messy before. The ride out here had done a number on it, though he found the tousled look appealing. It softened her business edges and made her seem natural, feminine, in an outdoorsy sort of way. All qualities he liked in a woman.

Abruptly, Katharine stopped drinking and handed the bottle back to him. "Thanks. I'm good."

Better than good, he wanted to say, but didn't dare. He was here to find a missing boy, not flirt with possibilities. Canyon cleared his throat. "Let's go."

Chapter Ten

Katharine followed Canyon through a forest of evergreen, her gaze continually scouring the landscape to either side of her. The morning mist had lifted, but the rich scent of trees and dirt remained heavy in the air, the nip from earlier now mild in temperature. If only the circumstances for this climb had been different, she might have enjoyed a leisurely hike with Canyon. He seemed competent when it came to the children. He seemed to understand them and speak their language. Did he know the mountain as well?

They weren't going down, or in the direction she'd expected, but instead seemed to be headed in the opposite direction. It didn't make sense. Did he have an idea he wasn't sharing? Was there a reason he wasn't searching the river? It would have been her first stop.

"Kyle!" Canyon called out. "Let's go—it's time to head out!"

If their suspicions were correct, and the boy had left voluntarily rather than lost his way, Katharine believed it unlikely he would respond to Canyon's repeated calls.

Stomping through an area of exceptionally heavy underbrush, Canyon held a clump of bushes aside for Katharine as she passed. Sidestepping him, she tried to ignore the fact that her body had brushed against his. It was unavoidable in the narrow space, though she didn't have to acknowledge it. He seemed content to overlook it, making no attempt at a customary, *Excuse me*. Why shouldn't she?

Besides, these weren't customary circumstances. They were anything but. They were searching for a missing boy, the mere thought of which gave her pause. "Kyle!" she called out, in need of something to do that would make her feel useful and productive. "Kyle, where are you?"

As they emerged into an open area, a wash of sunshine warmed her cheeks. Cupping a hand to her forehead, she searched the way forward. Something about it looked familiar.

"Where are we?"

"Back where we started."

"We are?" Katharine searched for landmarks. It was the standard mix of evergreen and aspen around them, grassy ground dotted with rust-colored rocks, pine needles and patches of dirt. Nothing jumped out at her. "Are you sure?"

Canyon pointed across the way. "That's the tree where Caroline sat."

Homing in on it, Katharine's cheeks flushed. *Son of a gun.* There it was, no different, except they had approached the area from a different angle. How could she have missed it? Katharine dropped the hand from her head. "Yes, I see that it is."

Canyon sniffed the air.

The move startled her. "Do you smell something?"

He shook his head. "No."

Had he expected to? When he didn't elaborate, she pushed, "Now what?"

"We head down."

"Down to the river?"

"Kyle isn't in the river," he said softly. "He's okay, I promise you."

Gripped by a sudden intensity in Canyon's eyes, Katharine swallowed, *hard.* For a second, she thought he was going to reach out and hug her, but the man made no such move. Feeling the near miss, she murmured, "Yes, you're right. I'm sure he is but we need to find him." It was more an affirmation for herself than a belief that it was true, but she needed to fill the void, the space she felt growing between herself and Canyon.

"We will," he reassured firmly.

Katharine wanted to ask him how he could be so sure. She wanted to ask him if he had a plan, if this had ever happened under his watch before. Frank had indicated as much. Had Canyon been with the ranch at the time? Had he found the missing child?

But unwilling to voice the first doubt, Katharine kept them to herself and followed him down the same trail the children had taken earlier. At least they were headed in the right direction—she hoped.

"Kyle! Where are you?"

Hiking down the trail behind Canyon, Katharine's knees throbbed with pain. They felt swollen, achy, reminding her of her old jogging days when she used to run through Central Park as a form of exercise, before she gave it up due to joint pain. Her parents had never liked the idea of her running alone, but she had assured them it was fine. She kept to busy, lighted paths, always kept her cell phone ready and trusted her gut instincts. If someone or something felt out of order, she didn't think twice. It was the way she felt about Canyon. Frank had to be wrong. This man couldn't be responsible for skimming accounts. He loved these kids. From the way he spoke to them, the time he spent with them, to the very fact that he was here, in the flesh, searching for one of them. Canyon Laredo clearly cared. It was easy to see why her mother had chosen him to take over the barn and stables. He was invested, from the inside out.

Invested. Pressure pushed into her stomach. Ranch investments were losing money. Frank. How could he let it happen? How could he have missed it?

Canyon stopped suddenly and Katharine barreled into the back of him. "Oh!" she exclaimed.

"Sorry," he mumbled, and dropped to a squat.

"What is it?" she asked, and leaned over him. "Did you find something?" Canyon picked up something from the ground and smelled it. He squinted and stared down the trail, then glanced through the sea of aspen trees around them like a Native American on the scent of his quarry. Katharine cocked her head and followed his gaze. But staring into a sea

of papery trunks dotted by black knots and covered in flitter-
ing green and gold leaves, she saw nothing. "What? What is
it?"

Canyon looked up at her and slowly rose. "Kyle's been
here."

Katharine looked at his hand but it was empty. Whatever
he had picked up, he'd dropped. She shook her head, overcome by a surge of frustration. "I don't understand."

Canyon grinned. "Beef jerky. Kyle is a nut for the stuff."

Katharine blinked. *Beef jerky.* "You think he dropped
it?" It was the obvious explanation and she almost felt stupid
for saying it aloud, but she needed to get this process rolling.
Canyon was a man of few words when she needed paragraphs
of explanation!

"Yes."

"And?" she pressed. "Do you think he followed the kids
down?"

"Possible."

Katharine wanted to shake him. "Okay…so now what?
You suggest we continue down the trail after them?"

Canyon pulled the two-way radio from his belt. "Weston, copy?"

Static erupted followed by the voicing of his name.
"Weston."

"Any sign of the boy?"

"No, but Jacob and the kids arrived a few minutes ago."

"Roger. I think Kyle might be coming down behind
them. Watch for him."

"Will do."

Canyon smiled at Katharine. "Okay, let's get to it," he
replied and headed down with a new vigor to his step.

Buoyed by his confidence, Katharine released a stream
of breath that pulled the tension from her lungs and chest.
Kyle was on his way down. That was good news. What Canyon would do when he found the boy, Katharine couldn't imagine. Would he punish him? Did the ranch have rules for
these types of infractions?

Katharine doubted her mother would have anticipated a child running away, or playing games with the staff members in the form of a practical joke. *It's happened before.* Frank's words reverberated in her skull. She couldn't believe it, but it had. Wainwright Ranch had lost a child and she'd never heard the first word about it. "Oh!" she cried out, grabbing a tree. Her boot had caught on a gnarled root stretched over the trail, wrenching her ankle.

Several feet ahead of her, Canyon jogged back to her. "You okay?"

"Yes, fine," she lied. Pushing from the tree trunk, she regained her balance. "I tripped."

"Did you sprain anything?"

"I don't think so." To prove it, she turned her foot to and fro. "See. All good." It was her knees that were killing her the most.

Canyon peered into her eyes. It was clear he didn't believe her, but he didn't argue.

Good. She could hold on. By her measure, they were halfway down. Rubbing the scraped skin of her palm, she balled her hand into a fist and focused on the narrow trail. She could make it to the bottom. Everything would be fine. Once she laid eyes on the missing boy, this would be nothing but memory.

Chapter Eleven

By the time they reached the base, Katharine's knees ached horribly. It felt like her knee caps were packed with swollen fire balls. Strange how the trip down had been harder on her joints than the trip up. But it was over. Soon, she could get off her feet and allow them to recover.

"Canyon!"

It was a man in his mid-twenties. Standing with a group of men, he called out the minute she and Canyon had emerged from the tree-covered trail. Fair-haired and surrounded by ATVs and a few men and women on horseback, the man was a stranger to Katharine. She assumed he was another staff member, most of whom she didn't know.

"Weston!" Canyon called back at once and strode over to him. "Where's Kyle?"

Katharine hurried behind him.

"Don't know," Weston replied. "We were hoping you found him."

Katharine's heart caught. She looked between staff members. "What? He isn't here?" she exclaimed then whipped her glance around the area, landing on the campers she'd met at the top. "You're saying he didn't follow them down?"

"If he did, ma'am, we didn't see him."

Canyon keyed up his radio. "Chase, copy."

"Hey, Canyon."

"Is Kyle with you?"

"No, sir. Haven't seen the first sign of him."

Canyon cursed under his breath. He looked at Katharine dead on and she could feel an underlying panic in his heated gaze. "We've got to go back up. We've got to call for back-up."

"Yes, yes," Katharine agreed. It was the right thing to do, no matter how much bad press it would rain upon the ranch. A child was missing. Kyle's safety was priority number one. "I'll call Frank. He can call the authorities."

"No need." Canyon pulled a cell phone from the front pocket of his jeans. "I'll call them myself." He dialed a number and in seconds was connected. "Wade, its Canyon. I need some help."

Katharine waited through the pause. Was Wade a friend of Canyon's? Did he know how to coordinate a search and rescue team with the authorities?

"Have Roan call my cell," Canyon said. "I'll call Walsh and get him on board. Yes, thanks." Canyon turned to her. "We'll run another ground search but this time we'll have a helicopter overhead."

"A helicopter? You called a friend with a helicopter?"

"I called the Chief of Police. He'll get things rolling on his end while we work the ground team."

Katharine stood stunned. Who was Canyon Laredo that he had the Chief of Police on speed dial? Roan, Walsh—who were these people? Shaking the cobwebs from her brain, she listened as Canyon made a second call.

"Walsh, it's Canyon. I need your help. We've got a missing camper on the mountain and we need a full scale search team. You know the area. I'm here with a team put together by Hal, but we came up empty. Yes, Lisa's great. Bring her along. And Walsh—grab Buck on your way over, will you? Thanks." To the group of staff, Canyon said, "Chief Davis is sending air power our way. We need to regroup and retrace our steps. Weston, take your men and begin again, but this time start three miles east of where you did before and stretch your search area three miles west. If Kyle lost his way, any one of those trails up there could drop him out on the other side and miles from here. I'm going back to the ranch to gather supplies."

Katharine stared as Canyon walked away and mounted his ATV. He hesitated, as though he realized he forgot something. She gulped. *Like his passenger*. Their eyes met and Katharine hurried over. She climbed on behind him and wrapped her arms around his waist as he gunned the engine. The vehicle took off with a jerk, racing over grassy terrain at high speed. Wind blew the hair from her face, nipped her skin with chill despite the bright sun overhead. Tucking her head behind Canyon's shoulder, Katharine tightened her hold and leaned forward. It was crazy. He was driving so fast, the bouncy wheels seemed wildly out of control, yet miraculously maintained contact with the ground. But despite her fear the ATV might flip at any second, she didn't utter a word.

Plastered to his back, her body secured against his, she ran through possible scenarios in her mind. Number one: they would find the boy and discover it had all been a prank and he was fine. Number two: they would find the boy injured, hurt from a fall or a tussle with a wild animal. Number three: they'd find him dead. Number four: they'd never find him.

Katharine's heart seized. The last was unimaginable. Possible, but unimaginable. She'd heard of hikers getting lost in the mountains, never to be seen or heard from again. A shudder raced through her. And those were adults, men and women with resources and phones, not a terminally ill child, entrusted to the care of Wainwright Ranch. Imagining the child lost and suffering unbearable conditions compounded an already difficult situation.

It couldn't happen. She couldn't let it happen.

When they reached the Wainwright compound, Canyon zipped around the barn and between buildings, braking to a stop in front of the administrative office. The vehicle lurched forward then tossed Katharine back. Arms wrapped around Canyon, she sat, her body vibrating with the idling engine.

"Need help getting off?" he asked.

She yanked her hands free and pushed back, her legs hot from the vehicle's engine. "No. I can do it." Swinging a leg over the back, she pushed off and landed on the ground with a jolt. Her thighs continued to hum with the energy. A bit wobbly, but firm.

"I'll let you know as soon as we find him," Canyon said.

"What? But I'm going with you."

"This could take a while," he said, dropping his gaze down the length of her. "You're not exactly dressed for the occasion."

"These clothes mean nothing to me," she rebuked, though she couldn't deny the idea that hiking in street boots loomed an uninviting one. She had no change of clothes in her car, nothing in the office. But she was going with him, whether he liked it or not.

Canyon held her in his gaze and dropped his tone. "You don't have to do this."

Katharine felt the hit. Canyon thought she was trying to prove something but he was wrong. She didn't have to prove anything to anyone. This ranch was her responsibility and she would not sit idle while one of its campers was in danger. "I'm going. If you have a problem with that, I'll find another method of transportation back to the mountain."

For a moment, Canyon's gaze darkened, but seemed content to let it go. "No need. I can drive you out there. After I gather supplies, I'll come back for you. Give me ten minutes."

"Ten minutes," she repeated, relieved to hear he wouldn't fight her on this. If he'd tried, he would have learned in short order it was a failing proposition. When Katharine Wainwright made up her mind, it was case closed. Her body ached, her throat was dry, but she would continue the search. Failure wasn't in her vocabulary. It was unacceptable. Change in course, revision, restructuring, yes. But failure?

No. Absolutely not. They would find this boy, because there was simply no acceptable alternative.

Canyon gunned the engine and sped away, kicking up a rooster tail of dust in his wake. Katharine watched him a moment longer then headed inside, swinging open the metal door to the office. Amanda looked up from her desk but her normally sunny smile was missing in action. Oddly, she didn't ask about the child. *Did she already know*?

"We haven't found him," Katharine said plainly.

"Found who?"

Katharine jumped at the sound of a strange male voice. A well-dressed man of about fifty rose from a seat in the small lobby. Staring at her with pale blue eyes, his hair was dark with a dash of gray at his temples. He wore a simple red button-down shirt, cowboy boots and jeans. Standard attire around these parts. How had she missed him? Tamping down a flurry of nerves, she asked, "And you are?"

"Steve Calhoun."

The name didn't ring familiar. Katharine looked to Amanda for explanation.

"Mr. Calhoun is with Dryer Textiles. He's here to see you."

Her? But Katharine hadn't made any appointments. Why would this man be here to see her?

Mr. Calhoun glanced around the office. "You missing someone?"

"A stable hand," she blurted. "Young man didn't show up for work and we've been trying to track him down." Sucking in a deep breath, she calmed the pounding in her chest, walked over to the man and extended a hand. "Katharine Wainwright.

He shook warmly. "Steve Calhoun. I hope you don't mind, but when I heard you were in town, I insisted on waiting for your return." All light went out of his eyes as he said, "I can't tell you how sorry I was to hear about your mother. She was an incredible person and will be missed by a lot of folks around here."

"Thank you." It was the automatic reply, the two words that expressed gratitude for a person's kind words without revealing how empty they made her feel. *Sorry for your loss. She will be missed.* Katharine had had a chunk cut out of her heart and people said her mother would be missed? Missed didn't begin to cover the gaping crater in her life but it was neither here nor there. This man was expressing his respect. She would accept it. "So how may I help you?" Katharine asked, redirecting conversation to easier terrain.

Glancing at the suite of offices behind her, his gaze cooled. "I'm here to discuss business."

Katharine's pulse thwacked between her ears. Instinctively, she knew what was coming next. Donors had been fleeing like a swarm of spooked birds. Was Dryer next? With no time for an impromptu business meeting—or bad news— and no way to walk out on the situation, she ventured, "Business of what kind?"

"I understand the ranch is experiencing some difficulties and Dryer's board isn't convinced your establishment will remain solvent."

"I assure you, Mr. Calhoun, that couldn't be further from the truth. Wainwright Ranch is a solid operation. Enrollment is strong, revenues are projected to rise... We are here for the long-term."

He smiled, though she thought it fell a bit short of genuine pleasure.

Seemed the man had his reservations. Katharine pushed her shoulders back and summoned as much conviction as she could, adding, "I've been going over the numbers myself. Our organization is on firm ground."

The lines in his face softened as his gaze released its indictment. "I'm glad to hear it. There have been a lot of rumors and I'd hate to think any of them are true. Your mother was a real dynamo. She single-handedly founded this organization and we've been proud partners from the beginning."

"And we thank you for your support," Katharine replied evenly, wondering what rumors he was referring to. "We're only as strong as our donors."

Mr. Calhoun's gaze clouded. With a glance askance to Amanda, he said, "Which is why it pains me to inform you that if we don't get a solid report from you during the fundraising gala we will be forced to withdraw our support."

It took every ounce of self-control Katharine possessed not to react. Withdraw their support? Losing Dryer Textiles would be a sizeable hit, one that could easily sink the ranch if they couldn't replace the funds with other donors. Paul Sutherland's face popped into her mind. A highly unlikely proposition, considering the man in charge of fundraising had no secret weapons up his sleeve. "You will," she assured him. "You will."

Angling near, he smiled. "I do hate to deliver bad news, but I am glad for the opportunity to meet you. Maybe I can steal you away for lunch one day while you're here?"

Caught off guard, Katharine suppressed her surprise and replied neatly, "I appreciate the offer, Mr. Calhoun, but frankly I'm swamped. Maybe some other time?"

Accepting the rejection in stride, he nodded. "Maybe." Casting an appraising glance over her, he ticked his head back. "Hope you find your staff member."

"Yes," she clipped. "We will."

Looking from Amanda to Katharine, he paused. "I'll see you at the fundraiser, then."

"Yes."

Steve Calhoun walked out of the office and once the door closed, Katharine gasped. Whirling upon the receptionist, she hissed, "If we lose Dryer Textiles, we're finished!"

Amanda peered up at her, a pair of soulful brown eyes mirroring the distress swimming through Katharine's heart.

Frank walked into the lobby, a mix of confusion and concern mingling in his gaze. "I thought I heard voices. Did you find the boy?"

"No," she snapped and strode toward him. "But Steve Calhoun just informed me that if we don't produce a positive cash flow report during the fundraiser next week, Dryer Textiles is pulling their donation. Did you know they were considering this?"

Frank's eyes hardened. "Yes, he said as much to me last week."

"This is horrible news, Frank. And we still haven't found the boy!" *Kyle*, she told herself. The boy had a name—an identity—and she needed to start using it. "Kyle is still missing. Canyon has called in a police search team and we're getting ready to head back up the mountain."

"You called the police? I told you not to call in the authorities." Frank's voice became heated, "If word gets out we had a missing child, you will lose more than Dryer Textiles. You'll lose the entire ranch!"

Anger rose sharply in her chest. "What did you expect me to do, Frank? Rely on good luck to find the child? He's missing. He's twelve. We need to find him and we need to find him quick—for *his* sake, not ours."

"You're not the only one with money at stake," Katharine. "You have investors to think of, employees."

"Money?" Nausea pitched into her stomach. "That's what you're concerned about?"

"Money makes this ranch possible."

"Money that's been disappearing from our accounts like someone left the doors to the vault wide open!"

Frank stilled as he registered the insult. Katharine kicked herself for delivering the news like this, but *dammit* he was coming down on her for putting the ranch at risk when it was *his* oversight that had been slipping for months!

Quickly capping the lid of her temper, she shifted her weight from heel to heel and felt the throb in her knees return. This was not good. Not Kyle, not Dryer, not Frank and his reaction. None of it was good but she had to keep her priorities straight. "I'm sorry, Frank, Wainwright Ranch might have a slew of problems but I refuse to add a missing child to the list."

An eerie distance slid into his gaze. "You're the boss."

Yes, she was. And with that title came tough decisions. If Kyle had wandered off intentionally, he would get a talking to from her. Her mother would have never tolerated such irresponsible behavior from a camper. She never coddled or pampered—she treated them like normal children. Which is exactly who they were. There would have to be consequences.

Katharine would check with Canyon to see what they should be, what her mother would have done. Until then, they had a job to do. Realizing the receptionist was staring at the door—at someone—Katharine flinched. Had Mr. Calhoun come back? Had he heard everything they'd just said?

Chills tingled down her spine and she slowly turned.

"Is there a problem?" Canyon asked. He stood quiet, arms by his sides, a pair of hiking boots dangling from his hand.

"No, no problems," she sputtered, the earlier panic draining from her limbs. "What are those?"

"Hiking boots. Your mother always kept a spare pair in the barn, in case she had to step through some nasty business. I thought you could use them."

Drawn to the boots, Katharine felt momentarily paralyzed. Those had belonged to her mother? Why did Canyon have them?

"It was your idea to call in police, wasn't it?" Frank accused instantly. "It's your fault they're involved."

Hearing the venom in Frank's voice, Katharine snapped out of her haze and addressed him directly, "No, Frank. It was my decision. We need help. This situation has moved beyond our capacity to handle it alone and I directed him to call. We're renewing our search efforts with the help of the authorities and I won't listen to another word to the contrary."

Frank became rigid. "You're making a mistake, Katharine. You heard Mr. Calhoun. Even if you find the boy, it won't matter. Dryer Textiles will only hear that you lost a child. It will be game over. Your mother would have understood that and handled it my way. Privately."

Anger churned in Canyon's gaze, soaked his tone as he shot back, "You have no idea what Eleanor would have done."

"Don't I? I worked side-by-side with the woman for the last thirty years which says I knew her pretty well, and I know she wouldn't have given in so easily."

Katharine reeled as the barb found its mark dead center in her chest. "He's right."

"He's not right," Canyon pushed back. "Your mother would have put the child first, pure and simple."

Katharine confronted Canyon. "Frank said this has happened before. Were you here then? Do you know what my mother did?"

Canyon shook his head. "No, but I know what she'd do today." Handing Katharine the pair of boots, he said, "She'd waste no time and spare no effort to find the child. Same as you'll do."

With a shaky hand, Katharine took the boots from him. All confidence in her decision evaporated. Evading Frank's pointed gaze, she said, "We have to find him Canyon."

"We will."

Chapter Twelve

"Everybody knows the plan," Canyon shouted to the group. Standing near the tree line where mountain met flatland, he spoke to the Wainwright staff members and mountain search and rescue teams who stood ready for his command, his dog Buck planted on the ground by his feet. There were men and women, young and old. Experienced. Everyone on hand had experience with search and rescue, save for a few of the Wainwright people, and Canyon felt they were on solid ground with regard to prospective outcome. There were no storm clouds on the horizon, temps were moderate. The situation was stable.

"We have about four hours until nightfall," he continued. "We've narrowed the search area to a twenty square-mile radius. It's a huge patch of ground to cover and we'll do it in teams of six, plus two choppers in the air offering assistance. Questions?"

"How familiar is this kid with the mountain?"

"Not very," Canyon replied. The lead search and rescue guy from the mountain squad had asked the question, but Canyon addressed the entire group, "I think he might have followed the group of campers down but detoured at some point." Canyon knew the beef jerky was a sketchy clue, but it was all he had. That section of mountain was private property and hiked heavily by the ranch. It made sense the jerky belonged to Kyle. What it didn't explain is why he'd veered off-track.

"Is he a nervous type that might stay put, or the kind to wander?" another fellow asked.

Kyle's face popped into Canyon's mind, his mischievous gleam clear as if he were standing before him. "Explore is a better word. He fancies himself as a real survivalist. I wouldn't put it past him to get caught up in the thrill of it and set off on an adventure just to come back and share it with the others."

"A thrill that can kill," McIntyre Walsh noted.

True, Canyon rued privately. An ex-Marine, Walsh, as he was known to his friends, had lived in the mountains for almost a year and understood better than anyone the danger that unfamiliar landscape could pose; the risk of disorientation, dehydration, panic. Kyle might fancy himself a survivalist, but Walsh was the real deal. "Yes, but we'll find him before he gets into any trouble."

Walsh slid a stern glance to his girlfriend. Standing beside him, she was a petite brunette in amazing shape and dressed similarly to Walsh in her khaki cargo pants, pullover T-shirt and hiking boots. Only she had the addition of a pink bandana wrapped around her head while his brown-skinned scalp was practically shaved bald. The two were a stark contrast in coloring. He was deeply tanned, grim-faced and menacing with his piercing green eyes and humorless expression. She, on the other hand, was fair-skinned, bright-eyed and perky. Her name was Lisa and she was Hal Richardson's daughter, a young woman with more experience hiking the mountainous terrain than even Walsh, though Walsh had proven himself capable by saving her hide this past summer under threat of a killer on the loose. But that was Walsh. Trouble loomed, he stepped in. The guy was solid—solid as a rock.

"Does this survivalist of ours have any supplies on hand?" Walsh asked.

"None."

Walsh grunted.

"But if he has a basic set of nature skills," Lisa Richardson piped up next to him, her brown eyes alert and focused, "he should be fine until we catch up with him."

Ever the positive one, Canyon mused. Except this time Lisa might be giving Kyle a little too much credit. Yes, the boy prided himself on his skills, but it didn't mean he actually possessed them. But they were wasting time. It didn't matter what Kyle did or didn't know. All Canyon needed was for him to keep out of trouble until they found him. "Okay, if there's nothing else, let's get to it."

The crowd broke. A dozen men hopped on ATVs, others headed into the forest on foot, Walsh and Lisa hung with him, along with Katharine Wainwright who had remained glued to Canyon's side. For a woman who had insisted on taking part, reiterating she was the owner and must be involved on every level, she sure had been quiet for the last hour. Strange, but it seemed to Canyon like she was finally realizing she was out of her league out here in the wild, a sentiment he'd bet didn't come easy. From what Eleanor had told him, Katharine was a high-powered Wall Street investment type who ran with the big boys. She worked with her father, a man who'd built his career on creating massive wealth, and massive wealth usually translated to massive ego. Where Katharine didn't outwardly flaunt a huge ego, she had no problem throwing her power around, beginning with her emergency board meeting and continuing with this search.

Maybe it was being surrounded by strangers that made her clam up. No longer hiking alone with one of her employees, Katharine was hiking alongside men and women who knew this area and how to handle the elements—a helluva lot better than she did.

Katharine looked up to him, her gaze nicked by concern. "You're not worried about Kyle, are you?"

"Not yet."

"He'll be okay," Lisa pitched in. "The temps are mild and we have a lot of time. We'll find him, don't worry."

Leave it to Lisa to pick up on the woman's distress and instinctively want to soothe. Walsh kept quiet, though Canyon could sense a comment peeling off his brain. Normally, the man had a comeback for everything.

"She's right," Canyon said to Katharine. "Let's retrace our steps. We'll head up toward the campsite and see if we can find any signs of him, then start fresh back down the trail."

"To where you found the beef jerky?"

Walsh perked at the mention.

Unwilling to entertain his buddy with details on his shabby detective work, Canyon merely muttered, "Yes."

For the next half hour, the four hiked in relative silence. Buck led the pack—usually by a dozen yards—followed by Canyon, Katharine and Lisa, with Walsh pulling up the rear. As they trekked upward, Canyon called out Kyle's name. Behind him, Walsh scanned the area with a trained eye, searching for what didn't belong. He'd explained to Canyon that it was a tactical method he'd learned while in the military. Scanning in an organized fashion, he combed the landscape looking for things that didn't fit in, seemed out of the ordinary, or simply caught his eye as oddities. It's how he met Lisa. She'd been hiking the high country researching her toads when Walsh spotted a flash of light in the bushes behind her. Being the good Marine that he was, he began pursuit of the threat. Canyon chuckled as he recalled the story. Wasn't exactly love at first sight, but after Walsh proved to Lisa there actually was a bad guy following her—and saved her from a gunshot wound from the same—the two managed to connect on a more personal level and have been together ever since.

Crazy how life threw people together. One minute a guy was minding his own business, the next he had a female on his hands—one he couldn't get out of his mind. Canyon's two-way radio erupted in static.

"Canyon, you copy?"

Snatching the handheld from his waist, Canyon keyed his mic. It was Roan Phillips, one of the helicopter pilots in the air. "Copy."

"We've got a sighting of possible fire over the east ridge," Roan advised, his voice competing with the heavy pulse of copter blades in the background. "Near Red Creek Canyon."

"*Red Creek*?" Canyon mapped the region in his brain as though seeing it from Roan's aerial vantage point. "But that's two miles out of our search zone."

"I'm just telling you what I know. Kelly says she spotted a thread line of smoke over there. She's moving in now for a closer look."

"Roger." Kelly was the other helicopter pilot in the air, a new hire for the police department. Unlike Roan, she was ex-military and darn good from what Wade Davis said, though Roan had his reservations. Reservations Canyon suspected might have more to do with competition within the department than anything based in fact.

"You want me and Lisa to cut over?" Walsh asked. "We can use Clarkson Pass and be there in less than two hours."

"Do you think it's Kyle?" Katharine asked.

Canyon shrugged, and whistled for Buck to halt. The yellow dog responded immediately then doubled back to the group, bounding easily down the narrow and densely wooded path. While Canyon didn't want to discourage Katharine, he didn't want to give her false hope, either. There was no doubt Walsh and Lisa could make it over there without issue, but Red Creek? Canyon doubted Kyle could have made it that far from the campsite. And fire? The boy had no means. It was more likely trespassers causing the smoke. Canyon fixed Walsh in his gaze. Overhead, the canopy of trees and shade lent an eerie appeal to Walsh's dark face. "Head over, but be prepared for surprises."

"Always am," Walsh replied, shooting back a knowing look.

In their silent exchange, Canyon was confident Walsh understood the danger. Trespassers weren't common in these parts but they were a reality and could mean trouble. Trouble Canyon was certain Walsh could handle. The man carried. He knew how to protect and defend. It's what he did. Canyon eyed him directly. "Keep in radio contact."

Walsh nodded. "Will do."

Walsh and Lisa stepped off the trail and trampled over heavy underbrush as they headed for Red Creek Canyon. They were experienced hikers, physically fit, and would have no trouble with the journey. If they found Kyle, they could get the boy to a clearing where Roan could fly in for a pickup. If they didn't find him, the two could easily spend the night and head home the next day.

Left alone with his dog and Katharine, Canyon stared into her eyes. His heart pinched. Naked, vulnerable, her gaze held it all. The ranch was in trouble, a child was lost, and she was smack in the middle of a crisis situation. But crisis called for calm and strength, not fear-laced hope.

Canyon pulled a plastic bottle from his pack. "Water?"

"No, thanks."

"You need to drink. Dehydration sneaks up on you."

"Okay." She accepted the bottle from him and drank, her throat bobbing rhythmically with each swallow. Her hair was combed and organized into a braid and pulled to one side. Her skin appeared flushed from the exertion, her lipstick long gone. Handing the bottle back to him, she wiped the drip from her mouth. "Thanks. That does feel good."

Canyon grinned. "You're welcome. How are you holding up?" he asked, squirting water from the bottle into Buck's eager mouth.

"Great," she replied, watching the dog slurp water, spilling almost as much as he took in. "These shoes really make all the difference."

"Figured they might," Canyon said, then squirted a stream of water into his own mouth. "Your mother knew the value of using good equipment."

Katharine's gaze softened suddenly, nearly tripping him. "It was nice of you to think of them."

Canyon stilled. The bandana at his neck grew warm. "Your mother would have wanted you to have them."

"You seem to know a lot about my mother."

"I don't know if I'd go that far," Canyon said, capping the water bottle, "but I sure did enjoy working with her."

"I bet she really liked you."

"I don't know how much she liked me..." The skin beneath his bandana flushed hot and he rubbed his neck, tossing a glance toward Buck. The dog stared at him, seemingly urging him to hurry up and resume their trek.

"Enough to entrust you with the management of operations," Katharine went on, "and bring you on as a board member."

"Yes, well, sometimes need dictates decisions more than desire," Canyon returned. Uncomfortable in Katharine's spotlight, he kicked his legs back into motion. Buck took his sign and ran up the trail ahead of them. Canyon ruminated over the statement. Couldn't mean that much. Eleanor had trusted Frank Dillard with the same vote of confidence and that man was as palatable as a mule.

Katharine caught up with him and said, "There's nothing wrong with catching the eye of the owner."

Did she think he was embarrassed?

Quite the contrary. He took pride in Eleanor's favor but she was gone and Frank was in charge. And where it was true Frank and Eleanor had a close working relationship, had known each other for years, it didn't negate the fact the man was a jerk. Canyon cupped his hands to his mouth and shouted, "Kyle!"

The sound of Canyon's voice echoed slightly in the trees but nothing came back in reply. Suppressing a flare of aggravation, he planned to string that boy up from the nearest T-bar for putting them through this exercise. The kid was fine. Canyon felt it in his gut. Kyle hadn't been gone long enough to put his life in jeopardy, and he wasn't stupid enough to get near the river where he could slip and fall. There weren't any dangerous animals prowling for food during the daylight hours, no bears to speak of in these parts, no ominous threats, which told Canyon the kid wasn't in jeopardy. No. Kyle was out on a self-hosted adventure and he was going to hear about it when Canyon found him.

"Why is it I don't remember you, Canyon?"

"Should I take that as a bad sign?"

"No, of course not. It's just that you seem to know so much about my mother. Why is it I don't remember seeing you around during my visits?"

"Probably because I spent most of my time in the barn or on a horse, rounding up cattle with the kids. Between that and our camping trips, I'm not surprised our paths didn't cross."

"Or at a rodeo," she added, a touch of disapproval in her tone.

Canyon chucked a smile over his shoulder. "Yes, I've always traveled the circuit—time permitting, that is."

"But my mother thought so highly of you, appointed you as a board member. I'm surprised she never introduced us."

She wouldn't have seen a reason to, Canyon mused. He was an employee. Katharine was her daughter. What purpose would it have served? Brushing aside a rush of irritation, he said, "The board member thing didn't come until recently. It was the year she learned she was dying." Uninterested in reliving the painful memories, he left it at that. Leave it to Katharine to fill in the blanks.

"But it's clear you love these kids," Katharine said, interrupting his thoughts. "Do you mind me asking why you were so willing to attend a rodeo instead of my emergency board meeting?"

"The rodeo came first," he tossed over his shoulder. Plain and simple.

"Before your work with the children?"

"The rodeos are about the children." The money, anyway. The challenge of riding the bulls was about him and only him. Canyon felt a surge of pleasure. But it was nothing this woman would understand. "I ride bulls and donate my winnings to the ranch," he said, grabbing a branch that lay across their path. Breaking it in two, he tossed it into a mass of low-lying green plants. "It's sort of my way to give back."

"You do? But why didn't you say so?"

At the growing distance in her voice, he realized that she'd stopped. He stopped and turned. "You didn't ask." Besides, it was no business of hers what he did with his free time, or his winnings.

"Is it a lot of money?"

He looked at her, threads of irritation pulling at him. "It is to me."

Katharine's cheeks flushed and she hurried up the trail to meet him. "I'm sorry. I didn't mean for that to come across as rude."

"No worries." Canyon brushed off the offense. It wasn't her fault he felt the edge. It was Frank's. For some reason, it irked the guy that Canyon donated his personal money to the cause and when he first learned of it, he'd made some pretty rude remarks, something she had no way of knowing. "Sometimes my winnings can be pretty hefty. This last payout was over thirty grand."

She sucked in her breath. "Thirty thousand dollars? Seriously? What do you have to do for that kind of money?"

Pleasure slid into Canyon and he smiled. "Stay on a bull for eight seconds."

Her eyes rounded. Her lips parted, and once again Canyon considered what it would be like to kiss that mouth of hers, the skin of which was bare and slightly puckered at the moment, dry from a day of hiking at high elevation. What he wouldn't do to slick them up for her and make her groan. "It's a challenge," he said, lingering a moment longer in his thoughts of her.

"And you do that for the kids?"

Canyon stuffed the lustful thoughts to the back of his brain and replied, "It would be a lie to say I don't enjoy it, but yes, I travel the rodeo circuit and ride to win. And winning allows me to give to the kids."

"Where else do you go?"

He cocked his head with a slight shrug. "Depends on the rodeo but I prefer to take part in the bigger events, mainly here in Colorado, down in Texas and other parts around the Southwest. The competition is tougher, but so are the pay-outs."

Mouth agape, Katharine stared at him, her expression softened by the filtered light from the trees overhead. "I don't know what to say..."

"There's nothing to say. We all do our part. You, me, the staff."

When she didn't say anything more, Canyon took his cue to continue their search. Cupping hands to his mouth, he shouted, "Kyle!" Then continued his trek up the mountain.

Chapter Thirteen

Katharine stared at Canyon's rising backside, overcome by a wave of disbelief. *Thirty thousand dollars? For riding a bull?* Her gaze slid down his body, then dropped to the ground, a trail embedded with rocks and roots and bordered by a miscellany of green foliage. Canyon couldn't be serious. Could he?

It would be an easy fact to check. He said he donated the money to the ranch. If it were true, there'd be a record of it in their account. But he wouldn't lie about a thing like that. It was too easy to follow up. *Thirty thousand dollars.* And he did this more than once? She had no idea rodeos paid money to their riders! She'd always thought of the events like the fair or the circus, a traveling show to entertain, not a competition where big money was at stake. Allowing her gaze to wander the length of his body, his long legs and broad back, she wondered, was it hard? Did he win often? Had he ever been hurt?

Laughter pulled at her. Judging by the size of him, she'd bet a bull had a hard time throwing Canyon off! Abruptly, the red bandana at his neck caught her attention. Did it serve a purpose? Did he wear it for his rodeos and then continue out of habit?

Stepping over a protruding rock, Katharine realized there was so much about this man she didn't know but suddenly wanted very much to know. Katharine dropped her gaze to the ground, landing on her shoes. *Her mother's shoes.* Walking in them, Katharine marveled at their slim fit. They weren't bulky or heavy and fit her feet as if custom made for her. The well-cushioned soles easily traversed the rugged terrain and her knees felt as if she could hike for miles. Had her mother been an avid hiker? Had she worn these boots often?

Katharine hated that there was so much about her that she didn't know. She hated the creeping feeling that Canyon had a better handle on her mother's ranch life than she did—her own daughter. But when two people lived thousands of miles apart, it was bound to happen. Distance seeped in. Conversations became summaries rather than lengthy discussions and shared feelings. Katharine had opted for the city, for the investment business while her mother had opted for western living and to help children. Sadly, hiking the land that belonged to her family, Katharine felt like a stranger.

Up ahead, Canyon's dog darted off trail, his golden-yellow body swallowed by the underlying brush. His tail wagged as though he'd discovered something interesting, but his master called him back. The animal obeyed without issue, reminding her of Cody. Katharine was certain he'd love to be up here instead of sitting in the office with Amanda. But she didn't think it was appropriate. Canyon's dog was trained for search and rescue. Cody was not.

When the dog rejoined Canyon, the two waited for her to catch up. "How you holding up?" he asked, a subtle concern simmering in his brown eyes.

"Fine." Expelling a sigh, she confessed, "What's not fine is the ranch."

Storm clouds pushed into his gaze. "Something new?"

"One of our donors stopped by today. Said he came to inform me that his company would be pulling out of the ranch if I don't give them reason to stay during the fundraiser."

Katharine hadn't wanted to burden Canyon with the bad news or distract him from the task at hand, but the stress of carrying the weight alone was killing her. Unseen forces were squeezing in and she needed room to breathe. If anyone would understand, it would be Canyon. He had a stake in the ranch. He'd understand the stress she was feeling.

His comprehension was swift. "Was that the fellow I saw leaving before I came back for you?"

"Yes. He represents Dryer Textiles."

"Dryer's talking about pulling out?"

The shock in Canyon's expression only served to underscore her concern. "Yes. And if we lose them, I don't know how we'll survive."

Canyon didn't immediately reply. Instead, he called out for Kyle, glanced from side to side, up into the trees, as though he expected he might see the boy sitting on a branch above.

Katharine followed his gaze but feared they weren't any closer to finding Kyle now than they had been this morning. Her pulse jumped. Was his silence a tacit indication he feared the worst, too? "Do you think we'll find him?"

"Kyle? Yes," he answered swiftly.

"If only I could be so certain."

"We'll find him, Katharine, don't worry."

"And the money? Frank is right. Once Dryer gets wind that we lost a child, they'll pull out. I don't know what I'll do if that happens, if I lose the ranch."

"We're not going to lose the ranch," he said. "We'll think of something."

"But what? We need money to operate and if Dryer pulls their money, who knows who else will follow? Once word gets out we lost a child, donors will fall like dominoes."

"We deal with the situation at hand. We find Kyle, we assess the finances, and we sell the value of the ranch during the annual fundraiser, same as we do every year."

She wanted to believe him but she didn't want to play games. "Canyon, these are big problems. Solving them in less than two weeks' time might be impossible."

"And it's also possible."

Biting back a rebuff, Katharine drilled her gaze into Canyon's back. She was not a negative person. She didn't give up without a fight, nor did she kid herself. Facts were facts. Numbers didn't lie. If they lost the funds to operate, the ranch would have to close. It was the last thing she wanted. If she could write a check and personally finance the ranch herself, she would. But she couldn't. And neither could Canyon. While she appreciated that he donated his rodeo winnings to help out the cause, it wasn't enough to sustain it. "Mr. Cal-houn remarked how they'd heard the rumors. Do you know what he's talking about? Is there something else at play be-sides my mother's absence?"

Canyon shook his head. "Not unless they're referring to Sutherland. Like I said before, the man doesn't seem to be doing a whole lot of good."

Paul. Canyon seemed to have it out for the man yet she'd seen nothing to indicate he was the sole problem. In all hon-esty, she laid more of the blame at Frank's feet than Paul's. Did Canyon know something she didn't?

Whatever. She couldn't deal with it right now. "Kyle!" she yelled out impulsively. "Kyle, do you hear me?" The ranch needed help. They needed money. Big money. They needed to find Kyle. "Kyle!"

As Canyon led the way upward, the forest opened to a sweeping view. Katharine cast her glance into the distance. Across the treetops she could see beautiful estate homes wedged into the mountainside at lower elevations. They were large, even by her parents' standards, and utterly breathtaking inside. Over the years, Katharine had been in many of them and remembered well the panoramic vista this mountain range made from a wall of windows.

The Wainwright mansion wasn't visible from this van-tage point. Her parents had chosen to build closer to the val-ley in order to avoid the icy winter drives required by the higher locations during the winter. Curvy hairpin turns were something her parents wanted nothing to do with, especially her mother, who spent months at a time here in the mountains alone.

Silver Creek had been her sanctuary, winter and sum-mer.

Admiring the landscape, the spray of colorful wildflow-ers over lush meadow grass, the intense blue sky, Katharine lingered on a cluster of cow parsnip. The white flower was a food source for moose. Succulent, the stems were stout while the array of blossoms reminded her of Queen Anne's lace. It was a beautiful flower. Technically, it was an herb, but beautiful nonetheless. She sighed. Summertime had been her favorite time to visit, when the air was warm and temperate, the land littered with flowers as it was now. She used to love how Silver Creek filled every space in town with wildflowers, from built-in planters dotting the square to dirt beds along streets and sidewalks. One literally couldn't walk the streets of the village without seeing flowers. Thinking about it now reminded Katharine of her flower boxes back home in New York. She'd need to bring them inside soon after her return. Come fall, the days would be getting shorter, her patio steeped in shadow, thanks to the high-rises surrounding hers.

Shaking an unexpected gloom, Katharine returned her focus to the land. On the trail ahead of her, Canyon and Buck appeared carefree and relaxed. If she didn't know better, they could simply be a man and his dog enjoying a day on the mountain. Seemed they hiked often. The campers hiked often. Had her mother joined them often?

Instantly, she looked to her feet. Walking in her mother's shoes—literally—plodding over the same ground her mother used to walk, served to make Katharine feel close to her mom. Eleanor Wainwright was a soft-spoken socialite who mingled in the halls of New York City's Fifth Avenue high society yet felt equally comfortable in the mountains of Colorado. Her mother was amazing. Nowhere on earth did Katharine feel her power more than here, traipsing across a mountainside in search of a missing boy. Strange, but the crisis made Katharine feel more connected to her mother than she had in years.

A breeze kicked up and cooled the skin of Katharine's neck, welcome under the bright sun and strain of exertion. Canyon looked back and an uncanny sensation overcame her. A column of tingles raced across her back and shoulders. The air hummed, and Katharine suddenly felt her mother's presence, almost as if she turned around, she might see her walking behind her. As Canyon disappeared into a section of forest ahead, Katharine couldn't shake the feeling. This was her mother's life, her mother's existence. Canyon, the campers, hiking, being outdoors...

And wholly opposite from Katharine's life in New York.

"Ground zero," Canyon announced when they reached the campsite, and glanced around the vicinity while Buck took an immediate inventory of the scents, sniffing anything and everything.

Katharine expelled a sigh, oddly overwhelmed by the vast empty space. The area looked the same as it had earlier this morning. It was a beautiful spot, surrounded by evergreens and boulders, the ground a matted carpet of short grass and fallen pine needles. A large fire ring was encircled by red and gray rocks. In the center, the blackened remains of fire could be seen but there were no ashes, as though someone had erased all evidence with fresh dirt. There was no debris of any kind, no signs that humans had been here. Other than the meticulous formation of rocks for the purpose of a campfire, the scene was undisturbed.

Brushing the back of her hand against her forehead, she wiped off a sheen of perspiration and looked to Canyon. To her, nothing seemed out of the ordinary. "So what do you think? Where should we go from here?"

"I'm going to take a look around. Jacob said that Kyle went missing right around the time they were packing up." Canyon pointed to an area off to the right. "He could have hidden over there and watched while they packed and called for him. Jacob and Becky wouldn't have left the kids to go search for him. Kyle would know that. I'll go see if I can find any signs of him."

"Okay."

Katharine watched Canyon walk into the edge of the forest, Buck close at his heel. The two moved in and around the trees. Canyon dropped to a squat from time to time. She doubted he would find anything. Other than a quick bite of jerky, what would a young boy take with him? And why would he leave anything behind? Canyon's reasoning didn't make sense.

Frustration welled as she checked her watch. It was almost three-thirty. She looked up into the sky. Clear and blue, it wouldn't stay light forever. They had to get going. And since Canyon had already voiced his suspicions about Kyle heading down the trail behind the others, why not start there?

Taking a few steps toward him, she shouted, "Canyon!"

He popped up from the ground and sprinted from the trees. "What is it?" Buck leapt between bushes and ran toward her as well. "Did you find something?" Canyon called out.

"No." She wanted to add that she didn't think they were going to find anything up here, either, and that they should get going back down the trail, but to voice it in such terms might be overstepping her boundaries. A nudge might work better. "But don't you think we should get going?"

Even from this distance, his scowl was unmistakable. Canyon walked back to where he'd been crouched on his haunches and resumed his search. Buck lingered out in the open, as though torn over which direction he should pursue but chose his master, darting back into the wooded section near Canyon.

Katharine crossed her arms over her chest. They were wasting valuable time. Kyle wasn't here. They needed to keep moving, keep looking. She glanced up into the sky. Clouds were few and far between. At the moment, the temperature was fine, but once the sun went down it would get cold. Very cold. Colder than a lone child could tolerate. Katharine skimmed the trees around her, the rocks and ground. Soon the animals would come out. They'd be hungry, looking for food. Nerves percolated in her midsection. If wild creatures stumbled across Kyle, there was no telling what could happen. It was a bad mix. A dangerous combination. Flicking a glance toward Canyon poking around in the trees, Katharine snapped. It was time to go. Rally the forces and cover more ground.

Marching toward him, a sparkle of light in a patch of grass caught her eye. Detouring, she went to the spot and bent over. There were two gray objects, rectangular in shape, and she wondered what they were. Secured together by a silver beaded chain, it almost looked like a set of dog tags. She picked them up and turned the items between her fingers. The larger piece felt like a flattened harmonica, the smaller was nothing more than a sliver of metal with a sawblade edge. Were they important?

Moments later, Canyon returned and announced, "Nothing. Let's start heading down."

Katharine stepped toward him and turned over her find. "I found this on the ground."

"Where?" he demanded.

"On the ground, over there," she said. "Is it significant?"

Canyon strode quickly to where she pointed and scanned the ground in short order. Buck was by his side, sniffing the dirt around Canyon's feet.

Katharine joined them, feeling a bloom of hope in her chest. "Is it significant?"

"It's a magnesium stick. Jacob carries one to start fires."

"You mean, like a campfire?"

"Yes. Striking a metal blade against the magnesium sparks a flame to set a fire."

"Oh." She looked around, somehow expecting to find something more. "But what would it be doing on the ground?"

He stared at her squarely and said, "Good question."

Canyon's radio erupted with static and a man's voice burst through the noise. "Canyon, copy."

Canyon answered quickly, "Copy."

"Red Creek is a bust. There's no sign of the kid, only a couple of lost hikers. I sent them on their way."

Canyon's expression darkened. "Okay, thanks Walsh."

"What do you want us to do now?"

"Head back," Canyon told him. "It was a stretch Kyle would have made it that far anyway."

"Roger," Walsh replied. "We'll head your way."

Listening to him, Katharine stared at the gray stick in his hand, all hope extinguished like a wet match. Back to ground zero. They had nothing. Except a looming disaster on their hands.

Canyon ended the communication and Katharine picked up a sense of disquiet. Was he at a loss on how to proceed? Were they at a dead end? The emotion churning through his gaze unsettled her. Torn between good news and bad, she searched his gaze. "Now what?"

Chapter Fourteen

With Buck sitting at attention at his feet, Canyon fought a growing pressure in his chest. Peering into Katharine's expectant gaze, he was losing hope. They should have found Kyle by now. It would be dark soon. Time was working against them. Temperatures would drop. Danger ratcheted up. Teams on the ground continued to criss cross with no luck. If they didn't find him soon, Roan and Kelly would be reduced to using searchlights and an infrared heat-seeking device from their choppers, a far more difficult proposition in search and rescue operations than a simple flyover.

Canyon had been on missions where hikers were found after dark with less than optimal results. Dark meant danger. Kyle had a backpack which meant he'd have a jacket, but he'd be hungry. Scared. Canyon didn't care how tough the kid tried to act, he was a boy, human. Normal. Kyle would experience the fear of being alone in the dark same as anyone would. Without a fire, he'd be vulnerable. Canyon ground his jaw, felt the muscles in his neck and shoulders spasm and tighten. Kyle had definitely planned this escapade. The magnesium stick proved it. He must have taken the stick from Jacob's backpack then dropped it on the ground, telling Canyon two things. The boy had had intent but had lost his chance. Stupid.

This entire scene was stupid!

"Canyon?" Katharine asked gently, as though afraid to upset him. "It's going to be dark soon."

"I know."

"What are we going to do?"

Settling on her face, he saw the tension in her eyes and felt a growing unease of his own. "We" was the operative word. "We" weren't going to do anything, he wanted to say. *He* was. "I need to get you down the mountain."

"What? I'm not going down the mountain until we find Kyle!"

"It's getting dark. You're not dressed for the cold. You have no food. It's no smarter for you to be up here than it is for Kyle."

She eyed his backpack. "Do you have food in there?"

"A granola bar. Enough for one," he said, heading her off at the pass. He didn't figure she'd take the news well, not when she'd been so adamant about taking part in the first place, but the situation was changing. While the last thing she'd want would be to head down, it was his first order of business.

"I'm not leaving until we find him," she said.

"You'll freeze in that outfit."

"I'm fine. I'm used to the cold of New York City. I can tolerate the dip in temperature for the time it will take to find Kyle."

"Problem is, we don't know how long it will take."

"Problem is, we have a missing child."

Canyon stared at her. She stared back. He'd insist, except she'd likely pull rank on him. Like it or not, Katharine was the owner of Wainwright Ranch and could fire him on the spot. Didn't matter that she didn't have any experience searching for a missing child—Kyle was missing from her ranch and that's what she cared about.

As much as Canyon didn't like the idea of her staying, he liked the idea of losing his job even less. "I need to check in with the others," he said, and walked away from her. A rumble of doubt twisted in his gut and he keyed up his radio. "Weston, copy."

"Weston."

"What's your status on the ground search?"

"Empty. Teams rode in from each direction and reported they saw nothing and no one. Teams on foot are reporting the same. I'm still waiting on a group out of the east, in the northern quadrant. I'll let you know as soon as I have something."

"Copy." Canyon re-clipped his radio and stared through the space of trees. The only patch of ground left to cover was between here and the river and beyond. If they picked up their speed, they could cover the area in less than an hour. He flicked a glance at Katharine.

If she could keep up. If she could, there was always the chance he could scare her with the threat of bears and wild animals, except doing so would only cause her more worry for Kyle's safety. Not that Canyon wasn't worried, he was. Unfortunately, now he had two to worry about. "C'mon."

Katharine and Buck followed. "Where are we going?" she asked.

"To the river."

Moving past her weighty gaze, Canyon ignored the fear in her eyes and his instinctual reaction to it and headed down the trail. He couldn't discount the possibility that Kyle had fallen in, no matter how unlikely he judged it to be, but he didn't have to dwell on it. *The kid was fine*. It was Canyon's search mantra and he was going to stick with it.

Searching for a dead body didn't key up his senses like a live one in danger did.

Buck darted around Canyon and took the lead, well-versed in the business of search and rescue and plain old-fashioned hiking. Maybe the dog could root out Kyle before he could.

"Do you think Kyle is okay?" Katharine asked, her voice fairly close behind him.

"Yes."

"Do you think we'll find him?"

"Yes."

"How can you be so certain?"

Because I refuse to accept the alternative, he thought and stepped over a gnarled root.

"Canyon?"

Frustration boiled over and he whirled upon her. "Kyle is fine. There are only so many places on this mountain he could be and we're heading to the last one."

"I'm all for thinking positive," she said, her voice catching as her stride landed hard on the trail before him, "but don't you think we should call up more people? More eyes on the mountain would make a difference, don't you think?"

"No. It's about quality, not quantity. We have to search smart. We have to think like Kyle, narrow down his whereabouts, and find him using a logical process of common sense."

"Yes, but you thought he followed the others down and he didn't. What makes you think he headed toward the river?"

It was all he had left. But to voice the same would only serve to unsettle her. "It's a forty-minute walk. You up for it?"

"Yes, of course," she replied. "I just don't want to waste any valuable time."

"I don't either. The river is one of Kyle's favorite spots. My bet is he's there."

"It is?"

"Yes." Satisfied she was ready to proceed, he turned and continued his trek down the trail. "In the three weeks he's been at Wainwright, he's been to the river four times."

"How often do you take the kids camping?"

"Weekly, for overnight trips, but some of the older kids like to head up for day hikes."

"What do they do there?" she asked, her voice bumping in sync with every step she took down the trail.

"Swim, explore, hang out—same as they'd do at any other river."

"Same as any other kids," she returned softly.

"That's right. Kids are kids. Illness doesn't change their desire. It only changes their body."

"Pretty significantly. Do you ever have issues with children unable to make the trip?"

"We assess each child's capability at the outset, eliminating any embarrassing situations before they happen."

"Of course," she replied, more to herself than to him.

Canyon wondered how much she knew about the nuts and bolts of the operation, how her mother had run things, how she viewed things. Wainwright Ranch wasn't an ordinary business. It was a specialized group of people, each highly skilled in their field of expertise. From the medical doctors to the stable hands, each and every staff member had a defined role to play within the organization. The ranch was a kaleidoscope of activities and programs, a prism that had to be viewed through the eyes of the heart, not the brain. There were countless circumstances and situations that had to be accounted for using foresight, not hindsight. If Katharine thought she could waltz in here and take over her mother's business and run it same as she did her investment firm, she was mistaken.

A branch cracked in the distance. Buck's body froze. His ears shot up.

Canyon stopped, his heart pounding in his chest. "Kyle!"

Katharine pulled up next to him. "What is it?"

He drew a finger to his mouth, signaling for quiet as he strained to listen for another sound.

She followed his gaze into the distance. "Did you see something?" she whispered.

Canyon shook his head then pointed to his ear. She nodded, her gaze intent. Seconds passed. Buck didn't move. Canyon heard nothing. Silence filled the space around him. As did Katharine's presence. He could smell remnants of her perfume, the scent combining with her perspiration for a soft and completely feminine smell. Canyon didn't look at her. He didn't want to split his concentration between her and the search, though it was hard not to the way her body touched his. She stood behind him, her head level with his shoulder as she scanned the distant trees. He could hear her breathing. He didn't dare look at her mouth. "Kyle!" he burst out.

"I don't see anything, do you?"

"No. I heard a branch break. It could have been him."

Topaz eyes rounded. She gazed down the trail. Leaves rustled overhead as a shaft of wind kicked through. Hints of dusk settled into the forest, hanging shadows within the trees around them. "Could it have been an animal?"

"Not likely," he replied. They knew how to sneak up on their prey, though he kept the thought to himself. No sense in troubling her any more than she already was. "Let's go."

Buck bolted forward at the sign of Canyon's movement.

Katharine followed without protest.

Battling a growing sense of urgency, Canyon focused on the hike. He didn't want to think about the prospect of Kyle *not* hiding out at the river. But if Kyle wasn't there, Canyon wasn't kidding himself. He had nothing. Knots formed in the pit of his stomach. And "nothing" wasn't gonna cut it. He could not fail. He could not come up empty-handed when a child's life depended on him.

Canyon blocked all thoughts of defeat from his heart and charged forward. The trail wound to the right, then dropped steeply to the left. Buck jumped and his body disappeared down the path ahead of them. Canyon waited and held a hand out for Katharine as she navigated the tight juncture of rocky trail.

Once down, she peered up at him. "What's that sound?"

Surprised that she'd detected the faint roar, he leaped down to the ground and stood beside her. "The river. We're close," he said, and shoved a branch out of her way as she passed.

Ducking, she remarked, "It's so loud. It must be big."

"You've never been to the river?"

She shook her head and continued picking her way through the narrowed path. Canyon followed behind, the trail only wide enough for one through this section.

"Did you not hike much when you came to visit the ranch?"

"We mostly rode horses."

That surprised him. Hiking this mountain was one of the highlights for campers and staff alike. Even Eleanor made regular stops. Why hadn't she brought her daughter along? "Not one for hiking, huh?"

"I'm not particularly against it. It just wasn't something we did."

"I see..." Canyon replied. But he didn't. If it had been his parents who'd owned the ranch, he'd have been all over this property, from the open range to the thick of mountain forest. He would have skied during the winter, hiked and ridden horses during the summer, slipping in his rodeo riding everywhere in between. He lived and breathed this land. Like the pummel of water ahead, it pumped through his veins, thundered through his heart and soul. He'd always believed the same held true for Eleanor. Maybe Katharine shared more in common with her father than her mother. Maybe she preferred the city streets to the rocky range.

Picking up the cool drifts of moisture in the air, he said, "Well, guess there's only so much you can fit in during a visit. Your mother sure enjoyed it, though, and used to join the kids for campouts. They'd roast marshmallows around the campfire and share stories about their adventures."

Katharine paused, and looked at him directly. "Canyon, it's not that I don't enjoy hiking, I do. It simply wasn't on the agenda during my trips here."

Agenda. Schedule. As though someone had to pencil in time to enjoy the great outdoors. "I understand."

"I love this land, Canyon, same as my mother did. It's why I'm here, to save the ranch for the children."

For the children.

They stood face-to-face, and Canyon saw a commitment steeped in duty, obligation. It was a vow to save the business, not a passion to preserve the lifeblood of a charity ranch. Katharine's was an admirable endeavor, one he couldn't fault her for, but at the same time, it placed them on opposite sides of the fence. For him, Wainwright Ranch was a way of life. It gave him purpose, filled him with joy. For her, the ranch was profit and loss. No donors equated to no operations. Canyon couldn't deny a need for money, but he would work with these kids with or without the ranch. He'd done it before with a local 4-H program and he'd do it again. It's who he was, what he did. It's how Eleanor had found him in the first place and offered him a job.

But this woman? Eleanor's daughter?

Canyon imagined she was chomping at the bit to get back to her New York City lifestyle. Colorado was a change in clothing, a change in scenery... It was a place her mother had refused to leave. Eleanor used to say that once the Colorado sunshine warmed your face and the Rocky Mountains filled your soul, there was no going back. New Yorkers could have their glittery Manhattan high-rise buildings. She preferred the diamond-punctured mountain night sky any day of the week.

"You don't think it's too late, do you?" Katharine asked.

"To save the ranch?"

She nodded and stepped aside, allowing him to take the lead as the trail widened, opening up to the rocky river bed.

"It's never too late," he said, "not in my book." A small smile tugged at her mouth and it took everything he had not to settle on her lips.

She moved wisps of long bangs from her brow and said, "Back to your positive thinking, I see."

Amused by the statement, he resumed hiking and said, "Don't tell me you're a pessimist. Your mother would roll over in her grave if she thought that!"

"Realist," Katharine lobbed back. "I'm a realist who likes to focus on problem-solving."

"Got me there," he replied, wondering at the upset in her voice. He'd only been teasing.

"But I can't solve a problem if I ignore it. My mother would have felt the same."

Bingo. Resisting the urge to look back at her, Canyon mentally checked off a box in his brain. *This one doesn't share her mother's tough skin*. He'd do well to remember it.

Up ahead, he spotted a white cascade of water where Buck was already scavenging the landscape. Canyon approached and surveyed the area for signs of Kyle. Fat evergreens stood quiet. Aspen trunks dotted open spaces in and around the area. Low-lying plants were lush but still, sprinkled with flowers and speared in places by protrusions of jagged rock rising from the earth.

Canyon tuned his senses to high alert as he neared the river. Kyle could be crouched between the trees, obscured by underbrush. He could be watching them, waiting. As he combed the landscape with a trained eye, a faint chill seeped into his skin. Night was near.

Advancing slowly, he stepped lightly and continued to scan the area until the crash of water took center stage. Rushing over flat boulders, the river spilled into a pool before flowing downhill via a narrow gulch. The sound of rushing river permeated him, saturated his senses. Canyon strode to an open area of dirt near the river's edge. Lowering, he registered the ground was clean of prints. Through the clear water, he could see rocks coated by patches of green moss and algae. Fast-moving, the water made deep thumping noises as it was sucked into gullies and dips downstream.

Katharine hovered over him. "What do you see?"

"Nothing," he muttered, noting Buck was actively hunting scents along the perimeter of river, the border of trees and scrub.

"So he isn't here?"

Canyon stood up in one fluid motion and turned to her. Katharine looked up at him, her gaze soaked in disappointment. Blonde hair fell over a manicured brow but could do nothing to conceal the sadness in her eyes. Katharine looked like she was about to cry. Steeling his emotions against the reality staring back at him, he replied, "It means I don't see anything yet."

Her glassy gaze shot up. She clamped her mouth shut, crossed her arms over her chest and evaded his direct gaze with a glance to the river. "This isn't good." She shook her head. "This isn't good at all."

Canyon experienced a sinking feeling. She had a lot riding on the ranch—they both did—but giving up wasn't going to help the situation. They needed to regroup, wrap their thoughts around the situation and come up with Plan B. Unfortunately, he'd wagered everything he had on Plan A.

Shadows crowded around them. A faint rise of cool moist air clung to the bare skin of his forearms. Things looked bad, but he couldn't let Katharine fall apart. Canyon placed his palms on her shoulders, surprised they were slender enough to fit into the cups of his hands. He'd known she was thin, but touching her brought it home for him. He swallowed. "It isn't good, it isn't bad. It simply is. Let me take a look around. There's a trail the kids take that snakes down the river to the swimming hole. Kyle might have gone down that way."

Katharine nodded, and to her credit, refused to allow the tears hovering in her lids to fall. Canyon savored a private smile. Eleanor would be proud. For a moment, he thought about taking Katharine into his arms and hugging away her distress, reassuring her that everything would be okay. Would she let him? Would she brush him aside?

With a wave of her hand, the moment was gone. "I'll go with you," she said. "Standing here is wasting time we don't have."

Canyon sucked back a lump of desire. "Agreed."

Chapter Fifteen

Katharine followed Canyon and Buck as they traveled down the trail, grateful for the small miracle that she had not broken down in front of him. Crying was a waste of time and would solve nothing. If they didn't find Kyle and soon, she'd have all the time in the world to cry and probably would. But not now. Now was the time to stay strong and stay positive.

Don't tell me you're a pessimist. Your mother would roll over in her grave if she thought that!

Exactly how well did Canyon know her mother? To listen to him, one would think they'd been close friends. And if not close friends, at least close working partners. Katharine felt the tumultuous flow of the river like a torrent of emotion streaming through her.

Well, guess there's only so much you can fit in during a visit.

Visit. Canyon spoke as though Katharine were a stranger and not family, not Eleanor's blood relative. But she was. She was her daughter—and current owner of Wainwright Ranch. She was the one with everything at stake, not him. She was the one who would have to face the parents if they didn't find Kyle, not Canyon. She was the one who would lose the ranch if they didn't convince donors to continue in their financial commitments. What did Canyon have to lose? A job? A source of income?

The ranch was her mother's legacy and all Katharine had left of her.

Canyon stopped suddenly and Katharine careened into the back of him once again. Slightly embarrassed, she bit back her reply and asked, "What happened?"

"I think we've solved our problem."

Katharine's heart leapt into her throat. "Kyle? You found him?" Instantly, she circled around Canyon. "Where?"

"There."

Canyon pointed to a clump of brown and green-leaved branches near the river. Propped against a tree, the mass was layered fairly thick and stacked next to a boulder. Katharine looked for signs of the boy but saw nothing except the backside of Buck's body as he rooted through the greenery. "Are you sure?"

"I'm sure," he replied, his tone smooth and calm. Canyon walked briskly to the branches where Buck stood and commanded, "Kyle."

A blond head popped out alongside Buck's body, followed by a toothy grin. "Canyon!"

"What do you think you're doing, young man?"

"We were worried sick about you!" Katharine exclaimed, disbelief peppering her skull.

Kyle looked back and forth between Canyon and Katharine, settling on her with a blank look on his face. Buck turned his body, bumped Kyle's cheek with a healthy lick then returned to Canyon's side, his entire body wagging with success.

"We've got the entire ranch and mountain search and rescue looking for you," Canyon scolded, and pulled the radio from his waistband to alert the others to their find. "Weston, copy."

"Weston here, go ahead."

"We found the boy, safe and sound."

"Roger."

"Spread the word, will you?"

"You got it!"

Canyon replaced the radio and demanded, "Why did you sneak off from camp this morning?"

Glancing around with a doleful expression, he mumbled, "I was trying to show you that I knew what I was doing, that I really can survive out in the wilderness."

"This isn't the way to prove a point." Canyon glanced at Katharine and said, "Ms. Wainwright here was about to call your parents. Do you know how upset they would have been to hear you were missing?"

Kyle hung his head. "Yes, sir."

"This is serious, Kyle. We might have to send you home."

The boy flipped his face up. "Home? But you can't—I still have two weeks left!"

"You know the rules. We can't allow campers to remain at Wainwright Ranch who don't follow the rules."

"But why? It wasn't like I was in any danger."

"What would you have done if we hadn't found you?"

"Stayed here, in my shelter." Kyle crawled out and stood. Swiping the hair from his eyes, he looked from Canyon to Katharine then back to Canyon. "I built it so it would be strong and warm. I also dug a hole inside where I could cover myself in case any animals came around. I have food, clothing, water..." His gaze lit up. "I've got it all covered, just like I told you I could!"

"You have no fire." Canyon pulled the magnesium stick from his pocket and held it in the air between them.

Kyle gaped at the fire starter. "Where did you find it?"

"At the campground, where you dropped it."

Kyle shot his glance to the side.

"Canyon," Katharine murmured, transfixed by an eerie sense of déjà vu. There was something about this boy that seemed familiar, personal. "Maybe this isn't the time to come down on him so hard."

Canyon looked at her but said nothing. He didn't have to, not if the heat blistering in his dark eyes was any indication of what was going on inside his head. He was not happy with her interference and apparently felt stern consequences were warranted. Would her mother have reacted this same way?

Katharine doubted it. When she was growing up, her mom had always asked questions first, debated consequences second. It had been more important to her to understand why Katharine had disobeyed than to simply dole out punishment for misbehavior. Looking back, Katharine believed it had been an effective method of discipline because it helped her to understand her choices, why she had made them, and what she had expected as a result. It taught her to think through her decisions before executing them, to understand her intended goals as well as potential pitfalls.

"Kyle," she addressed the child directly, stepping toward him. "I'm Katharine." She extended a hand of introduction. Kyle cautiously accepted the gesture. When she peered into his brown eyes, chills tingled up her spine. His hair was slightly overgrown and blended with his pale skin, skin that marked a boy in less than stellar health. And though she had never met this boy before, it somehow felt as if she had. Shaking the strange sensations from her mind, Katharine continued, "Canyon tells me you're a real survivalist."

Kyle brightened. "I am." Avoiding Canyon's direct gaze, he said to Katharine, "I can take care of myself out in the wilderness. I tried to tell everyone but they didn't believe me."

Glancing toward his rudimentary structure, she smiled. Extending from rock to ground, evergreen branches had been interwoven in a repeated pattern that did look pretty sturdy. He'd even made a makeshift entrance by propping several branches vertically on either side with another bunch padded around the base. "Yes, I see. And I agree, it looks pretty sturdy."

"It is." He tapped the roof proudly. "Waterproof, too. I tested it. No leaks."

Glancing to Canyon, Katharine suppressed a chuckle. "I'll bet. Where did you learn how to build it?"

"There's a show on television where a guy tests himself against nature. Every week he starts a new challenge and shows you how to survive it."

"Sounds like a great show."

"It is." Kyle stole a peek at Canyon then frowned. "I'm sorry if I worried you."

"You did worry me. You worried Canyon, Jacob, the other campers... The time and money we've spent searching for you. Everyone was concerned for your safety. And what about your health? What if you became weak and disoriented?"

"But I didn't. I'm fine."

Katharine smiled. "I know that, and you know that, but there are a lot of people who didn't."

Kyle peered up at her with a look that almost broke her heart. "You're not going to kick me out of camp, are you?"

"You did break the rules," she told him, drawing a pause in her tone.

"Only because Jacob wouldn't let me do anything," Kyle argued. "I told him I could help build the fire, but he wouldn't let me. It isn't fair. I mean, isn't that why I'm here in the first place? To learn how to do stuff on my own?"

Katharine exchanged a glance with Canyon who thus far had given her leeway on handling the issue. "Yes, you're here to learn how to do stuff, and to learn how to work with others and have fun. But, that entails a certain degree of teamwork and cooperation." Kyle stared at her. "What would happen if you had a hiking partner who decided he wanted to go for a swim in the river instead of help build your shelter?"

"I'd do it without him."

"And if he refused to help build a fire?"

"I could do it myself."

"And hunt for food?"

"I'd do it."

"What if he drank all your water?"

"I'd get more."

"And when you're scaling a rocky cliff and he's supposed to secure the rope overhead. What happens if he forgets and hikes ahead without you?"

A tinge of suspicion spread through Kyle's expression.

"You're on your way home," she continued, "a successful end to your camping trip awaits you, but there's this last challenge in your way. Your partner has already demonstrated he's not reliable, that you can't count on him. What then? What would you do?"

"There wouldn't be a rocky cliff I'd have to climb down."

"You don't know that." Katharine glanced around him. "Did the survivalist on your show ever run into a challenge he didn't expect?"

Kyle didn't reply.

"Did he ever find himself in a situation that stumped him, forced him to change course or get creative?"

A distinct retreat entered the boy's gaze.

"I'm no expert," Katharine said, seizing a window of opportunity, "but I imagine there must have been all sorts of unexpected situations he encountered."

"Yes, but he survived them all. By himself."

"He did." She nodded. "Because he understood the situation and prepared for it. He worked through potential positive outcomes as well as potential negative ones. I bet he trained with a team of experts in order to reach that level of skill. I bet he practiced over and over and over. In fact, I bet he was so practiced, he could almost do it in his sleep, wouldn't you agree?"

Kyle kicked at the dirt. "Yeah, probably."

"And I bet he let others know his whereabouts in case he didn't return when expected." Katharine placed a hand on Kyle's shoulder and said, "It's clear you're a natural out here and with a little practice I bet you'd be able to do anything that survivalist on TV can do."

"I could."

"But being an expert doesn't discount those around you. Instead, it adds a special layer of responsibility on your part. They needed you, Kyle. Your team needed you and you let them down." He peered at her and she hated the disillusionment filling his gaze, but it was necessary. The child needed to feel the consequences of his actions.

"I never thought of it that way."

"You're part of a team at Wainwright, and every member of the team needs to be accountable to the next."

Kyle dug his hands into the front pockets of his jeans. Buck sensed his distress and nudged his nose against Kyle's leg.

The gesture melted Katharine's heart. Giving a pat to Buck's head, she said, "How about we speak with Jacob and see if he can't give you some more practice on your next camping trip?"

"Really?"

"I don't see any reason for him to object, do you, Canyon?"

Next to her, he grunted. "Nope."

Katharine grinned inwardly. His one-word response belied the mutiny she detected behind those sealed lips of his. It was clear this wasn't the way he would have handled it, and while it might not be her place to step in and take control, she'd felt compelled to do so. It was a decision they could discuss later. At the moment, she wanted to get Kyle safely down the mountain. "Now, I'd say it's time to head down the mountain before it gets dark."

Kyle looked to Canyon as though checking with him first.

"Grab your backpack," he said. "Daylight is dwindling."

Chapter Sixteen

Showered and dressed casually in jeans and navy pullover, Katharine felt reinvigorated as she stood near the doorway of the Wainwright Ranch social hall, a silent bystander to the flurry of excitement swirling through the room as the evening program was set to begin. The space felt more like a barn than a living area, with its open rafters and enormous exposed wood beams, wagon-wheel chandeliers and rustic barrel table bases. A movie screen had been erected at one end with dozens of chairs lined up to create an improvised movie theater. The teenage campers had gone out on a campout of their own this evening, leaving the younger crowd to enjoy a G-rated movie followed by a marshmallow roast. Staff members moved in and out of the group, using red and white striped bags of popcorn to lure kids into their seats.

Earlier in the evening, Kyle had returned to a buzz of excitement and welcome. Boys quickly hammered him with questions about animals and danger, while the girls expressed concern about his safety and well-being. Caroline, the girl she'd seen crying this morning, was now overcome by joy. Her face glowed as she watched Kyle recount his escapade and Katharine wondered in a tickle of thought, *Did the girl have a crush on Kyle*?

Canyon did his best to direct everyone toward their normal activities, but the children wanted nothing to do with the scheduled agenda, instead only wanting to hear from their friend. That, and pet the dogs in their midst. Cody and Buck were smack in the middle of the action, lapping up attention from animal-loving children and generally soaking in the festive atmosphere. After the initial "sniff and greet" had been accomplished, the two dogs seemed fast friends, which didn't surprise her. Cody was as easygoing an animal as they came. It seemed Buck took other animals in stride, too. Probably because he was used to being around them, including horses, cows, and chickens. Together, the dogs reminded Katharine of cousins. They weren't the same breed—Buck was a Golden Retriever and Cody a Labrador—but definitely close enough to appear related. They were cute, actually. She chuckled. Two pups in the center of attention, with the addition of Kyle who was doing his best to relay the details of his adventure between bites of pulled pork. He'd missed dinner in the dining hall, but thanks to Canyon, the cook had prepared a to-go plate for Kyle so he wouldn't go to bed hungry. He wouldn't go to bed upset, either, thanks to her.

A fact that hadn't thrilled Canyon. As expected, when they reached the bottom and the boy was out of earshot, Canyon had told her exactly how he felt about her method of discipline, claiming it equated to letting Kyle get away with running out on Jacob and Becky. It sent the wrong message. Katharine disagreed. Kyle was here to live life to the fullest and sometimes that meant pushing the limits and boundaries. Not all kids were the same. Some thrived on the adrenaline of taking chances and pitting their will against authority. In her opinion, caging Kyle in would not serve the purpose of instilling a sense of pride and accomplishment. And after all, she had argued, wasn't that why the children were here?

Of course it was. Case settled. For her, anyway.

And while Canyon clearly disagreed, he let it go. The decision had been made, the crisis was over. There only remained the matter of calling Kyle's parents, but it was a call she'd make first thing in the morning. At this point, there was no emergency. Wainwright's doctors had checked the boy out the minute he returned and said all was fine. Considering the fact that Kyle's home was in the Eastern Time Zone, Katharine imagined a phone call at this hour might do more harm than good.

Watching Canyon edge away from the group of chattering children, Katharine felt a stir in her stomach. If he was coming to pitch his position again, he was wasting his time. She was standing firm. If only the sight of him, freshly-showered and dressed in jeans and boots, didn't send a quiver of surrender straight through her. His blond hair was combed, with tendrils curling behind his ears beneath his hat, a soft brown number that seemed as natural on his head as the red bandana around his neck. The man looked good. A squiggle of nerves ricocheted in her belly. Really good.

Taking a deep breath, she said calmly, "The children seem to be having a good time, don't they?"

"Sure do. Kyle has stirred up quite a commotion, hasn't he?"

Katharine hugged her arms to her body and replied, "I'd say he's injected himself into the center of things, yes."

Canyon smirked. "Those boys are tempted to try the same thing. I can see it in their eyes."

"They might be enamored with Kyle's adventure, but that doesn't mean they'll follow suit by running away."

"You watch. They'll try it. And if they don't run out during a camping trip, it'll be something else."

"How can you be so certain?"

"They're boys. I'm a man. I know what's going through their minds right now."

Canyon stared at her directly, making his comment feel more challenge than casual observation. Heat gathered beneath the silk fabric of her fitted sweater. "I'm sorry you disagree with the way I handled the situation, but I think I did the right thing, what was best for Kyle."

Canyon cocked a brow. "It's your ranch. You're free to handle any situation as you see fit. I'm just sharing my thoughts."

"But you think I'm wrong."

He paused, as though considering his words carefully. "Let's put it this way. I think a boy is like a horse." He slid a glance toward the group of them and explained, "They need lots of freedom to roam, but within very distinct fence lines. Without boundaries, they'll run clear off the ranch like a herd of wild Mustangs, never to return again."

She flung her arms open, swamped by disbelief. "Are you seriously telling me that you think Kyle would have responded better if you had threatened to send him home?"

"I think it would have made him think twice the next time, same as the others."

"By making an example of him?"

"By demonstrating there are consequences for one's actions."

"Which is what I did, but in a more thoughtful manner. Sending him home or making an example of him with the other kids would have only succeeded in making him angry."

"Anger isn't always a bad thing."

"Anger can also be very destructive, especially to a young boy's psyche. Look at him," she said, moving her gaze to the group of children. "He's in his element, thoroughly enjoying himself while entertaining the others. How can that be a bad thing?"

"Life isn't always about being the center of attention. Wainwright Ranch is about the team, doing your part, pulling your weight. Not special treatment."

Is that what Canyon thought she had done? Shown Kyle preferential treatment? "I didn't go easy on him."

"Didn't you?"

No. In fact, she wanted to point out that his young life had already endured too much anger and pain, but that would only feed into Canyon's line of thinking. "There's nothing wrong with a thoughtful approach to discipline. I reasoned with him. I explained that what he did was wrong and how he could have handled it better."

He slid his gaze toward the kids. "The boy appears pretty happy to me. Should he, after everything he put us through?"

"Kyle understands what he did was wrong. I told him that he let his team down. He won't repeat the episode." Turning more fully to face Canyon, she said, "Unlike horses, children have complicated emotions. You have to reason with them, let them know you understand how they're feeling.

Remember, these aren't ordinary kids. They're living with very difficult circumstances."

"And they come here to feel normal and be treated normally." Canyon's expression turned serious. "It's the whole point of the ranch. They come here to work, to be part of a team. When part of my team runs out on me, I let them know it will not be tolerated. It can't be. It's what makes their experience here unique and memorable."

Katharine stared, unable to form the words of a rebuttal. *My team*. This was his domain, not hers. These were his kids, not hers. Had she overstepped her boundaries?

"I'm sorry, but that's my opinion," he said, softening his tone. "And it's the way your mother used to handle things. I'm only following her lead."

Katharine's mother. It always came back to her and his understanding of her and her ways. *It's the way your mother used to handle things. It's how she would have liked it. It's what she used to do.* Katharine wrapped her arms around her body once again and stared at the boys and girls. They were her mother's kids. This was her mother's ranch. Suddenly, as its current owner, Katharine suddenly felt incompetent to run it. Why should that be? And why couldn't she make her own rules?

There was more than one way to ride a horse or raise a child. There was more than one way to view a problem or handle a situation. Why did everything have to be exactly as her mother had done it? Why must donors insist Eleanor Wainwright be at the helm and not someone equally as capable? From deep in the recesses of her mind, the answer floated forth. Because this was her dream and her vision and no one knew that better than Katharine.

Waking early the next morning, Katharine took Cody for a walk around the village of Silver Creek then headed into the office of Wainwright Ranch. Frustrated by her exchange with Canyon regarding Kyle, Katharine forced herself to push it from her mind and focus on the business at hand. She scoured

one document then another, but the words and numbers morphed into blurred lines against the white page. While Canyon
might not think her capable of handling the children the way
her mother had done, there was no discrediting her when it
came to the financials of the company—the situation she had
come here to solve.

She'd only been trying to help Kyle by showing him
kindness instead of temper. She'd used reason. Validation.
Why Canyon couldn't see that was beyond her, but she
wasn't here to change minds. She was here to solve problems.
Katharine gritted her teeth then yanked the pencil from her
mouth and smacked it to the desktop. Maybe Canyon should
remember that without her, the ranch would fail and he'd be
out of a job.

A knock at her mother's office door startled her.

"You wanted to see me?"

Frank Dillard stood in the doorway. Business casual, his
white shirt and gray slacks seemed at odds with the vibrant
colors of her mother's office décor, as did his sagging waist-
line. The man looked tired. Maybe it was the early hour,
maybe it was the strain. Katharine pushed her musings aside.
Whatever the reason, the two needed to clear the air.

"Yes." She set her papers aside and directed, "Please,
come in and have a seat."

Cody was up and circling Frank's legs. Frank didn't pet
the dog, apparently more interested in why she had summoned him than any pleasantries with the animal. "What's
going on?"

"As you know, I've been going through the files and I
have some concerns."

"Such as?"

When Cody returned to her side, circled and dropped his
body to the floor, Katharine stated, "The investment accounts,
to start. I don't want to question your judgment, but why are
we allowing Richmond Capital to churn our accounts?"

Frank tensed as he lowered into a chair. "Why would
you say that?"

"It's clear by looking at the numbers what's been going on. They're trading assets, earning commissions. Why aren't we letting our investments sit?"

"I didn't know that we weren't."

"What?"

"I'll give Richmond a call," he said, his cheeks flushing. "If they're churning funds, I'll put a stop to it."

That's it? Frank would call them? Why didn't he already know what was going on? But realizing she'd get nowhere with a man who had obviously unplugged himself from the situation, Katharine turned down a different path. A much more disconcerting one. "There's something else," she said, bothered by the detachment staring back at her. She opened a separate file on her desk, removed a piece of paper and slid it across the desk. "Why don't I have the banking documents for this account with First Federal?"

Frank scanned the document.

"It wasn't listed anywhere in the documents I had. It was set up earlier this year. Why? Was there a problem with our other accounts?"

"*Son of a bitch...*"

"What?"

"Paul." Frank's face reddened. "This might explain where the donations are going."

"Paul?" Dread saturated her limbs. "He has access to our bank accounts?"

"No, which is why he set up this dummy account."

Katharine was on her feet. "What do you mean *dummy* account? You don't know anything about it?"

"Of course not," he replied and stood. "If I had, you'd have received the reconciled statements."

"Frank, this is serious. There are hundreds of thousands of dollars in that account. The bank wouldn't give me any information because I'm not on the account as an authorized signatory. They asked for you." She'd originally hoped it would be their saving grace. If the missing money the ranch needed to survive wasn't gone, only lost in Frank's shoddy recordkeeping, there would have been hope.

"Paul must have used my name to set it up. He must be siphoning funds from donors through the account and into his own pocket." Frank slammed a fist on the desk. "Damn it, I can't believe I didn't see it!"

Katharine jumped, heart pounding. "But Frank, we need to prove it."

"We will. I'm going down to the bank right now and put an end to it."

Struggling against the shaky quality of her legs, she fought for calm as the enormity of the situation pressed in. "Let me know what you find out."

"Will do." Frank paused. "But, Katharine, do me a favor and don't let on to Paul that we know about this. I don't want him running off before we get a chance to get our hands on him."

"Yes, agreed," she replied. "We need to get our information confirmed before we make any move against him."

Frank folded the piece of paper and tucked it into the pocket of his dress shirt. He looked at her and shame scored his gaze. "I'm sorry about this. I should have checked into things more thoroughly."

"Frank, you couldn't have known. I only stumbled on it by chance."

He nodded, but the guilt in his eyes was clear. He was responsible.

"I'll call Richmond, too. I don't know how that got by me." Frank's shoulders slumped as he stared at her, his gaze dulled. "I guess a lot of things have gotten by me since your mother died. My brain hasn't been firing on all cylinders."

"It happens," Katharine said and came around the desk. Yes, the money management was his responsibility, but she felt hard-pressed to kick a man while he was down. Frank and her mother had been close. Her death had to have affected him. Why hadn't Katharine seen it? Why hadn't she been sensitive to what he was going through? "You've been working overtime, Frank. Everyone has."

"But still..." He turned from her. "I let your mother down. I let you down."

Katharine's heart sank. Frank sounded defeated, like the entire failure rested upon his shoulders when it didn't. Paul Sutherland was the bad guy, not Frank. Rising costs and apathetic donors were to blame. Paul might have managed to skim some of the money away from the charity, but Katharine knew for a fact that many donors were pulling out because of her mother's passing. Steve Calhoun was only the latest to threaten as much. "We'll get through this, Frank. Together, we'll make it happen."

He peered at her and pressed his lips into a firm line. He nodded. "Yes. Yes, we will."

With that he was gone.

Katharine stood staring at the empty doorway. A thousand emotions streamed through her, dissolving her previous anger and leaving only pity in its place. Frank was a good man. It wasn't fair that he should bear the brunt of Wainwright's troubles. Everyone had played a role. Everyone, including her. If she had come to Colorado soon after her mother's death to manage operations like Frank had asked her to do, none of this might ever have happened. She would have had her finger on the pulse of the company, would have known firsthand what was happening and could have stopped it.

But she had declined. The prospect of filling her mother's shoes had been too daunting at the time. Equally upsetting had been the idea of spending time in her mother's favorite place without her. It was why Katharine had stayed in New York until now. Guilt streamed through her. Only now it might be too late.

Canyon Laredo appeared in her doorway. "Knock, knock."

All thought escaped her. "Canyon," she uttered in a rush of breath.

"What's wrong with him?" he asked, tossing a thumb over his shoulder.

Katharine's gaze moved to the hallway behind him. "Frank is upset."

"I can see that." Moving farther into her office, Canyon smiled when Cody approached him—same as the dog did with all visitors—and stroked the animal's head. "Hey, boy. How's it going?" The dog nuzzled into Canyon's jean-clad legs. "What is it this time?" Canyon asked Katharine. "Someone call in sick? Forget to pick up Frank's hat at the dry cleaner?"

Ignoring the snipes at Frank, she replied, "We have a serious problem." Katharine wondered how much she should reveal to Canyon. He did sit on the board, was a trusted employee in her mother's eyes... Should she tell him what they'd discovered?

Canyon straightened and collected her in his sights. "How serious?"

"We might have uncovered an embezzlement scheme," she said. "We think Paul might be involved." Deciding against going into detail, Katharine deemed she and Frank should be the ones to handle the problem. It was their job to take care of the ranch finances, not Canyon's. His only concern was how to get his cattle expenses in line during this time of financial hardship.

Returning a thoughtful gaze, he said, "I wonder if it has anything to do with the man in the parking lot yesterday."

Katharine clicked to attention as the information registered in her brain. "Yes, you mentioned it." A fact she'd completely forgotten. But with everything that had happened in the past twenty-four hours, was it a wonder? She'd been consumed with locating a missing child, not ferreting out a potential embezzlement scheme. "Did you happen to overhear what they were discussing?"

"No, only that it was heated. The guy was dressed in a suit and standing next to a black sedan. I assumed it was another donor falling off the rolls."

Katharine turned the information over in her mind, mentally sifting through it for clues. "Why would they have been discussing business in the parking lot?"

"Because they didn't want anyone inside these walls to hear them." Canyon's expression hardened. "I never trusted that guy."

"Well, your suspicions may have been well-founded. We'll know more later, once Frank returns from the bank. Until then, we have to make a plan for repairing relations between the donor community and Wainwright Ranch."

"How do you intend to do that?" Canyon asked, dropping into one of the leather wingchairs without invitation. Cody remained by his side, patiently waiting for Canyon to return his attention to him.

"By beginning at square one," she replied. "We reiterate why the reason donors initially invested in the ranch remains strong and viable and will continue to be so."

Canyon said nothing and Katharine felt the elephant push into the room. Both of them knew the reason donations no longer existed, though it seemed neither of them cared to admit it aloud. Katharine dropped to her seat. It was irrelevant. They couldn't bring her mother back, no matter how badly each of them might want to.

Chapter Seventeen

Canyon's heart went out to Katharine. Sitting across from her, caressing the soft fur around Cody's neck, there was no denying it. She was in over her head and they both knew it. Sitting in her mother's chair, surrounded by a wall of books and the bold appointments that filled her mother's space, Katharine seemed dwarfed by comparison. Rugged landscape defined Colorado and the people who lived here. They were risk-takers, lived by the sweat of their brow. This was no place for a woman of refinement, a woman with a soft heart. She might know how to handle investments when it came to dollars and cents but out here people invested in people. Outlining the reasons why Wainwright Ranch was a good place to invest charitable donations was not going to be enough to change course, even if it should be. People invested in philosophies. They invested in passion, commitment. You could have the best idea for a charity on the planet, but if you lacked someone willing and able to execute operations, you had nothing, nothing but an empty hole to drop money in and call it a charitable investment.

Wainwright Ranch wasn't the only organization helping kids battling terminal illness. There were several camps and retreats across the country that catered to the children, most with talented, dedicated people at the helm. The reason Wainwright had flourished was because of Eleanor. Period. It pained Canyon to think Katharine didn't fully understand that concept.

As Katharine stared at him, a tinge of discomfort entered her gaze as if she could read his mind. "Was there a reason for your visit?"

As Canyon held her in his gaze, he damn near felt guilty about what he was about to say. He pulled his hand from Cody, and the dog immediately took it as his sign to return to Katharine's side. "There is."

"And...?"

"I'm having a problem with Kyle."

"What?" Her expression paled. "He hasn't run off again, has he?"

"No, but he is pushing back against his chores this morning, claiming his body aches from yesterday."

"Is he okay? Have you had the doctor check him for injuries?"

"Yes, ma'am. She checked him first thing this morning and reaffirmed what she said last night. The boy is fine."

"Oh, thank goodness," Katharine replied breathlessly, visibly relieved. "I haven't called his parents yet. It's next on my list this morning and I'd hate to have to inform them that he was ill on top of everything else."

The comment blared oxymoron. More ill than his leukemia? But Canyon understood what she meant. "Kyle's fine. On top of the world and that's the problem."

Katharine blinked. Setting flat palms to the desk, she said, "Okay. You're not making any sense now."

"Kyle is pumped from his little escapade yesterday and feels like he has free rein to do as he pleases, especially now that the owner of the ranch is on his side."

"*On his side?* Is that what he took away from our talk last night?"

Canyon nodded but didn't go into detail. There was no need.

In the silence that ensued, it seemed Katharine understood the gist of what he was telling her. Disbelief drained from her gaze. A wall began to rise. "You think this is my fault."

"I'm not blaming you. I'm stating a fact. I have a situation with one of the children and I know you have strong opinions on how to handle things. I just wanted to run it by you and get your direction on how to proceed."

"So I'm supposed to tell you how to do your job."

Canyon arched a brow. "Aren't you?"

"Canyon, my mother left you in charge of the stables and the children's activities with regard to the same. If she trusted you to handle them then so do I."

Resisting the urge to smile, he replied, "Well, I appreciate the vote of confidence..."

"But."

Canyon shrugged. "But nothing."

"I hear a distinct 'but' in your voice." Suddenly, her eyes glittered with challenge. "Care to elaborate?"

"I like to work with clear and distinct boundaries. I don't do well when left to run free, only to be yanked back to my stall unexpectedly." Watching the comprehension seep in, he thought, *Good. Now you're getting it.* And waited for her to make amends.

"This is about last night."

Sorry, sweetheart, but I'm not going to make it that easy for you.

"You're upset."

More amused at the moment, Canyon refused to budge. This was his rodeo and he was going to make her work for it.

Katharine swallowed and pulled her hands into her lap. "Canyon, I'm sorry for stepping in between you and Kyle yesterday. It wasn't intended as an insult to your capabilities. I simply acted on my gut, based upon the ways my mother used to handle me as a child. I thought I was doing the right thing."

You just did. Inwardly, he grinned. "Apology accepted," he replied. "And I appreciate your intentions, but you have to understand that these kids aren't the same as you were as a youngster. They're used to being coddled. They crave a dose of tough love, even if they don't know it. It's the way your mother wanted it, laid it out from the very first day the campers arrived. I'm only following her lead."

"The way my mother wanted it." Katharine exhaled a heavy sigh and pausing, her gaze lingered on Canyon. No longer confrontational, her eyes had softened to a creamy caramel. The lines around her mouth disappeared and her lips, well, her lips were nothing less than exquisite.

A channel opened between them, and he could feel the emotion spilling from her heart. Naked, vulnerable, it was a quiet moment between friends, between two people who cared about one another and wanted only the best for them. Suddenly, Canyon realized it was how he felt about Katharine.

"How is it that you know so much more about what my mother wanted than I do?"

"I don't," he said at once, batting back a surge of desire. "I only know what she wanted for the kids."

"And I don't seem to know a thing. I was here year after year. I spent time with her, the children..." Katharine's gaze darted out the window. "Yet I feel like a stranger. How is that possible?"

You were here as a visitor, he wanted to say. You weren't a staff member integral to the daily operations. But realizing the truth would break her heart, so Canyon simply replied, "It's a day-to-day thing, that's all. Working the front lines, digging the trenches... I don't know your mother better than you. I only know what she told me to do."

She looked at him and her eyes misted. "You're being kind."

"I'm being honest." And in that moment, if Canyon could have wrapped his arms around Katharine and pulled her close, he would have. She needed it. He wanted it. A lot. If only a quick hug to erase the sadness staring back at him, Canyon would do so if it would ease her pain.

Leaning forward he added, "I'm telling you the truth. You know your mom way better than I do. You grew up with her, loved her, spent years together." Encouraged by a grow-ing pleasure in Katharine's gaze, he continued, "Heck, you were all she could talk about when she wasn't talking ranch business! About how smart you were, how busy, how you traveled the world, kept your father in line when she couldn't be there..."

A faint smile touched Katharine's lips.

One that reached straight into his chest and revved his heart. "Your mother put everything she had into this ranch but that didn't mean she wasn't thinking of you, calling you, staying in touch."

"She did. She used to call me every other day." A wistful sigh escaped from Katharine as she glanced around the office. "Now that I'm sitting here, going through the files, the business side of the ranch, it's a wonder she had the time to call so often with everything she had going on here."

"She made the time. That's who she was, how she did things."

"You're right. She was a multi-tasker extraordinaire."

Canyon laughed. "I don't know if I'd call her a multi-tasker. She was pretty single-minded when it came to getting a job done. When she was talking to you, she was one hundred percent there. It's one of the reasons the kids liked her so much. She could be tough, but they always knew she had their back."

Sadness swamped Katharine's gaze and Canyon cursed himself, instantly regretting the comment. *Why couldn't he just shut his mouth and let Katharine do the talking?* Stop interfering with the woman's memory and let her remember her mom any way she wanted.

Katharine's smile returned. "I can see why she liked you. You speak your mind."

"Sometimes too much."

She waved him off and glanced at the wall behind him. Sunlight streamed through the office window, lighting up the paintings and making their colors pop. "You're fine. It's me. I'm the one overreacting to everything and everyone."

"You're not doing anything of the kind. You're saving the ranch. What more could anyone ask?"

"How about knowing a little something about what I'm doing before I attempt to do it?"

"You're being too hard on yourself."

"Am I?"

"Yes." The world wasn't a perfect place. Life had its pitfalls. "You're doing everything you can to save your mother's dream. Who could fault you for that?"

In a quiet plea, Katharine's gaze sought his. "Do you think I can do it? Do you think the investors will listen when I lay out our cause during the fundraiser?"

Canyon paused. He didn't want to lie, but he didn't want to discourage her either. "Depends."

"On what? I mean, if you have any bullet points on what they need to hear, I'm all ears!"

At her gush of desperation, he grew serious. "They don't want bullet points. They want dedication, commitment."

"I am dedicated and committed. Trust me, I want this ranch to survive more than anyone."

"Enough to take over?"

"What do you mean?" She paused, and he could see the meaning sink in. She pulled back in her seat and the tan sweater she wore outlined her small frame against the huge leather chair. "You mean on a daily basis?"

Canyon debated how far to go with this line. Should he really tell her what he thought? Did she really want to hear it?

Like a hawk on a snake, she latched onto him. "Canyon, if there's something you want to say, say it."

If the woman wanted the truth, he'd give her the truth. "Wainwright Ranch needs someone to run operations, someone who's passionate about the mission, the cause, not some braniac business person who thinks it's a matter of numbers."

"Frank is passionate about the mission. He worked side by side with my mother since the ranch's inception. If donors want passion, they only have to look so far as him to get it."

Frank was about as passionate as a dead fish. A thought Canyon kept to himself.

"We have an entire staff of passionate people dedicated to the mission."

Canyon couldn't disagree with her there, but she was missing the point.

"Like you," she said. "You're passionate. You're here."

"True."

"You're familiar with operations, are actually in charge of an entire department."

Canyon didn't like where she was going with this.

"Why, I don't see any reason you couldn't take over."

"I'm not a Wainwright."

The comment caught her on the chin. "What? What does that matter?"

"Almost everything," he replied. It had to be said. Katharine had to understand what was at stake here. Wainwright Ranch was a mission, not a corporate franchise that could be replicated and mass-produced. It was an idea that had been sparked by a woman's pain, transformed by a mother's love. Eleanor had lived the nightmare no parent should have to endure. She knew what it felt like to have a sick child and, like any mother, had wanted to make everything better, but she couldn't. And neither could he. Deep in his heart, Canyon understood Wainwright Ranch had been Eleanor's way of coping, of giving back, of honoring the memory of her lost child. Business school didn't teach you how to care like that. Life did.

"Canyon," Katharine began, more than a touch of irritation in her voice, "the ranch can survive without a Wainwright at the helm."

"Can it?"

"Of course."

"No hesitation?"

"None. Frank has done his best to keep the ranch alive."

Canyon didn't respond. Sunlight that had poured into the room now dulled, cut off by a passing cloud.

"Do you have a problem with Frank? I noticed from the first day I met you, there seemed to be an edge about you when it comes to him."

"Frank and I are not personal friends," he offered. "That's as deep as it goes."

"You work with him every day. You don't think not being friends gets in the way of business?"

"Not for me, it doesn't."

Katharine didn't buy it and Canyon didn't care. He didn't like Frank and Frank didn't like him. It wasn't a secret. It was a fact. Canyon rose from his seat. This conversation was over. Or should be, before he said something he regretted. "I'd better be going. You have a lot to deal with and I should let you get to it."

Katharine rose with him. Clearing her voice she said, "Canyon?"

"Yes?"

"I want you to know that I appreciate your candor. We don't have to agree on everything but we do need to be able to communicate."

If only the same held true for Frank. "Agreed."

"Your input is invaluable to me." She smiled at him, as if to underscore her point.

It wasn't needed. Her gratitude oozed from every pore of her body. Genuine to the core, Katharine Wainwright was definitely bred from the same genes as Eleanor. She was polite, intelligent, and cared enough to treat the people around her with respect. "Thanks."

The phone on her desk rang and she automatically picked up the receiver. "Hello? Yes?" Katharine's face blanched. "They're doing *what*?"

Canyon's heart tripped.

"The twelve o'clock news?" Her gaze darted about the room. "Yes, yes, I understand. We can get to the bottom of it later, but Amanda? Please direct all incoming calls from the media straight to me, okay? Thank you."

Katharine hung up the phone and Canyon asked, "The media is running a story about Kyle?"

"Yes," she replied, stunned.

"It wasn't Wade," Canyon said at once. "If he told you he'd keep it under the radar, he did."

"Do you think a member of one of the search teams would have told them?"

"Possible. They deal with this sort of thing all the time. But when dealing with a minor, I'd be surprised if they named names."

Katharine grimaced. "Guess it's a stretch to conceal the source, when you have helicopters circling the mountains over Wainwright."

Canyon remained mute.

"Well," she said, and circled the desk. "Someone called them and now they want a statement from me."

"No worries. Just tell them a boy was thought missing for a brief time but it turned out to be a prank."

She cocked her head and pricked him with a schoolteacher glare. "That's not entirely true."

"It's basically true. Kyle pulled a prank on us. He was missing for a brief time. End of story."

"I have to call his parents right away. They can't hear this on the news before they hear it from me."

"Do you want me to call them? I met the family during orientation."

Katharine peered at him with a quizzical look.

Alarm fired through him. "Katharine? Everything okay?"

She shook her head. "I'll call them. It's my responsibility." She pivoted and said, "I should have called them last night. Then I'll call the news station. They might think they smell blood in the water, but they won't get anything more than a scratch from me. I'll inform them of a small situation that was addressed at once by local authorities assisted by an expertly-trained search and rescue community. We had the utmost confidence in our staff and rescue operations and are pleased to announce the matter was settled within hours."

Canyon grinned. "You tell 'em."

Staring at him, she perched hard fingers on the desk and asserted, "The media I understand."

Sadly, Canyon heard in her tone everything else she did not. Katharine was out of her element on the ranch. It was unfortunate but true. A fact she was finally beginning to realize and admit. He wished it weren't the case. He hated to see the despair in her eyes. It meant a likely end to his life's work.

Chapter Eighteen

"Thanks for coming, Adele."

Adele covered Katharine's hand with one of her own and squeezed gently. "You bet."

Seated at one end of a picnic-style table, the two had decided to join the campers for a bite of lunch in the dining hall. Katharine thought it might make her feel more connected to the kids, giving her and them a sense of stability, continuity. But glancing around her, she only felt solitude. Around her the room was quiet. So quiet, she had expected the noise level to be decibels higher. Back when she went to summer camp, mealtime had been bedlam. Children's voices competed with the clang of dishes, shouts from the kitchen, counselors working to keep restless young bodies seated and on task.

But not here. Wainwright Ranch had to have the quietest lunch hour this side of the Mississippi River. Where Katharine could have used the noise to drown out the hum of her nerves, she had none. There was nothing but subdued conversation, similar to what she'd find in a restaurant. It certainly wasn't loud enough to prevent Cody from sleeping at her feet, the boy snoozing contently through it all. *Had this quiet space been another rule set by her mother*?

"I can't believe what's been going on," Adele said then took a sip of ice water. "First a missing boy and now a media storm? It's crazy."

"And leading the nightly news," Katharine added. "I spent all morning trying to play the story down with straightforward facts, yet it only served to heat things up. They're acting like Kyle had a near-death experience. He had an adventure. An unauthorized adventure, but an adventure nonetheless." Katharine shook her head and dropped her gaze to the bean salad on her plate. Holding her fork above her dish, she peered at the food, but her appetite was nonexistent. "This is going to kill us."

Adele squeezed her hand again. "Don't say that."

"Why not?" Katharine flipped her gaze to meet Adele's head on. "It's true. Once donors find out that we lost a child, it will be game over. No one will trust their money with us. No one."

"But you said Kyle's parents were fine with it."

"Only because they know their son and expected nothing less from him. The public doesn't know Kyle." As she tossed a glance about the dining hall, frustration practically peeled her out of her skin. "They're only going to know what they hear on the news and the media's slant. *Wainwright Ranch loses terminally ill child in the rugged Rocky Mountains*. No one's going to delve any deeper than the headline. They're going to stew in shock and tell everyone they know what a terrible organization we are."

"C'mon," Adele urged. "People are smarter than that. They'll read the story, hear the parents' account of their son and realize it was a simple hoax on his part."

"Who's going to tell them? The newspaper? The tabloids?" Katharine dropped her fork on her plate, the utensil clanging against thick white porcelain and irritating her already frayed nerves. "I've failed. I've failed my mother and the ranch is going to go under."

Adele pushed Katharine's shoulder. "Stop. You're being fatalistic. You sound like you're giving up without a fight."

"Shouldn't I be?"

"No. You're a problem-solver. You get things done." Adele's eyes sought Katharine's. Years of friendship pooled in her deep brown gaze as she said, "Remember when that bank in New York was going to be sued for discrimination?"

"Yes. They were being accused of not loaning to minorities."

"That's right. They were getting some of the worst press I've ever seen until you stepped in and took control. You introduced the bank manager to the public—a minority female—and explained the numbers being reported were skewed. Reporters weren't taking into account the entire community, but only a select few."

Katharine recalled the circumstances. The bank had developed a special program for youth living in the inner cities. The students had been given an opportunity to develop a charitable organization concept and the bank would serve as their partner and fund the venture. It was an initiative inspired by a local teacher. A rival school didn't like the favorable press they were receiving and filed a complaint. Because most of the applicants were of non-minority descent, the media picked it up, twisted the facts and the bloodbath was immediate.

Until Katharine righted the ship. It wasn't anyone's fault that the kids choosing to participate weren't from a minority background, despite coming from a school with a huge mix of ethnicities. Given enough time, all would have eventually jumped on board, and did. "It was a disgrace," Katharine spat. "The complaint was entirely disingenuous and easily proved wrong."

"Yes, but it took *you* to make that happen."

"I disagree. Anyone could have done what I did. I just happened to be the closest to the situation."

"And the one with enough insight to turn it around on them."

"You might be giving me too much credit."

Adele withdrew. Displeasure swirled in her features and turned her expression to one of distaste. "Why are you giving yourself zero credit? This isn't like you. You're a go-getter, a problem-solver. It feels like you're putting your tail between your legs and heading home without a fight. What's going on, Katharine?"

Katharine's attention leapt to the entrance. *The tall blond entering the dining hall across the room, that's what's going on.* Unable to pull her gaze from Canyon as he strode to the buffet line, she watched him grab a plate and heap food onto it. Pulled pork, baked beans, tater tots and corn on the cob.

Make that two cobs of corn and an enormous dose of melted butter. Raking her gaze up and down the length of him, she thought he definitely had room to put away the massive amount of food.

Adele followed her gaze and asked, "How's it going with Canyon?"

Katharine swung her focus back to her friend. "You know him?"

"Sure. He works with Hal on the search and rescue. He has a dog named Buck that I'm sure Cody would love to meet."

At the mention of his name, Cody's head popped up from his paws.

"Actually, they've met," Katharine said, stroking Cody's head to assure him nothing had changed. For him, anyway. Drawn to Canyon as though pulled by an unseen rope, Katharine couldn't say the same held true for herself.

Adele's mouth opened into a huge smile. "He's a beauty, isn't he?"

Katharine gaped at her. Were her feelings that obvious?

"I always think of you when I see Buck."

Heartbeats scattered in her chest. Adele was talking about the dog. The dog—not Canyon. Pushing food around on her plate, she asked, "You see him often?"

"Couple times a month."

"Huh." Katharine's attention moved back to Canyon where he took a seat at a table of children, many of whom she hadn't met. They were a younger bunch, she'd guess maybe six or seven years of age. Like him, their plates were piled with shredded pork drenched in dark brown barbecue sauce, white-bread buns and mountains of fried potato squares. Had her mother also approved of the menu?

"Penny for your thoughts?" Adele asked.

Katharine pulled her gaze from Canyon and the children and tacked it squarely onto her friend. "I'm surprised the ranch serves such unhealthy food. All children should eat a balanced diet but especially sick children, wouldn't you agree?"

"You know how I feel about food. I wouldn't put a toxic molecule in my body or anyone else's, for that matter."

"Me neither." Lingering on the group across the room, the easy banter between Canyon and the kids, the obvious affection, Katharine felt a tinge of envy. "I don't understand why my mother would allow such a menu."

"Probably wanted everything to be as normal as possible."

Katharine looked at Adele and snipped, "Healthy should be normal."

"You won't find disagreement with me," she replied with a hand held up between them. "I'm with you on this one." Adele's smile dimmed as her gaze clung tightly to Katharine. "It must be hard to be here without her."

Tears pricked Katharine's eyes. "It's the first time I've been back since she died." She glanced away and her gaze landed on a table inhabited by Kyle and several children from his camping exploit. He and two other boys were whispering feverishly to one another, completely excluding the girls seated beside them. "It's much harder than I imagined."

Part of her desperately wanted to be back in New York. The city pulsed with energy. It provided constant distraction, constant movement. In her job as Vice-President of Global Equities for Wainwright, Emerson, Katharine worked sixteen hours a day, traveled five months out of the year and loved every second. Add the cultural scene, the unlimited choices for dining and entertainment, the countless opportunities to meet new and exciting people, and there was no place she'd rather be—especially now, when memories of summers past haunted her with every step she took. In New York, she could avoid thinking about her mother's death, about all the missed opportunities to spend time together. In Colorado, she was inundated with it. Not only were memories and emotion swimming through her heart and mind, but warm recollections were being challenged, causing her to doubt the relationship she believed she'd had. Katharine felt as if she were losing her mother all over again, as though the woman she'd known was nowhere close to the woman who was, and now her only daughter was failing in the rescue of her namesake ranch.

Adele reached a hand across the table and re-covered Katharine's. "Time will help. One day you'll be able to return to Colorado and it won't hurt so badly."

"I'm afraid there won't be anything to come back to," she confessed. It was her biggest fear, the thought that she would fail her mother—her father—and return to New York with nothing.

"What you need is a shot of optimism to set you back on the right path," Adele said. "Maybe a steamy encounter with a cowboy while you're here would do the trick."

Katharine gaped at Adele then her gaze leapt to Canyon. "What?"

Adele laughed as she recognized the connection Katharine had made. "Canyon would certainly do, though I'm not sure you want to mix business with pleasure."

Katharine's heart thumped. Was she that obvious? Instantly besieged by visions of a night of passion with Canyon, Katharine reached for her glass of water and drank. Ice-cold liquid streamed down her throat, calmed her thoughts. "No, that would not be a good idea at all."

Adele shrugged narrow shoulders and picked up her glass. "But there's plenty more where he came from who would be more than willing to cheer you up with a hot fling."

Katharine laughed, warmth flushing her ear tips as she replied evasively, "I daresay that's not where I should be focusing my thoughts."

Adele frowned. "Tell me you haven't lost your libido."

"I've lost nothing of the kind," Katharine volleyed back.

"Then why so reticent?"

Katharine stopped and stared at Adele, wondering where this was coming from. "If I didn't know better, I'd say someone spiked your lemon water."

"Takes more than a spike to open these windpipes," Adele quipped, her dark eyes dancing.

"And you're seeing Hal," Katharine pointed out. "What do you know about hot flings?"

"Just because I no longer partake in them doesn't mean I don't remember them. On the contrary... Besides, you're single. Very."

True, Katharine mused, and fought every urge to look over at Canyon. It almost felt as if he was staring at her with a heated gaze, daring her to consider the idea.

Which was silly, of course. He had no idea they were having fun at his expense.

"Is it really so bad an idea?"

"What—having a hot fling with a sexy cowboy?" Katharine glanced around and replied, "Not in and of itself, no. But in the midst of a dining hall full of children, I'd have to say it's not the most appropriate conversation we could be having. Besides, like you said, I'm here for business not pleasure."

"No reason you can't add a little spice to the punch."

But not with Canyon. He was off limits. Adele said so herself.

Tightening her grip on her glass, Katharine spoke as nonchalantly as she could, "While I have to admit the idea does have its appeal, I'm afraid my time will be spent on less than thrilling prospects." Though she couldn't deny the reprieve from ranch talk had been welcome. In all reality, Katharine wasn't sure a fling with Canyon was such a bad idea. He was certainly a good-looking man, had a charming way about him. He loved dogs, was great with the children, had been approved by her mother...

Extinguishing her thoughts at once, Katharine redialed into the business at hand. The fundraiser would be here before she knew it and she had a thousand things yet to do. There was the media to stave off, the potential embezzlement to deal with, donors with whom she had to contend—a fling was the last thing she had time for, though oddly it had suddenly taken center stage in her mind. An affair with Canyon? Tingles of thrill raced up her spine. What would *that* feel like?

"Well, can't blame a girl for trying," Adele said glumly. "I hate to see you so wound up. Maybe we could settle on a glass of wine to relax you in place of a fling."

"Maybe." Katharine expelled a sigh and settled on the thought. "Pretty bad when life is coming at you like a bus head-on, huh?"

"I know what you mean." Adele pricked a bean from her salad and plopped it into her mouth.

"Speaking of life coming at you like a head-on bus, I saw Miles last week. He's losing the restaurant."

Adele recoiled. "He told you that?"

"You know Miles wouldn't reveal anything to me, but he didn't have to—the place is currently under renovation with a sign announcing new owners."

A slow smile spread across Adele's face as she savored the victory. "Serves him right."

Miles Lincoln was Adele's ex-husband and as smooth and slippery as 800-count bed linens. Granted, he was a good-looking man with wavy black hair and bedroom eyes, eyes that wrapped around women with offensive regularity, but he was a loser. Adele had met and married him while attending Le Cordon Bleu and refused to see the warning signs that hit Katharine like a city bus. Miles was charming and incredibly talented and Adele had been enamored from the start. Within six months of meeting, he had convinced her they were meant to be together.

Katharine had questioned his motives from the beginning. Not because she didn't think Adele was a worthy mate, but because Miles was not. He wanted to start a restaurant, and turned out, it was Adele's money he wanted to start it with. Once married, they worked side-by-side in their very own restaurant—a restaurant he stole in the divorce. "I thought you'd be pleased to hear it," Katharine said. "The man was never cut out for running a business, and once you were gone it was only a matter of time."

Adele raised her glass and said, "To leaving the big city where a lady can't trust her own spouse—unlike here in Silver Creek, where the air is fresh and the men are fresher."

Katharine raised her glass and tapped Adele's. "To Silver Creek," she toasted, stealing a peek at Canyon. Speaking of fresh men, this one was staring at her with a marked curiosity in his gaze. Something worth celebrating?

Unable to resist the irony, she took a quick swallow of water, grateful the man couldn't read minds! She'd be on the hot seat, for sure. The very hot seat.

Adele followed her gaze and turned back slowly. The mischievous twinkle in her eyes was unmistakable. "Am I too late?"

"Too late? What are you talking about?"

"You know what I'm talking about. You and Canyon."

Katharine smacked her water glass to the table a tad harder than intended. "There is absolutely nothing going on between me and Canyon."

"Would you like there to be?"

"No," she snapped, embarrassed by her sharp reply. Children's voices kicked up in the air around her and Cody was on full alert now, poking his head to the bench where she sat.

Adele laughed softly and slid another glance across the room. "Hmm. Looks like we'll have a chance to find out, won't we?"

Nerves singed the hair on Katharine's neck. *Canyon was coming over.*

Canyon was coming over!

Her heart pumped erratically and her ears flushed warm. The minute he stood near, Adele would see right through her. She would read her friend like the worn pages of a romance novel and call her out on it. Katharine gulped. Because there was no getting around it. The man was as fine as they came and there'd be no denying it. She jabbed a forkful of beans and shoved them into her mouth.

Canyon closed the distance between them in seconds and slowed to a stop at their table. Cody was on his feet, his head burrowed into Canyon's thigh for the expected affection. Adele smirked. Katharine chewed.

Towering over them, Canyon said, "Hey, Adele."

"Hey, Canyon."

Glancing between the two, he commented, "I didn't know you two were friends."

"The best!" Adele chirped. "Known her almost all my life."

"Adele and I met during college," Katharine clarified, disturbed by the unnatural pitch to her voice. It exposed her for the jumpy cat she felt like at the moment—a fact Adele wasn't helping with her repeated and obvious stares.

He nodded. "Small world. You two were toasting a minute ago. Can I hope that means good news?" he asked Katharine directly.

Adele cut in, "We were toasting my decision to move from New York to Colorado. Best decision I ever made."

"No doubt," Canyon replied. "And Silver Creek is certainly the better for it."

"Aw, thanks Canyon. You're so sweet," she said, waving him off.

It was not Katharine's imagination that her friend had drawn out the last word.

"So I hear Buck and Cody are friends," Adele added. "When did that happen?"

"Yesterday." Scratching Cody's head, Canyon said, "But what's not to love about this guy, right?"

"Right." Adele stared hard at Katharine. "Wouldn't you agree?"

"Of course," she returned, underscoring her words with an I-know-what-you're-doing-and-you'd-better-quit glare.

Adele smiled. Katharine grimaced inwardly.

Canyon stood by, silent.

Beneath the table, Adele tapped Katharine's shin with the toe of her boot. Katharine looked up at Canyon and said, "Well, I'm sorry if we got your hopes up with our toast. I wish we had better news about the ranch."

"No worries." He smiled at them both, though Katharine detected a shift in his gaze when he looked down at her. "Let me know what Frank learns, will you?"

"Will do," she replied, grateful conversation had reverted quickly to Wainwright business. There was no way Canyon could have missed the underpinnings of Adele's comments had he stayed much longer. It was sassy, coed doublespeak at its most blatant!

Watching him as he walked back to his table, Katharine pounced on Adele. "What exactly do you think you were doing?"

She grinned. "Pointing out the obvious."

"You're incorrigible."

"And you are not being straight with me."

Katharine rolled her eyes, picked up her fork and attacked her salad. This conversation was over.

Chapter Nineteen

Katharine's throat closed as she listened to Frank detail what he'd learned from his visit to the bank. "It's not good. As owner of Wainwright Ranch, they need to deal with you directly. I'll swing by and get you and we can meet with the branch manager together. We have an appointment at three."

"Thank you, Frank. I'll be ready."

As she hung up the phone, a sweeping sense of defeat washed over her. So it was true. The bank confirmed it. An account had been set up earlier this year and legitimate donations to Wainwright had been funneled through it and out of the country. Unbelievable. Katharine pounded a fist on the armrest of her chair. From his space on the floor, Cody peered up at her with sad eyes in an expression that mirrored the hurt that consumed her.

Unthinkable! Paul was stealing money from her mother's ranch—from the children—and had been since the beginning of the year. This ranch meant everything to these kids. She could see it in every face, every second she watched them in action. This ranch was a dream come true for them, a once-in-a-lifetime opportunity.

Lifetime. Lives that had been cut short. Katharine reached a shaky hand toward a pale blue envelope lying on the desk. Scribbled across the front of it was the ranch's address. With trembling fingers, she opened it. A child had sent the letter to her mother.

Dear Mrs. Wainwright,

When I first came to your ranch, you told me what the ranch was all about. You told me it was a working ranch, with real cattle that you needed to sell. At first, I wasn't sure if I was going to be able to do it. When I got cancer, I was told I couldn't do many things. But ever since I finished my treatments, I want nothing to do with talk about my limita-tions.

My cancer is gone right now, but they say it might come back. I don't care. My disease does not define who I was or who I am now. Some people call me "the kid with cancer." I just want to be a regular kid again and be normal. That's exactly what the ranch did for me. I was not held back or de-fined by the disease I had. You never went easy on me. You always told me I could do it. They were the best weeks of my life.

Yours truly,
Terri M.

Tears fell from Katharine's eyes. That's why she was here. That's why her mother had been here. Kids like Terri.

Folding the piece of stationery, Katharine slid it back in-to the envelope. Seated in her mother's office chair, she sought a wooden filing cabinet next to the window. She'd found the letter and many others like it in the bottom drawer. There were stacks of them. Genuine notes of gratitude and appreciation, personal statements about how a stay at the ranch had changed their lives. It broke Katharine's heart to think there would be no more campers. No more campers, no more letters, no more heartfelt words of thanks.

Because one greedy man had decided he wanted the money for himself. *Son of a—*

Katharine cut the words from her lips. Every cell in her body shouted—screamed—but she wouldn't. She would not let Paul Sutherland get the best of her. She would not let him drag this ranch into the ditch, either. To think that she had judged him as authentic. Incompetent, but authentic. She couldn't have been more wrong. The man was going to jail. He was going to jail and for a very long time. Once they stopped the flow of money from the foundation into his bogus account, she would consolidate accounts, reconcile every statement and create a workable budget. Then she would re-connect with every single donor the ranch had ever had and let them know the ranch remained in business and was going to be stronger than ever. She would also switch the investment funds to Wainwright, Emerson accounts. Propriety aside, Katharine could keep a better eye on the money if it was in-house with her father's firm than left with Richmond Capital.

Thoughts of her father popped into Katharine's brain. She would have to call him. She would have to give him an honest assessment of where things stood and reassure him they were going to get better. It might mean she'd have to be here a little longer than she had planned, but so be it. She would start from ground zero and rebuild her mother's legacy brick by brick, check by check, whatever it took. This ranch would not fail on her watch.

As determined thoughts and plans unwound inside her, Katharine forced her brain to slow down. Losing control wasn't the answer. Calm, cool objectivity was the key. Softening her focus, she moved her gaze from file cabinets to window to artwork. Breathe. Just breathe, she told herself. Focus on what's working, what's right. Focus on the way forward.

Perched on a table nearby was a bronze cowboy figurine. Her mother had the piece commissioned by a local artist, one that captured the spirit of independence that flourished in the Rocky Mountains. On the wall across the room hung a painting. It was a mountain range done in rich greens and reds and set against a deep blue sky which almost appeared off-color, unless of course you'd been to Colorado to witness the sky in person. There was no place on earth where the midday sky appeared as vivid—striking—as it did here in the mountains.

Expelling a sigh, she turned in her chair. Looking at the beautiful things her mother had accumulated over the years brought stabs of melancholy. People said you visit Colorado for the winters but you stay for the summers. They were right. It was the reason her mother had stayed. Katharine's pulse quickened. On a shelf in the bookcase, she noticed a small silver-framed picture. She'd seen it hundreds of times but the expression on the girl's face flipped a switch in Katharine's brain. Fixing on it, she realized at once what had struck her as odd before. Inside the frame was a portrait of her sister, Sarah, taken the year of her death. But it was the resemblance to the adventurous Kyle that struck her as uncanny. Fresh tears sprang to Katharine's eyes. The two could be siblings.

"Knock, knock," came a soft voice at her door.

Katharine whirled to see Canyon stroll into her office and choked back her emotion.

When he realized she'd been crying, Canyon came to her at once. "Katharine, what's wrong? Are you all right?"

She quickly wiped the tears from her eyes. "I'm fine." When she spotted the letter on her desk, she tucked it beneath a file folder and said, "Just a weak moment."

"Those letters will do it every time."

Katharine remained transfixed, pulled by the tenderness that had bathed his voice in understanding. Had he read the letters? Did he receive letters of his own?

Cody went to Canyon and he stroked the dog's head absently.

He didn't speak as Katharine continued to reel from visions of Kyle and her sister, the similarities, the connection between then and now. Finding her voice, she cleared it with effort and said, "They're beautiful, yes. And amazingly eloquent."

"I know what you mean. I've received my share, and nothing brings a man to his knees quicker than a camper who flays open his heart."

Imagining Canyon affected by the sentiments of a child touched her. Rugged on the outside, his cowboy persona seemed to have a soft center. It was a sweet image, incredibly so. Definitely the kind of man the ranch wanted around children. Katharine swallowed. To have around herself, too. Ejecting the thought from her skull, she said quickly, "But it's more than the letter. It's Paul Sutherland."

"Paul?"

"Frank spoke with the bank and it's true. Paul's been embezzling money from the ranch."

"You're sure about that?"

She nodded, finding strength in talk of business. "Very. Frank was at the bank and spoke with them directly. Seems Paul set up an account in the name of Wainwright Foundation and has been using it to funnel donations from our legitimate accounts into his."

"Son of a—" He whipped a hot glance around the room. "I never liked that guy. I'll bet that's why he was talking to that man out in the parking lot. He was out there heading him off at the pass so the poor guy didn't step into it with you and Frank."

"I'm sure you're right," she said, regaining some much needed objectivity. "And he's going to jail because of it."

"How are you going to prove it?"

"Frank and I are meeting with the bank this afternoon to learn where the deposits were directed and how we can tie them to Paul."

"But isn't that confidential information? Shouldn't you be calling the police, or FBI or someone? I doubt the bank can tell you anything without a warrant."

Katharine thought about that for a moment and decided to call Frank's cell. "You're right." As an investment broker, it should have occurred to her immediately. Dialing the number, she said, "Frank, its Katharine. Our meeting with bank this afternoon...did they indicate that they'd be able to share information with us, despite the fact that we're not authorized on the account?" It was feasible that a small town bank might feel comfortable operating outside the rule of law, but she didn't want to make any assumptions.

"Yes, I believe so. The manager didn't say otherwise. Are you concerned we might get the runaround?"

"It's possible. I think it's time we call the police in. They can get a warrant and force the man to answer our questions, in the event he chooses to be less than forthcoming with information."

"Good idea. Let's still plan on me picking you up and we'll go to the police station together."

"Perfect." Katharine ended the call and relayed the details to Canyon.

"Do you want me to call Wade?"

"No, I think it's better if Frank and I handle it personally, but I appreciate the offer."

"Just say the word. If there's anything I can do to help, you let me know."

Katharine stilled, a mix of gratitude and affection mingling in her chest. Canyon stood tall, his squared shoulders filled the office. Funny, but she found comfort in the sheer force of his presence. "Thank you, Canyon, I will. But really, the mere fact that you show up every day and work with the children is the biggest help. They adore you. I could see it in their eyes when you joined them for lunch. They really look up to you."

Canyon glanced away before returning a sheepish grin. "I don't know about all that, but we do have a good time together, don't we?" His cheeks turned slightly red. "I mean, me and the kids."

Katharine smiled, charmed by the boyish grin on his face. Suddenly, she wished he had meant what he hadn't meant to say. Hiking the mountain, finding Kyle. Buck and Cody...

And horseback riding. She imagined he must be a wonderful rider, what with his rodeo experience, galloping across the land, handsome in his cowboy hat and red bandana.

"Katharine?"

She blinked, momentarily lost in her musings. "Yes?"

"It's going to be okay."

"I know." She cleared her mind and recollected her thoughts. She was going to make sure of it. One way or another, she was going to pull the ranch from the jaws of defeat.

"And I mean it," he said. "You need anything, you just call me, you hear?"

Katharine nodded, biting back a more lengthy reply. "Yes, I will."

"Good." Pleasure blew the tension from his expression and he said, "Maybe when all this blows over, you'll let me take you for a horseback ride. I know this land as well as anyone and I bet I could take you to some beautiful places you've never been."

"That sounds nice," she replied, punched by memories of rides with her parents that quickly mixed with thoughts of riding with Canyon. A bucking bull flashed in her mind's eye, the quick shot of adrenaline it must be, the money he'd win, the charity... For a fleeting moment, Katharine couldn't think of anything else. She swallowed. "We'll make a date."

"I was hoping you'd say that."

In the pause that ensued, a current opened between them. Visceral, electric, it felt like the spark of something new.

Chapter Twenty

Canyon swore he saw more than a desire for friendship staring back at him, the softening in her gaze followed by a slow heating. It signaled a woman looking at him in terms of desire. It reminded him of the look in her eyes during lunch. From clear across the dining hall he'd detected a want in her gaze—a gaze he'd caught repeatedly glancing in his direction. Did Katharine feel the same way he did? Did she want to take it to the next level? And what would that look like?

Fancy New York businesswoman meets bull-busting rodeo cowboy. As Canyon walked back to the stables, he couldn't help but wonder. Beyond the ranch, beyond the crisis bearing down on them, he wanted to know if he'd ever see her again. Katharine had mentioned she'd be leaving after the fundraiser, after she put the cash flow into positive territory. Could he change her mind? Could he get her to stay on for a while so the two of them could get to know one another better?

Canyon cursed his foolish pride. And why would she want to do that? Give up her jetsetter life in New York for a cowboy who worked on a ranch? A ranch she owned?

He bet she had a ton of men after her, each offering a greater incentive than the last. What did he have to offer? A dog friend for Cody? A rodeo purse for the ranch?

He was a fool to think the two of them had a chance. Katharine was a different breed than him. She was rich and sophisticated, used to the finer things in life. Eleanor had been too, though you wouldn't have known it to look at her. She'd always been decked out in jeans and boots and the occasional cowboy hat, except for the annual fundraiser. For that one event, she'd pulled out the glitter, put a shine on her hair and looked every bit the wealthy New York City socialite. Mr. Wainwright would fly into town for the evening and together they made an impressive-looking couple. Canyon could easily picture them walking down the steps of a private jet or strolling the halls of a fancy theater. Not that he begrudged the Wainwrights their money. Anyone willing to work hard deserved it. And whether it was money earned from a complicated slate of investments or a ride on a bull, Eleanor Wainwright couldn't care less. She had treated every man, woman, and child the same—with equal respect or equal disdain, depending on which category you fell into. Canyon chuckled. God have mercy on the person who crossed her. He'd seen her tear off a man's head, then serve it to him on a dusty plate because he dared to insult her organization. Longing shot through him. Eleanor had been a feisty one but a lady he'd never forget. Unfortunately for him, he feared the same might hold true for her daughter.

"Canyon!"

He turned at the sound of his name to see Jacob waving him over to the henhouse. He had a frantic look on his face and Canyon didn't like it one bit. He jogged over. "What's going on?" he asked, looking past him into the small building. Plump hens sat in nesting cubbies lined along the wall, a few squawking and twitching, the scent of birds and hay heavy in the air. "Is there a problem?"

"Two of the chickens are missing."

Canyon ducked his head into the house. "Missing?"

Jacob nodded furiously. "Yep, and I can't find the dang things anywhere!"

Anger percolated in his gut. Canyon bet he knew where to begin looking. "Where's Kyle?"

"In the stables with the others. They're sweeping out the stalls."

"Have you checked their cabins?"

Confusion gripped Jacob's fair features. "No."

"I'll talk to the boys," Canyon said. "You go check their cabin."

"Yes, sir."

Jacob took off and Canyon strode to the stables. There wasn't a doubt in his mind where those chickens were. Canyon had read it in the kid's face this morning. Clear as the blue sky, the boy was up to no good. What he hadn't realized was that the mischief had already taken place. Only question he had now was who Kyle had enlisted as his accomplice. A boy couldn't handle two chickens on his own. He'd need help.

Turning the corner to the stables, Canyon called out, "Single file line, right now!"

Twenty feet away, bodies bumped and hurried as they obeyed his command. Becky did likewise, and stood at attention along with the rest of them.

Summoning his sternest expression, Canyon approached, raking his gaze over each and every one of them to ensure everyone knew he meant business. He prided himself on delivering fair discipline which came from immediate action and consistency, something Katharine had taken from him when she stepped in and unhooked Kyle from the consequences he'd been due. Now it was Canyon's mess to clean up, and he needed to be certain all the children were paying attention. "Kyle, step forward." Kyle did so, donning an expression shades less concerned than the boys standing behind him. "We have two chickens missing. Care to explain?"

"How am I supposed to know what happened to them?" he replied, then snickered, a gesture that grated on Canyon.

"Are you telling me that you had nothing to do with their departure from the henhouse?"

Kyle glanced away.

Canyon looked to the group behind him. Caroline and Melody appeared nervous while Garrett stood stoically beside them. Avery wore his emotion like a neon light, his freckles brightening as his fair skin flushed pink. But it was Derrick who was the dead giveaway. He swung dark bangs from his eyes and unable to suppress a giggle, he continually dodged his gaze to Kyle's back.

"Derrick," Canyon addressed him directly. "Is there something funny about missing chickens?"

"No, sir," he replied, and dipping his chin, he covered his mouth with a hand.

Through a heavy silence, Canyon scanned the faces peering up at him and allowed his disapproval to sink in. "Stealing is a crime. Lying is against Wainwright rules. I'll give you one last chance. Does anyone know what happened to the chickens?"

No one said a word.

Canyon exhaled and set his hands to his hips. "Then we wait."

"Wait?" Melody asked. "What for?"

"For the evidence."

Derrick's face reflected the hit. Kyle's left eye twitched and he darted his gaze over his shoulder, to the floor— anywhere but Canyon.

"We have a search team on the hunt as we speak," Canyon continued. "And when the chickens are located, the perpetrators will be punished."

"Er, Mr. Laredo—" Derrick spoke up.

"Yes?"

"What happens to the person who took them?"

"What does it matter to you? You didn't take them, right?"

Derrick shot an evasive glance toward Kyle, who smirked.

"That's what I thought," Canyon said, as though answering Derrick's reply. "Only the guilty need to worry about what happens next."

Canyon caught the leap in glances as Jacob entered the stables. Shock paled Derrick's brunette features while Kyle's body froze. All humor emptied from his gaze.

"Found 'em, Canyon!" Jacob exclaimed, a hen locked beneath each arm. "Right where you told me to look. They were closed up in the boys' bathroom."

"In these boys' bathroom?" Canyon asked, knowing there was only one. Wainwright Ranch had facilities for the boys, facilities for the girls.

"Yes, sir," Jacob replied.

"The one used by Garrett, Avery, Derrick and Kyle?"

"That's the one."

Canyon moved his gaze between Kyle and Derrick. Granted, there were a dozen other boys that would have access to that same bathroom, but Canyon didn't have any doubts as to the identity of his culprits. "That's odd," he said. "I just asked this group if they knew anything about the missing chickens and they said no."

"Guess they were lying, huh?" Jacob retorted.

"Guess so. Anyone want to change their story?"

Derrick buckled. "Mr. Laredo, it was Kyle's idea! He said we should take some chickens out of their cages for a joke!"

"And you thought that was a good idea?"

"No, sir!" Derrick's face reddened. "He made me do it!"

"Roped you like a calf, did he?"

Derrick clammed up but not Melody. She burst out laughing.

"Kyle?" Canyon prodded. "Care to speak up for yourself?"

Kyle kicked at the ground. "No, sir."

"Is Derrick telling the truth?"

Kyle appeared to be considering the idea of pitching his word against Derrick's, but when he looked into Canyon's face, he seemed to realize that would be a bad idea. A very bad idea. "It was only a joke. We didn't hurt anybody." He hitched his chin toward the hens. "The chickens are fine."

"Do you know that stress can affect their ability to lay eggs?" When Kyle stared at him, unconvinced, Canyon said, "It's true. Panic can decrease their production. And a decrease in production affects our food supply." Now that he held everyone's attention, he drilled the point home. "The kitchen relies on these hens for eggs. You campers rely on them for breakfast. Your bodies rely on them for protein." He paused. "Want to reconsider your statement about not hurting anybody?"

Kyle blew out his breath in a ragged sigh. "Sorry."

"Sorry doesn't cut it. This is your second offense, Kyle. Derrick, it's your first." Canyon was pleased to see the first signs of concern in Kyle's expression. Downright fear had begun to grip Derrick's. "To start, you two are going to clean the henhouse, top to bottom."

"What? No way!"

"That's disgusting!"

"Next, you're going to clean the bathroom," Canyon continued over their protest. "I'm sure your fellow campers don't want hen germs in their personal hygiene space. Hens can carry some pretty filthy business on their feet which they likely spread to the toilets."

Avery burst out, "Gross!"

His response was quickly echoed by several others.

"It is gross, which is why Kyle and Derrick here are going to scrub every toilet bowl 'til it shines."

"No way! You can't make us do that!"

Canyon ignored the outbursts. "I can and I will. Do you understand?"

Derrick looked like he was about to vomit as he replied, "Yes, sir."

Kyle mumbled, "Yes, sir."

"And afterward, Kyle, you and I are going to have a little chat with Ms. Wainwright and your parents."

"But Canyon—"

"But nothing." Canyon turned to Jacob and instructed, "Bring him to me when he's finished with the bathroom."

"Yes, sir."

"Boys," Jacob directed, sounding more like a warden than a camp counselor. "Let's go."

Chapter Twenty-One

Katharine sat immobile in her seat as Frank drove the Mercedes down the two-lane highway, unable to register what Frank had said. She couldn't accept it. Couldn't digest it. Her father had had a heart attack? He'd collapsed during a meeting with investigators from the SEC?

It was impossible. No one had called her.

Frank reached over and patted her arm. "Don't worry, Katharine. Amanda will field any more calls from New York. She has my cell. She'll contact us right away."

Katharine nodded dully. The New York office had called Wainwright Ranch, looking for her, but she and Frank had been en route to the bank. Amanda had called Frank. Frank had told her. Katharine's heart twisted. Harder, tighter, the worry sucked the life from her as she stared at the road ahead. They were headed for the airport instead of the bank. Frank had called ahead and ordered the jet to be prepared for take-off. They were leaving for New York at once. The business of embezzlement would have to be attended to after her father.

Katharine's heart squeezed. Cody. She'd left him behind for their trip to the bank, but Frank assured her not to worry. Once again, he'd taken care of everything. Amanda had instructions to get one of the ranch hands to drive the dog to the airport.

Yellow center line dots passed continually beneath Katharine's gaze as they headed for the small regional airport. Twenty minutes and they'd be there. Ten more, they'd be in the air and within a few hours, she'd be by her father's side. She closed her eyes. She felt like she needed to call someone. She needed to call the hospital, someone—anyone—but Frank was right. Who was she going to call? The New York office knew. Her father's personal assistant had called and spoke with Frank directly. To whom else did it matter but Katharine?

No one. Her father's condition mattered to no one but the two people sitting in this car. Katharine didn't know what she'd ever do without Frank. Crisis Management was his middle name. He'd taken care of everything. Every detail, every aspect, he was in charge. It reminded her of the old Frank and not the one allowing Wainwright Ranch to slip into insolvency.

During Katharine's eighth-grade year, when a scandal had erupted regarding her father's firm, it had been Frank who had handled the headwinds of accusations and media attention, leaving her father to handle the storm exploding within the company. The ordeal had consumed almost a year of their lives, and Katharine recalled how her mother had attributed their success to Frank, claiming that if he hadn't been in charge, she didn't know where Wainwright, Emerson would have landed. It had been the impetus for her move out West. Tired of being torn apart by treacherous business dealings, her mother had opted for the pure and serene life of Colorado. A year later, Frank had joined her.

There'd been speculation about the two of them, whisperings up and down the halls of Wainwright, Emerson, despite the fact they were baseless. Her father wasn't concerned, which meant Katharine wasn't concerned. Though she still hated how people talked, hated how they gossiped about things they knew nothing about. As she grew older, she'd learned it was unavoidable. Curiosity was a natural extension of human behavior. People would talk. No matter what a person did, how they did it or with whom, people would talk. It was up to the individual to guard against it.

Katharine inhaled, deep and slow, and calmed the sudden pounding in her chest. Now it was her turn to rely on Frank and his steadfast strength. He would get her to New York, get her to her father's bedside, all while handling the crisis at the ranch. Paul Sutherland would have to be dealt with but he'd have to be dealt with later. Turning her head to Frank, she said, "Thanks for getting Cody."

He smiled. "You know I wouldn't have done anything less. I know how much he means to you."

Tears pushed behind her eyes. Thoughts of her father and his condition infused her with grief. Having Cody near gave her comfort. If anything happened to her father, she didn't know what she'd do. She had to see him. She had to see him before—

Katharine's thoughts went to the last time she'd seen him. Recalling the sadness in his eyes, the heavy heart with which he left her became unbearable. It pained her to think that would be the last time she ever saw him again, the fate of the ranch hanging between them. Her father had been counting on Katharine to save her mother's legacy, counting on her to fix the ranch's financials and set the charity back on course.

Sorrow and doubt coursed through her, drowning Katharine with a defeat so great she feared she might not ever recover. Her father couldn't die not knowing the outcome. He couldn't die before she told him the ranch was solvent and secure—which hadn't happened, yet! Not yet, but it would. She'd make sure of it. Hot tears filled Katharine's lids, spilled onto her cheeks. *Your father had a massive heart attack.*

Dread iced her limbs and she turned quickly. "I can't lose him, Frank." Her voice cracked as she whispered, "*I can't.*"

"You won't. He's going to be fine," Frank reassured her, his voice supple and steady. "William's a tough old goat. It would take more than a little chest pain to keep him down."

She tried to smile, but somehow the gesture felt unnatural, grotesquely inappropriate under the circumstances. She knew there were no such guarantees. "He's been under a lot of stress lately. I was worried about him when I left, what this trip would do to him, the investigation back home..." Katharine's throat closed. Her father wasn't a young man any more. She understood the risks. Stress could be a killer for men in their fifties let alone a man in his seventies. She didn't kid herself. This was serious and no matter how badly she needed to hear them, encouraging words from a friend weren't going to keep her father alive.

Glancing at Frank, she clung to his profile, the line of his aging jaw, folds of skin around his eyes. He looked old, tired. This had to be hard on him as well. "I'm sorry I can't go to the bank with you, Frank. No matter what happens, my presence will be required in New York for the foreseeable future."

"I understand, and you know you have nothing to worry about. I'll take care of Paul."

"But the fundraiser next week..." Katharine couldn't bring herself to finish the thought.

Frank reached over and took her hand in his. Darting his gaze between her and the road, he said, "It will be okay. Our donors understand setbacks. Once they realize the ranch is back on track, they'll return in droves. Your mother and I have hit hard times before and we'll hit them again. It's part of the normal business cycle, you know that. We'll simply handle what comes our way and move forward, same as we've always done."

Frank smiled, but she could see it in his eyes. *We. Your mother and I.* He sounded like he was talking in the present tense, like he was forging ahead, fighting the good fight and carrying on with her. Peering at him, Katharine's heart split in two. He didn't believe a word of his own spiel. He was going through the motions. He was saying what he thought she wanted to hear. Needed to hear. Frank was a good man. A decent man. But he was in over his head. The churned investments, the embezzlement that occurred right under his nose... It all happened on his watch, under his supervision. Frank bore the responsibility for the failures at the ranch and they both knew it.

Katharine climbed the narrow, steep flight of stairs ahead of Frank and boarded Wainwright's private jet.

Through the cockpit window, she saw the pilot already in place, running through his standard pre-flight checklist. Jet engines hummed with the soft squeal of idle. Ducking as she entered, Katharine inhaled the scent of expensive leather. Similar to her father's Gulfstream, this jet was outfitted more like an office suite than an airplane. Cream-colored armchairs lined the front, separated by round, sleek blond-wood tables. In the rear, a matching sofa formed in an L-shape encircled an oval table, replete with oversized chenille pillows and a soft cashmere throw draped over the back. The carpet was a shimmery tan with flecks of gold, making for a gorgeous interior. Modern, cozy, the décor was entirely her mother, up to and including the bronze western-themed sculpture affixed to a short table stand. This was her plane, the one she'd used for the rare trips back to New York.

Sinking into the plush cushion, Katharine set her purse on the floor beside her chair and peered out the window. Airport crew moved about the tarmac as they saw to the final details of takeoff. She exhaled in a ragged stream. Within the half hour, they'd be ready for lift off.

Frank hovered over her. "Can I offer you a sedative?"

"No, thank you," she replied, pulling her gaze from the activity outside. "I'm fine. I just need to get to New York as soon as possible."

"You're sure?"

"Positive." She smiled. "Cody is the only sedative I need. How long do you think before he'll get here?"

"My guy said about another ten."

"Okay." Leaning back, she exhaled again and gently closed her eyes. The flight would take about four hours. With no communication inflight, she considered calling the hospital before takeoff. It was possible they had an update on her father's condition.

Canyon. Visions of him burst into her mind as it occurred to her that she should call him, too. They'd spent so much time together of late, it seemed she didn't make a move without him being there; the situation with Kyle, the news about Paul, and this afternoon, when he'd walked in on her after she'd read the letter. He seemed to understand exactly how it had made her feel. Canyon understood it all and was completely in her camp. Katharine opened her eyes. Except when it came to Frank.

Standing up front, Frank was talking with the pilot, finalizing details for the flight. The man was a godsend. Sure, he'd made some missteps but that was to be expected. Her mother's death had affected him deeply. And it wasn't as if they were problems that couldn't be solved. They could.

It was something else. For some reason, Canyon didn't care for Frank, alluding to some kind of personal differences—differences that could have arisen out of jealousy. Katharine understood men could be territorial when it came to their career and position, about the women they worked with and for. It was something she'd experienced in New York many times. Men and women were supposed to be equal in the workplace, but there was no denying nature. Men and women were equal, she mused, but different. A man couldn't completely detach himself from his instinctual need to protect and defend, or for that matter, his innate attraction to the opposite sex. Relationships happened, favoritism resulted, conflict arose...it was the nature of the human spirit.

Canyon had obviously held her mother in high regard with a distinct degree of affection. Frank, of course, had been devoted to her mother for as long as Katharine could remember, even following her to Colorado to help make her dream a reality. If the two men didn't see eye-to-eye, it could have stemmed from standing on opposite sides of her mother. But Canyon was like a Rubik's Cube. There were so many facets to him, so many twists and turns that she never knew what to expect from him. He rode bulls and donated his earnings to the ranch. He worked with the mountain search and rescue team, along with his dog, to save countless lives at his own peril. He was a natural when it came to working with kids, as gentle as any woman she'd ever seen yet equally as stern as any man. He was smart, attractive, yet humble as a quiet country boy.

Katharine shook her head. Canyon was definitely a puzzle, including his comments about a Wainwright running the ranch. Why was he so intent on that point? If he could run the cattle, he could run the ranch. Numbers were numbers, costs were costs. Maybe there was still time to convince him of the same. Katharine reached for her purse just as Frank turned, and pulled the main cabin door closed. She stopped mid-motion. "Frank, what about Cody? He isn't here yet."

Wordlessly, Frank locked the door. The whir of engines increased and the plane began to move.

Katharine dropped her purse to the floor. "Frank—" Panic stabbed at her. "We can't leave!"

Chapter Twenty-Two

Canyon strode out of the henhouse, satisfied the chickens were okay and the boys were paying their dues for their bad behavior. Jacob would make sure the boys cleaned the bathroom until they could eat supper from that floor. But that wasn't the end of it. Canyon believed Kyle should be sent home. The boy had broken the rules—more than once—and needed to pay the price. It was a conversation Canyon wasn't looking forward to having with Katharine, but he would. He'd explain to her in no uncertain terms that this was the way her mother would have handled it. Tough love, normal discipline, it was the bloodstream of the ranch. There were no special exceptions made, something the kids understood from day one.

During orientation, staff had explained in detail what the campers could expect and what would be expected of them. It was Eleanor Wainwright's philosophy to the core. Keep it simple, but keep it real. Canyon stopped. In the distance, he spotted Paul Sutherland whip his fire-engine red sports car into a parking space next to the administrative building. Anger rose sharply in his chest. Detouring, Canyon headed straight for him. Briefly, he wondered if Katharine was still here or if she'd already left for the bank. If she was here, she'd need a witness to any confrontation she had with an employee, and who better than him?

Paul entered the building and Canyon picked up his stride to catch up with him, thoughts and questions steamrolling through his mind. How did Paul think he was going to get away with stealing money from the ranch? Did he not think people would catch on? Eventually, the donors and owners would realize there was a rat in their midst and that rat was Paul.

Reaching the front door, Canyon swung it open. "Paul."

Amanda looked up from her desk and Paul turned. "Hey, Canyon. How's it going?"

"What are you doing here?" he demanded.

Paul shot him a queer gaze. "Uh, I work here?"

"Amanda," Canyon asked, shifting focus. "Is Katharine still here?"

Amanda shook her head. There wasn't a shred of flirtation in her dark eyes. Instead, they were unusually troubled. "No. She left with Frank a little while ago."

Canyon instantly assessed the situation. Katharine and Frank had gone. The two of them would handle the embezzlement issue and Canyon should respect her wishes. However, he was a board member with every right to question Paul about business dealings that affected the ranch—his livelihood—but they were business dealings he wouldn't have been privy to, if it hadn't been for Katharine. Need pulled at him, warred with loyalty. Canyon didn't want to overstep, but he didn't want to miss an opportunity, either. "Paul," he said impulsively. "Do you have a second?"

"Sure." Concern evaporated from his gaze as he offered, "Let's go into my office."

"How about we step outside?" Canyon suggested.

Curiosity churned in Amanda's gaze as she peered up from her desk. Ignoring the question in her eyes, Canyon pushed the door open for Paul who walked through and stopped. Canyon walked out past him and halfway down the front path. He stopped, and glanced around for onlookers. Other than a few stable hands working with the horses, he saw no one. No one was within earshot.

Paul joined him, squinting in the bright sunlight. "What's up?"

"I've been wanting to ask you about something," Canyon began casually, tipping his hat forward, alert for any unexpected intrusions before he stared down Paul.

"Shoot."

Capping a desire to knock a fist across Paul's jaw, Canyon reminded himself that calm, cool and collected was the way to go. "I saw you speaking to a man outside your car yesterday. Who was he?"

"Yesterday?"

Don't try to deny it, Canyon wanted to growl, but waited for the man to connect the dots.

"I don't know what you're talking about."

"Yesterday morning, before we got the call about the missing boy, you were in the parking lot talking to a man next to your car."

Paul shot his gaze to the sky then squarely on Canyon. "Oh yeah, I totally forgot."

"Since when do you conduct business in the parking lot?" Canyon charged, unable to control his urge for a confrontation.

"Hey, that was his choice," Paul replied defensively. "He's the one who didn't want to come inside, not me."

"Who was he?"

"Some guy asking questions about Ms. Wainwright and her family."

Confusion exploded in Canyon's skull. "What?"

"Yeah," Paul tossed back, glancing around as though suddenly aware this could be a problem. "The guy wanted to know what she was doing here, what Frank's role in the ranch business was, who handled their investments."

Canyon held up his hands. "Whoa, whoa, back up. Who was this guy? Did he have a name?"

Paul looked up to his left, paused, then shook his head. "Don't recall. I went in to tell Frank, but all hell had broken loose over the missing kid."

"You didn't leave a message?"

"I forgot."

"You *forgot*?"

"Yeah, I did, but I've got the guy's card." Paul screwed his expression. "What's with all the interrogation? Is there something going on I should know about?"

"What's the deal with the new foundation you set up earlier this year?" The question was out before Canyon could stop himself and now that it was, he had to know. "What the hell do you think you're doing?"

Paul angled his shoulders and said, "Hey, I don't know where you're going with this but you should be talking to Frank, not me. He's the one who set it up."

"For what purpose?" Canyon demanded, cornering Paul in his lie. If he thought he was going to squirm his way out by blaming Frank, he had another thought coming.

"It was trying to circumvent some new accounting regulations so the ranch could save on taxes."

"What new regulations?"

Paul's features contorted as he pushed back. "I don't know. I'm not an accountant. Why don't you ask him? He's the one who did it."

Canyon had an itchy feeling. "I don't believe you," he said, and took a step back.

"Well, you should. It's the truth. And what does it matter to you, anyway?"

"Did you direct donors to deposit money to that account?" Canyon continued, casting a wary glance around the immediate vicinity.

Paul glanced askance. "Yes, how else would I know about it? That's my department. Donations. Remember?"

"And Frank knew about it?"

Paul cocked his head and mocked, his blue eyes scathing in their rebuke. "He's the one in charge, last time I checked."

He's embezzling money from the ranch. Frank and I are meeting with the bank this afternoon to learn where the deposits were sent and how we can tie them to Paul.

Blood drained from Canyon's skull. Katharine was walking into the devil's lair. "If you're lying about this—"

"I'm not lying about anything! It's the truth, check it out for yourself."

Canyon's gut twisted. He would—now. Storming back into the office, he snapped, "Amanda, I need to get ahold of Katharine. Do you have her cell phone number?"

"I do," she answered with a brisk nod. "She gave it to me after the media started calling."

At the sound of voices, Katharine's yellow Lab trotted down the hall. The dog peered at Canyon with soulful brown eyes that seemed to beg for help. His heart pulled. Katharine had left her dog. She'd left the animal because she didn't expect to be long. Urgency tore at him as Amanda scribbled a number on a piece of paper.

She pulled it from the notepad and handed it to him. "What's going on?" Her gaze flashed to Paul, now standing behind Canyon in the office lobby. "Is there a problem?"

"Yes." Without elaboration, Canyon immediately punched the number into his cell phone and waited through rings. The call went to her voicemail. "Damn it," he grumbled under his breath. "Do you know which bank they went to?" he asked Amanda.

She shook her head. "I have no idea."

"The account was held with First Federal," Paul put in. "They're located downtown, across from the police station."

The very last place Frank would be. Canyon dialed Wade's phone number, but paused. Ending the call, he realized he didn't have enough to go on to call in the Chief of Police. Stuck between gut instinct and a lack of evidence, Canyon looked to Paul, then Amanda. Now what?

If Frank was responsible for embezzling the money and not Paul, he certainly wouldn't be at the bank. His call to Katharine would have been a hoax. But if he picked her up under false pretenses, where would he take her? When would he tell her it was all a scam?

Questions hammered. To his house? To a remote spot, some place he could dump her?

No. Frank wouldn't hurt Katharine. He was a friend. He'd been good friends with her mother, friendly with her father when he visited. He wouldn't harm her. *Would he?*

Doubt seized Canyon. But if it were Frank, what would he do?

The answer was swift. He would leave town. He'd get out of Dodge before anyone was the wiser. Except it was too late for that. Katharine had discovered his fraud, only she didn't know it was Frank's. Canyon redialed Wade's number. Evidence or not, he needed to call in a favor on this one.

The Chief of Police answered on the second ring. "Hey, Canyon. What's up, buddy?"

"Wade, I have a problem." His gaze darted between Amanda and Paul, both rapt on his every move. "Frank Dillard might be on his way to the airport. He's got Katharine with him. I need to know if you can send someone out to head him off."

"Whoa, whoa, whoa—hold up. Are you talking about Katharine Wainwright?"

"Yes."

"Why would he have her with him and why would I want to stop him? What's going on?"

"The ranch has been losing money and I think Frank is behind it. Katharine discovered it but didn't realize it was Frank." Dread seeped into Canyon. Though he bet she knew now. "I tried to call her but there was no answer. Frank picked her up from the ranch on what I think was a ruse and now they might be headed for the airport." He was spitting information out as fast as he could and hoped it made sense to Wade. "Wainwright has a private plane over there."

"Canyon, do you have any more to go on? I mean, I can't just send officers out chasing people on a hunch."

"I know for a fact Frank's the guy behind the embezzle-ment," Canyon said, smacking Paul with a hard glance. If he was wrong, if Paul was lying, Canyon would string the guy up by his bootstraps and ask Wade for forgiveness later. Right now, Canyon needed action and he needed it quick. "I'm headed toward the airport now." He headed for the door adding, "But they have about an hour on me."

Wade paused. "How about you drive over and call me if there's any trouble."

About to object, Canyon realized how panicky he must sound, like he was chasing wind. "Will do," he snapped.

"On second thought," Wade offered, "I'll send out a deputy, just in case."

"Thanks, Wade. I owe you one."

Ending the call, Canyon couldn't help but feel stupid. Slightly, but not entirely so. His gut warned he was right. Katharine was in trouble. Frank was on the run, and being on the hook for the amount of money the ranch had lost would make for a dangerous man. Canyon didn't care how good of friends Frank and the Wainwrights might have been. If he stole money from them, the relationship was history.

Speaking of relationships, there was a friend he needed to call. Canyon dialed Roan's number. The phone rang and he answered. "Buddy, I need a huge favor."

It was crossing the lines of protocol, but at the moment, Katharine's well-being trumped everything.

Chapter Twenty-Three

Frank walked toward Katharine, took a seat in the chair opposite hers. His expression had morphed from the familiar ease she knew and loved to a hardened detachment.

A lightning bolt of fear struck deep in her heart. "Frank, what's going on?"

"We can't wait for the dog," he said coolly. "We have to leave now."

"But Frank," she objected, and her voice began to shake, "I don't understand."

"I'm sorry, Katharine. The last thing I wanted was to involve you in any of this, but when you started digging through the files, it became inevitable."

"What's inevitable?" In an instant, she realized this trip to New York was a ploy. "Frank, is my father okay?"

"William is fine, healthy as the ornery goat he always has been."

Relief flooded her, mixing with a building fear. "What's this about, what's inevitable?"

"This, me." His shell cracked and the first hint of the old Frank poked through as he confessed in a sigh, "The money."

Katharine gasped. "*You* stole the money?"

He nodded.

"But why, Frank? Why would you do such a thing?"

"Because of your mother."

Katharine bristled. From the corner of her eye, she saw the pilot flipping switches, pushing levers. "What does my mother have to do with this?"

"Everything."

The word exploded between them. Katharine shook her head. "I don't understand," she said, trying to shut out the insanity coming from a man she knew and trusted. Although part of her did. Completely.

"I was in love with Eleanor." Casting a glance to one side, a tiny smile entered his tired gaze, followed by a razor-sharp knowing. "I'm sure it comes as no secret to you. I know people talked. I heard the gossip, the whispers behind my back, but I never cared." He shook his head. "I wanted to be with her more than I cared about what people said, so I made it happen."

Katharine's gaze darted out the window. They were slowly turning, the first steps to taxiing out to the runway. Her pulse ratcheted up. "But if you loved her, why ruin her charity? Why destroy the very thing you helped her build?"

The lines around his eyes softened. "For that exact reason—because I helped her build it." Anger returned to Frank's gaze as he said, "Your father didn't give a damn about her dreams, but I did. Me, Katharine. Not even you, her beloved daughter could see fit to join her out here. Only me. Me alone, and I will not allow it to be taken over by strangers."

"Strangers? Who? The board?"

"Eleanor and I built the charity together, without William, without you. She and I did that, together. It was built from love, and I won't let anyone take that away from me."

"Frank," Katharine objected, need closing in on her as the plane continued to move further from the buildings. "No one is trying to take it away from you. You're still at the helm. You're still in command. It's yours to continue, *I swear.*"

Ice seeped into his voice. "I know why you came here, Katharine. You came here to sideline me and take over the ranch."

She bolted forward. "I did no such thing! I came here to save it, that's all—my life is in New York, not Colorado!"

As soon as the words were out, the backlash hit her like a bus. *My life is in New York.* The words lodged deep, formed a pit in her stomach. Her life was in New York, not in Colorado with her mother—as Frank's had been.

Guilt poured into Katharine as she recalled how her mother had invited her to join her through the years, insisting she had a role in the ranch, that she would come to love it out west. But Katharine had declined, choosing to stay in the city and work with her father. Knives of accusation lodged deep as Frank stared at her, his knowing gaze gutting her to the core. He clearly felt Katharine had abandoned her mother. *Had her mother felt the same?*

"I'm going to Mexico," he announced, withdrawing all emotion from his voice. "Once we land, you can find a pilot to fly you and the jet back to the States. My pilot and I will not be joining you. We will be taking a different plane to Cuba, and from there I will disappear."

"Frank—I don't have a passport. You can't leave me there."

"You're a smart woman. I'm sure you can manage. You have the resources." His gaze clouded. "Call your father. I'm sure he'll help you."

"You don't have to do this," she urged him, growing frantic as the plane turned onto the runway. Katharine reached for his arm. "It doesn't have to end like this."

"It's already been done."

Removing her hand from his, Frank rose from his seat and walked back to the cockpit. Ducking inside, he spoke to the pilot once again. Katharine grabbed the cell phone from her purse. She pressed a button and the screen lit up, revealing Canyon's text message. *Frank is behind the embezzlement NOT Paul. Get away from him and call the police.* Apprehension pierced her heart. *Too late,* she texted back rapidly. *We're on a—*

Frank yanked the phone from her hands. "What do you think you're doing?" He read the message she'd texted and growled, "You're making this harder than it needs to be, Katharine. Don't you understand? I don't want to hurt you."

He dropped his gaze to her phone and warned, "But if you leave me no choice..."

"Frank—I'm sorry! I won't send it!"

"You're damn right you won't." He jabbed his thumb against the phone screen. "I deleted it," he said then slid her phone into his pocket. "Sit back and enjoy the flight. You'll be back in the States in less than twenty-four hours."

Katharine's gaze leapt to the window. Overcome by disbelief, she watched the tarmac as they rolled over it. She was going to Mexico. Frank was going to get away.

Canyon arrived at the airport, stopping his truck short of the fence line between parking lot and tarmac. Silver Creek's airport was a small facility, a single-story brick building that housed four commercial gates, including an office that dealt with private aircraft. Two mid-sized commercial jetliners were parked behind the building with a slew of smaller jet planes parked off to the right. Canyon located the Wainwright jet quickly. It was one of the larger ones, and parked on the runway about a hundred yards from him. Scanning the perimeter through his windshield, he ran through his options. He couldn't drive his truck onto the runway. The access gates were locked. His gaze shot to the sky. No sign of Roan yet. Canyon could call him, but if Roan was in the air, he wouldn't hear his phone over the chopper blades.

But he said he'd come. Although in the middle of flight instruction with a student when Canyon called, Roan promised he could be here in fifteen. Canyon checked his watch. That bird should be here any time. Scanning the horizon, he wondered, *Where are you, buddy?*

It occurred to Canyon that if Roan called Wade to clear it, he'd learn that Canyon had already tried to enlist Wade's official help without success. In fact, he'd been made to feel a bit like an alarmist. Moving his gaze back to the plane, Canyon trusted his gut. He wasn't overreacting. Something was wrong. The jet began to roll. What the—

Canyon shoved out of his truck and leapt to the fence. The aircraft was moving. They were taking off! Was Katharine in that plane? *Had Frank done something to her*?

Canyon couldn't let that plane leave the ground. Not without answers. Darting a glance toward the terminal, he realized he had no good options. Pulling his hat secure, he jumped onto the fence and clawed his way up and over, landing on the ground with a hard thud. He took off running. The area was crawling with staff—luggage handlers, ground control, fuel attendants—there was no way he could get past them without being seen.

Genius struck. And why wouldn't he want to be seen? Canyon sprinted across the tarmac, his heart pumping wildly as he shouted, "Stop that plane!"

The more attention he could call to himself the better. If air traffic control spotted him, they'd have to halt the planes. And that was the goal. *Stop that plane*.

Someone yelled at him. "Hey you—stop!"

Canyon continued running as fast as he could, his boots pounding hard over the pavement. The plane was halfway to the runway. Winded, he realized there was no way he could catch it on foot. It was too far, too fast. Dodging a service truck, he spotted his opportunity. A fuel truck sat parked next to a commercial airliner. There was no one inside. Canyon made a full-speed dash for the truck. Angry shouts followed. Body-slamming the vehicle, he hopped onto the running board and yanked the door open. His insides sang. The keys were in the ignition!

Canyon jumped in and gunned the engine to life then jerked the gear into drive. He spun the wheel hard right to avoid hitting a plane and headed for Wainwright's jet. "*C'mon, c'mon*,"—he crushed his boot onto the accelerator— "give me all you got!"

In his rearview mirror, he glimpsed a stunned fuel attendant staring after him.

Good. Now call the authorities and close down this airport!

The sleek white body of Wainwright's jet reflected sunlight as it turned onto the main runway. Canyon's heart pounded. If Katharine was on that plane, if Frank had hurt her—

For the first time in his life, Canyon wished he carried a weapon. His buddy Walsh never left home without one, something that sure would come in handy right about now. At the moment, his weapon had four wheels. There was no way that plane could take off with a fuel tanker in its path. But as Canyon trailed the jet now taxiing down the runway, he calculated time and distance and realized he wouldn't make it. The aircraft was already turning in preparation for takeoff.

Canyon ground his jaw. *Where the hell was Roan?*

Inside the Wainwright jet, Katharine sat, her body frozen stiff. This couldn't be happening. This had to be a dream. Frank couldn't be serious.

But as the plane picked up speed, she recognized that he was very serious. Deadly so. Suddenly, the pilot cried out from the cockpit. His words were unintelligible to her, but his emotion wasn't. Something was happening.

"I don't care!" Frank yelled at him. "Go!"

Katharine gripped the armrests of her chair. A flash outside caught her attention and she gasped. A helicopter swooped in over the terminal building and headed toward them. Whipping her glance to the cockpit, she could see it through the front windows. Nose down, it was headed straight toward them. She sucked in her breath. *It was heading straight for them*!

"We've got to abort!" the pilot screamed. "He's gonna hit us!"

"No he won't," Frank slammed back. "Go!"

"Are you crazy? He's coming right at us!"

"He'll back off."

"And if he doesn't?"

Frank leaned close to the pilot, his voice loud and clear over the engine noise. "If this plane doesn't get to Mexico, you don't get paid. You go to jail. Understand?"

The pilot was clearly having second thoughts, but he didn't voice another one. Instead, he pushed a center lever forward. Katharine's heart pounded so hard she thought it would burst from her chest. Frank was desperate. He was so desperate, he was going to get them all killed!

With a sudden calm she didn't completely feel, Katharine slowly slid the seat belt over her lap and pulled it snug across her hips. She mouthed a silent prayer and swallowed a painful lump in her throat, then braced for whatever came next. Through the cockpit window, she could see the helicopter continue its path without detour. Whoever was flying that aircraft had some kind of nerve. Nerves of steel, she mused. Unlike hers. Hers were a tattered mess.

As the plane sped forward, Katharine felt the nose lift from the ground. With her eyes glued to the helicopter visible through the cockpit windows, tears sprang to her eyes. The rapid fire of rotors thundered like chopping blades in her skull. She couldn't hear them, only the roar of jet engines that amplified the tension inside her aircraft. She squeezed her eyes shut.

Chapter Twenty-Four

A noise boomed. Frank shouted. The plane swerved and Katharine's body lurched against the wall. Her eyes popped open and she tried to comprehend what was happening. The helicopter had gone but they weren't slowing down. They weren't lifting into the air. She jerked her focus from window to cockpit. Between Frank's body and the pilot's head, she saw nothing but a wall of jagged mountain. An impregnable wall of mountain. Her breath caught. *Oh no*—they weren't up! They would crash if they didn't stop!

"What are you doing?" Frank shouted at the pilot. "We need to go up, dammit. Up!"

Katharine began to shake. Frank was a madman on the brink of sanity. A huge pop of color snapped her head back to her window. The helicopter was back. Angling toward them, it was circling back. Her heart jumped into her throat. It was trying to cut them off! Why would it do that?

Frank pounded his fist against a wall. "Get this plane off the ground—now!"

A grind of engines roared in her ears and her body shot forward. But the plane wasn't airborne. The pilot was trying hard to stop. He was trying, but it wasn't working. The mountains were coming at them too fast.

Regret plunged in her chest. She'd never see her father again. She'd never be able to tell him how much she loved him, how sorry she was for failing him. *Canyon*. She'd never see Canyon again. She barely knew him but felt connected in a way she'd never felt before. Katharine shot her glance out the window. The helicopter was gone. Because they weren't going anywhere.

It was over. The plane was barreling out of control.

Cody's image popped into her mind and her heart ached sharply. Her sweet, sweet boy... Tears flooded her eyes. Who would take care of him? Who was left? Adele. The answer was swift and certain. Adele would take Cody, no questions asked.

The wheels beneath her shuddered and the plane veered hard right. Up front, Frank was red-faced and screaming like a maniac. Outside, the runway fell away and Katharine instinctively folded her body forward.

The impact was sudden. She smacked her head onto the table then whiplashed back into the chair. A loud noise cracked and everything went quiet.

Shock rippled through her body. She couldn't move, couldn't think. Frank lay on the floor beside her. Blood oozed from his head. In the cockpit, the pilot's head swayed. Dazed, he was apparently conscious. Trembling, Katharine sat fixed in place. The aircraft had careened off the runway and planted its nose squarely in the ground. *They were alive*. Her gaze dropped to Frank. At least some of them were alive.

The helicopter swept down and landed at the edge of the runway. Then a truck swerved up beside the plane and jerked to a stop. A man jumped out and ran toward the aircraft. Her heart soared. Canyon!

Katharine tore at her seatbelt. Ripping the buckle open, she stood, adrenaline pumping through her limbs. Think. *Get out*. Canyon was here! Rushing for the door, she stepped over Frank and pulled at the handle. It didn't move. Panic lit into her. Throwing her entire body into it, she tried to force it open.

It didn't budge. It must be jammed. Fingers curled around her ankle and Katharine froze. Looking down, fear peppered her chest. Frank's grip became a steel clamp.

"Let go of me!" she screeched, pulling her foot from his grasp.

But Frank held fast.

Katharine's mind closed. No, no—this couldn't be happening—she had to get out of this plane! She turned back to the door and yanked at the handle again. Through the tiny window, Canyon appeared. Heart thudding her ribs, she called out to him. "Canyon! Help!" She pounded on the door. "Help!"

Canyon said something, but she couldn't hear his words, could only see his lips moving. But the concern in his eyes was unmistakable and nearly undid her. "Canyon!" she cried. "Yes! Yes, I'm here!" She beat at the door. "I can't get the door open!"

He surveyed the exterior then shouted again, but it was no use. She couldn't hear him. Frank's grip wound tighter around her ankle, his nails digging into her skin.

On the verge of panic, Katharine took a deep breath, calmed her thoughts, and took another look at the door. *You can do this.* She scanned the door for signs of blockage. Problems. Something was preventing it from opening.

Bingo. The lower corner had buckled inward. Assessing the damage, she determined the dent was minimal. Adjusting her angle of pull, she tried again, shifting her weight as she threw herself into it. The handle caught, then something popped and the latch released. "Yes!"

Katharine zapped a glance to Frank. Still in his clutches, she used her free foot and stomped his arm with the point of her heel. He screamed and released her. Escaping his grasp, she pushed the door open and out then tumbled into Canyon. His arms were around her in seconds. "Canyon!" she cried breathlessly.

Her toes barely touched the ground as he squeezed her tight. "You're okay. It's okay."

A thousand thoughts and feelings overcame her. Succumbing to the emotion, she buried her face into his chest. Nothing mattered. She was safe and in Canyon's arms. Soaking in his presence, she thought he smelled clean and woodsy. His body felt strong and warm with his arms secured around her body. Form-fitted against him, she could feel the mound of his chest muscles, the flat line of his stomach. As she lifted up to face him, his bandana brushed against her nose. Raw and masculine, it held the scent of *him*.

Inches separated them as she peered at him through fallen strands of hair. "I thought we were going to die...a helicopter was coming toward us and I thought we were going to crash and die."

Canyon's expression relaxed into a grin, though his embrace remained firm. "No worries. It was only my friend, Roan."

"Roan?" she uttered, her pulse fluttering in her breast.

"Best pilot in the Rockies. I called him in because I needed to make sure that plane of yours didn't take off."

She blinked. She knew the helicopter's presence must have been intentional, but it had been Canyon? How? When? Questions pummeled her brain. How did he know? "It was Frank," she said at once. "It was Frank the whole time!"

"I figured that out." Canyon frowned, his dark eyes deep and penetrating. "A little too late."

"What are you talking about? You're here!" She glanced at the truck, not entirely certain how he'd managed that feat but didn't care. Gazing into his eyes, she only cared that he was here. For her. "Frank's inside the plane. He's hurt, but alive."

Canyon scowled. "Too bad."

"No, Canyon, stop," she blurted, involuntarily rushing to Frank's defense. His admission had floored her, his plan, his feelings for her mother... There had been so much said and left unsaid that Katharine couldn't wrap her head around it. Not yet. Maybe not ever.

A good-looking brunette jogged up to them, his rhythm taut and measured, like that of an athlete. "Is everybody okay in there?"

Canyon looked to Katharine.

Brushing the hair from her eyes, she replied, "Yes. Injured, but alive."

"Wade's sending units our way," the man told Canyon.

Katharine continued to stare at the stranger. The man was lean and model-handsome. He could easily grace the side of any New York City building in an all-American ad campaign, sporting those aviator sunglasses and high and tight haircut. His red short-sleeved T-shirt revealed he was in incredible shape, as did his pair of hip-hugging jeans.

Canyon interrupted her thoughts, introducing him, "Katharine, meet Roan Phillips, my good friend and ace helicopter pilot."

She gaped at him. "You were the one flying straight into us?"

An embarrassed smile turned up the edges of his mouth. "Sorry if I scared you."

"You did that all right, but I'm grateful—you prevented us from taking off!"

He grinned. "That was the goal." Tossing a quick glance to her plane, he apologized, "I didn't intend for that to happen, either. The pilot should have stopped the second he saw me."

"He wanted to but Frank pressured him not to."

Roan shrugged then flipped a thumb toward the aircraft. "That's gonna cost a pretty penny to fix."

The sentiment reminded her of all the money Frank had stolen from the ranch, siphoning her thoughts from the accident back to the ranch and her troubles.

"Is Wade pretty steamed at me?" Canyon asked Roan.

"Nah. Once he got the call from the airport telling him they had a loose cannon on the runway, he knew instantly it was you."

Canyon laughed. "I tried to warn him!"

Roan smiled. "That's what he said."

"I didn't ruin your flight lesson, did I?"

"Nope. It was only Kelly."

"Kelly?" Canyon screwed his expression. "What can *you* teach her about helicopters?"

Roan drew back with a grimace, as if offended by Canyon's remark. "A whole heck of a lot. The girl can't hover on a dime for more than five seconds."

"Probably because she's used to flying at warp speed while shooting down the enemy like she's been trained to do."

Roan chopped out a laugh. "Child's play."

Katharine wondered who this Kelly was and why Roan seemed so defensive about her, though Canyon seemed to sense the underlying meaning right away.

He smiled and teased, "Seems someone is a little sensitive about his new trainee."

"I'm trying to teach her one of the most important maneuvers in search and rescue," Roan shot back, glancing at Wainwright's ditched jet plane. "If she can't hold the bird still, she can't make the team. End of story."

Lights flashed as an ambulance arrived on scene. Two paramedics jumped out and ran toward them. The older man asked, "Everyone okay?"

"No," she replied, "there are two men on the jet. A pilot and one of my staff. I'm okay, I think." Katharine felt a bit weak and unsteady, but it was nothing a little time and distance wouldn't cure. The more important question was what to do with Frank, the plane, the ranch—but those were none of this man's concern. They were hers.

"Those men on board need to be arrested," Canyon said.

Somewhat confused, the paramedic darted a hesitant glance toward his associate. "Uh, that's not our job."

"Wade has people on premises," Roan pitched in, then pulled out his cell phone and dialed. "He'll take care of the law enforcement angle."

Canyon nodded. "Yes, call Wade. I need to stay with Katharine."

While Roan called for help, Katharine was besieged by a paramedic. He inspected her head, her eyes, placed a hand to her wrist to check her pulse. She could feel an egg of a knot forming on her head, but it wasn't nearly as serious as

Frank's injuries. They should attend to him first she thought, watching the second paramedic climb the steps and board the plane.

Then they would have him arrested.

Sirens sounded the distant approach of police cars. Katharine looked up at Canyon. "This Wade fellow acts fast, doesn't he?"

Canyon didn't respond. Close at her side, he stood strong and solid, like a wall that would protect her from danger. She'd never thought about wanting a man like him around but at the moment it felt right. Really right. Watching him, she noted his expression had tensed.

"Canyon?" she asked. "What's wrong?"

Katharine followed his gaze over her shoulder and stilled. Frank had emerged from the jet, a line of blood streaming down his right temple and onto his cheek. In his hand, he held a gun aimed squarely at Canyon. "Frank!" she screeched. "What are you doing?"

Frank Dillard hovered on the top step. "I'm getting out of here, that's what."

Chapter Twenty-Five

"No, you're not," Canyon replied evenly, staring into Frank's vengeful gaze. Not on my watch, you're not.

Katharine stepped away from the paramedic at her side and exclaimed, "Don't be a fool, Frank. It's over—can't you see that?"

"The only fool I see is the one standing between me and freedom."

Canyon raised a hand to prevent Katharine from getting any closer then said in low and measured tones, "Listen to her, Frank. The police are on their way. You won't get out of here alive if you don't put down that gun."

Frank snickered. "You're the one who should be worried about getting out of here alive. In fact, I should shoot you right now."

Canyon's pulse ticked up. Frank was a wild card. There was no love lost between them. It wasn't a stretch to imagine he'd take a shot. Forget there were witnesses and Canyon was unarmed. Frank wasn't thinking straight. He was desperate. Dangerous. Someone could get hurt. Namely, Katharine. "Get a good lawyer and fight the charges," Canyon said. "The embezzlement charge will carry a far lesser penalty than murder."

Katharine gasped.

"Oh, you'd like that, wouldn't you?" Frank goaded with a sneer. "See me behind bars for murder while you waltz in and take over the board. You're nothing but a two-bit cowboy and I don't know how Eleanor missed that." His gaze darkened as he scowled, "Lucky for you, I don't have to kill you to get away. I only have to incapacitate you."

"It's a mistake, Frank." From the corner of his eye, Canyon registered Roan's expression. He was in. If Canyon wanted to take Frank down, Roan was with him. It was all he needed.

Canyon shoved Katharine into the paramedic and dove toward the plane, followed by Roan. A gunshot rang out.

"Canyon!" Katharine shrieked.

Frank stumbled backward and fired again. Canyon felt a crack of pain in his ears as he scaled the steps and threw his body on top of Frank's, halfway inside the plane.

"Get off me, you son of a—"

Canyon grabbed Frank's arm and slammed it against the metal doorway. The gun went flying.

Roan snatched it up from the ground then jumped several steps back, training the weapon on Frank.

Frank's eyes bulged with fury. His fists flailed and Canyon pinned them to the floor. Locking them together with one hand, he sank his free fist into Frank's jaw. With guttural pleasure, he muttered, "I've been wanting to do that for a very long time."

Frank's breath came in rapid bursts as he grunted.

A screech of tires signaled company. Canyon looked over his shoulder to see police burst from their vehicles and run toward him. Tightening his grip on Frank, Canyon slid down the stairway. His boot caught on the last step as he hauled Frank down with him, the two tumbled to the ground.

"Canyon!" Katharine exclaimed.

Leaping up, he yanked Frank up roughly and threw him toward the officers. Canyon would have loved nothing more than to drill another fist into him, but the terror piercing Katharine's gaze warned against it. "This is the one you want," he told them.

An officer stalked over and pulled a pair of handcuffs from his belt, hooking one onto Frank's wrist. Canyon stepped away and Katharine hurried toward him.

With a sketchy gaze, she skimmed his body. "Canyon, are you all right? Were you hit?"

"I'm fine." The knee he'd slammed against the edge of a step throbbed something fierce, but it was nothing compared to what could have happened. A bruise he could take. A bullet to the head he could not. Staring into frightened eyes, Canyon brushed the hair from her brow and returned softly, "I'm more worried about you. Are you okay?"

Canyon wanted to ask what she'd been thinking, going after Frank like she had, but realized in an instant she was a tough woman. Her core was made from the same stuff as Eleanor's and that woman didn't back down from anything or anyone.

Katharine nodded then bit her lower lip.

Canyon noted it was quivering and hugged her to him. "It's okay," he murmured into her hair. "Everything is going to be okay."

Shock could do that to a person. It could hide behind the adrenaline then wipe you out in the space of a second. Katharine had seemed pretty pulled-together a few moments ago but not any longer. Her narrow body was trembling against his, shaking like an aspen leaf. "It's okay," he hushed into her hair. Picking up the fragrance of perfume, he tried to ignore the feel of her in his arms, the soft strands of hair tickling his face, the connection he felt to her...

None of which was appropriate at the moment, but there was no denying it. She felt good. Really good. Warm and comfortable, Katharine was the kind of woman he could hold onto for a very long time.

Behind her, Roan handed the gun off to a third police officer, a guy Canyon knew well. He was one of Wade's newer hires, but experienced. Coming from Philly, he'd seen his share of action working the tough inner city neighborhoods. Struck by the thought, Canyon realized Philadelphia was probably a lot like New York—a bunch of buildings, crowded sidewalks, tough attitudes—and the city where Katharine came from.

It was a completely different world than Canyon had known.

As he released her, a strange mix of sadness and regret rushed through him. To think that Katharine would stay on at the ranch was a joke. She'd come here to fix a problem and once solved, she'd return to her life in New York where she belonged. Something inside Canyon tightened. At least Frank would no longer be part of the equation. The board would have to scout around for someone new, someone worthy of the position, and it wouldn't include Frank or any of his minions.

You're nothing but a two-bit cowboy and I don't know how Eleanor missed that.

Frank was wrong. Eleanor had believed in Canyon, enough to hand over operations of the cattle ranch to him. Maybe it wasn't a stretch to think he could take over the entire ranch. Someone had to. Katharine had suggested he take over. Could he?

When she rubbed the side of her forehead, Canyon's thoughts went to her. "Does it hurt?"

"No, not really."

When she didn't say any more, he realized it was time to move on. He couldn't continue to stand here and ponder new positions or old quarrels. He had work to do. After seeing to Katharine's injuries and Frank's arrest, he would head back to the ranch—where he belonged.

Parking his truck in the Silver Creek village public garage, Canyon opted to walk Katharine through town to her hotel, as opposed to dropping her with the hotel valet. After a grueling three hours with the paramedics, police and insurance people, Katharine was fading fast and he wanted to be there for her in case she needed something. Anything. All she had to do was ask.

She didn't. Katharine dealt with the madness at hand, leaving the rest to be handled tomorrow. She'd been professional, succinct and as stoic as they came. But like him, she must be feeling the turmoil of what came next. The fundraiser. It was the event where she was to convince donors to entrust their money with Wainwright Ranch despite the fact there was no actual Wainwright running the ranch. Despite the fact their manager had embezzled huge amounts of money right beneath their noses, and despite the bad press from scandal plus a missing child.

If Canyon thought it was going to be a difficult sell before today, he now figured it for a near impossible one. Like him, folks believed the ranch succeeded due to an abundance of passion and commitment, not dollars and cents. It succeeded because Eleanor had a vision and the wherewithal to see it through. Frank didn't have that. The board members didn't have it. Canyon had it, but convincing that stuffy board of Frank's to put him in charge might be a battle he couldn't win. Zeke Roberts would give him his vote, but Canyon wasn't as sure about the others. Thanks to Frank's treatment of him, they'd relegated him to bottom-of-the-barrel status.

But not Zeke. He was as grounded and sensible as they came. Unfortunately, one vote wouldn't win an election. Katharine could probably sway the board, except Canyon didn't make a habit of letting women fight his battles. Never had, and he didn't intend to start now.

Standing on the threshold of her hotel, Katharine peered into Canyon's eyes. Beneath the rim of his hat, he seemed distant, remote. The blood had been cleaned from his face, remnants from his encounter with Frank, though his pale blue shirt remained stained on the sleeve. He'd barely said two words to her on the drive home though he had to be feeling the same things she was—the shock of betrayal, the anger, the uncertainty going forward—yet he kept it in. He never let on how he was feeling or what was churning in that mind of his. Instead, only his quiet gaze revealed any signs of trouble. She wondered how heavy the day's events weighed on him. They felt like cement blocks tied to her shoulders. But in the wake of his silence, she had no way of knowing. "Thanks for the ride," she said simply.

"Don't give it another thought. I would have gotten Cody for you, too."

Katharine smiled, warmed by the offer. "Adele insisted. After she picked him up, she took him around town for a stroll to get his energy out so he could rest when I returned. The two had a grand time, from the sound of it."

Canyon smiled, the gesture small but genuine. "She's a sweet lady."

"She is," Katharine replied and tried to read Canyon's expression for clues as to what was going on inside him. There'd been no mistaking his affection at the airport. It had been etched clearly in his gaze, the strong wrap of his arms. Her well-being mattered to him and more than because she was Eleanor's daughter. Katharine would swear her life on it.

"We'll have to call an emergency board meeting for to-morrow."

Canyon nodded. "I'll contact the members. I'm sure everyone will understand."

It called to mind the first emergency board meeting she'd called, the one where Canyon couldn't be bothered to attend. Because he'd been at a rodeo. Winning money for the kids. Katharine cleared her throat of a sudden tautness. "Yes, maybe schedule it for the afternoon to give them all a chance to make arrangements to get here."

"Of course."

Staring into Canyon's dark eyes, she saw nothing but discouragement staring back at her. It pained her to think that he was giving up because it mirrored everything she felt deep in her heart. The ranch was finished. Once board members learned of Frank's deception, confidence would be lost, and Katharine knew from experience how difficult it was to re-build. Donors would disappear. The media would descend like vultures and the whole world would know that she had failed. Was there any point to even host a fundraiser? At this rate, what did it matter? Who would attend?

It might amount to nothing more than a complete waste of money, money the ranch didn't have.

Canyon placed a finger beneath her chin. "Don't give up, Katharine."

His touch sent tingles racing across her skin while the blunt statement pulled a strange smile from her. "Are you reading my thoughts, now?"

"I can see it in your face. You look defeated, same as I feel. But we can't give up. We can't lose the ranch."

Tears sprang to her eyes. But they were losing it. That's exactly what they were doing. They were losing. "Canyon..." she mouthed, more whisper than word.

He reached a hand to her cheek and with the pad of his finger brushed the tears from her eyes. It was a move so gentle—so natural—it made her crave for more. "You share your mother's spirit, Katharine. She wouldn't give up and neither will you."

Katharine's heart splintered. He was right. Her mother wouldn't have given up. She never gave up. Ever. How could she?

"We'll get through this," he said and dropped his hand, as though realizing he was taking liberties with her that their relationship didn't warrant. "It's what we do."

She focused on the word "we." She liked the sound of it. Katharine couldn't deny the attraction, and now, with the ranch in shambles, she wondered if she had to? If there was no ranch, there was no conflict of interest. At the same time, she didn't see how it could possibly work. Without the ranch, there was nothing for her in Colorado. Nothing but him.

Afraid Canyon would see her thoughts like a streaming movie in her gaze, Katharine turned away. "I need to get going. I need to check in on Cody."

Canyon nodded. "And get some rest. We have a big day tomorrow."

As he walked away, Katharine's gaze trailed his figure, the word "we" echoing in her heart. We. Him. It finally made complete sense what her mother had seen in Canyon Laredo. He was a special person indeed.

Chapter Twenty-Six

Katharine sat by the window of her hotel room, unable to feel the things she wanted to feel. Cody lay at her feet, snoring softly, rhythmically, but not nearly as calmly as usual. It was almost as if he sensed he'd come close to losing her today. Likely, he was picking up on her panicky energy. He understood she'd been upset, could feel it with an animal's instinct, and he wasn't leaving her side.

Casting her gaze out the window, Katharine exhaled a ragged sigh. *We'll get through this. It's what we do.* She wanted to believe Canyon. She wanted to believe that she could carry on and continue her mother's legacy despite the obstacles standing in her way, but the businesswoman in her knew the odds were against it. Once the scandal of Frank's embezzlement broke, donors would disappear, funds would dry up and the ranch would go bankrupt. Forget the story about a missing camper—there would be nothing left for the vultures to pick from after the financial scandal. Like a movie out of the Old West, one day you hit gold, the next day you went bust. Didn't matter that she and her father could make up the difference and fund the ranch going forward. Their reputation would be stained. Besides, it ran counter to everything her mother had wanted.

From the very beginning, she had insisted Wainwright Ranch must stand on its own two feet, and refused any and all family money. No handouts, no help from the Wainwright fortune. Her mother had wanted people who believed in her cause to carry the dream. It was a concept that had once made Katharine proud. Proud of her mother's independence, proud that she wanted to make this venture her own, outside of her husband's shadow. But recalling Frank's confession, Katharine's pride morphed into guilt.

Your father didn't give a damn about her dreams, but I did. Me, Katharine. Not even you, her beloved daughter, could see fit to join her out here. Only me.

Frank was right. As much as Katharine hated to admit it, neither she nor her father had worked to help build the dream. She'd been too busy pursuing an investment banking career, same as her father. He worked. She worked. It's what they did, it's who they were.

I know people talked. I heard the gossip, the whispers behind my back, but I never cared. I wanted to be with her more than I cared about what people said so I made it happen.

Katharine cringed. Was he inferring they had engaged in an extramarital affair?

The very thought of her mother in Frank's arms made her sick. Eleanor Wainwright had been above reproach. She'd been a picture of grace, a loving mother, a beautiful woman who had given of herself to those less fortunate, never asking for anything in return. Frank was dreaming if he thought she had any romantic feelings for him. She had viewed his assistance on the ranch as nothing more than the contributions from a friend. Whispers of shame echoed in the back of Katharine's heart. Because her husband and daughter had not—is that how her mother had felt?

No. Gossip aside, there wasn't an ounce of Katharine that could accept her mother entertaining those thoughts. She'd understood her husband was passionate about his career. She'd understood her daughter had dreams and goals of her own. At least that's what she'd always said. Had it been a lie? Had her mother only put forth a happy face to please them?

A knock sounded at her door.

Katharine's heart jumped but she remained seated, staring at the door. Suddenly, she felt alone, isolated, as though everyone knew her mother better than she. Over the years, the two had drifted, grown apart as distance settled between them. Though to be honest, Katharine had never felt an inkling of emotional separation. She'd only felt love from her mother. Deep and abiding love.

The knock came again, louder this time.

Abruptly, Katharine stood and walked over to the door. As she peered through the peephole, her heart leapt. She opened it, quickly engulfed in the arms of her friend. "*Adele*."

"Are you okay?" she asked, hugging Katharine hard. "I couldn't wait with Cody earlier but came the minute I could."

"I'm fine. A little shaken up by the events, but overall, I'm fine," she replied, soaking in the freshly-showered scent of her friend, layered with faint drifts of garlic and rosemary. Adele had been in the kitchen. She'd been at the restaurant but now she was here. And Katharine was grateful for her company.

"I'd be in shock." Adele pulled back, her eyes searching Katharine's as she exclaimed, "You could have been killed!"

"Lucky for me, Canyon was there. He took control of the situation, and now Frank is sitting behind bars where he belongs."

"That's what Hal told me," she said.

Walking into Katharine's hotel room, Cody appeared by Adele's side in seconds. He lapped up her attention, intermittently sniffing a white bag in her hand.

"I brought you some food. I figured the last thing on your mind would be to go grab a bite to eat, so I brought the eats to you."

Katharine eyed the bag, instantly famished. Fastening her gaze on her friend, she counted Adele as a major blessing in her life. "Thank you. Ever the food pusher, but for once I could really use it. I'm starving."

Moving farther into the hotel suite, Adele beamed. "I knew you would be."

Katharine smiled and the motion pulled a layer of tension from her body. "It's been a rough day."

"I guess. Frank?" Adele screwed her features in a disbelieving twist. "Who would have thought he was capable of such violence?"

Love does strange things to a person, Katharine wanted to say but didn't. She refused to lend any substance to his crazed claims of affection. Her mother loved her father. Period. Far be it from their daughter to allow anyone to smear the truth. "I guess people can change," she replied in a flood of breath, releasing streams of pent-up anger. "All I can hope is that we didn't learn the truth too late."

"You think this will affect the fundraising?"

"How can it not? Who will ever trust our judgment, now?" Katharine set the bag onto the granite counter of her in-suite kitchen and pulled out a container of salad. Beneath the clear plastic to-go lid, deep buttery green leaves were covered by an assortment of strawberries, chickpeas and avocado. The combination drew a rumble of hunger from her stomach. Drizzled with olive oil and balsamic glaze and sprinkled with goat cheese, the mix was one of her favorites. She also noted a small pouch of Adele's homemade granola tucked inside. That little gem would be saved for later.

Adele slid onto a leather barstool and stared at her pensively. "You can't take the blame for this, Katharine. It's not like it was your fault."

"I'm Captain of the Ship. If it goes down, I go down."

"Be serious. You have an entire board that should have taken note of Frank's betrayal far sooner than you. These people were privy to the inside operations. They were on scene, not halfway across the country. They should have detected a problem immediately and reported back to you."

"Frank was in charge. He ran the show, he controlled the numbers."

Adele blinked. Katharine sensed a retort hovering on her lips, but her friend said nothing.

Because she was smart. She understood it was Katharine's job to keep tabs on the ranch, a job she had failed to do because she was content to let Frank handle operations while she remained comfortably stashed away in her Fifth Avenue penthouse.

"It's my fault," she said then took a bite of salad. It *was* her fault they were in this predicament and it was her job to fix it.

You share your mother's spirit. She wouldn't give up and neither will you.

Once again, Canyon's words pulled deep longing from her. She wanted to be that woman, the one that rode in and saved the day, Colorado cowboy-style. It would be reminiscent of her mother's bold personality. And while part of Katharine believed anything was possible, an equal part of her believed otherwise. That was the problem. Taking another bite of salad, she savored the bursts of flavor erupting across her tongue and groaned inwardly. She swallowed, took another bite and focused on the taste. There was nothing better than clean, fresh food and nobody did it better than Adele.

"Well, I have good news for you," Adele said, watching Katharine eat. "You already have your first donations rolling in."

"What?" Katharine quickly covered her mouth, catching spits of food flying free. When she finished chewing, she blurted, "What do you mean, new donations?"

"The Fairchilds. Victoria Fairchild has pledged two hundred and fifty thousand dollars to your ranch and plans to make it official at the fundraiser this weekend."

Katharine nearly fell over. "Two hundred and fifty thousand?"

She nodded. "The minute she heard about what happened she told her daughter Kinsley, who told Lisa, who told her dad, who told me." Adele grinned. "How's that for 'news travels fast?'"

"I'd say..." Katharine murmured, momentarily stunned. Glancing around the luxurious appointments of her suite, the posh bedding and plush carpeting, the ornate window coverings and crystal barware, she acknowledged that Silver Creek had always been a playground for the rich, but two hundred and fifty thousand dollars, just like that? As she tried to wrap her mind around the news, she realized the residents of Silver

Creek rivaled even New Yorkers when it came to deep pockets and generous giving.

"Once word gets out that people are opening their wallets," Adele continued, "I think confidence in management
will be an easy assumption." She paused. "Have you thought
about who's going to take over for Frank?"

Any elation Katharine had felt over the Fairchild donation evaporated. "No." In fact, she had no idea. Canyon
seemed to think it should be someone from the family, but
that left only her and her father, neither of whom were in a
position to assume day-to-day operations. And while she was
ecstatic over the Fairchilds' donation, she wouldn't go as far
as to say people would be standing in line. "And I'm concerned. While it's a very generous donation, I don't know
how many others will follow suit."

"I think tons. But I do think they'll need to hear a strategy for moving forward."

Katharine frowned. "I've only made it so far as to call an
emergency board meeting. It's set for tomorrow afternoon."
She slumped against the counter adding, "I figured I'd toss a
few ideas to the group and see where it led. But strategy? At
this point, I don't have one."

Adele's black brow puckered. "Oh."

Yes, *oh*, a purely pathetic, one-syllable response that
said everything and nothing at the same time. Katharine had
nothing. Zilch. Zero. Like a weight dropped from the sky, she
was at a dead standstill.

"I'm sure it's not that bad," Adele said in a voice more
perky than was warranted. "What does Canyon think? He
always has great ideas."

Canyon. "He feels the family should be involved, specif-
ically that a Wainwright should be at the helm of Wainwright
Ranch."

"Do you think your father would take over temporarily,
until you could locate someone full-time?"

"No. He hasn't the time." Or the inclination, Katharine
added silently. His life is Wainwright, Emerson. End of story.

Especially with the investigation currently underway. She'd been lucky to enjoy his escort on the flight to Colorado. Asking him to stay focused on the ranch for any length of time would be like pulling a gamer from his video game and asking him to read a book. Wasn't gonna happen.

"What about you?" Adele ventured.

Katharine's heart thumped in her chest. "What about me?"

"Could you take over until someone else can be found?"

"I imagine," she replied, grateful that Adele couldn't see the heartbeats drumming loudly against her ribs. It was the obvious solution. Katharine should step in and assume management responsibility for the foreseeable future to reassure investors that all was well at Wainwright Ranch. It would prove difficult, but possible. It was the logical thing to do, only not what she wanted to do. Heaving a sigh, she said, "Yes, I could probably rearrange my schedule and stay on for an extended time, but I haven't any idea where I'd begin to look for a new manager."

"Maybe Canyon will do it."

"Canyon."

"Sure. He's got the experience, what with running the cattle end of things. It wouldn't be a stretch for him to take over general operations."

"Except that I already tried. He's not interested."

Adele blinked, her round brown eyes questioning. "Why not? It can't be that different from what he's doing now." She shifted in her seat. "Did he give a reason?"

"Other than he thinks family should be involved?" Katharine shook her head. And passion. He felt the individual running the show should be passionate about the cause.

"He needs convincing," Adele said, matter-of-factly. "Canyon is your guy."

Canyon. The name ricocheted in Katharine's skull. She'd thought about him a million times since the incident with Frank. Canyon worked with the cattle, he was hands-on

with the kids, the staff, and darn well knew almost every angle of Wainwright Ranch. Why not Canyon?

Because he wasn't a Wainwright? It was ridiculous. Adele was right. He was the obvious choice, only Katharine
didn't have time to convince him. She had business to attend
to in New York. She had a mess to clean up here. She had
obligations, obligations she couldn't abandon, obligations
that would take time. How much time, remained to be seen.
Fighting a tidal wave of stress, she knew that none of it would
be easy. Not replacing Frank, not convincing donors to hold
firm, not capping the media feeding-frenzy regarding Frank's
embezzlement. None of it. Katharine looked to Adele. How
much of her life could she devote to cleaning up this mess?

That was the billion-dollar question.

Chapter Twenty-Seven

From her vantage point at the head of the conference table, Katharine stared at her Board of Directors with a tinge of déjà vu. Seated around her were the same people with whom she'd met less than a week prior. Gary Levine, Chief Executive Officer for a hedge fund out of California, sat with a grim expression. Celia Glenn, the investment banker out of Denver, wore an identical shade of gloom, while Susan Billingsworth, the wealthy philanthropist from Texas, at least appeared hopeful. The grocer based in Boulder remained as calm and quiet as he had before. Next to him, Zeke Roberts conferred quietly with Canyon who sat beside him. There was no Frank today but instead Katharine had asked Paul Sutherland to sit in. The more options she could garner as they moved forward, the better.

Victoria Fairchild's donation of a quarter million dollars had certainly injected a needed dose of positive news, but it wasn't enough to cover one summer with over a hundred campers. Not at thirty-eight thousand per child, it didn't. They needed serious money—sustainable funding—not one-time donations from wealthy individuals who pitied their circumstance, though Katharine wasn't about to refuse a dime coming their way. She needed every single one and she needed them quick.

Clearing her voice, Katharine collected her thoughts and looked around the table, careful to make eye contact with each and every member as she opened the meeting. "It pains me to call you all in on short notice yet again, particularly when the news includes the embezzlement of Wainwright funds by our very own Frank Dillard, but the fact remains, if we intend to salvage Wainwright Ranch, time is of the essence."

It was the understatement of the year. With the fundraiser scheduled for Saturday night, the board had less than seventy-two hours to devise a plan capable of convincing donors to overlook mountains of bad press and stick with them. Canyon's gaze rested heavily on her as she spoke, which didn't help. It only pressed the burden deeper onto her shoulders. "I've asked Mr. Sutherland to apprise you all of our current status with regard to donations."

Paul responded on cue. Dressed in a navy suit with no tie, he straightened in his seat and lifted a piece of paper from the table before him. His brilliant blue eyes flashed a confidence she didn't feel as he read, "To date, we have commitments from Glazier Foods, Sunshine Films, Canyon Falls Foundation, Children United and Fogarty International, totaling two million, four hundred thousand dollars on a renewable basis. A few others have indicated their support but have sent nothing in writing so far."

"Do they know about our current troubles?" Celia asked, her dark gaze troubled.

Paul looked at her blankly, as if he didn't know which troubles she was referring to.

Because there were so many, Katharine thought glumly and responded to Celia, "The news of Frank's crimes has not yet been revealed publicly, however I have every confidence we can manage the crisis."

"More like earthquake," Gary pitched in. Glancing around the table, he was all business and matter-of-fact, underscored by his suit and tie attire. "After the missing boy, the media will have a field day with this story."

"You mean feeding-frenzy," Susan said, her usually upbeat expression souring. Even her brightly-colored cheeks couldn't camouflage her dismay.

"I think they'll stay strong," Paul rebuffed. "It's a write-off for them. So long as we remain a charity, I think they're good to go."

"Wainwright Ranch is more than a write-off," Canyon replied, the undercurrent of his displeasure loud and clear.

Dressed more casually than any of the other board members, in a chambray button-down and jeans, it was his red bandana that shouted cowboy—ranch hand—not serious businessman. But other than herself, he was more vested in the charity than anyone. "Companies and individuals donate their hard-earned money because they care about what we do. If they lose confidence in our ability to deliver, they won't deliver the money."

Katharine understood it was an insult to Paul, even if Paul didn't. Canyon was in it to win it. He believed in the cause. He lived and breathed it and had no use for anyone less committed than him.

"I agree with Canyon." Zeke spoke up, his attire only two degrees more formal than Canyon's with shiny pearlized buttons emblazoning the front of his cowboy shirt. "We need to prove we can stand on our own two feet or else nobody will give us a second glance."

The grocer remained silent, though Katharine could tell he was clearly dialed in to the conversation. Unfortunately, his broody expression summed up his thoughts without question.

"I second that notion," Katharine said. "Wainwright Ranch is not a tax-shelter. It's a place of hope, inspiration. We make a difference in kids' lives. If we can't continue to do the great work we do, then we close up shop. It's that simple." She paused, and skimming the faces around the room, assessed who was with her and who wasn't. Lucky for her, most seemed on board with any plan she put forth. Releasing a controlled breath, Katharine continued, "We're here today to make that decision. One way or another, it's the board's responsibility to determine the future of Wainwright Ranch."

A few board members looked at her queerly, as though they had nothing to do with the ranch's fate. She was a Wainwright. It was her call. They were ancillary to the cause.

A tide Canyon seemed to pick up on. "I think the primary question becomes who takes over for Frank," he said. "If we can replace him with an individual the donor community will trust, I believe the rest will fall into place."

Katharine didn't like the way he was staring at her. Or Zeke, for that matter.

"He's right," Gary said.

"Yes, you need to replace Frank at once," Susan agreed, and tapped a bejeweled finger on the table. "Without a solid manager in place, no one will want to give their money to the ranch, and you know how badly I'd hate to see you close its doors."

"Do you have someone in mind, Katharine?" Celia asked, her gaze pointed.

Katharine looked to her, then the others and wondered why it was solely her job to recruit a replacement and not a group effort. Did no one have any ideas?

"What about you?" Zeke proposed.

A pregnant pause consumed the group. Each glanced in her direction, but no one maintained eye contact. Instead, they drifted from one another as though rallying support for the suggestion.

"I can carry on temporarily," Katharine said, pushing back against the spears shooting from Canyon's gaze. Her ears flushed hot. Her heart pounded. She knew how he felt. She knew he wanted her to take over. "But with my obligations in New York, I'm unable to take over full-time." Her gaze darted about the room before landing on Canyon once again. It was hard not to. The man was making her feel like a pig stuck on a spit over the fire. Had Canyon been lobbying the board to support *his* cause?

"Seems like a no-brainer to me," Celia replied. "You're a Wainwright. With you as head of operations, donors should feel more than comfortable."

Except for the fact that she had a career waiting for her back in New York City! Or did Celia miss that part? Suppressing a swell of frustration, Katharine kicked back quickly, "While I'm flattered by your support, I don't believe I'm the right person for the job. It should be someone intimately familiar with operations, someone who knows this ranch and what it needs. Someone like Canyon."

All eyes turned to him.

Canyon visibly worked to conceal a smile—no, make that smirk, she mused—and returned slowly, "I appreciate your confidence, Ms. Wainwright, but I don't know how well the donors will take to accepting a ranch-hand as Wainwright's new CO."

Zeke objected and turned to him. "On the contrary, I think you'd be the perfect fit."

Several others wore their hesitation on their sleeves, giving Katharine pause. What's not to like about Canyon taking over? He understood the ranch, the kids, her mother's vision... If you asked her, he was the ideal candidate for the job. Why the reluctance?

But Katharine knew the answer even though no one voiced it aloud. In their eyes, Canyon was staff. Not management, but general ranch staff. Forget that her mother had entrusted him with cattle operations, that he had increased revenue by managing the herd more efficiently, and in fact, was scheduled to overcome a deficit he'd inherited with some respectable profits projected over the next five years, Canyon didn't look like management material.

As though reading her mind, Canyon returned a disheartened smile. He hadn't expected anything different. Why had she?

Katharine squelched a litany of responses. These board members had no idea the value of the man sitting in their midst. Even his henhouse was proving to be a smart return on investment! Canyon was an asset to the ranch. He could easily take over if handed the reins. Why couldn't the board see him for the man he was?

Her heart suddenly fell. Same reason she hadn't, initially. Canyon Laredo was cowboy on the outside, thoroughbred on the inside. Most people didn't look past the façade. They took him on appearance then continued on their merry way.

"Well," Gary put in, pulling her from her thoughts, "even if you don't take over for the long haul, you do intend to remain and assume management until a replacement for Frank can be found, don't you?"

Katharine looked to Gary and nodded. "Of course." There was really no choice in the matter. She would stay on until she could come up with a long-term plan. Whipping up some magic for the fundraiser would be her first task. "Until then, job one is money." She looked around the table. "Does anyone have any suggestions for new donors? Or reenlisting the old?"

"I'll make some phone calls," Susan offered.

"I'll call around, too," Celia chimed in.

Gary and the silent grocer seemed uninterested. Perhaps they felt the epitaph was already etched on the gravestone.

"I've got a few chits I can call in," Zeke chimed in.

Katharine paused. "Thank you." She made eye contact with each and every board member. "Let's reconvene by conference call prior to the fundraiser."

Canyon waited outside the conference room while the board members escorted themselves out. There was no fanfare, no enthusiasm, no "we can beat this" fight song. They were about as pumped as flat tires, men and women whose lives didn't depend on the success or failure of Wainwright Ranch. They probably considered it a favor to Katharine that they were even involved. Board Member was a title, not a passion. It was ink on a résumé.

"Chin up, Katharine. The gates haven't closed, yet."

She turned to Canyon, her spirits mired in a pile of muck. "Might as well. You heard them. We've got nothing."

"Correction: they've got nothing. We've got you and me." He winked. "I don't know about you, but I'm not giving up until my body is covered by six feet of dirt."

Katharine raised a brow. "Careful. I could have mistaken a few members back there for buzzards circling overhead."

Canyon laughed. "Let them. If a one-ton bull can't throw me, those stodgy old fools haven't got a chance."

Katharine stilled and held him in her gaze. From his sheer size to the gleam in his brown eyes, Canyon oozed strength and confidence. He was a man used to winning, a man comfortable in his ability, and he wasn't about to let anyone push him around or change his mind. The red bandana around his neck almost felt like a fighting flag. "You're really indomitable, aren't you?"

Canyon grinned. "When I set my mind to do something, it usually gets done."

Heaving a ragged sigh, she found his optimism hard to resist. "Wish I could say the same. I used to think I could conquer any obstacle, but now... I'm not so sure."

"I don't believe you for a second. Your problem is that you're allowing their negativity to get into your head."

"Am I?"

"I think so. I think we can fix the ranch's problems. The only question remaining in my brain is the identity and motives of the man who Paul was talking to out in the parking lot."

Katharine shook her head. "No questions there. He was here because of the investigation into my father. I received a phone call this morning. Seems they think there's more to my father's misdeeds than a superior edge in technology."

"Seriously?"

"Seriously."

"What kind of problem we talking here?"

"They think Frank's embezzlement is somehow tied to Emerson, Wainwright. He was a past employee and worked closely with my father."

"They think the two were in cahoots?"

Katharine smiled. "Something like that."

"Well, you set him straight, didn't you?"

"I did. But it doesn't fix our problem with the board members. Those people are worthless when it comes to brainstorming and problem-solving. How am I going to save the ranch on my own? Do they think I carry some kind of magic wand in my purse?"

Canyon stared at her. When he didn't say anything, she grew uncomfortable.

"You know what you need?" he asked then answered for her. "A change in scenery. A change in perspective."

She peered up at him and knit her brow. "Sounds lovely, but I don't think I'm going to get one of those between now and the fundraiser."

Bothered by the despair in her voice, Canyon paused, and an idea formed in his head. "How about you join me and the kids for our camping trip this evening?"

"What?"

"A group of older kids is heading up the mountain for an overnight stay and I'm scheduled to attend as a chaperone. Why don't you tag along? You said you enjoyed being on the mountain. How about enjoying it without the stress of searching for a missing child?"

"Oh, I don't think so, Canyon." She pushed hair from her face and evaded his direct gaze. "There's too much to do before the fundraiser."

"Like what?"

She paused, turned, and blinked. "I don't know if I can manage it right now. I have phone calls to make, donors to contact. I'm sure the police would like me to be on hand for any questions they might have regarding Frank and our bank funds."

"Nothing a cell phone can't manage."

"True, but donors need to be reassured we're still viable and worthy of their contributions. I have a list of people to call longer than my arm!"

"Isn't that what you pay Paul for?"

"Yes, but I also have to decide what to do about Kyle."

"It's already been done."

"Don't you think he should be sent home? I mean, after everything he put us through with the mountain search, he turns around and steals a chicken?"

"He paid the consequences."

"By cleaning the bathroom?"

Canyon shifted his weight from heel to heel as he stared into her questioning gaze. He hadn't wanted to tell her about the incident, not after everything she had gone through with Frank. It felt like he was piling on bad news after bad. Besides, he dealt with the situation—his way—and was confident there would be no more funny business from Kyle. Fact of the matter, the hen theft should have never occurred. Kyle should have been sent home after his stunt on the mountain, but once Katharine took those consequences off the table, all bets were off.

"It's a little too late for that now," Canyon said. "Calling his parents to send him home would be anti-climactic, if you ask me. I've got Kyle handled and I guarantee he won't be giving us any more trouble. Now, about that camping trip."

Katharine hesitated, as if realizing Canyon had backed her into a corner by eliminating her excuses. If she declined now, both knew it would be for purely personal reasons. Would she join him? It was an answer he suddenly wanted to know.

"Don't you think the kids will mind if you drag me along?" she asked him. "I mean, I'm sure they're used to a certain routine when they go camping. Wouldn't I be interfering if I suddenly popped into the picture?"

"Number one, it's your ranch and you get to make the call. I can't tell you how many trips your mother joined us on and the kids loved it. Second, there's nothing routine about camping, other than keeping tabs on your assigned buddy and reporting to staff on a regular basis. Everything else is at the whim of nature." When her features softened and he could tell she was leaning toward accepting his invitation, he pushed harder, "I promise you'll have a good time. Scout's honor," he said, and held up his closed fingers.

Katharine laughed. "With an oath like that, how can I refuse?"

Pleasure swarmed his insides. The thought of spending more time with her was like a light to his soul. "You can't. Trip takes off at four o'clock this afternoon. Let's say you come by around three-thirty and I'll make sure you have all the gear you need."

"Sounds perfect. That gives me enough time to collect some things and arrange for my absence."

"And bring Cody. Buck would love the company."

"Good, because I have no option *but* to take him along!"

Chapter Twenty-Eight

Shortly after four-thirty, the group of campers began their hike up the trail. Canyon pulled up the rear, accompanied by Katharine, allowing Buck and Cody to dart in and around the campers while Shannon Williams, an athletic brunette staffer, took the lead. A camp counselor for teenage girls, Shannon was a graduate student out of Boulder, majoring in planetary sciences and astrophysics. Toting a telescope that could see stars millions of miles away, she proved extremely popular on overnight camping trips. Inviting campers to peer through her powerful lens, she opened the star-studded skies of Colorado in ways these kids had never seen before. Talk about opening minds to the possibilities of life— Shannon was a master.

As expected, no one minded the "extra" camper. Instead, a few of the boys took a keen interest in Katharine, constantly stealing peeks her way. Canyon couldn't blame them. They were normal teenage boys with normal hormones and Katharine Wainwright was as pretty as they came. In great physical shape, she filled out her jeans with modest curves while her abdomen was flat beneath her light blue cotton pullover. Her hair was pulled back into a French braid but a few wisps fell free around her face. On her back she sported a small black backpack, and on her feet, her mother's hiking boots. But it was the white bandana around her neck that intrigued him most. Did she wear that with him in mind?

Canyon's signature bandana was often a point of discussion among the campers.

"Why do you always wear that bandana, Canyon?"
"What's it for?"
"Do you ever wash it?"

Canyon would laugh and reply, same as he always did, "It's part of my wardrobe. I couldn't leave home without it, same as you couldn't leave home without your pants."

From there, laughter would ensue and the question would be settled. Truth be told, Canyon had a dozen identical red bandanas and used them for all sorts of things, like wiping the sweat from his brow after riding a bull, keeping his neck warm in winter, or bandaging a wound when hiking alone. It was the main reason he wore the scarf around his neck. A few years ago, when he and his dog—the animal he'd owned before Buck—had been hiking, a sharp-ended stick had gouged a hefty gash in the animal's ear. The wound bled profusely. If it hadn't been for Canyon's bandana, the dog could have developed who knew what kind of an infection from the mountainous dirt and debris. For Canyon, it had been lesson learned. Ever since, he made it his strict practice to wear a bandana.

Trekking up behind Katharine, Canyon had to hand it to her. She looked right at home on this mountain, something he would have never guessed that first day he met her. Sporting a pair of jeans that seemed custom-fit for her body, she darn well looked perfect. Tamping back a swell of desire, he inhaled deeply and soaked in the fresh mountain air. From what he'd seen, the woman looked perfect in anything she wore. "It's beautiful up here, isn't it?"

Late afternoon sunlight cast sheets of gold through the trees, enhancing the occasional yellowing aspen leaves while cutting deep shadows in the evergreen. The air was crisp, rich with the scent of pine, and quiet save for the soft rhythmic movement of hikers.

"It is. I can see how you never tire of it."

"It never fails to set my head straight and get my thoughts back on target."

"Yes. And you're right about it being different circumstances. I didn't recall the number of creeks running in and over the trail. Is this the same way we hiked before?"

"The exact same." He chuckled. "But with each hike, your brain's in a different place. You see things differently, depending on your mindset."

"I wouldn't have believed it, but you're right. I don't remember all these carvings in the tree trunks, either. Is that legal?"

"Nope." He glanced around, disgusted by the black scars in the white-speckled tree trunks. "Not if the authorities catch you. If you're caught carving a trunk on public land, it's considered defacing government property. Doesn't seem to deter anyone, though."

"It reminds me of the graffiti in New York City. If there's a wall, someone is likely to spray paint it. It's against the law there, too."

"Vandalism is vandalism, I guess. Can't get away from people out to do the wrong thing, no matter where you live."

"Depressing thought, isn't it? Some people seem wired for misbehavior."

Canyon wondered if Katharine meant Frank, though his actions were a stretch deeper than misbehavior. What Frank did to Katharine and her family—the entire ranch—was downright criminal on so many levels. He had betrayed the trust of longstanding friendships, stolen money that was earmarked to help needy children, and seemed prepared to take a life. Incredible.

"Yes," Canyon said, "but there's a lot of good in this world, too." He eyed her rear. *And I'm looking at it.*

Katharine chucked a quick glance over her shoulder as though catching him in the act.

At her suppressed grin, he asked, "Something funny?"

"No."

He cocked a brow. "I don't believe you."

"I was just thinking that you, you're one of the good guys."

Warmth flushed his cheeks. *Not if she could read his mind, he wasn't.* "I don't know if I'd go that far, but I do try and give every situation my best." Something he'd like to show her, in more ways than one. "Doesn't mean I don't make mistakes, though."

"We all make mistakes, Canyon."

"Impossible," he hurled back. "What mistakes have you ever made?"

"I misjudged you, for one."

The revelation cut his pleasure to the quick. "What do you mean?"

"When we first met," she said, reaching for a branch to assist her climb through a narrow passage, "I pegged you for a selfish rodeo cowboy who cared little about his role at the ranch and I was wrong. Dead wrong."

Mixed emotions swirled through his gut. Is that the impression he gave to people who didn't know him? Or was it his absence from her board meeting that ticked her off?

More likely the second, he decided. Canyon Laredo was a lot of things, but uncaring about his role at Wainwright Ranch was not one of them. It was a sentiment he thought he'd made clear from day one. Apparently, he had not. But at least she seemed to understand him now. Or did she?

"You're clearly invested in the ranch."

Canyon liked what he was hearing, but in reality, they hardly knew each other. Katharine couldn't know him any more than he knew her. And he didn't. Not really. He could assign some of Eleanor's traits to her daughter, but Katharine lived in a world far removed from Colorado. She worked with financial reports, not children. She dealt in numbers, not hearts and souls. She was a businesswoman, not a rancher. And despite the fact that Eleanor Wainwright had once lived in New York City, she seemed more suited to the open ranch lands of the West than any city boulevard.

"Hey, Canyon—can I be in charge of building the fire?"

"You bet," he returned, switching his focus to the dark-haired boy, two campers ahead of him. He was the oldest teenager in the group and familiar with the process. "Right after we set up camp. And why don't you show Ritchie how to use the magnesium stick."

The boy grinned. "Sure thing!"

"Thanks, Canyon!" Ritchie hollered back to him.

Canyon smiled and gestured a thumbs up. Kids teaching kids. It was one of the basic tenets set up by Eleanor. She felt it bred teamwork among campers and instilled a sense of pride in those helping others. Staff counselors should step back whenever possible and encourage the kids to take as active a role as possible.

When the trail opened up to their established campsite, the kids immediately broke into groups, each getting straight to business. Buck and Cody dashed from tree to rock to random spot, picking up scents and whizzing accordingly. As a matter of protocol, the kids would set up tents first, then roam about and search for firewood. Once a fire had been established, there would be time for exploration, followed by mealtime, and later the group would do a little stargazing.

"Okay, girls! Let's show the boys how it's done!" Shannon shouted, and gently set her backpack near a stone. A perfect fit for these kids, she not only offered them peeks into the universe, but she entertained them with stories and history about the stars and planets. She was a natural teacher and her enthusiasm rippled like waves of excitement through their young minds, proving the ultimate distraction from what ailed them. When they learned the enormity of the universe around them, it made them feel more powerful, their illness a degree more manageable.

"You heard the woman," Canyon called out. "Chop-chop, guys! We can't let the girls shame us!"

"We're gonna sink you guys!" one of the girls taunted as she ripped open her pack. A blonde next to her laughed and tugged a tent from her bag.

Canyon chuckled and dropped his heavy pack to the ground. "Nothing like a little friendly competition to get the blood going."

Katharine watched the hive of activity and agreed. "Works like a charm, doesn't it?" Glancing about the area, she said, "Now that we're here, I do remember this area and the view. It is some kind of beautiful."

Sure is, he agreed privately. With her cheeks flushed from the hike, her eyes bright and alert, Katharine Wainwright was a thing of beauty. "The kids are busy getting set up. You and I should probably do the same. Shannon will take care of your tent, but I need to set mine up."

"I can help her."

"She won't need it. How about you catch your breath and get settled in before we take our evening hike?"

"I'm not helpless, Canyon." She glanced at a trio of teenage girls and needled him with a stern gaze. "No special treatment, remember?"

He grinned. "I do." Though at this point, her offer to help might only hinder Shannon. The gal was spot-on when it came to popping tents into place. "Why don't you ask her what you can do?"

"Fine."

Pulling the front of his hat forward, Canyon squared it on his head. "Meet you at the campfire in thirty?"

Katharine smiled, a gesture that made his insides go fluid. "Sounds like a plan." Turning, she called out, "Cody!"

The dog had taken off across the grounds, his nose picking up the scent of something near the line of trees.

"Don't worry," Canyon told her. "He won't go far. Buck's right there with him and he knows to stay near."

She slid him a wary gaze. "I hope you're right. I'd hate to lose him on the mountain. He has no idea where he is."

"He'll be fine."

Watching Canyon walk over to a patch of dirt near a group of boys, Katharine followed orders and headed for Shannon, mindful to keep watch on Cody. Canyon might think the dog would be fine, but she wasn't as convinced.

"Hi, Ms. Wainwright," Shannon said, and opened the top flap of her oversized backpack. "Did you enjoy the hike up?"

"I did, but please call me Katharine. Ms. Wainwright sounds so official."

Shannon beamed. "Will do."

"Thank you again for putting up with me imposing on your space."

"You're not imposing at all. Normally, I'd bunk with one of the girls, but under the circumstances, I think they're pretty content on squeezing three into a tent."

Katharine followed her gaze. Three girls were huddled together. Two were mid-motion pulling a tent together while the third yanked a cell phone from her pocket. She peered at the screen then held it for the others to see. To look at them, Katharine would never suspect they were battling health issues, but she knew for a fact that the tallest one was in remission from Hodgkin's, the middle was coping with the lingering effects of radiation from a bout with leukemia, and the smallest wasn't sick at all, rather struggling with her mother's terminal illness. Canyon had brought Katharine up to speed on the details of each camper on the trip, and each was heartbreaking, though the hardest for her to handle was a teenage boy battling a brain tumor. Her eyes went to the dark-haired boy. The man in charge of his tent crew, his surgery and chemotherapy had delivered positive results, but according to Canyon, the boy's body hadn't fully recovered from the treatment. He was slender and frail, his hair thin and his skin tone looked as if it hadn't seen the sun in years. It was amazing he had made the hike at all, but the teen was all smiles, his spirit shining through. Only his body seemed to reveal the toll the illness had taken.

"They do look happy, don't they?" she observed wistfully. "If I didn't know better, I'd swear they were sharing texts from a boyfriend."

"They are."

Katharine gaped at Shannon. "You're kidding me."

"Nope." She pulled the zipper on her backpack open and said, "Lydia is dating a boy she met during her stay at the hospital."

"Lydia's the one with Hodgkin's, right?"

"Yep. She feels like she's beat the disease and it's never coming back."

Katharine idled on the lanky teenager. "A boy will do that to a girl..."

"That, and this ranch," Shannon replied unequivocally. Lydia's been here for five weeks and I've seen her open up more and more over the course of her session. She's really come out of her shell. Learning to ride a horse like a pro, too!"

She looked like a rider with her long brown hair, her imperial nose and jawline, her distinct brow. Katharine thought she was gorgeous. Could probably model, if she chose to. A blip of pleasure skirted through her. And Lydia had a boyfriend. "That's wonderful to hear. She deserves it."

"They all do," Shannon said.

"Yes, they all do," Katharine murmured, her gaze drawn back to the boy battling cancer. If only they could all walk away from the ranch with a guaranteed survival rate. But they couldn't. Didn't. Her mother used to receive letters from the parents of those who didn't make it. Yet rather than expressions of grief, the letters were testaments of joy and gratitude. Katharine recalled how every single one had brought her to tears, but not her mother. She seemed to gain pride from reading them, explaining that life was about living. Not dying, not grieving, but living. There were no guarantees, no easy rides. Life was a gift and only as good as you made it.

Katharine thought some of the parents and children might disagree, but she couldn't begrudge her mother the sentiment. She'd lived the same nightmare and had chosen to make the best of what she had by giving back to those she could. Frank's image popped into Katharine's brain and she quickly erased it from her mind. He had no place here. This was her mother's domain, her mother's gift to the world, not his.

"If you want to grab this pole," Shannon said, "we'll get this tent set up in no time."

"Of course." Reaching for it, Katharine focused on the task at hand. She'd never constructed a tent before and instantly wondered how hard could it be? Glancing at the girls, she thought, if they can do it, she could do it. The girls had theirs halfway up, though how they'd managed the feat, Katharine wasn't sure. Between the cell phone and bouts of giggles, it was a wonder they could concentrate!

"Slip the pole through this loop," Shannon instructed, "then hold your end while I stake mine in the ground."

Katharine did as she was told and within no time, the tent was upright and ready for occupants. A perfect half-moon polyester construct. Or was it a more sophisticated material? Advances in snow skiing technology boggled the mind. She imagined the same held true for camping.

"You can toss your pack inside," Shannon told her. "It'll be safe in there while we're out hiking."

"Yes, I will. Thank you."

"Girls!" Shannon called out. "The boys are finished!"

All three whipped their heads toward the boys and squealed, "Hurry! Hurry!"

The boys leapt up, hooting wildly. "We beat you!"

Lydia screeched, but held fast to her cell phone, a sight that made Katharine laugh. The distraction of romance won every time. Canyon approached and she swatted a flurry of nerves. Speaking of romance...

"That wasn't too hard, was it?"

"Piece of cake," she replied coolly, noting his long-legged swagger with more than an ounce of delight.

"Sorry. No cake on this trip."

"No problem." Canyon was eye candy enough.

"Though you will have plenty of beans and stew to consume."

Katharine frowned. "Beans and stew? Is that what's for dinner?"

"Two of our most favored staples. Plus we have a side of corn and bread."

"Do you ever serve the children healthy meals?"

"What's not healthy about stew and beans? Plenty of meat and vegetables, a few beans to keep your insides moving." He wriggled his brow. "What's not to like?"

"Canyon."

He held up his hands and shot her a remorseful look. "Sorry, but some of the kids really get a kick out of it."

"I'm sure they do. But I'm serious," she replied, lowering her voice as she glanced toward the kids. "Why don't we serve more health-conscious meals at the ranch?"

"I'll bet you're a vegan, same as Adele."

Katharine pushed her shoulders back and stated proudly, "I am."

Unaffected, Canyon informed her, "Well, your mother was a meat and potatoes kind of gal and she created and approved of the menu."

"I'm surprised. She never served me that kind of food growing up."

"Eleanor cooked?"

"No, but she directed my nanny to prepare healthy meals."

Canyon laughed. "She must have mellowed in her old age, because out here it's nothing but the good stuff."

"Eating vegan *is* eating the good stuff."

With a tip of his hat, he said, "Sorry, but if someone told me I'd never see another plate of steak and eggs, I'd just as soon starve."

Katharine crossed her arms over her chest. "You're being melodramatic, don't you think?"

"Not me." He patted his stomach and asked, "Can you imagine this frame surviving on sticks and leaves?"

"I don't eat sticks and leaves." She angled her head and crossed her arms over her chest. "Have you been to Adele's? The food is amazing."

"Can't argue with you there. But Adele does have trout on the menu." He winked. "One of my all-time favorites."

Katharine rolled her eyes with exaggerated effect. "Well, if you ask me, I think these kids would enjoy a taste of healthy food. You'd be surprised how many young people are going vegan these days."

"Maybe. Doesn't change my appetite." At her pause he said, "How about we get to stoking some flames."

She started. "Excuse me?"

Canyon grinned. "It's time to build the fire, though I like the way you think."

Katharine's pulse quickened. There was no mistaking the twinkle of mischief in Canyon's gaze.

"Shall we?" he asked.

She stared at him, her mind stuck in his not so subtle innuendo and her more than obvious reaction.

Canyon held out a hand. "Fire ring is that way."

Katharine snapped out of her foolishness. "Yes, of course."

Chapter Twenty-Nine

After dinner and campfire songs, the campers gathered together on the point. It was a clearing that offered the least obstructed view of the sky, bordered on one side by forest on the other by nothing but sky. Scouting the area last year, Shannon had discovered it and used it as center stage for her telescope. Once the tripod was positioned, the telescope mounted and secured, she motioned for the kids to take turns. The reactions were always the same, followed by rapid-fire comments.

"There are so many stars!"

"That looks more like floating gas than a star."

"How do you know it happened millions of years ago?"

Canyon loved listening to the kids working to wrap their minds around the information. He could identify with their awe. It didn't seem possible that a telescope could capture images so far away—millions of years away—but the technology was here and Shannon had access to it. She even posted pictures to the university's website but it was nothing like seeing it from a mountaintop.

Sitting on the ground with one leg extended, Canyon perched an arm over a knee and dropped his head back to gaze at the fabric of stars. Without a blanket of cloud insulation, the air was unusually cold but made for amazing viewing. Stretched across the sky, the stars littered the black night like a canvas of white specks with the occasional streak from a shooting meteor. During certain times of year, the meteoroid showers were continuous and made for an amazing show. He'd love to share it with Katharine but began to doubt her interest. He'd managed to steal her away from the group for a bit of privacy, but noted she hadn't said a word since they sat down. Was she uncomfortable?

She didn't look it. Instead, she sat cross-legged and appeared to be taking it all in, quietly spellbound by the sheer magnitude of what she was seeing. "Penny for your thoughts?" he asked, trying not to stare at her profile, or dwell on her mouth. But it was hard not to. From the first day he'd met her, he'd been drawn to those soft lips of hers. Sitting on the ground next to her in the dark, their dogs peacefully resting by their sides, the urge to kiss her burned stronger than ever.

"I'm speechless."

"What did I tell you? It's a sight like no other, isn't it?"

"It's mind-blowing. The minute I try and consider the amount of stars I'm looking at, my mind moves to the stars I saw through Shannon's telescope. It's incredible. Truly unbelievable." Katharine turned to face him and through the darkness he could feel the intensity of her gaze. "I mean, it's not like her telescope is huge and mounted on the top of an observatory. She carried it up the mountain in her backpack!"

Canyon laughed softly. "I know. I remember the first time I looked through it. I couldn't believe my eyes. Some of what I saw looked more like gas floating through the air than a star. Then she starts telling me how what I'm seeing is millions of light years away, and my mind explodes. It just stops computing the information, you know what I mean?"

Katharine smiled. "Definitely not your average telescope."

"No, that's for sure. She has a camera she can attach to it and takes pictures. You should see her blog. It's incredible."

"I'll check it out, and you're right. It's the same way I felt when I looked through it tonight. When you realize you're nothing but a blip in the universe, it really makes you reassess your significance."

"We're small creatures in an endless sea of galaxies."

"Well said."

"Puts those troubles with the ranch in perspective, doesn't it?"

Katharine hesitated then nodded, returning her gaze upward. A sadness slackened her expression and Canyon almost wished he hadn't brought up the ranch. He'd been enjoying her company, her easy nature with the kids and an openness he hadn't much seen since she'd arrived.

It was a part of her he wasn't ready to let go. "We'll get through this, Katharine. We've been bucked off, but we're not out of the corral."

She smiled, this time a shade brighter. "I like the way you think, Canyon."

"But do you believe me? That's the question."

Katharine sighed, wracked by a slight shiver. "I do."

"Are you cold? Do you want a blanket?"

She shook her head.

"Sure?"

"I am. And I do believe you. One way or another, we'll get through it. I've never backed down from a challenge. I know it might not seem that way to you, considering I've been less than positive regarding our outlook, but saving Wainwright Ranch means more to me than saving any deal I've ever worked on, or impressing a client. And I'm not a quitter. It's just this situation carries a burden heavier than I expected."

"Nothing you can't handle."

At that, she turned to him abruptly. "Canyon, you don't know the first thing about me. I appreciate your kind words, but seriously, you don't. It's nothing but fluff and fantasy when you say those things, not hard-core truth based in fact."

Not sure whether this was push-back or blunt honesty, he paused. She had a point. It was the same thing he'd thought only hours earlier. They'd met less than a week ago yet he felt like he'd known her for years. Could be that he was lumping Katharine into the same category as her mother, as if they were two-of-a-kind. Could be they'd spent more time together in the space of a week than some folks do in months. Could be the crisis of the moment was bringing them together. Whatever the cause, Canyon felt like he knew

Katharine, at least well enough to know she wouldn't give up and she wouldn't fail. "That may be," he said tentatively, "but my gut says you'll pull it off."

"And if your gut is wrong?"

Usually wasn't, but saying as much would probably send her running. There was a new edge to her, one he wasn't sure how to take and definitely wanted to dull. "My gut works on logic. God knows I've heard enough about you from your mother, and the way I see it, you didn't get to where you are in your career without being savvy. You handled Frank's situation with a calm I don't see from most women. And Kyle? Well, that tells me you have an independent streak." Canyon flicked a gaze to the dogs at their feet. "Then there's Cody. Having a dog like him in your corner makes you a good person in my book. So..." His lips curled into a smile and he summed up, "Seems to me, I've got a pretty good handle on the pretty woman sitting next to me." When she didn't reply, he added, "As for hard-core truth, I'd put my hat in your ring any day of the week. You're a winner, Katharine Wainwright. I only wish you'd stay on here instead of returning to New York. I think the donors would respond, same as me. They'd be falling all over themselves to win your favor."

Surprised by his flash of crazy, Canyon wondered, had he really just said all that? His heart began to pound as she looked at him more closely.

"What are you saying, Canyon?"

Didn't he just say it?

Katharine held him in her gaze.

Lydia shrieked, but neither looked in her direction. It was a shriek of excitement, not of panic. Canyon swallowed and drew his knees to his chest. The only panic around here was unfurling inside him. What part didn't she understand?

Shifting his position so he could look at her more directly, Canyon decided to plunge forward. This might be his last chance. "I'm saying that I want you to stay. I think the ranch would be better off with you at the helm and not some stranger. I think others would agree."

"What about you? You're no stranger to the ranch. You could take over in a seamless transition of power, much more so than I could."

"Are we back to this standoff?" he teased, somewhat disappointed in her push-back. There'd been no misunderstanding where he was coming from, yet she'd detoured.

It was a detour he didn't want. He wanted her.

"You should think about it," she continued. "I think the ranch would benefit with you as head of operations."

He'd rather she follow his course of action and stay on. Talk about seamless fit, she was it, in more ways than one. The two of them working side-by-side, day in and day out. It would be the natural opportunity for them to get to know one another on a deeper level. A level he wanted to pursue. Canyon shot a glance toward the group of campers and said, "Katharine, I want you to stay. Call me selfish, but I think you're a natural fit for stepping in and taking over your mother's ranch."

"My mother's ranch," she said wistfully, as though saddened by the thought.

"It's more than that. I've seen you with the kids, I've seen you in this terrain. This is where you belong."

"Hm. I think my associates in New York would beg to disagree."

Let them. Canyon had her now and he wasn't about to let her go. "The kids need you. I need—"

"Canyon! Come here, you gotta see this!"

Canyon didn't want to see anything but Katharine's reaction. He wanted to know if she felt it, too. They had a connection. They had the beginnings of something special and they needed to pursue it. Holding her in his gaze as the seconds passed, he'd swear she felt the same, but surrounded by others, there was little private time to explore the subject.

"Canyon!"

Katharine nudged him with a knowing gaze. "I think the kids really want you."

And he really wanted *her*. Looking to the group of them, Canyon noted all eyes were on the two of them. Grunting under his breath, he pushed up from the ground and whispered, "This conversation isn't over."

A small smile formed on her lips. "I hope not."

When Canyon rose and walked off, Katharine caught her breath. Was he really going to suggest she stay on for him? The thrashing pound of her heart warned yes, that was exactly what was coming next. Canyon wanted her to stay on and take over the ranch, but not for purely professional reasons. And she had wanted to hear him say it. Breathing, she calmed the pounding her chest. She softened her focus and imagined the two of them together. If she stayed on, she'd see him every day. She'd work with him and the children. She'd enjoy hikes and overnight camping trips. Tingles erupted across her neck and shoulders, raced in columns up to her ears.

Next would come private camping trips, intimate evenings alone, dinners at Adele's. They could ride horses during the summer, snow ski during the winter. Anything was possible, if they lived in the same town. But they didn't.

She lived in New York.

Canyon lowered to look through the telescope with a passel of teenagers gathered around him. Shannon stood off to one side, clearly pleased to share her passion for astronomy. She definitely belonged on a mountaintop gazing into the night sky. And Canyon belonged on a ranch in the midst of children, surrounded by cattle and horses with a backdrop of rugged mountains. Buck lifted his head suddenly, as though alerted his master had left him. Without hesitation he lifted from the ground and joined the group.

Katharine would be returning to New York soon. Her business partners would be waiting, her father, all of whom felt so far away. Staring through the darkness, she lifted her attention to the sky. The moon drifted above, a pale white circle of light against a storm of astral activity. She'd never seen stars like this in Manhattan. It was impossible. City lights dominated the nightscape, erasing any existence of the world beyond. Crowded city streets drowned out quiet reflection. Colorado was beautiful. It made her want to stay forever. It brought her closer to her mother, brought her together with an amazing guy...

Canyon's ability with the kids was enviable, his ease with the staff a manager's dream. The campers, young and old, looked up to him. They admired and respected him while she was nothing but a name to them. She was some distant person who owned the ranch as opposed to a hands-on member of the team. Maybe with time, they would accept her. But could she accept them? Could she ever be happy with the slow pace of Colorado? It felt wonderful at the moment, but could she give up her investment career and stay full-time? Could she work with kids as her mother had?

Katharine wasn't sure she had it in her. Suddenly a boy let out a whoop and Cody's head popped up from the ground. Realizing Buck had gone, he looked to Katharine. Strings of melancholy pulled at her. "Go on, boy, see what all the fuss is about." She pointed with her hand and encouraged, "Go on, it's okay. I'll come with you." As she stood up, the fatal truth whispered through her head. Wainwright Ranch was her mother's dream, not hers. She had stayed in New York because the city is where she had wanted to be.

Canyon welcomed her with a smile that went beyond friendship. It was filled with want and desire and made every inch of her want to stay. She wanted to want to be here, wanted to explore a future with him. Unfortunately, she wasn't sure if she could fit in, no matter how badly she wanted to try.

Chapter Thirty

Canyon cut his time with the kids as short as he could, without coming off as uninterested in what they were doing—but truthfully he was more interested in continuing his conversation with Katharine. Standing next to her and a bunch of teens bantering back and forth, he grew impatient. He wanted privacy and he wanted it now. "Time to wrap it up, kids," he announced.

"What? No way," replied one of the boys. "We haven't checked out Venus, yet."

"Yes, way. We've got a schedule to keep. Reveille sounds at six-thirty tomorrow and there will be no excuses."

Groans broke out amongst the boys while the girls seemed oblivious to the news of an early morning. Canyon felt a tinge guilty but his desire to resume his conversation with her overrode all else. "Everyone give Shannon a big thank-you for hauling her equipment up here, then it's time to hit the sack."

Hit the sack. What he wouldn't give to hit the sack with the woman by his side and hold her close all night long. But rules were rules and if he expected to have any time at all to continue that conversation, he had to do it now. Waving the group off, he turned to Katharine. "Mind if we pull up the rear?"

She smiled. "Not at all."

When Shannon and the kids were out of earshot, he began to follow but at a snail's pace. "About what I was saying earlier... I want you to stay. I think you should stay."

"You're not playing the guilt card on me, are you, Canyon?"

Katharine smiled, but Canyon felt a distance that hadn't been there before. He shrugged it off and stayed on course.

"Not even close. I do believe you would be the perfect person to take over Wainwright Ranch, but I also want you to stay for purely selfish reasons." He stopped, and she stopped with him. Flicking a glance toward the group ahead of them, he lowered his voice despite the fact they couldn't hear him and said, "I want the chance to get to know you better."

Canyon smiled, struck by a punch of nerves. Saying the words aloud sounded corny to him, but he had no other way to say it. *I need you.* It was plain speak. The only kind he knew. And if he didn't get the words out, he'd never know. He reached for her hand and before he could think twice, gave it a gentle squeeze. "I need you to stay. I want you to stay...for me. I think you and I could make a great team, together. If you go, we'll never know."

Katharine didn't say anything, only looked up at him with a weighty gaze.

Was she not with him? Had he crossed the line, veered into hostile territory? "You're killing me," he said in a burst of nervous tension. "Did I say something wrong?"

"No." She shook her gaze. "You didn't."

When she dropped her gaze to the ground, Canyon almost felt it coming. *But...*

"But I don't know if it's a good fit for me." She looked into his eyes and must have sensed the impact, backpedaling quickly, "No, I don't mean you and me." She brought a hand up between them, then cupped her forehead. "I mean me and the ranch, Colorado..."

Relief flooded him but he kept it in check. He wasn't sure where she was going with this line. "What doesn't fit about you and the ranch? From what I can see, you're a natural with the kids, a pretty mean hiker to boot, and I'd bet my last dollar Cody would prefer Colorado over New York any day of the week."

Talk of her dog unclamped the strain in her face and she laughed softly, dropping her hand to her side. "I think you're right on that count." Her gaze went to the dogs. Parked on their rears about ten feet away, they were waiting for their masters before continuing back to camp. "Cody completely prefers it here to home." Katharine stilled. Her eyes misted but she didn't well up or cry, uttering, "Home."

The word was practically a whisper, and one that didn't seem to hold any joy for her.

Peering into his eyes, she said, "But my home is New York. It's where my career is, my father. Even if I wanted to drop everything and stay in Colorado, I couldn't. It's not possible."

"Could happen if you wanted it to happen," he said, struggling to keep it together. He felt like a heel for pressuring her, but was unable to stop himself. "Life is always about choices. If you wanted to stay here, you could."

"I wish it were that easy. I wish I could be in both places at the same time. These past few days have made me feel closer to my mother than I have in years. But my father..." Her voice fell away. "My father needs me."

"Your father can't live without you?"

"He can," she replied, shaking her head as though confused. "But he's all I have left. I'm all he has left."

"And you're content to live your life for him?"

"Is that what you think I'm doing?"

"Aren't you?"

As she stared at him, he detected an inkling of pity in her gaze, as though she were trying to let him down gently and he wasn't taking the hint. Abruptly, something inside Canyon closed. If Katharine didn't want to stay, she didn't want to stay. He would accept her decision and move on. Forcing a lighthearted tone he said, "Can't blame a guy for trying."

Her eyes shone, glittering stones of topaz in the wash of moonlight, but she smiled. It was a gesture that broke his heart. Katharine appeared grateful to be let off the hook. His hook.

Casting a longing gaze toward the moon, she posed, "Life is strange, isn't it? One day you're sailing on course, navigating smooth waters, and the next your entire ship is being tossed by the current, about to be overturned."

"Is that how I make you feel?" Canyon asked. If it was, he wanted no part of it. New beginnings should feel solid and strong. Any change he'd ever made in his life had been based on gut instinct. It either felt right or it felt wrong. If something about a new beginning in Colorado felt wrong to Katharine, it probably was.

As though reading his mind, she said, "It's not you, Canyon, it's me. I feel like I'm in way over my head and I don't like it."

"I'm sorry," he replied, and meant it. More than he'd meant anything in his life. Katharine Wainwright was a woman he'd take a chance on. She was a woman he believed could stand by his side for the long haul. He couldn't force her to feel the same. No matter how badly he wanted her to feel the same things he did, he couldn't. Taking a step away from her and toward camp, he cleared his voice and said, "We should catch up with the others, before they start wondering what happened to us."

"Yes," she agreed quietly.

With that, the moment was gone. The fullness of emotion, the overwhelming desire that had gripped him earlier vanished. Buck and Cody led the way back to the campsite, and Canyon followed, Katharine close at his side. Walking in silence, he pondered the void filling his heart. Guess it was true what they said. Some things weren't meant to be. Didn't matter how much you wanted to cram a round peg into a square hole, it wouldn't fit. It wasn't meant to be. End of story.

Katharine didn't sleep. Not because of the hard ground layered with rocks that jut into her ribs from beneath the tent, or the faint snores of Shannon who slept soundly by her side. She lay wide awake all night long, staring into the ceiling of her tent, feeling desperately alone—because of Canyon. The pain in his eyes when she'd expressed her fears had been clear and distinct. He'd taken it as a personal rejection. She hadn't meant it as one, but that's how he took it. Her words had hurt him. Any and all attempts this morning to under-score that it really wasn't him, it was her, went ignored. But it *wasn't* him. It was her. Totally her!

Jabbing a fork in and out of her salad bowl, Katharine ate. She enjoyed none of the savory granola Adele had made for her, none of the fresh fruit or lettuce. None of it. She couldn't taste the first bite. She could only think of Canyon and how there was no going back. Once the canary had been released from its cage, it flew. Far and away, it flew, leaving Katharine with a helpless feeling.

Things had escaped her control last night. Forget that everything she did, that every plan she had made her entire life had been about maintaining control, she'd lost it. In the space of barely a week, she'd lost control of her life and her heart. It was the latter that concerned her most. Lost revenue she could recover. Bad deals she could make right, but falling in love with Canyon?

That had ripped open the ground beneath her. It sucked her into a deep, deep hole where there was no escaping. Long distance relationships didn't work. Blending lifestyles that were polar opposite only disappointed. One couldn't recon-cile two thousand miles, two different career paths and two very different personalities. Take her parents. Despite their great love, they were on two different tracks, leaving them vulnerable to intrusion. Frank would never have been able to interfere if her mother and father were of like mind when it came to their passion.

Canyon's life was embedded in Colorado. And while Katharine loved it here, she had invested too much time in her career to walk away. It would be like building a skyscrap-er and tearing it down halfway through construction. How did one do that? How did they walk away and start fresh?

Maybe a steamy encounter with a cowboy while you're here would do the trick.

Katharine almost choked on the memory. Maybe she should have taken her friend's advice and left it at fun. But she didn't, and now Canyon had left the negotiating table. He had offered his heart and she had wounded his pride. She'd seen it as clearly as if it had been written in neon lights in those dark brooding eyes of his. Canyon had made his play and she had spurned him. In a cowboy's eyes, that was the end of the story. He was finished with the city slicker from New York. And she? She was simply finished.

Chapter Thirty-One

The Wainwright Ranch dining hall during lunch time was busy but manageable. Walking through the room, Katharine noted that kids and staff were in full gab mode. Compared to the last time she was here, the kids were loud. *Normal*, she mused, glancing around the room. Now at least they sounded like a dining hall full of rambunctious campers instead of a group of polite and proper kids eating in a library. It was almost as if there was an excitement underfoot, an anticipation that went beyond the day's activities. Which she found odd. Summer session was winding down. Kids would be going home soon, and where she expected a sadness on their part, there was nothing but euphoria.

Maybe it was her perception that was off. Because she saw storm clouds on the horizon, any shred of light and warmth was celebrated. But glancing around the room, she soaked it all in. The kids were happy. The staff was happy. She should be pleased. And she might be, if only Canyon hadn't relegated her to "stranger" status. Since returning from their overnight outing, the man hadn't said two words to her.

Choosing a table set for her in a corner near the back, Katharine lowered to a bench. She had invited Adele, her boyfriend Hal Richardson and his daughter, Lisa, to join her for lunch. Adele had suggested a brainstorming powwow and Katharine had jumped at the chance. These were the locals of Silver Creek. These were the people with the connections, the knowledge of who could be of help to the ranch and who couldn't. Fleshing out some last minute strategy also served to get Canyon off her mind.

"Thanks for coming," Katharine said and settled in. As her guests sat—Adele beside her and Hal and his daughter across the table—she realized there were settings for five and it dawned on her. "Lisa, was your boyfriend not able to join us?"

Lisa grinned, and a spattering of freckles over her nose and cheeks became pronounced, underscored by a bright pink shirt and naturally healthy glow. "Nah. He's here, but he decided to head over and see Canyon."

"Oh..." Katharine sat rigid.

"You don't mind, do you?" Lisa asked, her expression awash in concern. "We're here because you asked, but Walsh didn't feel like he had much to contribute to the conversation so he took a pass."

Katharine shook the hesitancy free and forced herself to relax. "Of course not. It's no problem at all." Walsh was with Canyon, his friend. Who cared that she'd begun to develop her own relationship with the man. She'd botched the other night and there was no going back. And if she had any doubts, Canyon's silent treatment was all the proof she needed.

"How are the numbers stacking up? Have you received any new commitments?" Hal asked. He was a fair-haired blond with his own share of freckles, hazel eyes, and a few strands of gray blending in with the blond. But that's where the resemblance between father and daughter ended. Lisa's features were those of her mother, as was her brown hair. Katharine knew part of his backstory from Adele. Lisa must favor the mother who had passed far ahead of her time.

"A few," Katharine replied. "Since you all put the word out, the ranch has increased its commitments by one hundred and fifty thousand dollars. That's over and above the Fairchilds' donation."

"That's great!" Lisa exclaimed.

"It is, but not nearly enough to sustain us going forward."

"How much do you need?" Hal asked.

"Wainwright Ranch runs an annual budget close to five million dollars." At Hal's soft whistle, Katharine felt compelled to explain, "It's an expensive proposition to staff a fully-specialized medical team, travel expenses for over a hundred campers, not to mention maintenance and repairs on an eight thousand acre functioning cattle ranch. Add property insurance, medical and liability and—"

Hal raised a hand. "Understood. The numbers are mind-boggling."

"Mind-boggling but manageable. We have considerable reserves to tap into, but I hate to deplete our cash when we might need it to cover unexpected emergencies. We also use those funds to bankroll family visits during the season, on a case-by-case basis, and sponsor scholarships for the kids as they graduate."

"What a great program," Lisa touted. "Kinsley told me that was one of the main reasons her mom donated. She's all about education and loves the fact you help the kids beyond their summer stays."

"Katharine's mother supported a lot of local charities as well," Adele put in, and looked to Hal. "Remember the year she donated money to help build the children's orthopedic wing at the hospital?"

"How could I forget? It wouldn't have happened without Eleanor's generosity. She also used to visit some of the kids in the hospital. She'd do so here in Silver Creek, as well as the larger institutions in Denver."

"Kinsley's mom said Mrs. Wainwright used to make the occasional trip to visit the families of previous campers," Lisa said. "Even helped out by offering to pay their hospital bills."

"Is that true, Katharine?" Adele asked.

"It is," she replied quietly. Her mother had always given generously of her time and money. Like an endless river laced with gold, her mother's love had flowed in and out of the ranch and the communities beyond. A flutter of heartbeats gave way to momentary weakness. It was yet another reason why Wainwright Ranch stood out among a crowded field of children's charities; her mother's devotion to the children went far beyond the fence posts of her land.

"Howdy, Ms. Wainwright!"

"Hi, Levi." Katharine looked up at one of the cooks, lugging a tray loaded with dishes and glasses. A thin brunette, he deposited the tray on the end of the table with remarkable ease.

"Here's your order of sautéed spinach, tri-colored bean salad and sliced tomatoes," he said and proceeded to hand out food and water.

Adele's eyes rounded. "Wow. When did these hit the menu?"

"This second." Katharine flipped her face toward Adele. "I asked the kitchen to prepare them for us so we wouldn't be subjected to barbecued beef and baked beans." After a minimal dinner last night consisting of a side of canned creamed corn and processed white bread, her stomach couldn't take anything less than healthy and wholesome today.

Levi beamed. "Louise had to special-order the spinach, but we had everything else."

Katharine inhaled a drift of fresh garlic and said, "Tell her thank you for me, will you? The greens look wonderful."

"Everything looks great!" Adele agreed.

"Sure thing," he said, and tucked the tray under his arm. "Anything else I can get for you?"

"No, Levi. Everything is perfect."

"Are we making these regular items?" Adele asked, and lifted a fork from the table as Levi walked away.

"I'd love to if I thought I could get anyone else to agree. Apparently, the kids around here expect chuck wagon food when they come to the ranch. Steak, barbecue, biscuits and gravy... The only healthy items on the menu are the lettuce and tomato for their burgers. Oh, and the sides of corn on the cob."

"Nothing that will kill them," Hal remarked wryly, and plucked his glass of water from the table.

"No, but that doesn't make it good for them," Adele rebuffed.

"I think it's a great idea to get the kids to eat healthier," Lisa said. "There's no reason they can't be taught to take care of their bodies, in sickness and in health."

"Good point," Adele echoed, and took a bite of spinach. She groaned loudly in approval and gave a thumbs up.

"You won't get any argument from me," Hal returned, "only a call for calm. Sometimes you vegans can get pretty voracious about your diets and forget that the rest of the population enjoys its red meat."

Lisa laughed. "Now you sound like Walsh!"

Adele stopped and turned. "Walsh uses words like voracious?"

Katharine could tell Adele was having fun and hoped Lisa could see it, too.

Lisa grinned. "Actually, Walsh is a man of few words. But I'm sure he'd use it if the situation warranted!"

Adele smiled. "Walsh is a simple man, pure of heart. It's a wonderful combination."

"He's wonderful," Lisa pronounced.

Katharine didn't join in their banter. Instead, she retreated from the din of conversation around her and gave in to the wheels spinning inside her head. Heavy scents of sautéed spinach and garlic permeated her senses. *There's no reason they can't be taught to take care of their bodies, in sickness and in health.* Lisa was right. All kids should be taught what was good for their bodies and why it mattered, especially sick children. How had her mother overlooked this fact? Was she so bound and determined to create a world of normalcy that she overlooked the fact that not all of "normal" was good for these kids?

Nutritionally speaking, a vegan diet was superior to cowboy fare. It wasn't fat-laden or over-processed, and despite Hal's assertion that the American population preferred its red meat, red meat wasn't vital for the human body to function. There were myriad sources of protein to choose from, beginning with spinach. She dropped her gaze to her plate. Granted spinach was an incomplete protein, but there was no reason these kids couldn't eat soy and quinoa. In fact, soy milk would be a perfect replacement for cow's milk. Quinoa could be served in lieu of rice and potatoes, flavored with a variety of vegetables. Edamame could replace baked beans. Katharine stared at her spinach. Tofu was another great protein, though it could prove to be a tough sell... A devilish thought lit up her brain. Unless she could hide it in their food somehow.

"Katharine?"

Startled, she looked up. "Yes?"

"The salad is wonderful," Adele replied, an odd look in her eye. "Everything okay with you?"

"Yes, of course, I was thinking about the food"—she laughed at herself—"and I think I became a bit carried away in my own mind!"

"Must have been some pretty dynamite food," Hal said.

"Tofu." Katharine glanced between them. "I was thinking how I might be able to hide it in the kids' food."

"Good luck with that." Hal smirked and skewered a stack of beans on his fork. "Adele tried that on me once." He slid a playful gaze across the table. "Once."

She plopped an elbow to the table and pointed at him. "The only reason you knew it was tofu was because you saw the empty package in the garbage. I had you totally convinced it was a bowl of plain old corn chowder."

"Did not."

"Did so," she quipped then took a bite of salad.

Katharine laughed. "What about that mock macaroni and cheese you used to make? That stuff was to die for," she said, recalling the creamy texture of the sauce. It had been one of Adele's cooking class creations, one her professor claimed for his kids at home. "I'll bet you could make that dish and fool every last camper!"

Adele turned to Katharine and finished chewing. "I bet you're right. I forgot all about that recipe, but you're right— these kids would love it."

Hal rolled his eyes. "Oh, brother. Wait until Canyon hears you're about to renovate his menu. I'm sure he'll love eating tofu mac and cheese, instead of hamburgers and pulled pork. The man will come out of his boots!"

Katharine chuckled and savored a private smile. *That would be a sight to see.* A very delightful sight to see. But distracted by images of Canyon, she quickly pushed them from her mind. "It's just a thought," she murmured. They were right. There was no way the bull-busting Canyon Laredo would be caught dead eating tofu mac and cheese. Or drinking soy milk.

"I think it's a good one," Lisa agreed and looked to Adele. "How come I haven't seen your mac and cheese dish on the menu at the restaurant? Sounds like the kids would love it."

"Forget kids," Katharine shot back. "I'd like to see it on the menu for my sake! It would make a great side dish, Adele. What do you think? Think you could whip up a trial dish for me, maybe as a side?"

"I'll consider it," Adele replied, and nodded thoughtfully.

"Are you growing soybeans in your kitchen garden?" Katharine asked.

"No. When I do use them for a dish, I buy them from a local supplier." A twinkle of mischief lit up her dark gaze. "Wonder how he'd feel about turning a few of his soybeans into soy milk and making tofu for me?"

"Is it hard?" Lisa asked.

"Not really," Adele said. "A little soaking, blending, separating, boiling and voilà—you have yourself fresh soy milk! Making tofu from there is a breeze. Basically, you add a coagulant to boiling soy milk, allow it to curdle, and then pack it into a mold. Remember when we used to make it during college, Katharine?"

"I sure do. What you could do with a mold of tofu makes my head spin."

Lisa laughed but Hal looked a bit leery. "Don't give her any ideas, please."

"I won't," Katharine replied, suppressing a giggle. Though she couldn't promise all this talk about tofu wouldn't give *her* any ideas. She had a bundle! Now, if only she could convince Canyon to keep an open mind on the subject, she might have a chance. Doubtful, but possible.

"Don't listen to him, Katharine." Adele waved him off. "Hal likes a good meal, doesn't matter what's in it. You simply have to make it taste good."

He shrugged. "Guilty as charged."

"Speaking of food that tastes good, how about your black bean burgers from the restaurant?" Katharine asked. "Or your cashew cream ravioli? The kids might really enjoy those items."

"The recipes are yours if you'd like to borrow them for the ranch."

Katharine grinned. "I'll keep the offer in mind."

Surrounded by friends, it felt good to be joking about tofu instead of stressing over the future of Wainwright Ranch. It brought her back to happier days, college days spent with Adele back in New York, her mother and father. They were good days. Wonderful days, back when her mother had only spent part of her time in Colorado, devoting the rest to her husband and daughter back home in the city. Once Katharine graduated and became fully involved in the firm's business, her mother made the transition, spending the majority of her time building her charity ranch. As an employee of Wainwright, Emerson, Frank was an ever-constant presence and eventually migrated out West with her.

Mulling over Frank's role, Katharine tried to recall how the chain of events transpired, the potential signs of infidelity. But same as before, she couldn't. It had seemed a natural transition at the time. Frank was a friend of the family. A trusted advisor. He'd offered to help her mother. Her mother needed the help. Katharine's heart soured. For him to take advantage of the distance was unforgiveable.

Hal's cell phone rang. He answered, "Hello? Hey, Donald. Yes. Yes, I'm actually sitting with her right now." His eyes widened with excitement. "Seriously? That much?"

Extricating herself from the tangle of memory, Katharine listened intently.

"Great. Yes, I'll tell her." Hal ended the call and beamed. "Donald Marsh has offered to donate fifty thousand dollars."

Adele's eyes became saucers. "He did?"

"Sure did!" Hal confirmed and set his phone on the table.

"That's wonderful, Hal!" Katharine exclaimed, her voice competing with a clamor from a group of girls seated one table over. "That makes eight physicians who have donated. What an amazing show of support from the medical community."

"It's a testament to an amazing cause."

"Yes," Katharine replied simply. "It is. Wainwright Ranch is an amazing place."

One that must continue. One that would continue. Deep in her bones, Katharine knew with a certainty they would win. The children would win. Her gaze moved about the room.

Wait staff weaved their way between tables, refilling pitchers of water and lemonade, picking up dishes and delivering extra baskets of bread. Mealtime was an active time, with kids popping up from their seats, scooping second servings onto their plates from a buffet where more staff was on standby to assist. Katharine spotted a slice of chocolate cake on one child's plate and cringed inwardly. Sugar. Meat. Fat. It was the normal American diet. Not her preference, but everyone here seemed to love it. Like Hal said, it wouldn't kill them. Exactly.

Bit by an unexpected yearning, Katharine redirected her thoughts. She might not like the food the children were eating, but it wasn't her business. Her job was to find donors. After lunch, she would return to her office and begin making phone calls. She'd call everyone she knew in New York until she had the money the ranch needed to stay afloat. With less than forty-eight hours to turn things around, it would be an enormous challenge, but she'd give it her all. Every last hour she had would be devoted to raising money, enabling her to announce during the fundraiser that Wainwright Ranch would remain open for business.

Chapter Thirty-Two

Katharine sat at the desk in her hotel suite, scribbling last minute notes for her speech as fast as she could. Dressed and ready to go with a driver scheduled to pick her up in five minutes, she couldn't stop the cascade of ideas reverberating through her skull. It felt like an avalanche. One thought ignited the next and the next and the next as a new concept formed in her mind. Desire and longing crystallized, and her vision fell into place. But that's the way her brain worked. When an idea was right, it fit perfectly. It was an organic process that flowed with ease to a positive outcome. There was no struggle, no second-guessing herself. Like when she had created her first hedge fund. Katharine had identified major shifts in financial markets around the globe and decided that trading in currencies and futures was the way to go. It was risky business, but her investors had signed on without a fight. Because her instincts had been spot-on, giving her a persuasive power she normally didn't feel. And true to her gut, she'd timed the market perfectly, earning her investors a fortune in less than twelve months' time. Her status in the industry catapulted overnight.

The experience had taught Katharine a valuable lesson. When she was slightly nervous but jazzed by the prospect of doing something new and uncharted, she knew she had herself a winner. Like now. Flipping through her notes, she ran through her outline and decided *Yes, this is a winning idea.* Removing the pen from her mouth, she blew out a sigh and chastised herself. *Darn habit.* Would she ever stop stashing the blasted pen in her mouth?

Katharine shook her head. Didn't matter. Tonight was the first night of the rest of her life. Once she made it through the fundraiser, there'd be plenty of time to recreate new habits. Jotting down another flit of an idea, she thought, *But first things first*. She had a car to catch!

Rising in one fluid motion, she closed her notebook and tucked it into her leather briefcase. "Time to go," she announced.

Cody lifted his head lazily and peered at her. Nestled in the corner, he'd been sound asleep on his new plush dog bed, the gift courtesy of Adele. She'd purchased it for him when she heard Katharine would be staying on for the interim, claiming Cody shouldn't have to suffer on the hard carpeted floor of her hotel suite. Adele had also offered her home to the two of them, but Katharine had declined. There was something about retaining her independence that appealed to her. It represented freedom and the ability to come and go as she pleased. One never knew when opportunity would knock.

Squelching a rush of nerves, she plucked her silk wrap from the bed and, passing a mirror, stopped. Katharine was struck by the sight of her black Chanel briefcase. It stood out like a blemish next to her creamy pink gown. Stark and sleek, the briefcase shouted business while her dress whispered elegance and privilege, as did the diamond earrings at her ears, the soft tendrils left to dangle from her professionally-styled hair. Funny, but her life was a combination of both. She felt equally comfortable in a hard-hitting boardroom as she did in the halls of a five-star hotel, similar to the one where tonight's gala was being held.

Turning to and fro, Katharine admired the cut of her custom-made dress, the way it flattered the narrow curves of her figure. She almost felt like a queen holding high court. Well-heeled guests would dine and dance in the most lavish of amenities and hopefully feel compelled to open their wallets to a great cause. As hostess, Katharine Wainwright would graciously encourage everyone to enjoy themselves and thank them for their generous support, followed by her outline for the future of Wainwright Ranch. Come Monday, she'd be donning boots and jeans along with a corral full of enthusiastic campers. Excitement sprinted through her limbs. At least she hoped they'd be enthusiastic. Her plans depended on it!

Calming a sudden thump of her heart, Katharine inhaled deeply and hurried to the door. "I won't be too late, Cody," she said and blew him a kiss. Her car was waiting and she couldn't be late. Tonight was too important!

Canyon Laredo hung out in front of the hotel, fidgeting as a constant stream of limousines and fancy cars swung around the circular drive. Met by dutiful doormen beneath a ceiling of glittering lights, elegantly dressed men and women emerged from the vehicles and passed by him on their way inside to the fundraiser. Dressed in a tuxedo for the black tie affair, he wondered if Katharine was going to make it in time. Sliding the white cuff from his wrist, he checked his watch for the third time in ten minutes. Where was she?

Donors had been arriving nonstop for the last twenty minutes yet there was no sign of her, the hostess for this fancy event. Did she not intend to meet and greet before her speech? Did she think she could simply waltz in here, say her piece and leave?

Canyon hoped not. He knew she didn't share his commitment to the cause, but he hoped she had the decency to play the part this evening. This was her shindig. The ranch's, really, but seeing as how she held rank as Chief Operating Officer until a replacement could be found, it was hers. Warmth flushed through him as he recalled her lobbying efforts on his behalf. *You're no stranger to the ranch. You could take over the helm in a seamless transition of power, much more so than I could. The ranch needs you more than it needs me.*

Katharine might have declined his argument for her to stay, but knowing that she believed in him helped soften the blow. At least that's what he told himself. Canyon hoped she meant what she said and wasn't merely trying to hand over the reins as quickly as she could, so she could get back to New York. He didn't kid himself. She'd made her position very clear. The ranch wasn't her home. The charity wasn't her passion. It had been her mother's.

Transported back to the moment when he divulged his feelings for her, Canyon felt stupid. Why he ever thought she would chuck everything she knew for a cowboy she'd just met dumbfounded him. What had he been thinking? Had he been thinking, or had he simply been feeling the moment? There he was, sitting next to a beautiful woman beneath a moonlit sky and all good sense left him. Carried away by the setting, he'd succumbed to weakness. Desire. Want.

But what did he expect? A man never did think straight when his thoughts were consumed by a woman. Evading the direct gaze of a gentleman escorting a female past him—a very young female who looked to be his daughter, though in all likelihood wasn't—Canyon felt the void. He wanted a woman in his life, a real woman who wanted him for who he was, not for what he could do for her. He wanted true love. Not a trophy on his arm. Not a business arrangement or a close-enough-you'll-do kind of woman. He wanted true love.

It was an aspect Canyon had always admired about Eleanor's husband. William Wainwright could have traded her in for a younger model like so many wealthy men did, but instead, he seemed proud to escort his wife of thirty-plus years. Smitten, even, the way he doted on her around the ranch during his visits, taking a back seat while she ran the place. It was refreshing. Encouraging.

And the kind of relationship Canyon wanted. Except he wanted his full-time. No visits, no every-once-in-awhile. He wanted a woman by his side, one he could dote one and take care of. A black limousine pulled around the front drive, met by a doorman who opened the back passenger door. Canyon's heart skipped a beat as Katharine emerged. Their eyes met and she smiled, a gesture he returned. Thankfully, he wasn't close enough for any more to be required of him. At the moment, he couldn't speak. He could only stare at the strapless gown hugging her curves with draped pink satin, a material that flared at her feet in a style so feminine she appeared angelic. Her hair was swept away from her face and clipped in an elegant twist behind her head, yet several softly curled wisps were left to dangle around her face. Canyon swallowed. Katharine Wainwright was stunning. There was no other word to describe her.

She took a step toward him and Canyon kicked into action, closing the distance between them in seconds. There was no way he was going to let her walk into the hotel alone. Besides, it might be one of the last times he could get this close to her.

"Katharine," he breathed her name, tamping back the hungry longing thrashing inside him. "You look beautiful this evening."

"Thank you, Canyon." She briefly dropped her gaze and remarked, "You dress up pretty nicely yourself."

"I look the same as every other male in the vicinity."

She laughed lightly, the familiar sound calming the twister of emotion erupting inside him. "Very few men look like you, Canyon, trust me."

"Well, I'm going to take that as a compliment."

"Please do," she said, and paused, peering up at him with an odd expression.

"Something wrong?"

"No." She shook her head. "I just realized this is the first time I've seen you without your red bandana."

Canyon touched his collar and noted the absence. "Didn't seem to fit the outfit."

Katharine's gaze softened. "Bandana or not, you look very handsome for the occasion."

Ribbons of desire wound through him. She wasn't making this easy. All he wanted to do was to take her into his arms and kiss her. Cover those satiny-glossed lips with his and show her exactly how he felt. But standing front and center of a ritzy hotel where guests were coming and going didn't seem the right place for their first kiss. A kiss that likely would never happen.

Instead, he held out his arm. "May I?"

"Please," she replied and looped her hand over his elbow.

"I was worried you weren't going to show," he said, slightly unnerved by the scent of perfume swirling about her. It was flowery and sweet and underscored her allure, as did the glow of her skin, the slight curves of her cleavage. Forcing his brain to switch gears, Canyon asked, "Did you run into problems on the way here?"

"Only my own. I was finalizing my speech for this evening but was carried away by distraction."

"Care to share?"

She tipped her head up then shook it slightly. "Not yet."

Sliding doors opened as they neared. "Nothing ominous, I hope."

"No." Katharine's eyes danced as he whisked her through the entrance. "At least I hope not! I hope it will be anything *but* ominous."

"Why so mysterious?" he asked as they crossed the lobby of the hotel, the site where she would make or break their case for the ranch's future.

"I have a good feeling about tonight and I don't want to jinx it."

Canyon nearly busted out laughing as he paced the flow of guests headed for the ballroom. Beneath sparkling chandeliers, the diamonds at her ears sparkled. "Tell me you don't believe in jinxing."

She whipped up a hand and crossed her fingers between them. "Jinx, good luck charms, I'll take whatever I can get, so long as it works!"

Good luck charms and jinxes were the last thing he expected to hear from the no-nonsense New York City businesswoman he'd come to know and love. Canyon's mind froze. Love. He at looked her and gulped. *Loved*?

That was a secret he'd have to keep to himself. Nerves fired on all cylinders as he said, "How about I focus on counting dollars. If we can cover the bottom line for the next fiscal year, I think we can figure out a future from there."

"Agreed."

Slowing as they entered the ballroom, Canyon sized up the event. Round tables had been organized in rows across the room, their tops covered by white tablecloths and fancy table settings. In the center of each were vases filled with yellow, purple and orange flowers. Like him, men were dressed in tuxedos, most of which were traditional black and white, though a few men boasted red, blue, and even pink ties. Canyon shook his head. If that was fashion, he was lacking. Women wore gowns in every size, shape, cut and color and gathered in clusters. A stage had been set up opposite the entrance doors with a giant screen hanging behind it. It would be the focal point of the evening, where Katharine would state her case imploring donors to continue their support. Until then, soft music drifted in the air, and waiters circulated through the crowd, handling trays of bubbly for the taking.

Canyon turned to Katharine. "Looks like we've got a packed house tonight."

"Yes," she said, her gaze sweeping the room from one end to the other. "We actually had to add three tables to the mix after a few last-minute requests."

"Really?"

She smiled. "Yes, and I'm going to take that as a sign."

He grinned. "Tell me you're not into astrology, too."

"I'm not. But like I said, at this point I'll take all the positive indicators I can get!" She followed her words with a laugh, as if to underscore her point.

Canyon detected a nervous quality to her enthusiasm, an insecurity that echoed his own. Katharine hadn't shared the numbers with him, but one phone call to Paul Sutherland told Canyon they were close, close enough for breathing room to operate another year, and that was all he needed. He'd figure out where to go next after he saw the results from tonight's purse. "Shall we mingle?"

"By all means," she said.

As if on cue, Kinsley Fairchild and her mother approached.

Canyon's gut tightened. Kinsley wasn't one of his favorite people. It was because of her that Buck had nearly lost his life during an explosion that rocked a ski patrol hut on top of the mountain. It had been during the peak of ski season, when Palmer International had been announcing its expansion plans. Kinsley's group of activists decided they were going to stop progress by setting a bomb and scattering tourists. One of the ski patrol staff members had been seriously hurt in the explosion, along with Canyon's dog, Buck. The animal had suffered second degree burns, and if it hadn't been for a plant in the group of protestors tipping them off prior to the explosion, Canyon wouldn't have been able to react in time to save his dog.

Bitterness blistered his thoughts, but he dialed back his personal animosity and remained cool. Kinsley's mother was here to support the cause and for her, he would remain civil.

"Hello, Canyon," Victoria Fairchild acknowledged evenly, her tone rich and silky.

Kinsley stopped, and stood close by her mother's side.

Victoria Fairchild was a beautiful woman. Dressed in a sleeveless black gown with a neckline layered in sparkling white crystals, her face and hair done to perfection, she was definitely model material. Kinsley wasn't much different. While he didn't care for her activist tendencies, he'd be lying if he didn't acknowledge her good looks, especially in the red, strapless, body-glove dress she wore. Both women shared the same long, dark brown hair that fell in waves past their shoulders, along with the same sultry dark eyes and narrow figures.

"Good evening, Mrs. Fairchild. Thank you for coming tonight."

Victoria smiled. "Canyon, you know I wouldn't miss this event for the world, especially during such trying times." Her attention darted between him and Katharine. "I understand you've been faced with some difficult times, and I wanted you to know how firmly in your camp I remain."

"Thank you. It's much appreciated."

"Hello," Katharine extended a hand before Canyon had a chance to introduce her. "I'm Katharine Wainwright."

Mrs. Fairchild's eyes lit up. "Eleanor's daughter..."

"Yes." The two shook hands. "I wanted to personally thank you for your extremely generous donation. Without patrons like you, the ranch couldn't survive."

"Which would be an injustice, darling." Victoria's gaze moved seamlessly between Canyon and Katharine. "Your mother's organization does such wonderful work with the children, I couldn't dream of a Silver Creek without it."

"Thank you. I couldn't agree with you more, and it's your continued support that ensures we continue our work."

Canyon didn't miss the fact that Katharine used the word "we" for the first time since discussing her role with the ranch. Normally she assigned credit to her mother, or Canyon, or Frank, but at the moment she was taking credit. Was it another so-called "good sign?"

Victoria gestured a hand to her side. "I'd like you to meet my daughter, Kinsley. She is a huge fan of the ranch as well and has also offered to make a donation."

Kinsley smiled, and Canyon noticed she avoided direct eye contact with him, focusing solely on Katharine. "On behalf of my blog, *Wildlife Neutral*, I'd like to pledge a donation of one hundred thousand dollars."

Canyon released a soft whistle under his breath. *She was giving one hundred thousand dollars?*

As though reading his mind, Kinsley flicked him a glance and added, "I will have a check delivered first thing Monday morning."

"Why thank you, Kinsley," Katharine responded. "That's extremely generous of you."

"Yes," Canyon spoke up. "Thank you."

"Silver Creek wouldn't be the same without Wainwright Ranch," Kinsley replied. "You're a top-notch organization, a real benefit to the area."

Except for the fact we sell cattle for meat. But to voice the same would be an insult to a donor and completely unacceptable. Kinsley had stepped up with a sizeable donation, and for that, Canyon was truly grateful. "Thank you."

"It's a pleasure to meet both of you," Katharine picked up quickly. "I can't tell you how gratifying it is to know the ranch receives such generous support from the community."

"I think you'll see a new swell of support this year," Kinsley told them. "Dr. Richardson has been pleading the cause and he's a hard man to say no to!"

Katharine laughed. "Yes, I know. I must thank him again!"

"Well," Victoria said, "we know you have a flurry of people waiting to see you. We won't keep you any longer. Good luck this evening." Dark eyes fastened on both of them and she held up two crossed fingers, one with a massive diamond ring glittering from it. "We'll be crossing our fingers."

Canyon laughed inside. He sure hoped the ranch had more to go on than putting stock in good luck symbols tonight! He didn't like to think of his future dangling from the stars in the sky. He preferred solid ground and all things certain. As he watched the Fairchild women take their leave, he could feel Katharine staring at him.

"So it's true," she said quietly. "You don't care much for her."

"For who?"

"Kinsley Fairchild."

How in the heck did she know that? Had it been written on his face?

Sucking back a retort, Canyon realized he was going to have to do a much better job of hiding his feelings. "Kinsley and I have our differences," he said briskly. "Let's leave it at that."

"Adele told me."

Canyon wondered why Adele would reveal something like that but figured friends talked, especially women. "Then I'm sure you can understand why I keep my distance."

"Do you not believe in forgiveness?"

"In my book, forgiveness isn't a gift. It's something you have to earn."

"I hope it's not too hard."

"Too hard?"

What did she mean by that? he wondered.

But the question fell on deaf ears. Katharine had walked away from him. Promptly assuming role of hostess, she introduced herself to guests, engaged them in conversation and never looked back. Canyon was confused. Why would she care whether or not he forgave Kinsley?

Chapter Thirty-Three

Silverware clinked against dishes as Katharine approached the podium. Voices fell to a scatter of isolated conversations. Surrounded by Zeke Roberts, Gary Levine, Susan Billingsworth, two doctors from their staff and the ranch accountant, Canyon sat back in his chair, a bit uneasy over the prospect of her presentation but ready to listen. He hoped she had a bombshell to deliver because that's what these folks needed to hear.

"Good evening, ladies and gentlemen," Katharine began, "and thank you all for coming."

Flanked by huge potted plants topped with sprays of purple-blue wildflowers, she paused, and glanced around the room. The screen behind her was currently lit up with an image of Wainwright Ranch's cattle brand. It was the one Canyon helped Eleanor design years ago, the one that adorned the hides of Wainwright cattle and met visitors at the front gates in the form of an iron emblem. Canyon took pride in the symbol. To him, it represented the epitome of everything he loved, everything he'd worked so hard to achieve. In the beginning, his role had been limited, with most of his time spent between rodeos and mountain search and rescue. But over the years, his focus had shifted, mainly because Eleanor had pulled him in, handing him more duties, more responsibility, giving him more satisfaction than he'd ever known in his life.

"It's with great pleasure that I stand before you today," Katharine continued, "to share in the cause that's touched so many of our lives." She moved her gaze over the crowd, as if attempting to make eye contact with each and every member of her audience.

Canyon had to hand it to her. She was a vision of confidence.

"At Wainwright, we create a setting where children can push their limits and learn the impossible is possible, that despite their illness, they are normal, as normal as any other child. By fostering a community of personal responsibility and a commitment to others, one that includes friendship, inclusivity, laughter and even a little bit of mischief, our kids develop a self-confidence they've lost. They learn they are not helpless simply because they have an illness, rather they are stronger for it. It's an incredibly powerful experience with real healing capability. Tonight, I'd like to begin by conveying a few of my experiences at the ranch, and the extraordinary way these children transform a person simply by sharing the ordinary day-to-day business of their lives."

Canyon had a sinking feeling. Was that her strategy? A rerun of "a day in the life?" He didn't even want to look around the table. The others must be feeling it, too.

"As you know," Katharine continued, "Wainwright is a working ranch and the children take part in activities ranging from caring for the animals and harvesting eggs to rounding up and branding cattle, each according to age and ability. And I tell you," she said with a small escape of laughter, "no matter the task, these kids throw themselves into the job fully. They become a team, no member more important than the next.

"Besides working with the animals and around the ranch, they learn to hike and camp, build fires, identify plants and animal tracks. Even poop." A collective giggle erupted from the room at large and Katharine smiled. "They have a lot of fun, but in the process they learn how they are connected to the world around them, how they coexist with nature and wildlife and just how much of it they can control." She paused, glanced around the room, and Canyon almost heard the words before they left her lips. "We have one young man who prides himself on controlling his environment—through his survivor skills. With encouragement from the staff, the boy has learned to start a fire, build a shelter, weather the elements, and become accountable for his actions. In essence, he's learned to depend on himself. He's not the weak child or the sick child. He's not the pitied child or the lonesome child. He's the strong child. Powerful. Illness does not define him. He defines it."

As Canyon listened to her describe Kyle, for a moment he felt as if she were discussing a completely different young man. But she wasn't. She was merely looking at him through a different prism. It reminded Canyon of her discipline style, her reasoning and her goal.

He sucked back a spurt of ego. Maybe her way hadn't been all that bad. Kyle was a kid. He was a prankster. He was normal, same as so many other rebellious twelve-year-old boys with a surplus of energy.

"We have children at the ranch who have never seen horses and cows, let alone ride them or feed them," Katharine went on, her voice pulling him back to her. "But with us, they do all of the above. They immerse themselves in the experience and learn the words 'I can' like they've never learned them before."

Katharine unfolded a piece of paper on the podium before her and began to read.

"Dear Mrs. Wainwright, I had to write to you because you have to know what a great time I had at the ranch and how much I miss it. When I first arrived, I wasn't sure what to expect. I was scared it would be hard. I was nervous about meeting new people. Before I went to the ranch, I didn't have many friends, because I spent too much time at the hospital. But after the first couple of days, I really started to enjoy it. And not because it was fun, either, but because I felt like I could really do stuff. You showed me that I could take care of calves, ride horses, hike in the woods...it was awesome! And best of all, I met my new best friend, Amy."

Listening to her reminded Canyon of the day he walked in on her at the office. He'd seen the opened envelope on Eleanor's desk, the tears in Katharine's eyes. He also remembered the vulnerability, the softened space between them as her emotion took control. It was the day he'd felt they'd crossed a line—an important line—moving from business to personal and everything in between.

"I'll never forget everyone at the ranch," Katharine read aloud. "You, Canyon, Jacob, Shannon...everyone was so nice and I miss you already. My parents say I might be able to come back next year. Would that be okay? I hope so, because being at the ranch has been the best part of my life."

Katharine quietly folded the letter and slid it back into an envelope. She looked up, and Canyon could see her eyes glistening beneath the bright lights overhead. He wasn't sure if she knew the history of the child who wrote the letter, but he did. The girl had attended the camp during Eleanor's last summer, a summer he would never forget.

It was the summer Eleanor revealed she was dying.

"Even after reading only one letter," Katharine said, "it's easy to see why we work so hard to ensure that Wainwright Ranch prospers. We change lives, and in turn, our lives are changed. It's an incredible process, one I wouldn't trade for the world. It's also the reason I stand here today." She paused, as though collecting her thoughts before continuing, "Since my mother's death, Wainwright Ranch has undergone the usual changes one would expect after the passing of a significant member of the ranch family. It's been an adjustment, but each and every person on our team has stepped up to the challenge, continuing business as usual."

Canyon noted the omission of Frank, and felt a deep sadness radiate from her. He looked around the room to see if anyone else saw it. But slowly pushing his attention back to the stage, he realized no one had. They couldn't. They didn't know her the way he did.

"We've also experienced a few difficulties of late," she said. "But I am here to tell you that nothing will prevent us from moving forward and continuing the great work we do."

Despite the determination and grit he heard in her voice, Canyon thought it an understatement. Frank had stolen almost a million dollars from the ranch in the wake of Eleanor's death, money he'd stashed away in an undisclosed account, in an undisclosed location. Katharine had assured Canyon that the authorities would be able to track it down, but he had his doubts. Frank wasn't a stupid man. Greedy, corrupt, but not stupid. He probably planned to get the money when he got out of jail. Canyon ground his jaw. He would prevent that, if it was the last thing he did on this earth.

Shaking off the animosity, Canyon tuned back in to Katharine. This event wasn't about Frank, it was about them.

"But we can't do it without you." Katharine summoned a quick smile adding, "I'm proud to announce that through the generous support of so many of you sitting here tonight and many others not in attendance, we've raised nearly three million dollars!"

Canyon shot forward. *Three million dollars?* Applause exploded across the ballroom and Canyon's hands instantly went together. That was quite a bit better than Paul had indicated earlier. But this draw could have been attributed to the pity factor. Without a solid gold plan that donors could hang their hats on, the ranch would be in the same predicament next year.

Katharine gazed out over the crowd, glowing with pride. "In light of these results, I'm confident we will continue to thrive." She brushed over Canyon, but not before they exchanged a knowing look. Wainwright Ranch would survive another year. It was a tribute to her efforts.

Their efforts. As the applause settled down, Canyon sat back and shared smiles with the group at his table. Tonight could be counted as a success. The board members felt it, the staff felt it, he felt it. Katharine had scored and he couldn't be more proud of her. She was beaming. Beautiful. The crowd was hers.

"Tonight is the culmination of the hard work of so many people too numerous to name," she said, "but each and every single one of them is as important as the next." Then her eyes found him once again and this time, held firm. "But there's one man in particular who I believe is responsible in large part for making Wainwright Ranch the success that it is, and that man is Canyon Laredo."

A spattering of applause broke out at the mention of his name.

Warmth flushed hot beneath his collar and he glanced around nearby tables, tipping his head to those he knew, and those he didn't. Canyon hated the spotlight. He'd much prefer working behind the scenes but he couldn't ignore the friendly faces staring at him. He smiled, even though it wasn't true. There were a host of people responsible for making the ranch what it was and he didn't want to shine brighter than any of them.

When the audience settled, Katharine continued, "He not only runs the cattle operations, the horses, our new henhouse, and donates his own hard-earned money, but he also works one-on-one with the children who all adore him."

Faces turned toward him again and he felt his cheeks warm. Did she have to continue singing his praises? One mention was enough, he thought, and shifted uncomfortably in his seat. Let it go, he willed silently.

"Canyon's love for the children is unmistakable. Even when the mischievous ones get into trouble," she tossed out with a playful smile, "they know Canyon's got their backs—because he cares. He's right there with them. He's part of their team. It's the magic ingredient that makes Wainwright Ranch unique. We're not just a summer destination filled with fun or duty. We're a second home, a family where everyone is equally treasured and needed, to pull their weight in order for the ranch to function." Katharine paused. "Thank you, Canyon." Her gaze hovered on him before moving to the crowd at large. "And thank you to our entire staff."

More applause followed and Canyon settled back into anonymity. Not that he wasn't glad to know that he was appreciated—he was—but he was more interested in hearing the details about the future of the ranch and his role with regard to the same. Three million dollars? That was incredible. But what about a plan? She hadn't mentioned anything about the details going forward. Had she found Frank's replacement? Did she know how long she'd be staying on?

Katharine continued her spiel about the ranch activities, the staff and how hard they worked, citing their roles and how crucial they were to the whole. Canyon sat spellbound. If he didn't know better, he'd swear it had been her creation, her dream that lived and breathed every day through the lives of others. But it wasn't. Her dream lived and breathed in New York City.

Katharine cleared her voice and announced, "I'd like to take this opportunity to announce a new project."

Canyon's ears perked. *New project*? He swung his head from side to side, checking with those sitting around his table. Anyone heard of this before? Jason looked dumbfounded while the board members seemed perplexed. Zeke Roberts wore a tinge of suspicion in his gaze. Seems the group of them were clueless, though keen on hearing more.

"Cattle have been the centerpiece of Wainwright Ranch," Katharine said, securing Canyon's complete attention, "but moving forward, we're going to incorporate an organic food line into our menu."

Canyon pulled back. *A what*?

"In our pursuit of normalcy, we serve the most normal of foods, much like the average American child's diet. Unfortunately, it's filled with fat."

A hush fell over the crowd and fear swelled in his gut. *Uh, oh.* Katharine was galloping off property without a clue as to where she was going. But there was no way he could rein her in from here. He slid a wary glance around the room. From the doubt creeping into the gazes of the crowd, this new idea wasn't going over well.

Katharine smiled, excitement blossoming in her gaze. "This year, Wainwright Ranch is going to begin a garden. It will be a totally organic garden where the children will learn to work the land and grow their food in addition to their existing responsibilities on the ranch. Once established and the children are able to harvest their produce, we will bring them into the kitchen and make them a part of the food preparation process. From properly cleaning the fruits and vegetables to cooking them, the children will play an integral role in the process of nourishing their bodies. Ours will be a farm-to-table dining experience, using only meat that is free of hormones, antibiotics, or any unnatural supplements."

Whispers spread across the room and board members shot Canyon questioning stares. He sat rigid and groaned under his breath. *She's kidding, right?* Tell me she's kidding, he mused, avoiding Zeke's heated glare. The man looked the same as Canyon felt. Was Katharine trying to push the cattle out of the ranch equation?

"Our vegetables will be heirloom only, and free of any toxic pesticides and fertilizers. We'll provide our own eggs, and any food we're unable to produce on our own will be secured from area farmers. On a commercial level, we will hire a specialized staff trained in the art of food development that will help guide us as we begin our Wainwright-labeled line of specialty food products, recipes determined and approved by our very own campers."

Katharine paused and Canyon's heart went out to her. The room was dead silent.

People were looking from one to the next, uncertain as to whether or not they should be excited or not. Cheers suddenly exploded from somewhere behind him. The room became engulfed by applause and Canyon's mouth dropped open as he turned to stare. It was thunderous. Men, women, and campers alike were cheering Katharine's new venture.

Completely speechless, he turned back to face her. From the podium, she looked down at him and his heart ripped open. *God, she was beautiful*. She was so enamored, so completely blown away by the support for her new venture that she reminded him of a camper who'd just learned they could do something they'd previously believed impossible. Canyon fell back into his seat, stunned. But a garden? A food line?

Gary leaned over and whispered, "What do you think? Is this going to be a good idea?"

"I have no idea, but it sure sounds like everyone else thinks it's going to be a winner."

Susan smiled, clearly pleased by the new direction, but not Zeke. He sat stone-still, shadowed by a cloud of gloom over his head.

Katharine went on to announce the scholarships, calling a teenager up onto the stage and handing him a certificate that read, "I'm going to college!"

The scholarship program had been another one of Eleanor's brainstorms, Canyon mused. It happened one day when an older camper had walked out of the ranch on the last day with tears in her eyes. Eleanor had asked her what was wrong and the girl replied, "I've learned so much this summer, but now I'm going home with nowhere to go and nothing to do." It seemed her family had spent their life savings on getting their daughter well, there was nothing left for college.

Eleanor told the teenager to keep her chin up and not to worry. Where there was a will there was a way. When the girl was out of earshot, Eleanor told Canyon, "Wainwright Ranch is going into the scholarship business. Let's go tell Frank so he can have the paperwork drawn up."

It was the way she operated. Eleanor saw a need and she filled it—on the spot, no turning back. Pride flared hot and fast inside his chest and his gaze went to Katharine. *Guess the apple doesn't fall far from the tree.* But seriously, who did Katharine think she was going to hire to oversee this new department of hers? She'd said she wanted him to take over for Frank, but Canyon didn't know the first thing about food production. Was Adele going to be a part of this new venture? It would make sense.

Question after question pummeled Canyon until his brain missed the entire scholarship presentation. As the trio of teenagers trotted off the stage, Katharine turned to the room once again. "In closing, there's one more announcement I'd like to make."

Canyon tensed. He wasn't sure how many more surprises he could take.

"In light of recent changes to our staff, I've decided to take over as Chief of Operations for Wainwright Ranch, permanently."

Canyon nearly fell out of his chair. *What*?

Her gaze landed squarely on him and his heart began to pound. "As I make the change, I will be required to travel frequently between New York and Colorado and will rely on Canyon Laredo to help oversee operations in my absence. With his help, I have every confidence it will be a seamless transition, one I hope to complete by the end of the year."

Emotion swamped him. As she elaborated on her decision, Canyon tried to digest the news. Katharine was staying. He could only hope it had something to do with him. He had put his heart on the line. He'd confessed his desire in no uncertain terms and she would have to take that into account with her decision to stay. Because he wasn't going anywhere, and his feelings were here to stay.

Chapter Thirty-Four

As the crowd dispersed, Canyon stood in place and waited for a group of guests surrounding Katharine to finally take their leave. It wasn't a wonder she'd been swarmed. Donors would want details about her upcoming plans, how they could invest, how they could take part, or how it was actually going to work. The announcement of an organic food line was no small undertaking. It would require money, and lots of it. It would take an entire organization devoted to the project—manufacturing, marketing, sales, distribution—Canyon's mind reeled. He had to hand it to her. The woman had certainly laid out some lofty goals for the next fiscal year, but could they achieve them? Could they work out the logistics?

As quickly as the questions came, the answers followed. Katharine Wainwright could do anything she set her mind to, of that Canyon was certain. And he would do everything in his power to help her. Pleasure unfurled inside him, filling him with warm sensations replacing all remnants of the wounded feelings he'd been nursing of late.

Katharine was staying. She understood what that meant to him. *She had to.*

When Katharine thanked the last guest, she walked toward him. The fundraiser was over, but they were just beginning. Slowing as she neared, he noted a flash in her eyes. "Can you forgive me for not seeking input from you and the board for my new venture?"

"You know you don't have to get input from the board," he said, more interested in the part where she was staying on. "It's your ranch, your decision."

"Do you think I'm overreaching?"

He wanted to support her, but he needed to know her motivation, the reason behind her change of heart. "I think you can do anything you set your mind to do. But I'm more interested in the part about you taking over for Frank." His gaze darted back and forth across hers, searching, willing it to be true. "You're staying and I need to know—did I have anything to do with it?"

Her eyes danced and she swung her head down and away from him with a coy smile. "Why Canyon Laredo, don't you have everything to do with it?"

Canyon dipped his head and peered into her eyes. "I was hoping..."

Katharine reached for his hand and pressed it between her own. "Yes, you have everything to do with it."

Pleasure soaked him. Dropping his gaze to their hands, he took both of hers into his. The soft quality of her skin reminded him of everything he wanted, everything he needed. "Let's say we go for a walk. I hear there's a full moon out tonight."

She grinned, and her cheeks tinged pink. "I love full moons."

Canyon pulled the wrap around her shoulders and helped her adjust it before securing her hand within his. Keeping her close by his side, he led Katharine through the lobby and out the back entrance to a wide stone patio. Several guests mingled in small groups. A few men eyed Katharine as they passed. *That's right, fellas. She's with me.*

She's with me, he savored privately. And it felt good, really good. It had been too long since Canyon had spent time with a woman who made him crave her presence, made him want to peel open the layers of his heart and expose his very core, but that's what Katharine did. She made him feel things, made him want to share things.

Nerves zipped through him but he held them in check. Nerves were a good sign, he mused. It meant the next few seconds mattered. A lot. Happened every time he mounted a bull. Nerves would tear through him right before a ride, sending his body on high alert, same as it was now.

Spotting an area away from prying eyes, Canyon glided Katharine to a stop. He glanced upward, the sky pitch black save for a full-bellied moon surrounded by a pale white glow. A scattering of stars blanketed the background, but he wasn't interested in stargazing. He wanted to talk. "See," he said. "Just like I promised."

She looked up and instantly his attention was drawn to her mouth. Her lips shimmered with a pale peach gloss, one that looked entirely natural against her light skin.

Overcome by an urge to kiss her, Canyon whispered, "I'm glad you decided to stay."

"Me, too." In the dim light, her gaze became fluid.

"Would it scare you to know I'm falling in love with you?" Canyon asked, his voice but a whisper between them.

She shook her head. "I don't scare so easily."

Well, that made for one of them. Canyon couldn't shake a sense of fear riding through his veins. He wanted Katharine more than he'd wanted anything in a long time and the thought of running her off because he moved too fast, gave him pause. But Canyon never walked away from a challenge. Not ever.

Cupping a hand behind her head, he drew Katharine to him and covered her mouth with his. Desire surged deep in his loins as he pressed firmly, gently, reveling in the sweet taste of her lips, the way her body sank into him, encouraging him. This was something he'd wanted for a long time. A very long time. Hungrily, he probed deeper, seeking her response.

Katharine surrendered, succumbing to the swirl of feelings rushing through her. Canyon felt hard and warm, yet comfortable, loving. It felt as though they were melting into one, a greedy desire cutting deep between them then threading them together. It was urgent and patient at the same time. She'd never been held by a man so towering, so commanding, yet utterly tender. Katharine couldn't think, couldn't reason, she could only feel. And this felt right.

Canyon pulled away but held her close, his gaze moving quickly across hers. "Is this okay?"

"It's better than okay," she replied breathlessly. "It's perfect."

Pleasure consumed his expression and he kissed her again, this time soft and careful, as though savoring her skin. Katharine dropped her head back and indulged in the way his mouth moved down her neck, back along her jawline. It stirred urges deep in her belly, pulled yearnings she hadn't unleashed in a long time. No longer was she a busy career woman but a sensual being enjoying the raw pleasure streaming through her body. Canyon paused at her neck, and nipped behind her ear. The move sent tingles racing down her breast.

"What changed?" he mouthed into her skin, his breath warm and moist.

What changed?

Katharine wanted to laugh. Everything—him, her, Frank's betrayal, nearly losing the ranch—her entire life had been turned upside down. What she thought she wanted, she didn't. What she never dreamed she desired, she did. Looking into Canyon's dark gaze, the strength of his arms wrapped around her, Katharine never dreamed this was where she wanted to be. Ever.

But she did. More than ever. *I changed*, she mused, taking a moment to fully grasp what she had done this evening. The new line of food, the garden—they had been ideas that struck like lightning. One minute she had no intention of starting any such venture, the next minute she knew it was meant to be. It was her destiny. Like the children had changed her mother, they had changed her. More precisely, her experience with them had changed her.

And this man... Katharine giggled like a schoolgirl. He asked if he'd had anything to do with her decision. Joy ripped through her. Only everything!

"Did I say something funny?"

Katharine expelled a stream of pent-up want. Laced with anticipation, excitement and a healthy dose of uncertainty, she smiled up at him and said, "I was just thinking how drastically my life has changed and most of it is because of you.

And the children, the ranch. I never envisioned myself here, not for any length of time, but as I was preparing the speech for this evening, it hit me. I couldn't imagine returning to New York and leaving you, the kids, the ranch..." She shook her head, as if it would set everything right in her mind. "I've come to love it out here. The thought of going back to the concrete jungle of New York City was so unappealing. Yes, I loved the city," she admitted, "the nightlife, the energy, I loved everything about it! Does that make any sense?"

Canyon grinned. "It makes perfect sense. You're Eleanor's daughter."

"I'm serious, Canyon." She grasped his upper arms. "I've been to Colorado every year since I was a little girl and never felt this way. And now I'm ready to uproot my entire life for a permanent move? That's an incredible turnaround."

"I'll take the credit for that part." He pecked her nose. "I'm irresistible. Go ahead, say it. You can't imagine your life without me."

She couldn't, though falling into his hands so easily didn't sit well with her. Straightening, she pushed her shoulders back and drew the wrap snugly around her shoulders. "You are gorgeous, yes, in a cowboy sort of way." Canyon shot her a wounded look in which she took pleasure. If Canyon Laredo thought she would be a pushover for him like Amanda, he'd better think twice. Katharine had developed feelings for him—serious feelings—and he'd better not take them lightly, but she wasn't a pushover.

"Canyon," she stated abruptly, overcome by a rush of emotion. "You said you were falling in love with me. Would it scare you to know that I feel the same? That I'm in deep and there's no turning back?"

"Not for a second. That's the only way I fall—hard and deep."

Nerves skittered through her pulse. "I've never met a man with a heart like yours, one who communicates from the soul. You're honest and genuine, you're loving, compassionate, yet you're tough as nails." Katharine shook her head. The scene with Frank had proven to her that Canyon wasn't afraid of anything. Yet with the children, he was easy and sweet—except when it came to discipline. Kyle's situation came to mind and reminded her that Canyon knew how to draw his boundaries. "How does that happen?" she asked him. Katharine had met a lot of men in her lifetime, and they usually fell into one of two camps—tough and jaded or soft and sensitive. "How does a man develop a tough exterior, yet remain tender on the inside?"

"Life."

"Life?"

Canyon looked around the patio then shot his gaze out into the dark night. Lights dotted the mountains, marking homes and businesses in the distance. The still air penetrated one layer deeper as she waited. But studying his features, she was surprised by the distance entering his gaze, followed by a pain that was unmistakable. He looked as if he were about to cry. "Canyon?"

After a long moment, he pulled his face back to her. "Her name was Rebecca."

Katharine's heart stopped. Rebecca? Was there another woman?

"She was eleven, I was twelve. The doctors told her she had lymphoma."

Oh, no...

Katharine's stomach dropped. Staring at him, she couldn't move, she couldn't breathe.

"We pretended it wasn't real." Canyon laughed softly. "But once the treatments began, there was no denying it. She looked sick and felt sick. The doctors said she was going to die."

Tears filled his eyes and nearly broke Katharine's heart. She touched his cheek. "Canyon..."

He looked her directly in the eye and growled under his breath, "I was so angry. I remember it like it happened yesterday. How could anyone say that to her?" he whispered fiercely. "How could anyone be so sure?" Canyon turned away. "It was nothing less than cruel. People were cured all the time. They could fight, they could heal. But taking away her hope as she traveled back and forth to the hospital? I could feel she was giving up." He shook his head and his voice cracked. A tear fell onto his cheek. "I couldn't let her do it. I couldn't let her give up without a fight, so I convinced her not to think about it. I talked her in to getting back on a horse, against her parents' wishes."

Katharine could feel his pain, could feel the scene as it played out in his mind. She reached up and brushed the tear from his face.

Unfazed, he continued, "I told her I wasn't giving up on her. I wasn't going to treat her like she was a fragile egg. She was my friend. How could I?"

"You couldn't," Katharine told him, hot tears rolling down her cheeks, chilling her skin in their path.

"It worked for a while. She began to feel better and started to act like herself again." Canyon laughed again, but this time Katharine picked up a cord of anger. "The doctors declared her in remission. Her parents were so happy, they apologized for all the things they said to me. But I didn't care. I never cared what they said. I only cared about Rebecca."

"Oh, Canyon, what a beautiful story," Katharine exclaimed.

He turned to her. "She died four years later."

Katharine stilled.

"Rebecca swore to me that she'd never been happier than she had the last several years, but this time she was finished. It was too hard. She couldn't bear to see her parents suffer anymore. She was worried about them, not herself. She was worried about them."

"Oh, Canyon, I...I..."

But the words fell away. What did one say to a man who'd lost his best friend? And so young? Turning inward, Katharine knew there were no words. There hadn't been any for her when her mother had died. There hadn't been any for her mother when Sarah had died.

Words were horribly inadequate.

Visibly collecting himself, Canyon took Katharine into his arms. "You asked me what makes a man tough on the outside and soft on the inside? Life," he said. "Loss." Canyon paused. "Love."

"What doesn't kill you makes you stronger, right?" Katharine wasn't sure how the saying popped into her brain, but it seemed to sum up the situation fairly well.

Canyon smiled. "If you let it." He tilted her chin up to face him and murmured, "Your mother understood these kids. I understand them. It hurts, but it keeps me going, keeps me focused. Does that make sense?"

"Completely."

"I love you, Katharine Wainwright."

Her insides flipped and she smiled. Guess some words do have power.

"It's cold out here," he said. "Let's go somewhere warm."

Chapter Thirty-Five

Nestled in the crux of Canyon's body, her bare feet pulled up and tucked beneath her, Katharine allowed her gaze to drift through her hotel room. Cody slept soundly on his plush bed in the corner near hers, oblivious to the couple seated. The dog knew she was home, and that's all that mattered to him. What mattered to her was the man by her side and the future that lay ahead of them. Canyon's touch swam through her body, filled her with a longing she'd never known. After they left the fundraiser, he drove her back to her hotel. He'd wanted to take her home to his place, but she'd declined. She couldn't leave Cody alone in a strange hotel room for any longer than necessary, and she wasn't ready for a night alone with Canyon. She needed to take it slow. She needed their first time to be right, despite the desire that coursed through her, filling her with a deep longing.

She wanted Canyon, but one kiss warned her that she would surrender quickly. She had no defense strong enough to stop her body from saying yes. She would succumb, and she would enjoy every minute. Speaking of minutes, her eyes sought the clock, glowing red across the darkened suite. It was 5:30 a.m. Time had disappeared, lost to midnight conversation and intimate whisperings. "It's late, Canyon. Are you sure Buck is okay without you?"

"He's fine." Canyon put his lips to her head and murmured, "The boy doesn't even know I'm gone."

"Won't you need to let him out?"

"I have a neighbor who steps in when I'm gone."

She turned her face to him. "A neighbor?"

"I have an old guy who lives next door and checks in on Buck when I'm traveling the rodeo circuit. One text and he's happily on duty."

Katharine's heart softened. "That's nice. You're lucky to have him."

"I am." Pulling her to him, Canyon added, "I'm lucky to have you, too."

"I'd say I'm the lucky one."

"Not nearly as lucky as me."

Shoving a gentle hand into his side, Katharine was struck by the solid wall of muscle. No longer wearing jacket or tie, Canyon's dress shirt was thin and she could feel every round of his ribs, every flattened angle of his abdomen. She wondered what he would look like without it. She imagined his body would be amazing. Perfection in the flesh.

Pushing the distraction from her mind, she asked, "So tell me, really, what do you think of my idea?"

"Not sure how I feel about it, to be honest."

Katharine would have given anything to be able to read the look in his eyes. She didn't want him to play along with her because he felt he had to, because she owned the ranch. She wanted him to like it and fully support her in the venture. "Don't you think the kids will have fun with it?"

"I think the girls will enjoy most anything that has to do with gardening."

"Not the boys?"

"If there's dirt involved, I guess they'll be okay with it."

"Not just dirt—composted cow manure."

"You're kidding, right?"

Katharine laughed softly as she visualized his surprise. "No, sir. It's the best darned plant food on the planet! That, and worm poop," she added, just for fun.

"Since when does a city girl know anything about gardening, let alone cow poop?"

"Since I've been researching on the Internet. I've learned a lot over the last two days."

"Two days? You're launching a food line from your own ranch garden after considering the idea for *two days*?"

The total and complete shock in his voice amused her. She folded her arms and nestled into him further. "Yes. All great businesses start with a great idea before they become huge corporations. Think of it, we'll be able to make our own tomato sauce and ketchup. We can make squash spaghetti and corn chowder. Adele has a phenomenal recipe for it."

He chuckled and kissed the side of her head. "Well, I might be convinced if I saw that you could get the kids to actually eat it."

"What's not to like about tomato sauce?"

"Nothing, if it's served on a pizza. Try and pass a bowl of squash off as spaghetti and I think you're going to get some push-back."

"Nonsense. They won't even know it's squash. In fact, Adele can make macaroni cheese out of tofu that would fool even the finickiest campers."

"You think so?" Canyon posed skeptically.

"I know so."

"I'll need a little more proof before I agree that swapping pork and beans for squash and tofu is a good idea."

"I'll give you all the proof you need, you'll see."

"How about I hold that card back for a while."

"Suit yourself."

"And I'm still selling the cattle for beef."

She shrugged. "Whatever." Now that she was staying, she had plenty of time to convince him that horses would be a better industry for Wainwright Ranch. At least it wouldn't involve the slaughter of animals, though at the moment, the man didn't seem inclined to change his ways.

Running a finger along the length of her arm, he asked, "So tell me, what else have you learned researching this latest venture of yours?"

"Actually, I've learned a lot in the last two days." Beginning with how much she'd been missing out by not having a man like Canyon in her life. He was a man who said "ours" and "we," a man who looked forward to a shared future with her. Katharine wondered what that future would look like, what it would feel like, what *he* would feel like. So far, she liked it all!

"And...?"

Tamping back her mischievous thoughts, Katharine giggled. "How much time do you have?"

"For you? All day."

Katharine turned in the darkness and ran a hand over his chest, sliding it between the opened buttons of his shirt. She leaned near and replied in a breath of voice, "Liar. I know for a fact you have to be at the ranch in an hour."

Canyon grunted. "You got me there. And my new boss is a real bear."

"What?" She punched him lightly. "You better watch where you're treading, mister."

"Ouch!" he exclaimed exaggeratedly and grabbed her arm. "Watch where you're throwing that thing."

"Watch who you're calling a bear—and lower your voice, you'll wake Cody!"

"What? You didn't seem too concerned a few hours ago."

Katharine's cheeks flushed hot. "What?"

Canyon groaned and grunted.

"We were only *kissing*."

"And as I recall, you were enjoying it—a lot."

She smacked his shoulder and leapt up from the sofa. Her dress caught and she tumbled forward. Katharine would have hit the ground face first, except Canyon was too quick. He caught her and locked her firmly within his grasp, pulling her to a stand. "Careful—you'll wake Cody."

"Grrr—"

Canyon silenced her with a kiss.

Katharine struggled but locked in his arms, there was no getting free. Nor did she want to. His hands migrated down the back of her, arousing a deep need. There was no place she'd rather be than right here, in his arms. Everything was erased from her mind, but him. Canyon Laredo. Bigger than life, tougher than a bull, he was also gentler than a lamb. Canyon was her equal in many ways, yet her complete opposite. Born and bred from the rugged Colorado terrain, he was sexy with the easygoing swagger of the West. His was a lure she couldn't resist, a man who would stand by her side and allow her to lead without being threatened by her success.

Canyon would follow her heart's whim, because it was headed in the same direction as his. It was enormously freeing. No rivalry, no egos or competing careers, a life with Canyon promised a security that made Katharine's heart soar. Adele was right. The men of Silver Creek were a different breed than the men of New York City.

And the only kind she wanted. This one, in particular.

"Canyon!"

Startled by the sound of his name, Canyon turned from the plump hen in his hands to see who had called him. One of the birds had escaped her perch and he was returning her to her roost. Angling backward, he caught sight of Jacob through the doorway. He was standing near the paddocks, waving wildly and pointing toward the office. Following his direction, Canyon's heart skipped a beat. Kyle Stevens' parents were walking up the path to the administration building.

Canyon bolted for them at once, hurrying over to head them off at the pass. If they were here to discuss their son's exploits, Canyon imagined it would be more confrontation than friendly conversation and one he should be a part of. Katharine was still new and needed him for backup. Jogging to a stop, he called out, "Mr. and Mrs. Stevens—hello!"

His arrival drew odd stares from the couple. Realizing he still clutched the squawking hen in his hands, Canyon tucked it beneath an arm and shrugged it off. "Sorry. I was busy in the henhouse when I saw you but wanted to come and say hello. What brings you to the ranch?" Kyle wasn't scheduled to go home for another three days.

"We're here to speak with Ms. Wainwright," Mr. Stevens said as he took the lead, his attire a profile of conservatism in his khaki slacks and penny loafers, thin navy pullover sweater and pinstripe stiff-collared shirt. His wife reflected the same in her navy slacks, white button-down and yellow cardigan, the color of which set off her shoulder-length blonde hair. They were an attractive couple, though slightly aged by the stress from living with Kyle's illness.

"About anything in particular?" Canyon asked, working to appear as casual and uninterested as possible for a man who'd just jogged over with a hen in his hands.

Mrs. Stevens smiled. "We're here to thank her."

Canyon gaped at her. "Thank her? For what?" Last he heard, Katharine had called the Stevens to inform them about their child's exploits on the mountain and his subsequent hen theft and *they* were madder than an old wet hen to hear about it!

Mr. Stevens stepped forward. "For what this ranch has done for Kyle. He's a changed young man."

"Changed?" Canyon wanted to ask how so, but he was already intruding as it was. They were here to see Katharine, not him. But curiosity got the better of him. Slanting a gaze toward the office front door, he asked, "In what regard?"

"Kyle has signed on for Boy Scouts," Mr. Stevens replied. "He wants to start with our local troop as soon as he gets home. I've been a member of the organization since I was eight"—he beamed— "and have tried for years to get Kyle to sign up, but he said it wasn't for him. He was a survivalist, not a Boy Scout."

Seemed a natural fit to Canyon, wondering why the boy had resisted.

"But everything's changed," Kyle's mother said. "Because of his experience here at the ranch." Shadows crossed her gaze as Canyon heard her silently add, *because of his experience up on the mountain.*

"That's great," Canyon replied. "I'm glad to hear it. The Scouts is a top-notch organization. He'll learn a lot from them." And while he was happy for the family, it didn't explain why they needed to come for Kyle early.

Katharine walked out of the building and stopped. Dressed in a pair of black riding boots that rose clear up to the knees of her slim-fitted jeans, a jean jacket pulled over a white button-down, she was beginning to look more at home on the ranch. Of course with that long blonde hair of hers blowing lightly in the wind, she could have been a model playing the part.

Her gaze went straight to the hen under his arm. "Canyon?" she asked quizzically.

"Hen was loose," he explained briskly, the bird wriggling against his grasp. "Then I saw the Stevens and wanted to come over and say hello."

Katharine's gaze flew to the couple. "Kyle's parents?"

"Yes," Mr. Stevens replied pleasantly. "I'm Tom and this is my wife, Beth."

"Hello," Katharine said, shaking hands with both of them. "Welcome to Wainwright Ranch." Looking to Canyon for explanation, she asked, "Is there something I can help you with?"

"Not exactly. We're here to thank you."

"Thank me?"

Canyon felt a sense of déjà vu. Seemed Katharine shared his sentiment.

"Kyle is joining the Boy Scouts," Canyon told her. "Because of his experience here."

Katharine's gaze became guarded. "But I don't understand," she said, directing her response to the couple. "When we spoke on the phone, you mentioned your displeasure with the ranch over the incident, for which I fully understood and sympathized. Forgive my confusion, but I don't understand your change of heart."

"Yes, well..." Mr. Stevens pulled a small white envelope from the breast pocket of his jacket. "A day later, we received this letter from Kyle."

Taking the letter from him, Katharine opened it and read. Shock wrestled with her refined features as she looked between the Stevens and Canyon. "May I?" she asked, handing the letter to Canyon.

Mr. Stevens grinned. "Sure thing, considering he's mentioned prominently."

Canyon's stomach tightened. Heat gathered beneath his shirt, despite the pleasantly cool air temperature. Taking the letter from Katharine, the bird's head bobbed up and down as he read.

Dear Mom and Dad,

I'm sorry for the mess I made of my time at the ranch. I didn't mean to, but no one listened to me. Just like at home, no one believed I could do anything. Until Ms. Wainwright. She listened to me and didn't get mad when I ran away from Jacob. She understood that I knew what I was doing, that I was a survivor. Then I took the chicken. I don't know what I was thinking, but I'm sorry. I'm really sorry. Canyon said I had to come home. He said those were the rules and Ms. Wainwright had to send me home. But she didn't. She said there were going to be new rules now that she was in charge, and if it was okay with Canyon, I could stay on with one condition. They made me group leader. Canyon said I had to be in charge of my cabin and be responsible for everything they did. Garrett and Derrick were terrible! They did everything they could to get me in trouble, but I didn't let them. I told them they weren't gonna get away with anything, as long as I was in charge. That's when I realized how bad I was. I did the same kind of stuff they did—to Canyon and Jacob and I'm sorry. I shouldn't have, but I never understood what it meant to be a leader until now. If it's okay with you, I'd like to join the Boy Scouts when I get home. You always said I could and now I want to. They understand outdoor skills. They have leaders. I think it will be fun.

Love, Kyle

Canyon clenched the letter in his hand and looked up at Katharine, then to the Stevens.

"Your tactic was very effective," Mr. Stevens said, peering at him as though the two men shared a secret. "Making the boy walk a mile in your shoes... It worked."

"Wish I could take credit for it, but it was all her." Canyon hitched a hen-filled elbow toward Katharine, brimming with pride and love as she looked at him with nothing less than adoration. A lump lodged in his throat. Kyle had learned his lesson because she had given him a second chance—a point Canyon had fought her on. He had come up with the idea to put Kyle in charge of the others, but it never would have happened if the boy had been sent home in the first place.

Katharine shook her head and folded her arms over her chest. "It was a team effort. Like the letter said, without Canyon it wouldn't have happened."

"You make a good team," Mr. Stevens returned.

"Thank you," Katharine replied, adding quietly as she stole a peek in Canyon's direction. "I think so, too."

Canyon's heart kicked.

Mr. Stevens continued, "This is the first time Kyle has started acting like a regular kid instead of manipulating the emotions of others to get his way." Kyle's mother glanced away but his father didn't miss a beat, "We've known we're part of the problem, but I tell you, it's hard business to be tough on your child when they've already suffered so much. Kyle's only twelve and he's endured more pain and sadness than most adults I know. It makes a guy go soft, I guess, but no more." Mr. Stevens shook a weariness from his gaze. "From now on, Kyle is the same as any other child in our home. No more special treatment—or exceptions."

Canyon would have commended the man, if he could have gotten the first syllable out of his throat. But he couldn't. It had swelled shut. The Stevens reminded him too much of Rebecca's parents. They struggled in the same fashion and he knew how that story ended. Canyon wanted different for Kyle.

"Thank you for sharing the letter," Katharine said. Walking over to Canyon, she took it from his hand and returned it to the Stevens. "It means the world to us to have made a difference in Kyle's life."

Mr. Stevens smiled. "You've made a difference for us, too."

"May I ask?" The expression on Mrs. Stevens face changed. "Is that a garden we passed walking in?"

"It sure is." Pride lit into Katharine's voice as she explained, "It's a new program we've started here at the ranch. The children will be working an organic garden, harvesting the vegetables and preparing them for their meals during their stay."

"Really? I used to have a garden when I was growing up. It taught me so much," Mrs. Stevens said, her lashes fluttering as she looked to her husband. "I wish we had been able to share the same with Kyle and his sisters."

"Maybe you still can," Katharine prodded gently. "Kyle played a big part in digging up the ground and preparing our beds. I think he enjoyed it, too. Perhaps you can convince him to start a garden at home?"

Mrs. Stevens brightened. She glanced over her shoulder toward the garden—currently a patch of neatly tilled rows of dirt—then back to Katharine. "Maybe."

"Kyle's a strong young man," Canyon spoke up. "He can do anything he sets his mind to." And in that instant, Canyon wished he'd expressed that confidence to Kyle early on in his stay. It might have made a difference and saved them all a truckload of heartache. A young man who felt valued, felt less of a need to prove himself.

Pausing, Mr. Stevens took his wife by the arm. "We appreciate your time, but we won't keep you any longer. We've said what we wanted to say. We'll be back for Kyle this weekend. Until then..." He drew his wife closer. "The Missus and I have decided to spend a few days in your fine town of Silver Creek."

"Wonderful!" Katharine exclaimed.

Mrs. Stevens smiled. "The girls are staying with my sister, allowing us a private getaway."

"You must have dinner at Adele's, on me. It's the finest restaurant in Silver Creek, serving the freshest ingredients you'll ever find."

Husband and wife stood stunned.

"The owner is a personal friend of mine." Katharine winked. "She's also my partner in the new Wainwright line of organic food. She'll be thrilled to have you."

"You're creating your own line of food?"

"We are, beginning with the best barbecue sauce this side of the Mason-Dixon line. We're going for the gold and the kids will be involved from the ground up." She flashed a smile to Canyon and quipped, "How's that for a Colorado metaphor?"

Canyon laughed and the hen in his arms started squawking. "Perfect." As perfect as Katharine was beautiful, he mused, and stroked the breast feathers of the hen to calm her.

"Do you have time for a quick tour?" Katharine asked the Stevens. "I'd love to show you the garden and get your input. We've marked the area and have brainstormed a marketing plan. Adele has some super recipes the kids will be taste-testing here at the ranch, but I'd love to hear what you, as parents, think."

"We'd be delighted!"

Katharine beamed. "Wonderful. Shall we?" As the Stevens fell into step, she prodded, "Canyon, would you care to join us?"

"I'll catch up with you—as soon as I deliver this little lady back to her home."

Home. Canyon was home. At the ranch, with Katharine. It's where they both belonged.

# # #

The End

Strawberry & Goat Cheese Salad

Assortment of fresh from the garden bibb lettuce & spinach leaves
4 strawberries, washed and stems cut
1 TBSP goat cheese
Organic olive oil
Balsamic glaze
Freshly-ground pepper

Wash and dry lettuce and spinach, then combine in your favorite salad bowl. Slice strawberries and drop over greens. Drizzle with your preferred amount of olive oil over top, swirl a round of balsamic glaze, and then sprinkle with goat cheese. Finish with freshly-ground pepper.

About the Author:

Dianne Venetta lives in Central Florida with her husband, two children and part-time Yellow Lab Cody-boy! An avid gardener, she spends her spare time growing organic vegetables, surprised by what she finds there every day. Who knew there were so many amazing similarities between men and plants? Women, life and love and her discoveries along the way provide for never-ending fun on her garden blog: BloominThyme.com. When she's not knee-deep in dirt or writing, Dianne also contributes garden advice to various websites.

You can also find her on twitter @DianneVenetta and facebook.com/DianneVenetta. Plus, learn how you can become a member of her street team, Bloomin' Warriors, where you'll be eligible for special discounts, advance excerpts, author swag and unique gift items throughout the year. For full details, be sure to check out her website, DianneVenetta.com.

Other novels by Dianne Venetta:
Mystery/Romantic Adventure Fiction
Silver Creek Series:
NOT WITHOUT YOU #1
BECAUSE OF YOU #2
ALL ABOUT YOU #3
ONLY WITH YOU #4

Mystery/Romance Fiction
Ladd Springs Series:
LADD SPRINGS #1
LADD FORTUNE #2
HOTEL LADD #3
LADD HAVEN #4
LOSING LADD #5
LADD CHRISTMAS #6

Romantic Women's Fiction
The Gables Trilogy:
JENNIFER'S GARDEN
LUST ON THE ROCKS
WHISPER PRIVILEGES

Women's Fiction
CONDEMN ME NOT